From Bogey to Birdie - Against the Odds

David Geoffrey Adams

Published by David Geoffrey Adams, 2023.

Table of Contents

Dedication

To my darling wife, Marion
and to our great-granddaughter, Elsie,
born the week I finished this book.

Acknowledgements

No book is written solely by one person and I willingly record the support of my lovely wife, Marion, who has read the manuscript from top to bottom, editing and making suggestions, most of which now form part of the final book.

The characters in the book are, of course, entirely fictitious apart from those tour golfers named who, I hope, will feel complimented by how I portray them. Naturally the scenes in which they appear are also entirely from my imagination. The tour golfers are, of course, Rory McIlroy, Tony Finau, Tyrell Hatton, and Tommy Fleetwood.

Any book fiction or non-fiction involving golf cannot avoid references to the Greats: Jack Nicklaus, Lee Trevino and, of course, Tiger Woods.

Mr Grump is not, **I repeat not**, based on any individual broadcaster.

Each of the courses referred to in the book were researched using their various web sites. If there are any errors or omissions, they are my fault and no-one else's. Hopefully any such errors will not reduce the reader's enjoyment of a story which, I hope, can take the golfers amongst us on that journey we would all, at some point, have dreamed of making, before we woke to our reality!

For those of you who do not play golf. I hope you can enjoy the personal battles Sophie and Rob must deal with.

PART ONE – SOPHIE BEFORE

Nightmare.

Screech! The terrifying sound of metal being twisted and torn. We jerk round, far too late, the monster has broken through the barrier. The blazing eyes of the beast blind us. I hear Dawn's yell. "Look out, Sophie." Her violent thrust throws me against the side wall and I fall. Even as I do there is a thud and I see my friend somersault through the air before crashing down to the ground, whimpering. I scream as the beast's claw rakes my body. I try to reach out for Dawn but the beast comes back, its eyes now a fiery red. With another thud it runs over her and her moans die. I scream again as the monster crushes my leg. Darkness.

The Terrible Reality.

My screams bring my brothers to my bedside. Gradually I hear their soothing words. "Sis, Sis. It's OK. It's all right. You're safe. You're at home."

I have two brothers, both older than me. For years they had been little more than irritating siblings, always knowing better than their little sister how things should be. Until my fifteenth birthday that is. Twelve months ago, now.

Tomorrow I will be sixteen and, despite the efforts of the prosecution team, I will celebrate my birthday giving evidence in court against the bastard who killed my friend and caused me to lose my leg. They had tried to get an adjournment arguing that the emotional trauma of those events last year would be far worse for me. Somehow the defence have managed to convince the judge that this was not a good enough reason to delay.

There was a time when I would have found it difficult to believe that I could hate anyone. That changed on that fateful evening.

Usually, I would have been at the local golf club practising. On the range or the putting green. If I missed, the club professional, who was a close friend having effectively become a member of my family, would be ringing my mobile to check I was OK.

Ever since he had seen me, aged seven, messing around with my brothers who enjoyed hitting golf balls with gay abandon, he was sure I had the talent to be a successful golfer. I had got the dregs, as always, perhaps a dozen balls and a cut down eight-iron, if my memory is correct. But Alan noticed that I was, as he remembers it, swinging smoothly and the balls were going straight and, he says, quite a long way.

As we started to leave to go home, Alan called us over. Given my brothers were older he asked them if they had considered lessons. It was obvious, with hindsight, that he was more interested in teaching me. My brothers laughed at his question telling him that neither they nor our parents could afford lessons.

That was true though I had no real understanding of how hard life was. That was hidden from me by our parents who worked all the hours they could to ensure that we did not go hungry and had decent clothes to wear. Perhaps the only hint was that we only had short holidays in England or Wales staying in caravans, while our friends regularly took off for Spain or Greece and other exotic places.

Alan was not deterred, getting my brothers to tell him where we lived and, a few evenings later, he knocked on our front door. That visit led to the first major change in my life. I was never told what was said between him and my parents but the outcome was that he would provide me with lessons and other support such as clubs and, eventually, access to the local club where he was the club professional and he would meet all such golf related costs, if I was prepared to do the work, the hard part as he put it. That a stranger believed I could be good at anything was amazing. Remember that I was only seven and my brothers, though I love them, tended to stamp on their little sister if she showed any gumption or said she wanted to do something they didn't feel was right.

I don't believe I really thought about the work that would be needed to get anywhere but golf had two attractions. Firstly, I could escape the confines of home for the fresh air and my brothers admitted they didn't really want to play golf. I do know, now, that the family had a council of war after I went to bed that night and all four agreed that they would take it in turns to go with me, to my lessons and my practice sessions.

Eight years on, Alan's investment of time and not a little money was paying off. A lot of hard work by me, meant that I was already one of the best teenagers in the country with a handicap, almost unbelievably, that was better than scratch. Far better.

But, on my fifteenth birthday, two of my friends claimed me for the evening taking me to the local ten-pin bowling alley to celebrate.

As we got ready to leave and walk home an older man from a group that had heckled us earlier in the evening, our bowling wasn't great, came across. To our astonishment and fear he pushed Dawn against the wall trying to force a kiss and pawing at her breasts. She pushed him away kicking out against his groin while Chrissie and I grabbed him by the arms and pulled him off her so hard that he fell backwards landing on his backside.

I remember the laughter of his mates but that was overshadowed by his snarling threat as he regained his feet and tried to attack Dawn, this time with his fists. Fortunately, the centre's security reached him and, having restrained him, threw him and his mates out. We waited for a few minutes before leaving, keeping a couple of police officers between us and them as we looked to walk up to catch our buses. Chrissie reached her stop first and was able to board a waiting bus while Dawn and I turned up a pedestrianised arcade, towards our own stop.

We were halfway along when there was an horrendous crash and scraping sound as a car smashed its way through the barriers. We looked back in amazement as the headlights lit up the street and the car, trailing debris, accelerated towards us. Dawn reacted first pushing me to one side as she, too, tried to dodge the vehicle without success. Even as I fell, I knew she had been hit while I was dragged aside by the edge of the front wing which raked across my side and leg. The pain was such that my scream died, as I lost consciousness. Dawn had been hit full-on and run over as the car crushed her. As if that was not enough, I learned later, the driver had reversed and run over her again, killing her and catching my leg, severing it at the knee.

To this day I do not know why I did not die too. Even the doctors told my parents not to get their hopes up too high. Despite the miraculous efforts of the paramedic who was the first responder, I had lost large amounts of blood and my leg, which had been crushed beyond any possibility of repair. I was in surgery for more than six hours as they fought to save my life.

Afterwards they told me that police cars had blocked the other end of the street and arrested the driver who, though unhurt, was trapped by the damage caused to his car. I would have hoped he might have been subdued by his actions but I heard that all he said was "They had it coming to them, the bitches."

After forensics had confirmed the details and eye witnesses had been interviewed, the driver was charged with a series of offences up to and including murder.

For me the following months were difficult, as I slowly recovered from my injuries.

Eventually I was deemed fit enough to be measured for an artificial leg. The limb would be matched to my other leg to help me with my balance when I was finally able to walk again.

Walk again! I've lost my leg! I cried to myself as I sat by my hospital bed. That was what hurt the most. The two major scars that crossed my body, one on the back, the other on the front, where the car's wing had twice scythed across it had healed as far as the medical teams could manage. Even the cosmetic specialists had been unable to completely hide the damage but they would be hidden by my clothes. I do not think that I had any thoughts as to how they might affect my future, not then anyway.

Then I found out that Dawn's funeral, much delayed by the coroner's court and other legal processes, was to take place. I had four days. Maybe that was the kick up my rear end I needed. I was determined that I would attend it and I made life hell for the team on the prosthetic rehabilitation unit until they completed their work and fitted me with that first, temporary, limb.

"You will need crutches at first, Sophie. Walking will be a case of having to learn how to again. Once you achieve that hurdle, we can start work on a better solution."

They told me, then, in answer to my plea. "Maybe not with this first prosthetic, but in time you will be able to play golf again. It will be hard work just walking a golf course let alone playing. But, with your spirit, we see no reason why you shouldn't manage to return to playing the game."

That was the boost I needed and I set to, during several exhausting sessions, to learn how to walk again. I believe that my progress was far quicker than the medics would have thought possible but, three days after that basic limb was fitted, I was finally allowed to leave hospital, albeit still on crutches.

My Mum and Dad were not really in favour of my going to the funeral but, to be honest, I gave them no choice. Dawn had saved my life and, despite their own grief, her parents had visited me while I was still in recovery. I had told them how I wished things were different. I would have swapped places if I could. Her father was quite blunt.

"You must not think that way. We know what good friends you were and we know that, if you could have saved her, you would have. The best thanks you can give her is to make a full recovery and get back out playing that silly game of yours."

He grinned suddenly at my look of horror. "Sorry, Sophie, I know what golf means to you and it isn't silly, just not for us. Go out there and sock it to them, girl." He leaned forward and gave me a gentle hug. "Do it for our girl, lass. That is what she would have wanted. She told us how good you are. It'll be a long road back but I'm sure you can make it."

After they left the ward, I wept for hours until sleep claimed me.

Funeral

The church was crowded. Family, friends and schoolfriends including several I would not have expected to be there. Maybe there had been a three-line-whip as they call it. I don't know and I never asked. It seemed wrong to do so. As I reached the doors, I passed the crutches to my Dad, giving him no choice but to carry them. The walk was slow and painful. I was still not ready to do without support but there was no way I was going to admit it.

The vicar looked down the aisle to this figure creeping towards the front and was not, I think, amused by the ripple of noise that happened as people recognised me and realised that I was walking. I must admit that at one point the hospital had confiscated my mobile as its constant buzzing, from texts and emails from schoolfriends and even teachers, was disturbing the ward. It was obvious from those messages that my injuries were hardly a state secret.

Eventually I reached the front of the church. Before I sat, I limped over to the vicar who I didn't know, my family were not avid churchgoers, and asked that I be allowed a few words, very few I promised. He seemed a little put out by an apparent stranger making such a request, especially one who had already caused a certain amount of disturbance. Only when I explained who I was did he nod and give a gentle smile.

With that I managed to sit down near the front as members of Dawn's family made room. The relief to be able to sit was immense such that I found it difficult to hide it. Even as I did so, the church organ changed its melodious background sound to that of the funeral march and the coffin, followed by Dawn's Mum, Dad, and her brother, entered the church. The service was not long, though I refrained from standing for the various hymns.

After the formalities and eulogies were almost complete the vicar beckoned me forward without a word. I had had time to think about what I wanted to say but nearly froze once I reached the lectern. For a long minute I simply stood saying nothing, before.

"I was Dawn's friend. She was my best friend. I am standing here because and, with apologies to the wonderful medical teams at the hospital, only because of her. I wish I could change that. All I can do is to do my best to show that her sacrifice was worth it. That will be my goal from now on. You all know the saying that there is no greater love a person can show than to give their life that their friend might live. Dawn was that person and I am better for having known her."

I know I was close to tears again and unsure how to walk back to my seat. I was saved any indignity of falling by Dawn's mother who swiftly rose and came to my aid supporting me back to a seat next to her. Despite her own emotional state, she smiled to me and her few words, which I will not repeat here, gave me much solace in the coming months as my rehabilitation continued.

The Trial.

Over those months I still struggled with the idea that the man who had killed my friend had not come to trial. I had occasional messages of support from the detective who had been given responsibility for collating the evidence and proof that it was the same person we had had the confrontation with in the ten-pin alley. Finally, I was told that a date had been set for the case, just a week before my sixteenth birthday.

"I swear by almighty God that the evidence I shall give is the truth, the whole truth, and nothing but the truth." I sat down, to the visible annoyance of the defence counsel. Witnesses should stand but I had been given leave to sit. My second prosthetic was a great improvement but I still tired quickly when standing still. Although, to the bemusement of everybody including myself, I could already walk quite long distances with seemingly less fatigue.

During the next few minutes, counsel for the prosecution asked me several questions. I was asked to tell the court what had happened that fateful night. Could I identify the man who had attacked Dawn? I could, pointing to the individual in the dock. "It was him." The defence counsel took over to begin his cross-examination.

"Miss Jordan. You identified the defendant as the person who, you claim, attacked the deceased in the bowling alley. Was he the driver who hit you by accident later that evening?"

I was startled, he must have known that I could not.

"No. You know I can't. I never saw who was driving but he was the person in the driver's seat when the police arrested him."

"Just answer the question, Miss Jordan. Did you see the driver?"

"No, I've already said that."

"Now perhaps we can turn to events earlier in the evening. Your story is that the defendant assaulted your friend without provocation. I put it to you that that is a lie, that you and your friends regularly bowl and always look to attract the young men, giving them glimpses of your underwear, teasing them until they approach you and then laugh at them."

"Objection, my Lady. The court has already heard independent evidence that the assault was without justification."

The judge was clearly not happy about the line the questions were taking but the defence counsel responded.

"My lady. It is essential to my client's defence that he was provoked beyond reason. This impacted him such that he lost control of his car as he made his way home. That the accelerator jammed and he had no way to avoid the collision. Only Miss Jordan and her friend can dispute this. There are, as my Lady is aware, significant views on social media supporting the idea that these girls enjoyed acting in a way to cause young, immature, men to react inappropriately week in and week out."

"That's not true." I blurted out. "I had never been there before that day nor had my friends, unless with their families."

"Really, Miss Jordan, really? Then what did you do every evening?" The question would have made me laugh on any other occasion.

"Practice at my golf club, what else?"

"You expect the court to believe that a fifteen-year-old girl practices at a golf club? Every evening? And how good a golfer are you? Win anything, did you?" His sneers enraged me but I bit my lip before answering.

"I played off a handicap of plus five." I paused. "Do you understand what that means?" I could not entirely hide my anger at his attitude and emphasised the "you" in my answer. Especially as I didn't yet know if I would ever play to that standard again. There was a gasp around the courtroom. Clearly there were people who did understand.

"Five, and that is good, is it? I suggest, Miss Jordan, that you are a liar. That you live in a fantasy land and have made up this flimsy excuse to divert the jury's attention from your contribution to the events of that night." His ignorance was amazing but before I could respond there was an interruption.

"My lady, if I may approach the bench." Counsel for the prosecution, it seemed, had finally lost patience.

There were a few quiet words before the judge looked up. "Court is adjourned until two pm. Counsel, in my chambers."

In the privacy of the judge's chambers, we learned later, the prosecution explained that there was CCTV footage from inside the bowling rink and covering the spot where the car had hit us. The prosecution had hoped that they would not need to use it due to the content but the defence had given them no choice.

The judge had pointed out that introducing such evidence so late was irregular then demanded that she and the defence be shown the footage.

We returned to the courtroom in time for the restart at two o'clock, when I found that I was not required back in the witness box.

The judge's next words caused a degree of consternation, mostly amongst the press it must be said, as she instructed the ushers to clear the court. She made it clear, that she considered that it was inappropriate for some new evidence to be considered in open court.

I asked the prosecution what the evidence was and then asked the judge to permit me to remain as it clearly impacted my personal understanding of the events that had led to the death of my friend. She did not reply immediately, waiting for the rest of the court to empty and the mumbling dissension to die away.

"Miss Jordan, you understand that you will be forced to watch video evidence of the incident. It may not be an image you will wish to see. It could reopen wounds that only now are possibly healing."

Her words gave me scant comfort but I was determined. "My lady, my friend died saving me. I believe that unless I can see this through, the wounds may never fully heal."

"In that case you may stay."

She then instructed the usher to bring the jury in. As they returned to their seats it was apparent that they had not been warned that the court would be largely empty.

"Ladies and Gentlemen of the Jury, the court has been cleared because, in my view, the evidence that you are about to see should not be shown in open court. The prosecution had hoped that it would not be needed and, because of its nature, I am inclined to agree. However, that situation has changed and I regret that you will be forced to watch video footage which contains graphic images of violence."

Before the footage could be run, the counsel for the defence spoke.

"My lady, following the new evidence produced by the prosecution and having consulted with my client, I must advise the court that he wishes to change his plea of not guilty to guilty to the charge of causing death by dangerous driving."

The judge looked to the prosecution asking if that was sufficient.

"No, my lady. The prosecution considers that all the evidence supports the more serious charges."

"In that case we will proceed. Dim the lights please."

The next twenty minutes were, I confess, such, that there are times when I do wish I had never watched them. On the other hand, for my own mental state, I am glad that I did. There was nothing to support the defence's claim that we had encouraged any sexual activity and the coverage obtained of the streets where he had driven, like a madman, were terrifying.

There was no doubt left in my mind that he had intended to kill us, all three if he could have. The car had smashed through bollards, hurtled up the walkway at a speed, we were told, exceeding sixty miles an hour until it had hit Dawn and me. She had clearly realised the danger and I could see her push me hard to one side before she tried to dodge herself, far, far, too late.

The driver had then slammed the brakes on and reversed back over us before trying to race away. The damage from the bollards, finally caused him to lose control as he headed onwards to where the blue lights of police cars could be seen, before crashing into a shop window as he tried to turn into a side alley.

I tried desperately to hide my tears but failed miserably. I was, though, not alone as the jury looked on ashen faced and with some crying as well.

With no further witnesses the court adjourned until the following day to allow for the final speeches from the prosecution and defence before the judge's summing up during which she made several points. The one I remember most was her comparison between manslaughter and murder. If they, the jury, had any doubts that the defendant had intended to kill then they must return a verdict of manslaughter. She did not suggest that there was any other possible verdict.

The jury retired to consider their decision just at the lunch recess and there was much discussion around the court as to what verdict they might bring. Given that the final evidence had not been seen, the general opinion was that the most likely outcome was that of manslaughter. As someone said, killing with a car did not seem to ever be seen as serious as a stabbing or other method.

Then came the news that the jury was coming back in, less than three hours after retiring and that included the lunch break. The judge took her seat and the jury filed in looking, unsurprisingly perhaps, downbeat.

The court clerk turned to the jury. "Foreman of the jury, have you reached a verdict on which you all agree."

I had to remind myself that it was necessary that the legal process be followed. They'd been out for such a short time they must have agreed on something, the question burning in my mind was what verdict.

"We have."

"Defendant, please rise and face the jury." It looked as if he was going to object for just a moment before he obeyed with a shrug.

"To the charge of murder, how do you find the defendant? Guilty or not guilty."

"Guilty."

I felt myself breathe again before realising that I had indeed stopped doing so. The rest of the process was of little interest, the verdict was the right one for me. I do remember the judge deferring sentence pending some report or other and then thanking the jury. She also made the decision, that for a short trial was unusual, excusing the jury from any future jury duty. "This has been a case of great emotional weight and you faced the rare necessity of having to view the actual events. There is no doubt in my mind that you have reached the correct verdict. Court is adjourned."

We were back in court three weeks later. We being me, Chrissie, and Dawn's family to hear the sentencing. There were, as expected, the press and, unusually I believe, some members of the jury.

I had had to make a victim's statement as to how I had suffered and/ or been affected by the actions of the guilty party. When I look back, I realise that I still had not thought through the impact, not so much of the loss of my leg, but of the scarring to my body.

The judge was mercifully brief but extremely harsh in her words.

"Thomas White, you have been found guilty of a vicious, nasty, and deliberate act of murder. It is only by sheer luck that it was not two murders. I delayed sentencing in the hope that those tasked with reporting on your attitude and state of mind might find reason for me to be lenient. That you might be showing some evidence of remorse. It is clear, that that hope was wasted. You have shown no such remorse, continuing to blame your victims and you seem incapable of accepting responsibility for your actions. The crime of murder carries a mandatory life sentence and I hereby sentence you accordingly."

At that point White interrupted with a howl of triumph. "You wait, bitch." Looking at me. "That means seven or eight years. I'll see you before you're thirty and then you'll pay."

The judge looked at him. "I hadn't finished, Mr White, but that outburst supports the rest of my ruling. I had considered giving you a whole life sentence but, unfortunately, there are rules restricting me in that vein. Nevertheless, you will serve a minimum of thirty years before you may be considered for parole."

"Thirty years! You can't do that. You'll pay, bitch!"

The judge looked back at him before saying quietly. "Take him down, before I question if I should increase that period."

The warders had to force the swearing and shouting man away from the courtroom.

With silence returning the judge spoke to Dawn's parents and to me. "I am sorry that no sentence can replace your loss. I hope that, with time, you will be able to remember Dawn with love and recall the good times. Sophie, you will carry your injuries for the rest of your life. I am told you still hope to return to playing golf at the highest level. I wish you well in that venture."

The end of the trial and its result was, I think, the end of the beginning of my true recuperation mentally. Physically, I know, I was improving much faster than the experts had believed possible. Mentally, I continued to carry the scars, deeper than they realised.

A Long Road Back.

"We now come to the main awards, firstly the winners of the Orders of Merit. I, perhaps, should have said winner, as you all know. For the first time in the history of the Club. At least as far back as I could check, no-one has previously won both the Men's and the Ladies competitions."

Sitting near the top table, I was almost trembling with emotion. It had been a hard climb back from that new start, exhausting and painful to say the least. I was now on my fourth leg and how things had changed. New technology had allowed the team at the hospital to devise a prosthetic which responded to the needs I placed on it when swinging a club.

The first year had been difficult. Simply playing eighteen holes was hard enough without competing but the support from most, if not all, the members had given me repeated boosts whenever things got on top of me. Alan, my coach, was well, Alan. He never doubted me, even when I was close to throwing my golf clubs in the lake on the fifth.

There were also the other restrictions my injuries forced, at least in my own mind. Swimming would have been good physically, my artificial leg was waterproof, but I simply could not face being seen by others in a costume that could not cover the scars. I also found that quite a few of my acquaintances, clearly, they had not been real friends, found plenty of reasons to avoid me. The few true friends, especially Chrissie, made up for that but it did hurt when I was feeling depressed, which was more often than I care to remember.

After that first year, when I completed barely a dozen rounds and even fewer in competitions, I headed into the second year with a mix of hope and uncertainty. By mid-June my playing handicap had dropped to one, a full six shots worse than before I lost my leg and, for a time, I began to believe that I would only ever be a decent low handicapper. Then I got that fourth replacement leg and suddenly I found my old swing beginning to return.

It may seem odd but I had no idea then, that strings were being pulled to keep me on a fast track for regular improved prosthetics, that someone was pushing for this on the basis that I was the ideal opportunity for developing a process that would help others in the future.

Within a month I had broken the junior course record, something that had eluded me even when playing off plus handicaps. By the end of that summer, I had played well enough to win the Junior Order of Merit and my handicap was back in positive territory. I began to look to the future with a more hopeful outlook and, oh yes, things did get better, if a bit crazy.

I worked through the winter with Alan trying to improve on my areas of weakness. By the end of March, he complimented me on my whole game. It wasn't that he didn't encourage me all the time but he did reserve such wide compliments for very occasional use. "Don't want you running before you can walk" was his reasoning when I had felt that I was solving problems and he wanted me to do more work. That was when he dropped a bombshell on me.

"I have spoken to the club committee and they are happy for you to compete in the Men's competitions as well as the Ladies."

"Really, Alan." Noting his slight grin. "What's the catch?"

"You'll have to compete off the medal tees. Look, before you clout me with that putter, you need an extra edge to your game. We have good juniors and Ladies in the club but, if you compete with the Men, you will add a challenge that will boost your game when you play in the county and national competitions."

"Wait a moment, do you think I could play at that level? Already? And remember, I still haven't got the strength to carry my bag, not yet anyway."

Alan looked at me, his grin now a wide smile. "First, you will be ready, at least to enter them. This year, I am guessing, it will be more for experience. I'm not expecting you to win much, if anything, but it will add to your overall game. As for carrying your bag, there are two solutions. Either a caddy, always allowed, or using a trolley. And, before you ask, I have already checked and you can get a medical exemption from the usual ban on them. So, are you up for it, Sophie?"

Was I up for it? Of course, I was. Three weeks later I played in my first monthly medal with the Men. My top ten finish engendered a few rude comments about bandits but it was mostly the good-natured banter that every golfer gets when they do a lot better than expected. In any case, it was nothing compared with the comments when I won the next two comps. Suddenly the extra distance required from the medal tees seemed nothing, my swing was back and the balls seemed to fly better and further.

Junior competitions, around the country, did provide experience and quite a few compliments from the other players. Not surprisingly they had never come up against a player with an artificial leg and my use of a trolley always required an explanation, and occasionally a challenge. My brothers did caddy for me a few times but deep in their degree courses they had little opportunity to do so with any regularity. I did learn that a caddy would be essential in the bigger national competitions where trolleys were simply not allowed, even in my case, but that was for the future.

The Club chairman continued his, to be honest, rather boring speech, as he complimented the runners up before finally calling my name. "Everyone, please applaud the winner of both Orders of Merit, Sophie Jordan."

As I struggled back to my table carrying both trophies, I heard my name again. "And the Ladies Champion, Sophie again please."

In some ways it was the compliments of the Men's Champion that meant the most, John Deeley had won by one shot beating me into the runners-up position on the final hole. To my chagrin I had three putted both the seventeenth and eighteenth holes. John's comment that I deserved to have won drawing more attention to his luck on the closing stretch when three long putts had dropped. Ones, as he put it, that could have ended up as far worse. Rubbish really and I knew it. I had bottled it on the last green and no compliment was going to change that. Still, it had been a good year; the next year I would no longer be playing in junior events at all. Now eighteen I would be playing with the big girls, as my Dad called it.

The email was quite clear and totally unexpected. "We would like to invite you to join the Curtis Cup team at a pre-match session to be held at Wentworth GC."

I read it again and again, what could it mean? Was it real? My season had started well, though not, I thought, exceptional and an invitation such as this was crazy, for a rookie who had only one win under her belt from the end of the previous year.

I called Alan, was there any way I could confirm that it wasn't a hoax? There was a laugh at the other end of the phone. It wasn't a hoax. He had already been spoken to and the invite was not to play, though that might be possible during a practice session, but the Cup captain had seen me in action and felt that the team would benefit from hearing my story and learning of the battle against the difficulties I faced.

"She saw you play at the Forest of Arden and believes that you have the makings of a future Curtis Cup candidate. The team face a very strong US side and your story should boost their moral and motivation."

I almost gagged. I was no good at public speaking. Even the necessary thank-yous at the club prize giving had been hard for me and I said so. Alan was quite comforting.

"It won't be in public. Just a couple of dozen people some of whom you have already met. If or when, I should say, you go on to be a successful player on the tour you will need to be ready to speak with reporters, often on camera. Take this chance, Sophie. Nothing wrong in raising your profile!"

After we finished talking, I went back to my laptop and started drafting a reply accepting the invitation. Halfway through the process, I suddenly stopped. What had Alan said? A successful player on the tour?

It was the first time he had ever uttered any suggestion of my being able to move on from being an amateur. Even if I did occasionally dream of turning pro. Did he really think that I had it in me to make that huge, to me anyway, leap? He had always been totally honest with me whether holding me back from advancing too quickly before the incident and even more so afterwards. At the same time, he always encouraged me to try harder when I was feeling down but this went way beyond any previous support. I resolved to have it out with him back at the club when he returned from playing in his own competitions.

In the end we wouldn't get together for some weeks. I received a letter addressed to me, care of the Club, offering me a wildcard invite to a French Championship based, presumably, on my win at the Forest. I hadn't, I revealed to my brothers, even heard of the event and it took a little research to find out that the last English golfer to win it was Rachel Jennings in 2008 and it was a seriously big event. The French International Lady Juniors' Amateur Championship!

To be truthful it terrified me. I had still only played a handful of tournaments since moving out of the regional junior competitions and had never played in any of the significant English or British Junior Championships. My attempts there had been scuppered by the earlier loss of my leg. Now I was being invited to compete in an international tournament! It took another long-distance call to Alan, thank God for mobiles, to get his backing.

I had managed to save a little money from my part-time job in the pro-shop, the question I had, was where could I raise the rest? The Championship lasted five days and I knew that I should look to arrive early enough for at least one practice round on the course. I would need to be prepared for a stay of seven or eight days in the unlikely event that I made the cut after the two rounds of strokeplay.

When I look back, I am still not sure that the matchplay days really came into my mind then and certainly not the idea that I might need to play two rounds of golf a day culminating in a total of five or even six in three days.

Putting that to one side, I started looking to see if it was possible to raise enough by selling any of my bits and pieces. Bits and pieces, of course, they were and not worth the effort. Mum and Dad offered some cash but I knew that that would probably mean them missing out on a holiday they really needed and, even then, I would not have enough.

With my recuperation getting in the way there had only been one trip for any of us. During that first winter, Chrissie's family had insisted on taking me to Spain, arguing that the warmer weather would help me. Mum and Dad had taken the opportunity then to take a few days by the coast but Dad had not been too well and they did need to get away again.

The idea of missing out on what might be a one-off opportunity had me so down on myself that it affected my work. I knew that the club members enjoyed my normally positive outlook, what I didn't know was that they had realised something was wrong as I became rather short when serving them.

After two days of this, Richard, the part time pro, pinned me, metaphorically that is, in the back room of the shop and demanded to know why I was being such a misery guts. It was the last straw. He was a nice guy and we got on well together. Now he was both berating me for not being my usual happy sort-of-go lucky person and telling me he was sorry if he had upset me! It finally hit home and I dissolved into tears.

It took Richard several minutes to get the whole story. He then told me to dive into the ladies and make myself presentable as he needed me to run the shop on my own for a few minutes. "And, for heaven's sake, put a smile on it. There are far worse things in life."

I couldn't argue and, in any case, he was quite right and I knew it. A few minutes later I was back behind the counter and gave him a beaming, well maybe not beaming, but a smile anyway.

"Better, Sophie. Now I'll be back shortly. Try not to turn any more members into gargoyles, yes?" And he vanished. And I did try, at least, to really welcome the half dozen members who came to confirm they were on their way out on to the course.

Richard's "few minutes" dragged on before he returned more than an hour later just as I was thinking I might have to miss my lunch break and time on the range. I raised an eyebrow to ask without words where had he been.

"Sorry, Sophie. I had an errand to fulfil and it took a little longer than I expected or hoped anyway. Go and get your break. I may need to vanish again after lunch so take it out on the balls!"

I had to laugh, his humour was always infectious, as he knew I tried very hard never to take anything out on the golf balls, after all that didn't help at all.

"Apology accepted. I'll be back in an hour." And off to the range I went. We had the latest ball tracking technology and part of my pay for helping in the shop was unlimited access to it. At least, I thought, I could check if my depression was affecting my swing at all.

I had arrived back for my afternoon stint serving when a figure appeared in the shop doorway.

"Miss Jordan, might I borrow you for a moment?"

My heart jumped. It was James Caunter, the club secretary. James was a very precise man who was also always highly polite. First names were for social occasions, not when in or around work and he seemed able to remember every member's name. That was a skill I would have loved to have had. I had only met him once and that was when he came to talk to Alan, Mr Dawson to him. Alan had introduced me, to a laugh from James. He already knew exactly who I was and why that was important to him. Now he wanted to talk to me, apparently in private.

I followed him back into the clubhouse nervously worrying that a member might have complained at my attitude. It was a bit like being summoned to the school head's office when you don't think you've done anything wrong but are desperately finding excuses for whatever the Head wanted to see you about.

We entered his office and he indicated a chair in front of his desk for me to sit in. As he sat down on his side he suddenly smiled, a smile that changed his entire appearance, and altered the atmosphere. Suddenly I felt as if this was not going to be a telling off or the sack for that matter. I wasn't totally correct in that moment of relief.

James spoke gently. "Sophie, may I call you Sophie?"

That was unexpected and I could only nod in response. "Of course, sir."

He laughed. "I do have that reputation, don't I? It can be very useful at times. While in private, James, please."

I could only nod again.

"Now then, Sophie, I have a bone to pick with you." My heart dropped; I was in trouble after all.

"I know about the invite to the French Championship. Such wildcards are much sought after and rarely get sent without someone asking or even begging. And you are considering returning it! That is unacceptable young lady! When you play there you will be representing the Club."

I could almost feel the capital in "Club" but kept silent. In any case he clearly already knew that I couldn't go. Richard. It must have been Richard, I thought. Boy, is he in trouble when I get back.

"Sophie," James continued. "I really am disappointed. Did you not consider telling me, or the Chair, of your need? You must know that the club provides help for all the juniors when they enter regional or national competitions. Even if it is only the entry fees."

"I know, I know that." I stuttered. "But this isn't the same, it's not just an entry fee, James." I gulped.

"And you felt that it was wrong to seek help at this level?"

I nodded miserably.

"Well, you should have remembered that this invite is a compliment for the Club. In fact, you should know that the letter, that accompanied yours, was an invitation to the Club to send you and allow you to compete."

"I didn't know. I'm sorry." I was switching between more misery because I had upset him and the sudden glimmer of hope in my mind. What was he really saying?

"Sophie, cheer up. You are a remarkable golfer and you've only got that good by a single-minded approach. Alan saw that potential back when you were seven and he had that conversation with the committee of that time. I only came a few years later. How your family would not be able to pay for you to play but that he would give his time if the club could provide the cost support, no membership fees and so on. He said, even then, that you had a gift, an underlying talent and we should look to support you as far as we could. He promised us a good player, perhaps very good, but even he, I believe, never expected a golfer of your ability."

"Thank you, James, I don't know what to say. I will try and find a way to go to France and do you proud."

"Sophie, you need not worry. The Club will pay your expenses. I know you will do well but at the end of the day simply do your best and you will prove us right. The committee consider it a good investment both in your future and the Club's own reputation."

"I don't know what to say, thank you, thank you, James. Oh Lord, I'm sorry."

I was dissolving, for the second time that day into floods of tears. My dream was still on track. France here I come, I was thinking, even as I stumbled out of James's office and into the nearest ladies. Typically, it wasn't empty. The Ladies Captain must have been lunching and was now tidying up, presumably before joining others for a friendly round.

"Sophie? What on Earth's the matter? Who's upset you?" Linda was more than capable of taking issue with anyone she felt was out of line and upsetting the club's best player, in her view, was very much out of line. She had no time for the idea that any of the ladies could outplay me or any of the male players for that matter. I might have disagreed but it never seemed a good time to argue.

"Oh heck. Sorry, Linda, nobody has upset me. I just got the best news possible. I'm happy. Really!"

"And that reduced you to floods? This, I have got to hear. Spill the beans, young one."

"I'm going to France after all. I thought I wouldn't be able to but the club is going to help with the costs."

She smiled. "I'm so glad you accepted, Sophie. Now, just to put a bit more pressure on you."

"What? How?" I was back getting nervous again.

"I was already arranging a trip to support you. That means that a dozen members are not going to be disappointed, now we know you are going. We'll be there to lift you to the top of your game. Whatever, you won't be on your own. The only issue might be that you'll have a lot of people fighting over the honour of being your caddy."

"You can't be serious, Linda. I've never played at this sort of level. What happens if, when, I don't make the cut. All that way just to watch the other golfers."

My heart was racing. What if I really didn't do well enough? I already knew that some of the other entrants would have loads more experience at national level championships. They would be from all over Europe, maybe even from the USA. I gulped, feeling almost nauseous at the idea that so many would be looking to me to perform.

"Sophie, oh dear, perhaps I shouldn't have said. Look. We will be travelling in hope. I know I think you can lift the Esmond Trophy but to do so means maybe eight rounds of golf in five days. All you need to do is play as well as we know you can. If others play better, well so be it, you can't control them and maybe, just maybe, your best will prove better than the opposition. I intend to enjoy the trip whatever. Just seeing you tee up on that first day, well that will be great. Now go on back to the pro shop. I suspect that Richard may need some help."

I nodded before suddenly stepping forward and giving her a hug of gratitude. "I'll do my best." I whispered before almost running back to the shop. Yes, that was how good that leg was, although perhaps a trot back would be more honest.

As I reached the door, I hesitated. Richard would still have to pay. After all, he should have warned me as to his intent. Opening the door and finding no-one there apart from my intended victim,

I turned around and closed the door before continuing my way towards the counter and simply glared at him.

"And your excuse?" I growled. He went ashen with shock as I approached him menacingly.

"I, I, I." He stuttered unsure what to say as I closed the gap. Then he didn't say anything for a long time as I pulled him into an embrace and a long kiss. It took only a moment for him to respond before the door opened and Linda walked in with a wide grin.

"You guys might want to think about getting a room." She laughed, clearly pleased to see me in a better frame of mind, even as my face went bright red and Richard also looked embarrassed.

"What can we get you, Linda?" He asked and managed, somehow to serve her with his usual sunny disposition.

After Linda left, he turned around to where I was sort of hiding behind the drinks' fridge. "Sophie, I'm not sure. Was that for real?" I hesitated, unsure myself at what had happened. Richard had always been fun to be around but I hadn't seen him as a boyfriend. To be truthful, since I had lost my leg, I hadn't thought I would ever be able to find someone who might be able to cope with that.

"I think so." I said quietly. "If you want it to be. I mean its ok to not want to be close to a hop-a-long." I was struggling with the whole situation realising, for the first time that I did want to be with someone and that that someone was Richard.

"A hop-a-long?! Now that is daft, Sophie. I sometimes need to look twice to even realise your leg isn't real. Look, why don't we go and have a drink tonight, after you've finished practising. We can see if we can work out how we want to go. Yes?"

I gasped. "Yes, that would be good." I took a step forward and we kissed again, just a gentle peck really but it seemed more important that way.

That evening was rather weird. I mean we liked each other but we were both wary of getting closer than just being friends.

Richard told me he found my golf almost unbelievably good and would love to be a part of that. That he was a scratch golfer planning to head that autumn to pro-school seemed, to him, to be a minor detail when compared with my plans. He had always assumed I would find a way to go on the tour without that need and that would mean we would be parted for most of the years ahead.

On the other hand, I both feared and longed for the closeness of a real boyfriend. Longed because I had never had one, feared a little because I was still a virgin but mostly because of how a boy or man, and let's be fair Richard was a man three years older than me, would react when they saw my scars. After all they would not be able to avoid them. They crossed my body with wide gashes from the tops of my thighs to my neck. More than once I had looked at myself in a mirror and wished that the surgeons had not managed to save me. In the end we decided to give it a go but promised each other that if it didn't work out there would be no recriminations. How easy that seems now when I look back.

Of course, I had the preparations for France, only four weeks away, and a smaller Open to play before then. Despite that we found ourselves together most evenings after practice or an occasional round of golf when we could both get out of the pro-shop.

Those evenings are some of the best, I can remember. Richard seeing me home after a drink or a takeaway, making sure I was safe. Our kisses grew more intimate as time passed until, I think it was at the end of the third week together, he invited me back for a coffee, as he put it. Of course, I knew exactly what he was hoping for and, to be honest, so was I, despite my misgivings as to how he might react. I was just praying that he wouldn't simply recoil and say it was a mistake. That he couldn't go through with it.

Richard had a one bed flat near the city centre. He'd bought it with money he had been left by his grandparents who had both died within a few months of each other. It was a lovely place. I guess he might have tidied it up before I saw it but I suspect that he was, of his nature, generally careful to look after his things. We did have a coffee but it was only a form of foreplay as we kissed and cuddled before moving into the bedroom which, thankfully, did have a double bed. I had decided to keep my leg on, its surface was soft enough to pass muster as skin and Richard had simply put on a soft side light. If the lighting had been bright, I doubt I would have had the nerve to let him undress me as he did, gently caressing my body as my clothes fell to the floor.

"Oh, my love, you are beautiful." Words that were probably the last I expected to hear. I knew better, even without the disfigurements, I was no more than good looking with a little shapeliness as Mum had once told me.

I decided that I had to remove his clothes while I could. He was taller than me and more muscular than I had ever realised. Our hands kept roaming as we dropped on to the bed. I had been warned, my Mum had always been practical about sex just hoping it would not be a one-night stand for my first time, that it might hurt, but Richard took his time not attempting to go the whole way until he was sure I was ready.

I suspected that he had more experience than I was aware of. He told me later that his first lover, if you could call her that, was an older woman. Not sure that late twenties could be deemed old, he said, but he was only eighteen at the time. She had guided him and helped him to learn how to satisfy his future lovers. Whoever she was, I said thank you in my mind. Richard was a kind and considerate lover. At least that was how I found him.

So, unlike some of the stories told by my friends, it was, I have to say, wonderful. And the second time was even better. I think we might have gone a third time, though that could just be wishful thoughts in my dreams later.

It was only after we had cleaned up in the shower that Richard reacted to my scars.

"My god, Sophie, if I could get my hands on that bastard, I swear he would never harm anyone again."

Somehow, I was sure then that, though we might, if I had my way anyway, have more nights in bed together, it would in time become a platonic relationship. That of close friends, I hoped, for the rest of our lives but not that of lovers. Richard deserved more than the fleeting moments we would be limited to if, by some miracle, I did make it on to the tour.

France and an Evening with Sophie.

It was, perhaps, a good thing that I was due to head for Paris a week later. The nights before then were fantastic, but exhausting, and it was with mixed feelings that I boarded the train for London that Monday, en-route to catch the Eurostar. It turned out that James had a few contacts in the French capital and I would be met at the Gare De Paris Nord. Monsieur Bois had promised to drive me to the hotel in Garches where I would be staying for the next fortnight.

It was a little nerve wracking for me to make this journey or maybe I should say terrifying. I had never been to London and to travel abroad on my own was another major step. I did reach Paris in one piece and Phillipe, who had taken on the role of chauffeur at James' request. He was, I am glad to say friendly, cheerful, and amusing. He was also fluent in English which was just as well, as my French was limited to the phrase book I had bought. My school language studies, such as they were, had involved me trying to learn Spanish and not very well at that.

I finally arrived in Garches in the early evening. Phillipe guided me through reception and ensured I got the best room still available, an upgrade I had not expected. Linda and the others were not due to arrive until the following Saturday. The Championship, itself, would start in earnest on the Monday.

I had managed to book practice rounds every day from the Wednesday and had been cleared to use a pull trolley, not ideal but better than having to carry my clubs. In the event the club, having learned of my false leg, lent me one of their part time pros to act as caddy and his knowledge of the course was to prove a great help to my preparations. Other competitors had also arrived early and most of the rounds were played as two or three balls. It was all very friendly; the weather was kind to us and the golf itself was enjoyable. By the Friday I felt that I knew the two courses that were to be played. For Saturday and Sunday, I planned work on the range, in the practice bunkers and on the putting green and, as it happened, some time with my fans!

Monday duly arrived and Linda had claimed my bag. With an early afternoon tee-time and among the last to start, I could see that I would need to play well. A score of level-par was unlikely to leave me above the likely cut line but as Linda said there was a lot of golf to be played, wishing me luck as she passed me my driver.

"On the tee, from England, Sophie Jordan." The English translation after a French introduction gave me goose pimples, as after the brief applause, I settled down going through my routine. Then just as I was halfway through my swing there was the sound of what seemed to be a gun going off. I wish I could have pulled out as I jumped, startled. My ball, far from going down the centre of the fairway, vanished left, deep into the thick trees. The tournament referee and other officials were immediately in conference before they turned to me. "M'selle. We are sorry but we cannot allow you to retake your shot."

I think that Linda was about to explode but I nodded, it was as I expected. The rules of golf are clear on this point and I resigned myself to playing another shot off the tee. The first shot had apparently gone out of bounds, so three off the tee it was. I could not recover the lost shots and my European experience got off to the worst possible start with a double bogey.

The wind had risen during the morning and the afternoon conditions were much harder. As the round progressed my fellow players were steadily dropping shots. With a little difficulty and with intense concentration, I managed to avoid that. Unfortunately, I could not find the necessary birdies. At the end of the day, I finished, still two over par and placed forty-first, three shots back from the cut-line. I went back to the hotel after spending an hour on the range, somewhat depressed but aware that I was out in the first hour the next morning and needed some rest.

The next morning, I was up with the sun determined to climb the leader board. More time on the range and the practice green before I made my way to the first tee. The conditions were a little better than the previous afternoon but it did seem that we might suffer the worst of the weather both days.

Linda had pulled rank on the others and claimed my bag for the second day. As we stood on the tee, she looked around the crowd with such a glare, I swear that a few backed away from the immediate area. This time there was no noise only a flutter of applause as this starting shot hurtled down the middle.

A few minutes later I ran a twenty-foot putt into the hole for what proved to be the first of seven birdies. The only blemish on my card was a bogey on the last hole after my approach bounced sideways into a bunker and I could not manage the sand save needed.

Still, I knew I now had a chance of making the cut at four under with the officials suggesting that three under would be the mark, though with a quarter of the field still to start that was by no means certain.

Linda refused to let me mope around as she put it.

"Come on, Sophie. You've done all you can and what a round that was today. I checked. Six under is three shots better than anyone else so far. Now, we are off to get some lunch, I suspect that you haven't eaten properly since yesterday morning."

She was right, of course, and I gratefully settled into a seat at the restaurant the others had found near the golf course. Thanks to their company the time passed quickly.

Finally, I returned to the golf club around four in a state of nervous anticipation. Had I done enough?

As I walked into the area where a leader board had been set up, I was met by the tournament referee who had ruled, correctly don't get me wrong, against my implied request for a second start the day before.

"M'selle Jordan, merci. And I **mean**, thank you. You were courteous and pleasant yesterday when you must have felt like screaming. We have not been able to find the culprit who brought shame on the club and the federation. I am happy to be able to tell you that you will have made the cut, despite that start. There are a few players still out there but you have qualified. Today you played better than the field by a long way. May I wish you the best tomorrow."

"Monsieur, merci. It was not your fault yesterday and I can look forward to tomorrow now."

I raced back out to find Linda. "We made it, Linda! We made it!"

She beamed. "No, Sophie. You made it. Now its matchplay and you don't need to fear anyone after today's performance."

Wednesday and the knockout matchplay began. I woke that morning aware that I would need to arrive for a session on the driving range early. Of the sixteen matches to be played in the morning mine was the eleventh with a tee-time of half past nine. I remember that my biggest concern was that if I did win, I would be faced with a second round later in the afternoon and I hadn't played thirty-six holes in a day since I was fourteen. Oh well, I thought, let's cross that bridge if I need to.

Another club member took over from Linda, carrying my bag. Ginny was a Scot and I learned, later, that threats had been made, if Linda didn't back down and share the load.

If I am honest, that day became something of a blur. In the morning I got off to a flier, winning four of the first five holes. My opponent regained a little self-esteem pulling one back at the second of the par threes but I lost no other holes and eventually won six and five. The end was not that friendly. The handshake at the start proved much warmer while that after I had sunk the winning putt was short and cold, there was no well done or similar words.

As the younger girl quickly marched away, I suspect in tears, I started towards her to commiserate. Ginny stopped me following her, guiding me to the scorer's office alongside the official who had followed our game. "Let her go. Remember, you would have been pretty upset if you had lost by that score especially since she didn't play badly. You simply showed your class."

Showed my class?! I still found it difficult to understand that other people considered me to be that good.

The afternoon game proved harder, partly because I found fatigue setting in and my leg was hurting more than it usually did, but mostly because my Irish opponent grabbed the lead at the first hole and was not about to lose it. By the time we reached the turn I had begun to wonder if she would make any mistakes. That my tournament would be at an end and then it happened.

Her drive on the tenth strayed into the first cut. That would not have been a problem, but there were trees cutting off her second shot to the green. To this day I do not understand why she did what she did. Was it because I was in perfect position forty or so yards in front of her? Whatever, she tried a shot I would never have risked, trying to cut the ball around the trees and on to the green. A few moments later there was a scream of anguish as the ball vanished into the water on the left. Her game fell apart and I won the next five holes before the match ended on the fifteenth when she missed a long putt before turning and shaking my hand with surprising warmth, saying. "Sophie, well done. You played well, sorry for my meltdown on the tenth."

I could only give her a hug admitting that I had been wondering if I would find anything capable of beating her before that happened. We parted on friendly terms while I started to realise that I was into the last eight. I needed rest, maybe another two rounds tomorrow?

Day four and the quarter finals would be in the morning. The golf was as difficult as I anticipated. After all, the players left were the better ones across the board, although there had been one shock. My win on the previous morning had, unbeknown to me, removed one of the joint favourites. Now I was attracting more attention, whereas on the first few days I had been an unknown.

Surprisingly, when I look back, the morning was the harder match going, in the end, to the second extra hole. Again, my opponent was unable to hole a long putt for a birdie leaving me with a shorter, knee trembler of seven feet for mine. This time we walked off the course arm in arm as she warned me, she would get her revenge at the Amateur Championship before wishing me all the luck in the semi-final.

Semi-final, oh wow! And I had only half an hour to rest and get a snack before heading back out!

"Ridiculous, absolutely ridiculous!" Ginny's sister, Fiona was not amused. "They should have given you at least an hour."

This time I was faced by a junior champion from the previous year and she had had a couple of hours rest. Of necessity I had to force any thoughts of fatigue to the back of my mind and focus. Fiona, now on the bag, muttered about bananas and I smiled. "Let's go, my friend."

I don't know whether the other girl had taken the time for a little practice in her break but, if she had, it hadn't helped her. As a champion it was also difficult to believe that nerves were getting the better of her. I could not and cannot believe it was anything to do with my own earlier performances but for some reason her early play was unbelievably poor.

Her choice of shots, even allowing for the deteriorating weather, was not even close to good and for the second time in two days I raced into a four-hole lead. As the round continued her demeanour and approach visibly worsened despite almost constant conversations with her caddy.

I would be lying if I suggested that this did not affect me and my own play suffered. It made no difference though and I was winning, or at least halving, holes with bogeys as well as pars. Overall, when I look back, it was my worst eleven holes of that week, as we finished on the twelfth fairway after my second shot landed on the green. Already seven down, she threw her iron back in her bag, walked over and, with the briefest of words, conceded.

For a few moments I stood there a little stunned. I was in the final! Just how, I was struggling to absorb without allowing my emotions to show, when all the girls from my club broke across the fairway to mob me in delight.

As we walked back to the clubhouse the exhaustion suddenly hit and I stumbled. Only my friends saved me from a bad fall as they caught me and brought another meaning to the description of supporters.

Bed was very welcome that night, even if Richard wasn't around. Linda and her cohorts had ensured I got a decent meal before helping me back to my room. Linda insisted that she would help me get ready for bed as the near fall had left her worried that I might fall again when dealing with my leg. I tried to get her to let me alone but, to be honest, her help was welcome. Only the fact that, inevitably as she helped me undress, she saw my scars, truly upset me.

"Thirty years he got, didn't he? I tell you Sophie, if it had been up to me, he would be locked in a deep cellar and the key thrown away." She thought for a moment. "Or maybe I'd just have him cut into large pieces."

"Don't Linda, I know I must live with this and do my best to be positive. Believe me I still have nightmares where I have him at my mercy. You wouldn't want to know what my dream self looks to do."

"Let's hope they don't come tonight; you need your sleep."

"They aren't as frequent as they were and I have better things to dream about." I smiled, before dropping back on to my bed. Within a few minutes, I suspect, I was deep asleep. Even my nervous anticipation of the next day failed to keep me awake.

I woke early the next morning, mainly because of the banging on my door. Ginny was there. She had been talked into being my escort to the golf club and to make sure I was up and ready in time for practice.

The final would be over thirty-six holes and we would be starting at eight o'clock. Oh boy, I thought, I do hope I can keep going. The previous two days had taken their toll and both my legs were feeling the strain. Only the presence of my fan club, as I was now thinking of them, provided the drive to not let them down.

Back home my parents, Alan, and Richard had all sent best wishes as had the Club Secretary. James in a rather lengthy text had emphasised that I had already done the Club proud. Just one more match now, before you can take some real rest!

We shook hands and my opponent, Francine, went first. That first eighteen holes will stick in my memory for a long time. It was quickly apparent that both of us had brought our A-game to this final day. As we returned to the clubhouse for the half-time break the match was all-square. In fact, we had shared every hole up to that point with five birdies and thirteen pars each. It was fun! Was it competitive, of course it was, but it was enjoyable as we fought to match each other's shots.

As we headed out to the first tee for the afternoon session, I thought for a moment that I could see family in the crowd, but I knew that they were back in England. Oh, I should say that I had never played in front of so many people, several hundred were tracking us as we moved around the course.

With Linda's help, she was back on the bag, I managed to put them to the back of my mind and focus on my game. For five holes we continued to match each other before I made a mistake on the sixth. Francine hit her approach to about seven feet for a clear birdie opportunity, while I did not allow enough for the wind with my ball landing in a bunker. One down with twelve to play!

Uncertainty in golf is, I guess, no different from any individual sport and, boy, was I suddenly unsure of my game. Then I realised. I had seen someone I knew. Alan was there, I was sure of it.

Now I had to play, but Francine was indefatigable matching me stroke for stroke until we reached the thirteenth. Her tee shot on the short par three hit the green and spun back to a few feet. I knew I had to at least match her, two down and I suspected it would be a lost cause.

Linda muttered about my club choice, the wind was gusting, and I decided to club up before taking a few breaths more than normal. As the ball left my club, I knew instinctively that I had hit it perfectly. Turning through the wind the ball dropped on to the apron, bounced once onto the green, and then ran up to the hole. For an agonising second it stopped and then slowly toppled in for my first ever hole-in-one.

The high fives around the tee were joyous. Everyone involved loves to see an ace, even opponents. Suddenly the roar from the crowd broke my desire to shut them out. Back to all square!

I seemed to grow with that shot and the fifteenth was just what I needed. Despite the issues over my swing with my artificial leg, I was still outdriving my opponent by twenty to thirty yards. On the par fours that had not proved particularly useful but this par five gave me a real chance. For me it was reachable with a good drive. For Francine it would be difficult even with two perfect shots. A few minutes later I was standing over a reasonable putt for eagle, on the other hand she was facing a shot from a deep bunker short of the green.

Her sand shot was not bad either but the ball raced away across the green and when her resultant fifty-foot putt came up short she conceded the hole. I never did get that eagle.

We halved the next two holes, which was now all I needed, and I was able to play conservatively at the eighteenth. Francine could not and her second shot aimed directly at a difficult pin position ended up in a bunker. I was able to simply aim for the centre of the green and two putts were enough.

Francine's hug as, I stood in shock, was the best moment as I realised – I was the Champion!

"I think there are some people who want to say hi, Sophie. Well played, we will meet again, I hope."

As she finished, she stepped aside to clear the way and then all hell let loose, as a pile of people descended on me. My first thought was that the girls had given way to their impulse to crowd me out, then and only then did it sink in that Alan really was there and so were my parents!

"Alan organised the trip when he knew you had reached the semi-final but swore us to silence and to keep towards the back of the crowd until now. He worried you would be put off if you knew we were here." It was my Dad whispering as Mum tried to hug me without crying.

I turned to my long-time supporter. "Alan, thank you."

"There is someone else here, Sophie." Alan replied and nudged another figure forward. It was one of the prosthetics team from the hospital. I gasped with delight.

"Doctor Patel, how wonderful to see you here."

"Sophie, your golf club told me of your success in reaching the finals. I had to come and watch you play. The team all send their congratulations, I just called them, and they wanted me to say what I would have said anyway." Anita responded with a smile. "I don't pretend to follow golf and I needed Alan to help me understand what was going on. You continue to outperform far beyond what we could ever have hoped to see. You're the best advert for the new technology yet."

"Thank you, you know that without your work over the past four years I could never have managed this. It is a bonus to see you."

"And am I a bonus too?" The voice came from behind me and my heart leapt.

"Richard, how?"

He grinned. "Sophie, you didn't think I was going to miss this. The club sorted out cover for Alan and me. I think James may be serving in the shop! And, wow, was it worth coming! You played great." I shut him up with a long kiss, a little to his embarrassment, I think, but I was over the moon that so many of my family and friends had been there to see me win my first big championship.

At the prize giving, a short time later, Alan had come up trumps again with a list of thank-yous I had to make. To the greenkeepers, the club, and the officials and, of course, to all the other players but especially to Francine who really deserved congratulations and had been gracious in her words after receiving the runners-up trophy. I had not prepared a speech; I had simply found it too difficult to truly believe I could win.

For the first time in a long time, I started to look towards the future with belief. Belief that I might really be able to become a half decent golfer.

I returned home with a bounce in my step that brought back memories of my early teens. Those thoughts did not last long but engendered a desire to do something I will admit I had been neglecting. Despite being tired from the journey back, I had one place I needed to visit even before I went home and I had to do that alone, despite the protestations of my Mum.

The nearby florist was happy to provide a small bunch of carnations and I caught a bus across town to the crematorium. Dawn's grave was always being looked after by her family but, when I arrived, there were no fresh flowers and I found that helpful. Having placed my bunch in the water holder, I knelt talking to my late friend under my breath almost silently. They tell me that such words are never wasted. I was still there, lost in my thoughts, when a quiet voice gently disturbed me. Dawn's mother had also come to visit her daughter's resting place. We spoke just a few words together before I left her alone to tend to the grave and add another few flowers to mine.

I got to the house much later than the family had hoped but my brothers had stayed in to greet me. We had a small celebration before exhaustion finally caught up with me and I headed for my bed.

The next few days felt a little unreal as everyone at the club seemed to want to congratulate me and ask about the tournament. In the end, Alan, who was back from the club pro competitions he had entered, was forced to intervene, more than once.

After discussion the Club decided that there would have to be an "Evening with Sophie." where I could tell my story and answer questions.

Conscious that I would have a lot of travelling expenses in the coming months, as I looked to compete in the bigger competitions, the Club committee decided that the evening should act as a fund raiser for me with a nominal charge for admission. I only found out later that the nominal charge was an eye-watering, to me anyway, twenty pounds. James had argued that it was easily affordable for most of the members and that a separate session with the juniors would be easier on numbers.

To say I was more nervous than when I had teed off in the final is to understate. The only comfort was that the audience would be friendly, I hoped.

Organisational issues meant, in the end, that I had my first presentation with the juniors and that was not as easy as I thought it would be. My success seemed to have irritated a few of the older players who constantly questioned how I had got the wildcard sent to the club and not one of them.

Jake, the juniors' captain listened for several minutes looking askance before finally intervening.

"I have listened, with an increasing level of disbelief, to the whinges and moans from the last three or four members and to Sophie's calm responses. It is perhaps apparent, or should be, that that calmness is one of the reasons she is, by far, the best player in the club. And I mean in the club, not just amongst present company. You may have forgotten, or simply ignored, the fact that she won both the Ladies and the Men's Orders of Merit last year."

"She didn't win the junior one, though, did she?" The shout came from a seventeen-year-old, Daniel, who I recall had a playing handicap of two. He had something of a problem with his temper, having been known to break clubs if he hit a bad shot and, I remember Alan saying he would never make it big until he learned to control his emotions.

"That is right, Daniel, and that is because she didn't compete in enough junior events. Her time was taken up with the adult events, invitations, and Opens around the country. I might add, nor did you win the Order of Merit, as I recall. Had Sophie played in even half of the qualifying events I suspect she would have had enough points to beat us all. And remember, the wildcard was for a Ladies event, so most of you wouldn't qualify."

Jake took a breath as he clearly tried to control his own temper before continuing. "Oh, and for the record, the letter to the Club was sent by the French Golf Federation. It didn't ask us to nominate anyone. It was an invitation to send Sophie to compete and included a letter offering her the wild card."

"That's rubbish! They don't write to Clubs!" Daniel shouted before he stormed out of the room, hurling a final insult. "You wait, you'll see. I'm entering the Amateur Championship and I'm going to win it! She's just a flash-in-the-pan."

Jake grimaced. "I'm sorry Sophie, that was nonsense and I hope you know it."

James had been sitting quietly at a table in the corner and his expression did not bode well for the, as he later called him, spoilt brat.

A few days later, I was to learn, the Club ended Daniel's membership and told him to leave. At first, I worried that this action was simply a response to his words aimed at me but Richard told me, later, that the truth was, he had upset too many members with his tantrums when playing in various competitions. I was sad that it had had to come to that. With a little restraint he could have been a very good golfer but despite Alan's attempts there had been no progress in correcting his behaviour. I would not come across him, personally, again. He did find another club, and did try to win the Amateur Championship but that was not in my future.

After the mild, I think, hostility of those few juniors, the evening with the adult members was not difficult at all. Alan chaired it, fielding questions and ensuring I was given the time to answer those I could.

Telling of the exhilaration of scoring a hole-in-one during the final was the highlight of the evening. My explanation of how everyone, including Francine, had high-fived me was received by the audience with awe, I sensed.

"You know, we've seen it on the television when the professionals score an ace, how everyone is happy for them. It was no different for me." I said.

I think that the idea that I could have enjoyed the final and found it fun, had not occurred to my audience and I had to reiterate that when you and your opponent are playing the best golf you can together, the challenge of finding a way to beat them was, perhaps surprisingly, less of a strain. Harder though when you fall behind!

The final question almost stumped me for an answer that did not sound big-headed. "Sophie, can we look forward to you bringing back the Amateur Championship trophy in the Summer?

I thought for a moment before replying. "It would be nice. And I'll give it my best shot but don't hold your breath anyone, I'm not even sure my ranking is good enough to be more than, perhaps, a reserve. If I don't make it, I might try and qualify for the Women's Open but that's a pro competition and much tougher."

Alan nodded in approval before calling an end to the evening, commenting that he hoped they had had their money's worth and thanking me for my patience.

I managed one last comment. "You know, of course, that were it not for Alan, I wouldn't be here. It has been he who has been my guide for more than a decade. Please give him a round of applause, and thank you for coming."

There was a call from the audience, to friendly laughter. "True that may be, Sophie, but it is you who has to go out there and play and, boy, you really do that!"

The next day Alan and I got together for a council of war. It was as I had feared, the win in France had helped but my World Amateur Golf Ranking was still only one hundred and sixty-five.

"You haven't been able to play enough Elite events yet." Alan told me. "Most of the top one hundred will have played more than twenty, some more than thirty. You've been limited to playing in

England with a couple of tournaments in Wales. And March was the cut-off. We'll look to put you on the reserve list but you are going to be relying on enough players dropping out."

"So, I'm looking at next year really?" It was depressing to know that I had not done enough to qualify. Now I had to try and play more Elite events and play well. I couldn't, for the moment, entirely shake off a feeling that I just wasn't good enough to compete on the world stage.

Richard stuck his head around the door and interrupted. "Alan, you're needed for your next lesson."

"Right. Sophie, have a look into the Women's Open rules. That is, as I understand it, a genuine open but you will have to enter pre-qualifying."

I had to explain to Richard about my ranking not being high enough as far as we could tell.

"I need to enter as many Elite competitions as I can this year. If nothing else, that will give me a chance of making it into the Women's Amateur, next year."

He thought for a moment. "I did think it was an Open, not the case anymore then?"

"No. It isn't. How can I tell people that I haven't made it?" I suddenly felt down, there were so many people rooting for me and it looked as if I would disappoint them.

"Sophie, don't forget you are still only eighteen. You have time on your side, if it takes another year, well it takes another year. Look. Go check those details and we'll have a drink after you work out on the range."

A drink sounded good, with the implied promise of other exercise later, and I grinned my agreement.

My research into the Open showed that I would be accepted for the preliminary qualification although I did gulp when I recognised how many of the world's best would likely be there. Perhaps I was moving too quickly, I thought, but then I remembered that I was still an amateur. Just qualifying would be good and then if, by some miracle, I made the cut then that would be success. Forget winning, it had been a long time since an amateur had won.

My plans involved a lot of travelling and I would have struggled to get to some events except that my brothers had found the money to buy me driving lessons once I was seventeen and then, with Mum and Dad's help, had given me a small car for my eighteenth birthday.

The weeks passed and my form held up well. Another win at an event at the Belfry plus seven top ten finishes saw time fly past with the Amateur Championship looming on the horizon. I had sent my entry in but as expected my ranking was not high enough for automatic acceptance. However, there was some hope. Although the field was full, I was on a reserve list. I thought about that hope but soon realised that it was, really, only a gesture. The headline reserve list was twelve long and guess who was twelfth?

During this period, I spent a fun weekend at Wentworth with the Curtis Cup team. We did play a round of golf but, as Alan had told me, it was the Q&A session that provided a telling example of how different players would react to my lost leg. The Captain told them that all they had to do was emulate my determination and the USA would have to watch out.

I decided that, even though the Championship, itself, would start on the Monday with practice rounds, I would still play in the prior week's event. There were no other Elite events, in the UK, during the week of the Championship, not surprisingly, and I decided that I would go and take the opportunity to watch and learn from those who had qualified from around the world.

Perhaps the thoughts of the next week affected me but my own performance suffered with a finish outside the top twenty for the first time that year. The ladies from the club had been taking it in turns to caddy for me and Ginny, who had the bag that week, was distraught with the idea that she had not found a way to drive me into the top ten. Truth was, and is, that Ginny was the best caddy among my friends and she made me laugh at that idea anyway. I had simply ignored her advice too often.

Amateur Championship

By Monday morning, that phone call I had been praying for had not, as I truly expected, happened and I decided to set off to watch the practice rounds. Royal Lytham & St Anne's is a beautiful spot and has hosted The Open frequently. It was also where the Championship had first been played in 1893. To walk through the gates was quite something even as a spectator. Having decided that I would spend part of the day following one or two groups as they practised, I set off to gently walk around.

At lunchtime I settled down to eat my sandwiches sitting in one of the locations that allowed me to see two greens. It was fascinating to see how these top players dealt with the undulations when they missed the green and I decided that I would try and claim the same spot on at least the Tuesday for the first qualifying round.

Much as I enjoyed relaxing there was frustration that I could not be out on the course with the others and, believe me, I saw some awesome shots. Finally, as the afternoon progressed, I made my way towards the clubhouse to watch players as they finished the course. I was stopped as I looked to enter the stand at the back of the green. For the first time since I had entered the grounds, I was asked for my pass. As a reserve I had been provided with a basic players pass for the week, not as valuable as the pass if I had made the entry list but something that made it feasible for me to attend. I would have struggled to find the money for a week-long ticket, that was certain. "Miss Jordan, you are Sophie Jordan?" The steward seemed quite excited which, given I wasn't even competing was a little disconcerting and for a moment I thought I might be about to be thrown out.

Nervously, I replied. "Yes, that's me. It is my pass. Is there a problem?"

"We have been asked to find you if we could, we were told the organisers understood you were somewhere here and they need to talk to you. Please wait a moment." He moved away speaking on a radio link before turning back to me.

"Miss, you are needed in the clubhouse. Just follow the path round and go up the steps to the recording office." He paused with a smile. "And good luck, lass."

To say I was disturbed and yet suddenly excited is to say the least. I made my way around to the recording office and nervously knocked on the door.

"Come in, come in." The voice sounded guarded but gave a sense of urgency as well.

I went in to be greeted by a smiling gentleman, at least that was the way I saw him, dressed in a suit and tie despite the warmth.

"Miss Jordan, I am so pleased to meet you and I am sorry we did not find you earlier. Like the other reserves you have been rather difficult to contact. You have your mobile switched off?"

"Yes, I tried to follow the rules, but how did you know I was here?"

"In the end, we contacted your club and they told us. Sophie, I am pleased to invite you, if you still wish to, to play in the Championship."

I gasped, if I wished to? Of course, I did but I didn't have my clubs or a caddy. Could I organise it?

"Of course, I do but..." I went on to explain what I needed to do. "I was twelfth on the list, I never expected to get an entry."

"I don't blame you for that. I'm not sure we have ever had to go that far down the list either. We had four last minute withdrawals but haven't been able to contact anyone else other than the first three. I admit we were just about to give up when you arrived at the eighteenth. If it helps, your tee-time tomorrow will be in the last group off the first tee. That will be around three forty-five. Can you manage to handle that?"

Could I manage that! I would have borrowed a second-hand bunch of clubs to get that opportunity!

"I'll be on the tee, Sir."

"That is good, I am sorry you could not have a practice round."

I left the room in something of a shock, scrabbling for my phone and finally getting it working. Who should I call? In the end the first call was an easy choice.

"Richard, you won't believe it. I'm in!"

"How?" His own excitement was tangible.

I explained and then told him I really needed someone to bring my clubs, I would borrow a putter, if I could, and practice putting before hitting the range if I could get my clubs. Even as I was speaking, I was suddenly worried, what if no-one could make the trip? Surely Richard would.

"Sophie, don't worry I'll get them to you somehow. I can't do it myself, I'm not at home. I'm away now and won't be able to get back in time. Who would you like as your caddy?"

"Oh, Richard! I'd hoped you could but if you can't then I'll ring Ginny. She's the best of the other caddies."

I don't know why but Richard not being able to join me hurt more than it should. It wasn't as if our relationship was out of kilter but I hadn't realised that he was away. He hadn't told me of anything special happening and this wasn't the time to ask more questions. He promised to do what he could by phone but left me to call Ginny, who wouldn't be expecting to hear from me.

"Sophie, that's great! But you want me to caddy? After last week?"

"Ginny, last week was not your fault. I trust you more than anyone else to advise me. Please, are you able to do it?"

She was, without a question, and promised to head north as soon as she could get my clubs from home. With the time as it was, I was sure my Mum, at least, would be in and promised to call her and warn her that Ginny would be knocking on the door to claim my clubs and spare balls. Mum, of course, was over the moon that her little girl would be playing in the big tournament, although she still found it difficult to understand why some were bigger than others. Golf had never been her game and she relied on others to explain each step and how I had to work to get better.

Ginny was as good as her word, arriving later that evening. Fortunately, I had managed to get her a room at the same B&B that I was staying at, no grand hotel for us, but it was comfortable and the owners pleasant and helpful.

My real concern the following morning was the lack of a practice round which meant that I had little real knowledge of the course beyond what I had seen as a spectator. Ginny solved that by doing what a caddy does. While I headed for the range and the practice areas, she set off to walk the course.

I am still not sure how she did that in the short time she had but she was back in time to have some lunch before I headed out for some last-minute practice. In due course, just after three twenty, we reached the first tee, where, to my amazement, I found Francine preparing to start. We had a warm embrace as she made a mock groan.

"No chance for the rest of us now, ma Cherie! How are you here? I did not see you on the entry listing, which did surprise me a little."

"A long story, I'll tell you later." As I responded to the beckoning starter.

"On the first tee, holder of the Esmond Trophy, Sophie Jordan." There was warm applause and, thankfully, I struck a decent shot down the fairway. I stepped back as Francine moved forward.

"On the first tee, the French Junior Champion, Francine Bonnevoir." I jumped, I had not known just how good Francine was and now I knew. How the hell had I beaten her?

As I ruminated over that mystery the third player in our group was announced and, apparently shaken by playing with the French

Champion, duly missed the fairway. To this day I am sorry to say that I cannot remember who that player was except that she had a terrible day. It was as if she had never played on a links course in windy conditions and her game fell apart.

Even Francine struggled with the wind but, like myself, she clearly had some experience of similar conditions and while not setting the course alight, we managed to complete decent rounds of one and three over respectively. I would like to think that my lack of a practice round cost me but, as I had experienced the day before, the conditions were very different.

Last back in the clubhouse we found quickly that both our scores were very respectable. There were joint leaders, at two under par, and two more players who had shot level par. Francine was well placed one further back and I was surprised to find myself still only ninth.

Wednesday, and the rains came as the forecasters had warned us. And how. We were due to be first off, the tenth tee, and reached it only to be sent back to the clubhouse. The officials had decided that the combination of high winds and flooded greens made it necessary to suspend play even before it began.

The next few hours dragged until finally the rain eased off and the ground staff were able to clear the greens. At almost one o'clock we finally got away as a two ball. Our playing partner from the previous round had withdrawn, apparently unable to face trying to recover from her disastrous performance the day before.

By the turn, as we reached the first tee, I was beginning to feel as if that unnamed individual had had it right. Despite Ginny's best efforts my clubs were getting wetter and harder to handle and even our waterproofs seemed to be failing. How the greenkeeping staff were managing to keep the greens playable was a mystery.

Francine was no better off and found simply keeping the ball in play, hard. The rain had returned although not as bad as at the start of the day but it was the winds that were the worst. We were told later that if they had been any stronger play would have had to be abandoned. It was only because the greens were so wet, I felt, that balls did not roll in the blustery gusts. Still, we battled on as did most of the field, although a few gave up and withdrew. I rather think that they were not in any real contention.

Finally, and to our relief, we completed our rounds. The end of round, handshakes were brief, no-one wanted to stay outside any longer than they had to and having dealt with the necessary paperwork in the scorer's tent we headed into the clubhouse where we all did our best to dry out before getting a much-needed drink.

Francine and her caddy had nabbed a table with a view over the eighteenth green and Ginny and I joined them and spent a while watching our fellow competitors coming in, some looking as if they were even wetter than we had been. That, Ginny commented, was impossible but the amount of water flowing off the waterproofs suggested that it might be true.

Juliet, Francine's caddy, suggested that quite a few of the field might not have very good weatherproofs, as she put it. "They come from warmer places and some will never have had to face these conditions. We know your English weather quite well though." She laughed.

I should say that I was still wondering if I had done enough to make the top sixty-four who would face off in the first round of the matchplay the next day. It was easy to say that all the scores would be higher than usual but I was sitting there with a total of nine over par after a seventy-eight. Francine was eight over and I knew that those scores would not have been good enough the previous year when the cut had been at two over.

Ginny was quite sensitive to my mood and my French friend, as I was beginning to think of her, was no more upbeat than I. Ginny finally stuck her oar in.

"Look you two, I know you are worried and in none of the last three years would either of you have made the cut but I did do a little studying of the competition earlier this year. The conditions both yesterday and today are easily the worst seen for at least a decade. The leaders only managed, what? Two under, yesterday? The way the weather has been, I'd be surprised if the cut isn't well into double figures over par. So, can we have a little cheer? Please?" If she had used sign language, she might have had more success, as we watched the rain finally stopping with a good portion of the field still out on the course.

Francine put it in a nutshell, with a sigh. "We'd better hope they have all had bad starts because they are certainly going to find it easier now."

It took a while but slowly the scoreboard filled up. The conditions had made it difficult for the live scoreboards around the course to work and so we had had no chance to see how the rest of the field were managing. Quite well, it seemed, as it developed. Shortly after the rain stopped the live board lit up. Neither of us was on the first page of the leader board nor on the following two pages, and it looked as if several players had finished well under par. The idea that we would be going home tomorrow was looking more likely by the minute.

Francine was muttering. "That cannot be correct. Some of those players scored worse, a lot worse, than we did yesterday. To be returning scores of around par for both rounds would mean that they have shot eight or nine or more under today. Even Tiger Woods could not do that in this weather! Could he?" Her voice rose in pitch as she questioned what we were seeing

"We'll have to wait and see, I guess." I wasn't optimistic but it did seem crazy, particularly when one of those who had led overnight had returned an eighty-four to be one stroke behind me.

Finally, Ginny could not continue to sit in such a dismal grouping and vanished. To my surprise I saw her heading down the course to where she would be able to see one of the scoreboards near the fifteenth. I didn't see her return but a little while later she crossed the bar triumphant.

"You look far too happy." I grouched. "Don't tell me. You know you won't be out getting soaked again, tomorrow."

"Lord, Francine, see what I have to put up with." Ginny's smile took the sting out of her response. "Now look, guys. No promises but it seems that one of the team of scorers has managed to get the inputs wrong. Nobody, as I understand it, has managed to complete a sub-par round yet and no-one out in the park is under par or anywhere near it."

"Then we have a chance?" Francine perked up.

"Chance? This is from the scorers. The best player, at the minute, and they are out there still, is seven over today and seven over for the tournament. I reckon that once they correct the error, and revise the board, you two will be in the top half dozen. Now could I have a smile or two?"

I held my breath. Top half dozen and I hadn't even played well! Straight into the second round of the match-play without needing to start in the preliminary round? Really? I decided to breathe slowly and, just in case, not get my hopes up again.

"How long before we know tee times, if you're right of course?"

"They should have everything done within a few minutes of the last group finishing." Juliet commented.

"Yes." Ginny agreed. "They are already building the structure now based on current scores. Of course, it will change a little as the final numbers are filed but I think it would be safe to say we'll all be out there at some point, just not together."

And she was right. A few hours later the draw for the first or preliminary round and the second rounds were announced. There was, for the first time, no need for a preliminary round as no players had tied such that more than sixty-four qualified and we were in the top ten.

As we split up to return to our B&B and Francine to her hotel there were mutual offers of good luck. I didn't know, but it looked as if we were now in opposite sides of the draw and, I was certain, wouldn't meet again. I truly found it difficult to believe that I would make much progress, let alone the final.

One round at a time, Ginny reminded me. "Remember, Sophie, you never expected to do well in France and yet...."

By comparison to the first two days of competition, the third day was uneventful. We woke to clear skies and the wind had dropped, perfect weather for links golf or for any golf to be truthful.

I recall being very thankful that the day only required a single round. The previous round had been quite exhausting and I had suffered a restless night with my leg providing irritation. I had always wondered how amputees could claim to still be able to feel their lost limbs. Believe me, it was nights like that that demonstrated just how crazy it can be.

Despite that, we were up early, I had drawn the fifth tee time just before nine o'clock and that meant heading for the course not long after seven. Our hosts were very understanding, and a little excited, Ginny thought, serving us with a good breakfast much earlier than they would normally have done.

I found myself playing an American who hailed from Boston. Ella won the toss and decided to go first. I admit that Ginny and I had talked about this and had decided that if I had won that toss, I would have chosen to go second, so I was quite happy.

A little to my surprise Ella's first drive was with her three-wood rather than her driver. Nevertheless, the ball ended on the fairway around the two-hundred-yard mark. A sensible if constrained start. I, as ever, took my driver and duly also hit the fairway but much closer to the two-hundred-and-fifty-yard distance and that is how the match continued.

From the start I played well, perhaps not to my best but that wasn't needed as I was reaching most of the greens in regulation. Ella was having to rely on a chip and putt game which might have worked on an inland course but failed on the links as she was unable to get up and down, much of the time. As a result, I was winning holes with pars as well as a few birdies. Only on the par threes did Ella threaten and by the thirteenth I was six up with six to play – dormie. For the first time she opted for her driver and struck a monster drive comfortably over three hundred yards. Unfortunately, for her, the ball ended up well right and out of bounds.

Showing little or no emotion she turned to me and shook my hand, saying "Well played, Sophie. No point in finishing this hole now. Good luck tomorrow."

Her caddy was also friendly, being a local introduced through the club. "You played, I suspect, within yourself today, Sophie. You managed the course well. Keep that up and you will be difficult to beat even by the best of the players here. Ella will admit that this was as far as she expected to get, we talked a lot over the first two days, but she couldn't resist the chance to play here. It'd be different if she were back home."

With those thoughts, I invited Ella back for a drink and we spent an hour or so talking about places where we had played. Finally, I couldn't resist asking why she had not used her driver more.

She grimaced at the memory, still raw. "You saw what happened when I did. I still have work to do on my swing. I tried it yesterday and it was a disaster. You know, I only just made the cut?"

It had not occurred to me to see how she had performed, after all strokeplay and matchplay are quite different and I apologised for not knowing.

"Not a problem." She grinned and we went back to talking about different courses we liked. I think she was surprised that I had not travelled more and played more Elite tournaments outside the UK. In the end I had to explain about my false leg and the loss of that year. At that she sat silent, stunned, I think.

Finally, she spoke, quietly. "That is amazing. First that you could come back from such a traumatic event and second the technology in the prosthetic. It allows you to have a swing better than most despite what should be a major constraint. There are two members at my club who are amputees and neither of them have a great swing and they can't even walk the course. They have no choice but to use buggies. Don't get me wrong I still think it is great that they can even play the game. But you, gosh, Sophie, you are headed for the top! Remember me, when you get there, because when you come to my side of the pond, I'll be gunning for you!" She smiled before embracing me and heading off to change.

Ella's departure left me in an emotional state. More compliments, suggesting I could make it big time. Not just from her, which was nice, but also from her caddy who must have known the course well and have seen many golfers play.

Finishing early meant that I could rest up before the next day which might involve as much as thirty-six holes and I was for the first time starting to get an unreal sensation, for me anyway, that I might be good enough.

Before we finished eating that evening, I confessed that feeling to Ginny. She was rather surprised, she said, that I still didn't realise how good I was. But stay that way she told me, and she would help me keep my feet on the ground. "Stay nervous, my friend. That way you'll play your best. I might be thinner and my legs shorter but that would be good, Sophie."

Another early start and a long match against, this time, a German player. She was friendly enough but I had to think there was a sense of the Teutonic nature in her play. This was my hardest match, probably since the final in France, and the lead swapped several times though neither of us could manage a two-hole lead. We went to the eighteenth with my opponent one up.

This was it, I had to go for it. A half would not be good enough, only a win. The hole is a four-hundred-and-ten-yard par four. It isn't the hardest hole on the course but fraught with danger with multiple bunkers. In the earlier rounds I had only used my three-wood, this time I knew I would have to go with my driver unless Dagmar made a mess of her drive. Some chance of that, I thought, as I watched her shot appear to be fairway bound. I took my driver and with an extra deep breath struck, probably my best drive of the day. Despite the wind, I knew it would be close to two hundred and fifty yards leaving only a mid-range iron in.

In the event Dagmar's drive had drifted off the fairway and her second shot was impeded by gorse bushes. A few minutes later and we were headed for the first hole, into sudden death. At a par three, for heaven's sake! Having the honour, I hit a decent shot only to see it bounce right and down into one of the pot bunkers. Dagmar, seeing this, played a conservative shot into the heart of the green, giving her two putts for a par, a winning position, she must have thought.

For me the only plus was that I had landed in the bunker furthest from the hole and I had some green to play with. Crazily, I was still nearer the pin than Dagmar who duly ran her putt to only a couple of feet with a sense of now you get up and down, Sophie. I did make her mark her ball and then focused on my sand shot, conscious that my tournament was about to end if I couldn't get reasonably close. Thinking with sudden clarity, I stepped down into the bunker. Make sure you get clear of the fringe, I told myself. Standing there I realised that I couldn't even see the hole and climbed back out to better judge the green and its undulations. Turning back to Ginny,

I switched from my usual sand iron to my sixty-degree wedge. At her questioning look, I reassured her. "I need more height if I'm to get near that hole." She nodded quietly, the most I could hope for. Reasserting my focus, I stood for a moment before following my training. My club struck the sand and then the ball lifting it into the high arc I had intended. Deep in the bunker I was blind to the resultant bounce and roll of the ball. As I tried to get out quickly to see what I had left there was a roar from Ginny and a shout of "Nein!" from my opponent. "Go on, get in!" Ginny's words confirmed the remarkable outcome. The ball had run across the green and hit the flag. Just as I got high enough to see, it dropped into the hole to win the match.

My commiserations to Dagmar were politely received but with no emotion. Unsurprisingly, perhaps, she was not that happy with victory suddenly snatched away by a shot that smacked of luck, but then that is golf. She did, at least, wish me good fortune in the next round.

The afternoon match that followed was tiring but satisfying. No give and take in this one. I grabbed a three-hole lead after five holes and could relax matching my opponent, a fellow English girl of sixteen, hole by hole and, in the end not conceding one. I finally won on the fifteenth. It was enjoyable, for me at least, and I did not need to strain as I had had to that morning. I was into the last eight!

Quarter-finalist! This was better than I could have hoped for and now just two rounds before the final. I knew that the golf would only get tougher as I faced the world number six, a Japanese teenager of the same age as me. I had always, and certainly wrongly, felt that players from the Far East were smaller than me. After all, at almost a metre eighty I am not short. Aiku, it turned out, was not only taller but well built.

What little research I had been able to complete the night before, thank goodness for Google, warned me to expect her to be the first of my opponents who would be likely to consistently out-drive me off the tee. Oh, and she was, is, a brilliant putter. Everything told me that I would need to be on top form just to make a match of it. Winning? Well, I suspected, I might need to rely on her not being on top form. Ridiculous, of course, she too was in the quarters.

Having won the toss, I decided to go against my usual routine and play first. Driving distances were less relevant with the par three facing us and I felt that I should try and put pressure on her while I could. I would also have played before she could be announced on to the tee. I sensed that that detail might be jaw droppingly powerful, leaving me back wondering how I was even there. As it happened, the announcement was short, referring only to her having won the Asia-Pacific Open a few months before.

This time my tee shot had found the green leaving me with a putt of around ten feet, no unlucky bounce this time. Then there was a surprising delay in Aiku playing. The wind was stronger than the day before but not, in my opinion, enough to cause problems. She had selected a club only to put it back in her bag picking a second out. This led to a surprisingly heated argument with her caddy. For several minutes they discussed, to put it politely, the pros and cons of her choice. This went on long enough for the match official to finally step forward and indicate that she would be penalised if she did not play immediately.

I was uncertain as to what the punishment might entail but took a little comfort from the idea that Aiku did not appear to be operating on all cylinders. That comfort increased when it became clear she really had got the wrong club, as her drive cleared the green landing in a bunker twenty yards further on. Her cry of anger at her caddy as well as at herself gave me a boost immediately. A few minutes later I was ahead.

That lead would not last long but each time I lost a hole I found the means to regain the lead on the next hole. This involved a degree of, as Ginny would put it later, magic play with my wedges. The match remained on a knife edge until we reached the twelfth, the last of the par threes. Here events took something of a turn for the worst. My tee shot came up short of the green landing on the apron. Not the worst result as the flag was at the front left edge of the putting surface. Aiku for a second time misjudged the wind badly and her tee shot, although finishing on the green was about as far as possible away from the hole as it could be and she had to putt before I needed to decide on my own shot. Her putt was good but rolled a few feet past the hole.

She strode across the green, obviously expecting me to concede the return, and was quite taken aback when I asked her to mark her ball. I had previously not asked her to do so on several putts of similar or shorter lengths but I suddenly felt that now was the time to test her reputation.

It became apparent that her relationship with her caddy had not improved. Having marked the ball, she picked it up and threw it at the other woman angrily demanding that she clean the object. This did not go down well. The caddy cleaned the ball before throwing it back and then turned away clearly intending to march to the next tee and wait for Aiku there. It was then that the accident happened. Ginny was waiting for me to decide on which shot I would play, while holding the putter ready as a guide to what she felt would be best. The Japanese caddy didn't look where she was going and walked straight into Ginny knocking her aside with a solid barge. Ginny fell into the pot bunker she was standing next to, landing with a cry of pain. As I rushed to help her, with a glare at the back of the other woman, who hadn't stopped, I could hear the match official yelling through his radio for medics. Down in the bunker it was clear that Ginny had damaged, if not broken, her arm as she had bounced off the rivetted wall of the pot.

There was some delay as the medical staff assisted my friend, no longer just my caddy, out of the sand. It was clear that she could not continue and, as she was helped away in tears, I was left to request a trolley. This had Aiku in a rage. Not being aware of my disability she believed that that was not allowed. My own temper was not being improved by her selfishness and I angrily retorted. "Fine, have it your way."

As I bent to collect my putter and prepare to take my shot there was a voice behind me, it was Ella's caddy from the first knockout match. "Thomas, I assume that Miss Jordan could have a replacement caddy?"

Thomas, it became clear, was the match official. "Captain, yes, of course she can. Are you offering?"

"If you'll have me, Sophie." His words gave me a warm lift but, he did it for money and I couldn't afford it. It was as if he had read my mind. "Don't worry, I'm happy to help and I don't need paying."

"Then, yes, please."

My new caddy nodded his approval of my choice of the putter merely indicating that he felt I should aim a good five feet right of the pin, far more than I had intended. But I reminded myself, he was a local and regularly caddied, I took his advice. My strike was not perfect, if it had been I might well have holed out, still, I felt that at only four or so feet, just outside Aiku's marker, I had managed to get my half.

The next putt was not entirely straightforward but my hours of practice paid off and I read the borrow perfectly. Now came the moment, the Captain had said quietly, don't you dare concede that putt, it isn't any easier than yours.

Aiku's annoyance at having to hole such a short putt, may, I emphasise may, have had an effect. She stood over it and much too quickly, I thought, struck the ball hard directly at the hole. Did she believe that she could ignore any turn and send the ball straight through, I don't know. Whatever, the ball simply missed the hole completely and for the first time I had a two-hole lead with just six to play.

I look back still with a doubt in my mind as to what really happened from there on. The disagreement between the two Japanese must have hurt Aiku more and within three holes I had won four and three. She was coldly formal at the end simply nodding in respect before leaving the course.

"For a race that prides itself on its etiquette that was unbelievably insensitive." Captain commented as we walked back to the clubhouse.

"I know, not what I expected, Captain. Thank you for standing in but I know you are a professional caddy and I can't afford to pay you."

"Sophie, first it's Steven. I'm only referred to as Captain because I have a bit of a reputation being ex-army and there are also two more local caddies with the same name! Secondly, yes, I would have been available to caddy for a fee at the beginning of the tournament but I don't need the money and, hey, you're good. You can go all the way and that will be fun for me. So, you can buy me a drink after you win. That'll be more than enough payment. I don't imagine I can match, it's Ginny isn't it, in terms of the relationship you have as a team but I'll do my best. Now let's go and find out how she is, shall we?"

As we got to the clubhouse a taxi arrived and a smiling though pale Ginny got out with her arm strapped up.

"Sophie, you won? And this is?" She said with an approving look at Steven.

Having introduced Steven and explained the result, I asked the question. "How bad is it?"

She hesitated. "Maybe not as bad as it might have been but it could have been better. I've dislocated my shoulder so won't be back in action for a month." She went for the jugular. "Steven, you were on Ella's bag earlier. How much to stay with Sophie for the rest of the week?"

Steven laughed out loud. "A pint after each round will be more than enough, Ginny. I'm more than happy to carry that bag. Don't get me wrong. I really wish you were going to be carrying it. I watched how you both worked together, not just against Ella, but in your later matches. With no-one needing me, I could enjoy watching the golf as a true spectator. Now I can help, if you want me."

Ginny really laughed before grimacing as the pain shot through her shoulder. "Steven, I did check up on you after Sophie beat Ella. You intrigued me. Sophie, the locals consider this man the best caddy in the area. I'm an amateur, he is one of the best. With him on the bag you're even more likely to win. Now look, you need lunch. You're due back on the first tee in a couple of hours. Good luck. Now, I need to rest so I might not be able to watch your whole game."

"Watch how you go." I gave her a gentle squeeze and we headed for the clubhouse via the scorer's tent.

A little later, I found myself facing another outsider, Denise, who hailed from Dublin, calling the K Club home. Like me she had been on the reserve list now one of us would be playing in the final, how about that?

And after eight holes it looked as if Ireland would have their first finalist in many years. Denise had played unbelievable golf. I rather think she only needed seven putts, having chipped in on the first and despite my best efforts I was five down and looking out. This was where my new caddy proved his worth. Steven gently overruled my choice of club on the par three ninth. Denise had for the first time erred missing the green right. Having looked at Steven with a quizzical look I decided to follow his guidance.

"Just hit your normal shot." He said, which was a little counter intuitive since the ball was likely to end up short of the green. Having made the decision to follow that advice, I did just that and to my surprise the ball hit the apron and bounced up on to the green rolling across it at some speed. In the end it stopped a few feet short and we walked to the tenth with a little more spring in my good leg. Suddenly I felt that I still had a chance and by the seventeenth the match was all square. A game almost of two halves. I was starting to struggle though, with my right leg feeling the strain where my prosthetic joint linked the upper and lower parts.

As we reached the eighteenth tee, I spotted Ginny in the crowd smiling as she gave me a thumbs up, it was the best boost I could have got and I relaxed. A solid tee shot was followed by a second that spun back to finish close for a birdie finish that Denise could not match and I had completed the comeback of my nascent career!

"Wow, Sophie, I thought I had you before the ninth. You don't give in, do you? Well played."

"Denise, what can I say. You gave me the fright of my life and I did think my fun was going to end. Keep at it, next time it will be you going the whole way."

What was I saying? I was in the final of the biggest event I had ever played in! That I nearly didn't manage to qualify for. Bring on Francine again. I wanted to show, to those juniors back home, that I wasn't just a flash-in-the-pan. I rather think my mind was struggling with the reality of making the final against all my own expectations. I didn't need to prove anything to Francine, she had seen me play and would no doubt be up for reversing the result at Garches.

Naturally, as Francine had, till then, been the best player I had ever competed against I had assumed she would be my opponent in the final. I had seen her before my semi-final long enough to wish her luck in her own match and thought she would take a steady smooth journey into the final.

How wrong can you be?

As I walked up to the clubhouse, I saw Francine already there and her expression told a story. I find it difficult sometimes to empathise with other people's emotions but I knew, without asking, that she had lost and lost badly. What on earth had happened?

A Californian is what had happened. Ranked in the world top ten, she had played what Francine called golf that was almost out of this world. Golf that she could not cope with and she had subsided, her words, to a loss on the fifteenth.

"Ma Cherie, you will need to be on top form tomorrow and, possibly, hope she has peaked too soon. You can beat her but be ready to see some amazing golf. I think she must be on the way to being World Number One this year!"

I think it helped Francine to talk about her loss though I am not so sure I benefitted. If she could lose that heavily, what chance did I have?

Ginny and Steven combined forces to give me a good talking to over dinner later. Ginny had dragged Steven away from the club bar with the promise of a meal.

"This is what you have worked for, Sophie, remember that. Yes, she ranks higher and is a good player. So are you. And if you don't meet the best, then how can you ever beat them?"

I had to admit that for the first time I had had a glimmer of hope that I could win. Now, well I knew I wasn't that good really. Ginny rolled her eyes at that. "Steven, have you ever heard such rot?"

Steven was a little less harsh, though that may have been because he had only known me a few days. "Sophie, just remember that when you tee-off tomorrow morning you will just be two golfers, bloody good golfers that is true, but still just two golfers. Francine was correct, the American may have peaked a day early. It doesn't matter, any professional golfer will tell you how hard it is to play at a consistently high level. Maybe Woods managed for periods but look how rare it is for the professionals to win two weeks on the trot."

"I know that," I mumbled back, "but that is in my head. I just struggle to believe it."

"So, I gather. Ginny has been telling me all about you. Now listen up. Tomorrow, you go out and play your best. If she performs better and beats you, well you'll have to take it on the chin. But you have had your worst round today and still came back to win, tomorrow it may just be her turn to drop below what is a very good level."

With that we all headed out. Steven, I assumed home, while Ginny and I went back to the B&B.

I don't know whether it was the pressure of the final or just fatigue but the nightmare recurred for the first time in months. In fact, I had begun to think that I could really put those hideous events behind me. I woke to find Ginny by the bed trying to calm me, much as my brothers might have done.

"Sophie, Sophie, what is it? It's all right. You just had a nightmare, I think."

As I tried to collect my thoughts, it suddenly struck me. "Ginny, how are you in my room?"

"Your screams woke me and the landlady came into our wing, sound carries. She let me in." She turned her head. "It's okay, Mrs Turner, just a nightmare, she's all right."

"Are you okay?" Her voice echoed real concern. "It sounded awful." I was still trembling with the carnage flitting through my mind but, after a moment, explained the background.

"Will you be all right? Do you want me to stay?" Ginny sounded very worried and I had to admit having her stay was attractive.

"Would you? I don't think it's a necessity but I wouldn't want to wake you again." I made my excuse. There was plenty of room in the double bed I had but then I hesitated. "What about your arm? Do you think you will be okay?"

"I'll be fine. Now just roll over and let me get in."

The warmth of my friend calmed me faster than I had done in the past. What was odd for me was that the other person in the bed was female and it was the first time I had ever shared my sleeping quarters. I hadn't even had a sleepover as a kid and, for reasons I am not sure we could have explained, I had not stayed overnight with Richard. This was new.

I woke the next morning to find Ginny and I wrapped around each other. It was an unnerving experience for me. Girls were for friends! Ginny slowly opened her eyes and jerked away from me. "Sophie, sorry. Nothing happened, did it?" Her nervous cry made me wonder for a moment before reassuring her that it seemed we had simply rolled together in our sleep before I asked a question that was refusing to go away.

"Why? Did you want it to be more?" As soon as I asked, I wanted to reverse time and avoid the implication. I had never been physically attracted to another woman but then even men had been a bit of a mystery to me, before Richard at least.

"Oh Lord." Ginny replied. "I'm not sure where to start."

"At the beginning?" Now I was intrigued.

"Well, it goes back to my uni days. I fell for another student. I had had boyfriends but this was a strong-minded woman. To cut a long story short, I found myself in what I thought was love. Now when I look back, I was a fool but at the time I was lonely and she took advantage.

After we graduated, we got married. It lasted two years before I realised that what she really wanted was a servant not a partner. It was painful not least because she tried to claim that I only had money because she had given it to me, a real lie. She was reasonably well off but didn't have anything like as much as I had inherited. The money was in a trust until I was twenty-one. As soon as I was old enough, she pushed to manage my investments, as if I was incapable. That was the final straw. The divorce took more than a year. I never want to go through that again. Waking like that, I worried that my past might have caused me to do more than just sleep."

I sat there shocked. My friend was gay, or was she? I did say again that nothing had happened, before. "You said you had boyfriends? You never found the right guy then?"

"No, and the one lad that got me in bed was not exactly great at sex! When I look back, I'm not even sure that it was the sex that encouraged me to stay with Meredith, as I say I was lonely. I hadn't long lost my Mum and my Dad passed away when I was nine. Fiona was living in the States making her own marital disaster. Meredith was forceful, not sure she really gave me a choice but that was then. Today, I'm far more likely to drive any relationship and I suspect it will be with a man. They'd have to cope with my past or at least understand it. I don't feel that I could ever trust a woman to that extent again."

"Wow, I would never have guessed, Ginny. I knew you were divorced but I always assumed your previous had been a husband. Daft, sorry."

"Not really, same sex marriages are still relatively new and follow on divorces are, for the moment, rare. Look Sophie, we need to move. You are due on the tee at eight-thirty. Need any help getting ready?"

I didn't need any and was down for breakfast before half past six with Ginny coming down a few minutes later, obviously not yet adept at handling her shoulder. We finished quickly, settling for fruit, cereal, and toast. Steven was at the door for seven o'clock with "Come on, you need the range, young lady."

He looked at Ginny. "Do you want to come with us? Or will you make your own way later?"

I watched with a little hidden amusement. Both were looking at the other, much as I sensed Richard looked at me and vice versa. Really, I thought, they've only known each other for a few days. Mind you, I thought, they've been together long enough, at some point, for Ginny to tell Steven all about me. Wow! I do hope it works out, sounds like Ginny could use another love but I wonder why Steven is on his own, if he is?

Ginny smiled at him and said she would follow.

Day five, the Final, and I arrived at the first tee still having to remind myself that I was there on merit. Now it was showdown time. "On the tee, from California, the Texas Amateur Champion, Anna Bull."

Anna had won the toss and elected to go first, possibly I thought, to try and put me under some pressure with first tee nerves. She waited for the crowd to quieten again before with a smooth easy swing she launched the final with a beautiful shot centred on the fairway.

As she turned back to make way for me our eyes met. "Nice shot, Anna." I said quietly and I sensed a little startlement as if my compliment was an unexpected reaction.

"On the tee, from England, the holder of the Esmond Trophy, Sophie Jordan." The applause was much louder and there were a few cheers. It should have been obvious to me before but I suddenly realised that the crowd was likely to be largely on my side. Taking my driver from Steven, I followed my usual routine before sending a shot that was the equal of Anna's. That seemed to soften the competitive edge as she gave me the same acknowledgement. The final was under way and we led the way down the first.

It might be surprising but the morning was not that exciting. At different points we both took the lead only for the other player to fight back. Unlike previous rounds there were no tantrums or upsets and few bad shots. If we won or lost a hole it was because, typically, our approach play was better, or worse without being terrible, than our opponent's. Only on the eighteenth did I slip up finding a fairway bunker and being unable to reach the green in two. We went in for the lunchtime break with Anna two up.

The crowd had been typically fair to both of us, though the groans when I lost a hole were as loud as the applause for Anna when she struck a good shot.

The afternoon was hard for me, my leg was starting to suffer from the volume of golf during the previous days, but with Steven's guidance I managed to keep going and Anna could not increase her lead. Hole after hole was halved and by the ninth-hole I began to realise that unless I could pull a rabbit out of the hat and soon, I would not be winning my second big tournament.

Perhaps Anna made a mistake at the turn by needing to take a comfort break. This gave me time to discuss a change of tactics with my caddy. Steven was reluctant to argue against my suggestion but he knew that simply continuing with a conservative approach was not going to be enough.

"I understand, Sophie, and I can't disagree. Better to try and win and if it doesn't work out lose four and three rather than two and one. Go for it and let's try and upset her apple cart."

Anna was, like me, playing steady sensible golf and, no doubt, felt that, if she continued in that vein, she was good enough to withstand the style of golf she was seeing me play. Don't get me wrong, it was not that she had no respect for my golf, just that she had the confidence that hers was my equal.

Back on the tee, Anna, with a gracious apology for delaying matters, struck her usual quality shot using her three-wood. A sensible two hundred and twenty yards. I looked at Steven, who nodded passing me my driver. My drive split the fairway and utilising a slope finished almost three hundred yards down wind. Anna's face was a picture. Her second shot was good but, perhaps because she was still a long way back, she was unable to generate any spin and her ball ran to the back of the green, finishing in the first cut of rough and on a downslope. With only a wedge in my hand I hit a peach of a shot and was able to watch as the ball landed just past the pin and spun back to finish barely four feet away.

As I may have mentioned, the game had been played in good spirits and this could be summed up by Anna's reaction as she crossed the green. Personally, I would not have conceded my putt. I knew how hard the greens could be to read even with the help of Steven but, as she walked past the pin, Anna bent and picking my ball up tossed it to me with three words. "Great shot, Sophie."

Having considered her own shot, she eventually decided to try a chip. In other circumstances it would have been brilliant and I watched as the ball rolled end-to-end towards the hole. She had, of course, left the flag in and I held my breath as, for moments, it looked as if she might have saved the hole. To my relief the ball ran across the edge clipping the flag before spinning to a stop barely a foot past. Would it have dropped if the flag was not there? I don't know but all I could do was to say.

"Hard luck, Anna."

She grinned. "Would have been good, wouldn't it? Onwards we go."

The par-five eleventh was halved, it's a long hole and there wasn't anything I could do to outplay an opponent who was well able to outdrive me if she chose to. The par three twelfth was a different game. I have fond memories of that hole, indeed of all the par threes and this time was no different. My tee shot landed just past the hole and spun back, not for a hole-in-one but near enough as it stopped only a few feet away. Beat that, Anna, I thought, and she didn't. She did make me putt but then it certainly wasn't a gimme. We went to the thirteenth all square but I felt that the momentum was in my favour.

And it was. We would remain level until the sixteenth a shorter par four and again I used the driver to great effect. Anna felt obliged, I am sure, to follow but that was not her favourite approach and she misjudged the dog-leg finding the thick rough on the right. A few minutes later I was one up and that was it. We halved seventeen and with Anna needing to win the eighteenth to take us to extra holes, Steven convinced me to revert to my normal play on that hole and it was enough. To my stunned amazement I had managed to win my second big tournament and one of the Amateur majors.

As we walked off the green having shaken hands, Anna turned to me. "Sophie, I simply don't know how you did that. I don't think I made any mistakes until the sixteenth but you stayed in there all the way. Francine told me I would need to be better against you and I found that difficult to believe. Truth will out they say and you stepped up when you needed to. Tell me, though, that what I was told is wrong? That your right leg is not real?"

I had to admit it and it was then that my leg almost gave way under me. I had said that fatigue might stop me but somehow over those closing holes I had pushed the pain to the back of my mind. Now I needed Steven and Anna to help me to the scorers' hut.

Aftermath

I never seem to be able to remember award ceremonies very clearly and this time all I wanted to do was to lie down, remove my leg and ease the throbbing ache.

Ginny had joined us, at the end, overjoyed to see me collect the trophy and greeting me with a gentle one-handed hug. Her shoulder was still causing her to be careful as to how she moved and she had used a taxi to reach the course rather than drive. It was left to me to drive us back to the B&B where I was that exhausted, I refused the offer of a meal from the Turners, heading straight to my room and slowly collapsing on to my bed. Ginny did help me up the stairs but left me to deal with things as I wished. In truth I didn't even remove my leg, falling asleep as soon as my head hit the pillow.

I woke, three hours or so later, now ravenous. I thought that Ginny might also be hungry but there was no answer when I knocked her door. Slipping out I took a gentle, and not very quick, walk to the local pub which turned out to have a carvery. I gratefully claimed a table just before service ended.

As I ate, I suddenly heard familiar voices. Ginny and Steven were somewhere in the bar chatting like old friends. I grinned to myself, sounded good between them, then I thought again could I be about to lose my favourite caddy? It wasn't difficult to put that selfish idea behind me, Ginny had become a good friend and if she had found someone else then she deserved it.

I decided to stay low and not interrupt them, the old adage of two's company, three's a crowd, came to mind. That idea was blown away as the table next to mine suddenly got quite noisy.

"I tell you that's the girl who won the Championship, Sophie what's-her-name."

"Can't be, she wouldn't be eating in here and on her own. She'd have her caddy or that woman who joined her before the prizegiving."

The woman who had, of course, correctly identified me, turned her chair, and called over. "I am right, aren't I. You did win today, didn't you."

I could only nod.

"Oh wow! See Mike, I'm right. Could I get your autograph? Please?"

To say I was staggered is to understate the shock. A stranger wanted my autograph!

There was, of course, only one answer. "Yes, of course, if you've got a pen and paper."

"Better than that, how about a ball with a sharpie?"

She came over and as I rather shakily signed my name, she asked how it was to win such a big competition. "You never looked as if you were going to lose, even when you were behind."

"You play yourself then?" I asked, wondering how she could have seen that.

She laughed. "I do, sort of. More like a nice walk in the countryside spoiled! On the other hand, you looked as if you were born with a club in your hand. Thank you, Sophie, and good luck in the Open. Now can we buy you a drink?"

I had finished eating and, to be honest, the idea of a drink was suddenly attractive. "That would be nice, if, you're sure." At the same time, I was wondering how to tell her that I still needed to qualify for the Open.

"What's your poison, then? By the way, they call me Phil." She laughed, obviously delighted that I hadn't just done a runner.

"Just a small glass of white, Phil." I'm not teetotal but I don't drink a lot and nothing at all during competitions, so I was wary of anything stronger given how worn out I felt.

It became apparent that the group were regulars, as Phil marched into the bar calling to the barman. "Come on, Jordan. Let's be having a small glass of your best white. We have another Jordan here, who's rather special."

Jordan looked across the room towards me. "I thought so, but I felt Miss Jordan deserved a bit of peace and quiet. Not your rowdy bunch! Now she's going to have to put up with our lady golfers' society all looking for autographs and handshakes. They're in the function room."

Turning his attention to me. "Want me to throw these so-called golfers out, Miss Jordan, give you that peace and quiet?"

I didn't think he was serious and I laughed, feeling better than I had for some time. "I'll survive, Jordan."

As I sat down near the bar, a rather sheepish looking Ginny appeared. "Sophie, sorry. I thought you would be out for the count and, well, I had an invite to dinner. Didn't expect to see you here."

"It's OK, Ginny, you can't babysit me all the time. Oh, and I think I know who you were or are with. I heard you talking when I sat down to eat. Good for you."

I'm not sure that I had ever seen a grown woman blush in the way that Ginny did, after all by my reckoning she was in her thirties, she just nodded. "Thanks, Sophie."

The rest of the evening went quickly, although I conceded a couple more glasses of wine, I think.

It wasn't long, before one of the golfing society members appeared and begged me to go through and meet the others. Phil and Ginny insisted on accompanying me as moral support. I suspect Phil felt it worth doing for the possibility of a free drink but her friendly defence of me as the crowd rushed to greet me was a real lifesaver.

Before going in, I had nudged Ginny in the direction of the Ladies where I asked her how to explain that I still needed to qualify for the Open. Her laugh must have disturbed the rest of the pub.

"You really didn't expect to win, did you Sophie?"

"Ginny, until Monday evening, I didn't even think I would be playing. I worried about reaching the knockout stages at all, let alone the final. You know that."

"You know, I still can't understand why you don't recognise how good you are. Look, I'll take you through the automatic tournament entries you get, later. But, for heaven's sake, how could you not have known that the Amateur Champion gets a place in the Open without having to qualify?"

I was for the second time that evening stunned. Ginny's disclosure was way beyond anything I had expected, I had never looked to see what the winner won. The Trophy and the Gold Medal were exciting enough.

The evening was now as good as it gets, though having to point out that the Open was a professional Major, that even making the cut would be success for me. One retort summed it up.

"Don't do yourself down, Sophie. You're the best English golfer in years, since Charley Hull and Georgia Hall at least. Just because an amateur hasn't won since before the war doesn't mean it's impossible. You'll do good. We all saw you this week and how you handled the ups and downs. You've got what it takes and we will be watching you."

They finally let me and Ginny free and we headed back to the B&B. Back in my room and having got ready for bed, I decided to Google my prizes. Ginny seemed to think that an entry in the Open was only one of the prizes. It took a few moments before I sat back in astonishment. The list of competitions to which I would be invited seemed endless:

Women's Open

Augusta National Women's Amateur Championship,

Chevron Championship, USA

Evian Championship, France

US Women's Open.

And a Ladies European Tour Event! I almost screamed with disbelief not just at the number but at the quality. Then I groaned at the locations. Three top US opportunities but how was I to find the money for them? I could save the money for the Evian and a European Tour event, if it was in the UK, but I could never find the money for three trips to the States. Not even one. I didn't sleep that well and was up early the next morning.

Ginny didn't laugh at me over breakfast. "We will find a way, Sophie. These are not chances to turn down. There must be some route we can use. Now eat and then we both have long drives home. Before you ask, my shoulder is a lot better. I'll just take it steady."

Home was almost another trial. For the second time, I had to fend off multiple congratulatory approaches from friends and relatives and even more from the Club and I had to do it without Richard, who now admitted he was overseas.

We exchanged texts and a couple of phone calls but he was reticent about the reasons for his trip, only promising me he would tell all when he got back in a week's time. During that week it was difficult to focus on the future other than thoughts of the Open and I was missing him more than I ever believed possible.

I was still desperate about the financial implications of the US events. No matter how I looked at it there was no way I could raise that sort of money.

Then, Linda came up with an idea. "Why not set up a website on Crowdfunder? I'll bet that there are a lot of your fans out there, ones you don't know, who would want to help."

We agreed that I should look in to it but, in the end, I simply decided to put off any decision regarding anything other than the competitions I was already entered for and the build up to the Open. The others were a year away.

Richard came home as promised but only with news that hurt. I know that I never thought it would last but I had hoped we would be together at least until I managed to turn professional, even if that was simply as a club pro. That first evening after he returned, we went for dinner and then later, back in his apartment, he explained that he would be moving to the States later in the year. His parents had taken jobs at a university in New England and they had managed to negotiate a scholarship which would allow him to try for the Korn Ferry Tour.

When I look back, I fear that I lost it in a way I have never done before. Why hadn't he told me before he went to the US? Didn't he trust me? I threw a real tantrum before collapsing in tears. Daft as it sounds, we made love with even more passion than usual. And when I think about it now, I really mean made love, not just had sex.

The two months before my trip to the home of golf were well occupied. When not working at the Club including as much overtime as I could twist out of James, practice dominated while I had typically two tournaments to play every three weeks, on average. These kept my competitive edge going, not least because, suddenly, I was the player to beat.

I had mixed results during that period as is not unusual for the sport. Winning every week is impossible nevertheless I was doing enough to help my already improved ranking after the jump into the top one hundred as a result of the Championship win. I managed to finish in the top ten every time and achieved two good wins, one at Sunningdale and the second at Celtic Manor. Both wins were particularly satisfying as the fields were strong and the courses difficult. The Celtic Manor win came just two weeks before the Open which suggested that I was on the right path to be in good form for what would be the biggest challenge of my life.

Ginny had agreed to carry my bag again as Steven was away and couldn't be there, other than in spirit as he put it. She also had finally come up with a suggestion as to how I might raise the money for the overseas trips next year - sponsorship.

"But I'm an amateur, Ginny. Amateurs can't earn money from the game and anyway who'd want to sponsor me?"

"I didn't think you could either but James pointed out that the rules changed a few years ago. All we need to do is find a few local or national business' that would like to be associated with your name and face."

I giggled. "Someone who sells brown paper bags big enough to cover it, you mean!"

"That's daft. Haven't you noticed how the men, and a few women for that matter, turn to watch you walk past, on and off the course?"

Now she had me blushing. "Look, okay, I'm not exactly ugly but, come on, I'm no beauty queen either."

Ginny looked at me, trying to gauge how to disagree with my down-to-earth view of my looks.

"I give up. Has no-one ever told you that you have looks that go way beyond the plastic of beauty queens. There are a lot of women out there who would kill to look as good as you and that's without the golf skills. OK! OK! I know I'm not going to convince you unless I find those sponsors. Leave that with me."

It suddenly sank in that my friend was quite likely to go out and do just that. "Ginny, what type of work do you do?"

"I don't, these days. I graduated in Public Relations and Sociology and then built a small business but I sold it after the divorce. Got enough to top up my inheritance and, now, I don't need to work unless I want to. I still have a few contacts though, so watch this space. Or rather don't. Go and focus on your preparations for St Andrews."

Thanks to my overtime I was able to head north almost a week early and, as a result, had the chance to practice on the Old Course in different conditions. The weather was in typical summer mode. Hot and sunny one day, blowing a gale the next and throwing it down with rain the day after. Watching my ball refuse to stay still in the wind left me wondering if we would be able to play through the following week. Still the experience would hold me in good stead when the real work began, I hoped.

Ginny arrived on the Monday and we walked the course together, allowing her to make notes in her yardage book. "This place is really special, isn't it?" I told her as we walked over the Swilken Bridge.

"How can it not be? I mean it's been around so long. It's that special, the greatest golfers have posed on the Bridge in a farewell, signalling their retirement from the Open. Then look at the first tee. No moving that back for the pros."

"Don't remind me. I've seen so many golfers make a mess of that shot during the last week. I tell you, Ginny, all I will want to do is play something that looks as if it belongs here."

Ginny, as she usually did when I down played my golf, just laughed. "The first shot's the easy one! It's the second over the burn on to that tight green that would worry me."

The Open.

Thursday found me walking on to the first tee just after midday. The weather was relatively warm but the wind had picked up as the day went on and was almost straight in to our faces.

"Typical links weather." I heard one of my playing partners mutter to her caddy, before she turned to shake my hand. "First pro tournament, Sophie?"

I nodded, still trying to grasp that these players earned their living playing the sport I loved. To say that my stomach was generating kittens was to say the least.

"You'll be OK. Just breathe deep. We've heard that you're the one to beat this week, so you aren't in the wrong place, no matter what nerves you have. Good luck."

The third player in the Group smiled. "Ignore the player to beat bit, she always overstates everything and after all she is the favourite! Play to your strengths and you will do OK."

Two announcements and two great tee shots later it was my turn to enter the gauntlet. "On the tee, the Amateur Champion, Sophie Jordan."

There was a roar from the crowd, some only a few feet away, and several cries of "Go, Sophie" as I tried to go through my normal first tee routine. I know that all players are on edge until they have played their first shot, professional or amateur. But that's not here, that's not St. Andrews, the Old Course, not the Home of Golf, crossed my mind.

Still, I settled down and swung my club. Into the wind there was no chance of reaching the burn that runs just in front of the green but I had decided that my three-wood would, if I got it right, leave me the better distance for my second shot. The wind was not totally head-on being a little left to right and, remembering the advice from the starter the previous week I aimed towards the left of the fairway. With the ball in the air, I gasped, it looked a wonderful shot even to me and the applause echoed that thought.

A good start, which rapidly went downhill. Ginny was right, the second shot was the harder and I got it wrong, or maybe the wind gusted at the wrong moment. Whatever, my ball hammered into the bank of the burn and bounced back into the water. Even though I recovered to only drop one shot, my first pro tournament was off to almost the worst start possible.

My playing partners were sympathetic but they had their own games to play and things settled to a quiet process. I am not sure how I really played and Ginny struggled to boost me but I reached the turn five over. Five bogeys meant that my dreams of making the cut looked already in tatters with only a quarter of the holes played. The scoreboards, at that point, showed that the leaders were as much as five under par as they came towards the end of their rounds. Ingrid, who had muttered about links wind, was level par and wasn't happy. "Just our luck, winds were light first thing and it looks as if those guys have got the best of the weather." Her caddy nodded. "Luck of the draw, boss."

I do wonder, now, if it was that comment that gave me a mental boost, that I wasn't the only one suffering. It made me chuckle inside. She was five ahead of me and not happy!

I took a sense of "what the hell" to the tenth trying to make myself relax and look to enjoy things. Heck, I said to myself, this chance you might never get again, let's not waste it.

Into the wind on the front nine but as we made that turn for home there seemed to be a softening in the weather. The gusts were no longer as strong and suddenly it felt a little warmer. My downbeat approach just vanished at that point, to Ginny's relief. A good drive followed by the best wedge shot I had played all day left me a four-foot putt for birdie. By the time I reached the eighteenth tee, I had managed three more. Talk about a game of two halves.

Then came Tom Morris, the eighteenth, the Road Hole. It is frightening not only because it is surrounded by the crowd but it is not the easiest finish. To add to that, you are treading in the footsteps of the Greats. The men can and often drive the green or, to be honest, miss by just a little and then leave awkward chips or wedges. I couldn't hope to emulate that and was considering my fairway wood rather than my driver. That was until Ginny stuck her oar in, pulling my driver out of the bag and handing it to me. No arguments, her face suggested, the nearer that green the better.

Ten minutes later, I was stood over a putt from the apron. My tee shot had simply bounced, and bounced, and run, and run, only just failing to reach the green, to the muted astonishment of my playing partners and even more so to mine. Ginny was ecstatic.

I say I was standing over a putt but I really considered using a wedge. The hole was at least a hundred feet away on the opposite side of a huge green. Ginny came to my rescue. "This is links golf, use the putter, you've got a better chance of leaving a tap in for a three than if you try and chip from here."

I walked all the way across the green to try and get the line. Half way the hole suddenly seemed to get bigger to my eyes. It is something I have seen before. In my mind's eye I was seeing exactly the right line from there. Now that was all I needed. I went back and played the shot of my life. The ball ran across the green, smoothly swinging right to left as it neared the hole, before to the amazement of everyone, me, Ginny, my playing partners, and the crowd, it dropped in for an eagle two. They must have heard the roar from the crowd across the town let alone the course. It was all I could do to stay standing, waving my cap to the crowd in delight. We all shook hands after the others had finished before heading to the scorers' hut to complete our cards. En-route, a young man ran up to Ingrid. "As soon as you are finished, please."

Ingrid, who had finished four under having also had a good back nine, grimaced to herself and nodded. "Five minutes."

I looked over. She grinned. "Part of the cost of sponsorship and television. Sky want me on their interview cart. That's the downside of being a pro, Sophie, they expect an interview with anyone they think is in with a chance or, on occasion, no chance. Can be hard if you've just had a bad round but they who pay the piper, and so on. Look forward to seeing you tomorrow."

I nodded. "Good luck, Ingrid."

Having finished for the day, Ginny and I were headed for the changing rooms only to be intercepted by the same young man. "Miss Jordan? Sky Golf. Could you spare us a few moments?"

Ginny chuckled. "Looks like you're going to be on the telly, Sophie."

"Do I have to?" I pleaded, more nervous than I had been on the first tee.

"Strictly not, I think, as an Amateur. Is that not the case, young man, Simon, if I am reading your badge, right?"

Simon stuttered at the idea that I might not want to be interviewed. "Well, no, Miss Jordan, you don't but I know they want to chat about a putt you sank on the eighteenth. I didn't see it myself but everyone is raving about it. Please."

I gave up, I shouldn't hole out like that I thought. "Give me a few minutes, I just need to check out my leg." Which wasn't a lie, as it often did after a round, it ached. If I left it, my thigh muscle would only hurt more. Simon nodded but his quizzical face at my comment demonstrated that my prosthetic was not obvious.

"Don't worry, Sophie, it'll be a doddle." Ginny tried to encourage me. "Won't be anything bad. They'll just want to show you that putt and ask you about it."

And she was right, although the idea that Sky considered it the best shot of the day struck me as crazy. The interviewer finished up.

"Good luck, tomorrow, Sophie. Play that well and you'll make the cut comfortably."

There was a gap afterwards and she asked, off camera, if she would be seeing me at the US Open. I smiled.

"Maybe, if I can raise the money to travel." She looked a little disconcerted at my answer. I was to learn later that she had spoken with Ginny about how they might help in finding a sponsor.

Back home, the Club erupted with the sight of me being interviewed. My parents didn't see it live but BBC showed the putt and the follow up as part of their highlights reel later that evening. Alan and James, apparently, simply looked at each other with mutual satisfaction, Linda would tell me later.

That next day dawned sunny and the winds of the previous day had dropped away leaving almost perfect conditions for golf. For once I was far from happy. This would work in the favour of the many players who would expect to shoot low scores as a result.

My second round was due to start a little after three and I spent the first part of the morning relaxing before heading out to the practice ground. Passing the scoreboard behind the eighteenth I could see that my prediction was correct. Red scores dominated. Two players back in the clubhouse, had shot rounds of nine under, close to the course record. It was clear that another round of one under would not be enough to make the cut and I felt rather depressed.

In the changing room Ginny calmly banged her head against the nearest wall. "Sophie Jordan, sometimes I despair of you! Always running yourself down. Yes, there are some good scores out there but you can do that too. At least enough to make the cut."

And, as usual, she was right. With no real excitement I steadily compiled a round of sixty-nine with just the three birdies. With the cut line finally set at three under my own score was enough by a stroke, though I was still seven shots back from the leader. I say that as if it was important and, of course, it wasn't. For I had done what

I had hoped I might, winning had never come in to my thoughts, but Ginny was stuck with my bag for another two days.

"No interview for me today!" I said to Ingrid as we parted company. She would be in one of the later groups tomorrow having played an almost perfect round of six under placing her just one shot back. "Good luck, tomorrow."

Her laugh would have been infectious in other circumstances but her words would echo in my mind for a long time.

"You did well, Sophie. Best amateur for you, I expect, but I think I need to look forward and try to win this week, before you turn pro and tie it up for the future. Good luck to you, too."

Day three dawned to peaceful summer weather with little wind and I was able to take advantage of those conditions, early in the day, to reach nine under with a round of sixty-seven.

This time I couldn't avoid the TV and the questions were a little more pointed, as the interviewer talked about winning Best Amateur. It turned out that I was six shots ahead of, of all people, Francine, who was the sole remaining Amateur aside from myself. That was easy enough but the last question stumped me completely.

"Sophie, you are just three shots off the current clubhouse lead. Can we expect you to make a move up the leader board? Perhaps set a target?"

"Are you serious? There are loads of great players still out on the course and they'll finish ahead of me. I don't think that twelve under will still be the leading score tonight."

"Well, I'll wish you the best of luck tomorrow. Thanks for making the time, Sophie."

As expected, the breeze picked up later in the day which did hinder the leading groups. Ingrid seemed to find this a challenge to which she rose better than the others, finishing a shot ahead of everyone except for one of the early starters who had moved into that lead with a round of sixty-five.

By now, everyone back home had been glued to both the live golf, where they could watch it or to the evening highlights. Back in my bedroom, I was resting when the highlights programme began with, for some reason, my interview as the first part of the programme. I was quite relaxed at first. The brief chat had only touched on one of my birdies and was soon over. As they looked to move on the commentator made one last comment which had me bolt upright with shock.

"And there you have it, folks. The best amateur in England if not Europe and, if she can raise the money, she will be competing in all three of the other Majors next year. Oh, and I'm not betting against her winning one of them, though tomorrow might, only might, be out of range."

Even as I sat there wondering if I had heard right, there was a knock on my door and an excited Ginny was there. "Did you see that, Sophie? Tell me you've been watching the highlights! You have, haven't you?"

When I nodded, she grinned. "Didn't expect to be the headline story, did you?"

I looked at her, suddenly remembering what her career background had been, and suddenly felt angry. "You've opened that big mouth of yours, haven't you? How else would they know about my finances? You should have warned me, Ginny."

She looked suitably abashed for a moment. "I'm sorry, Sophie, you're right, I should have. It was just too good an opportunity to miss when they nabbed me after your first interview. I won't do it again. Not without your say so. Now are we going to give those pros a shock tomorrow or not?"

"Don't be daft, Ginny, I'm not Justin Rose, you know."

She looked thoughtful for a long time, as if trying to marshal her words. "No, you aren't a Justin Rose, not yet anyway. It's just that anyone that has seen you play would probably feel that you are better than he was at the same stage. He finished fourth in his first Major and that was as an amateur. You could match that or do even better. If you would only believe in yourself, just a little."

Sunday came and with it my parents and a group from the Club. James, who was among them, admitted that they had decided to put together a coachload even before the tournament started. "We never doubted you'd make the cut, Sophie. Missing cuts isn't in your game."

Oh dear, I thought, didn't they realise how close I had been to doing just that?

I arrived at the course quite early and was able to see Francine tee off. Being so far back from me, she told me she just intended to enjoy the final round, however she played. We had a good chat before she did, with her usual smooth drive, and with mutual "good lucks" ringing in my ears I set off for the practice area.

Lying joint twelfth meant that I would be going out only five groups behind the leaders but the practice range was still busy. I had almost finished my routine when Ginny nudged me. Ingrid was walking down the path.

"Go on. Wish her luck."

I smiled but didn't need to move as Ingrid came over to my place on the range. "Mind if I swing next door, Sophie?"

Mind!? This was one of the top players in the world asking me, if they could practice next to me?

"Of course. I'm almost done anyway, heading over to the bunkers now. Good luck, Ingrid. Thanks for the encouragement earlier, it meant a lot to me."

"You play well, today." She grinned. "Just not too well!"

An hour later my drive off the first tee set up a perfect wedge into the green for the best start, a birdie. By the sixth hole I was enjoying myself. Three birdies meant I really was moving up the leader board and a sneaky look at the display over the sixth showed that Ingrid had dropped a shot at the first, falling into a three-way tie for the lead only one shot ahead of me. Of course, I had already played five holes more and I knew there were multiple opportunities for the leaders to pull away from me. But that leader board looked great, for a few moments anyway.

As I expected, Ingrid and one of the other players both picked up birdies on the front nine although the others did not and by the time, I reached the fourteenth, still at twelve under, I was four shots behind. The back nine was not playing as easily as the front nine but, somehow, I managed a fourth birdie at that hole and two more at the fifteenth and seventeenth. Incredibly I got another at the eighteenth to take the clubhouse lead at sixteen under par and joint first!

It couldn't last, I knew it couldn't. But as the rest of the field closed in on the last few holes it became clear that they were struggling, why I do not know. Ingrid's playing partner had already fallen away but the favourite was holding steady. I avoided any Sky personnel by heading back out to the practice range after Ginny pointed out that there was the amazing possibility of a play-off and I should ensure I was loose enough to go back out. I also dodged my family and friends leaving them a little bemused.

"I don't understand what is happening, Ginny. Ingrid must get a birdie, if not at the seventeenth then at the last."

"Sophie, true but you would have expected her to already be one or two shots to the good. The wind picked up just after we finished and it looks as if that has hit them hard. Everyone else is out of it, barring an eagle at the last or a birdie-birdie finish except for Ingrid. So, get your swing going, just in case."

And I did, focusing on what I needed to do completely unaware that a cameraman was watching and the commentators were approving of my actions.

Ingrid could only par the seventeenth and, in the end, I could bear it no longer and moved to watch a nearby video screen as she played the last. Her tee shot hit the fairway and the second shot was out of this world, finishing just a foot from the hole. I think that I had stopped breathing but I managed to drop my club back in the bag and start back to the clubhouse reaching it as Ingrid reached the green and marked her ball pending her partner finishing.

A few minutes later she tapped the ball into the hole before raising her arms to take the cheers from the crowd. She was immediately captured by the Sky team looking for a quick word with the winner. Even as they spoke to her, she looked past them and saw me applauding her along with the crowd.

Her words at that point enraptured the viewing audience, at least that made up by my family and friends. "Anne, there is the person you should really be speaking to." She pointed to me and beckoned me over, to a little consternation among the officials. "Sophie Jordan. The Best Amateur. She gave me the fright of my life. She was four back at the start of the round and I end up needing a special birdie here at the last. I remember saying on the first tee on Thursday morning that I had heard that she was the one to beat this week. How true was that? What a player and she's not even twenty yet."

I found myself wishing I could hide my face as the emotions threatened to overwhelm me. Ingrid saw my tears starting and gracefully cut the interview off. Taking me under her arm as it were she guided me into the clubhouse to allow me the chance to collect myself.

"Sophie," she said, "we have the prizegiving to come. Just remember that I meant every word. The idea of a play-off against you, and I knew that was possible, terrified me. One word of advice, don't turn pro yet, please. Enjoy the other tournaments you have been invited to. I'd also like an extra year with the chance of winning before you join the fray. All the best, my friend."

The prize giving was, as ever for me, something of a blur but, as I accepted the Silver Medal, I was just able to make my thanks. "Thank you for this. I just need to thank everyone here at St. Andrews for the course and the hospitality. Thanks to all the professionals I played with in the various rounds, their encouragement was warm and helped me. Thanks to my coach and family, I know you are somewhere but this time the most thanks go to my caddy, Ginny. She has no time for me when I'm down, just kicks me back to the game. Thanks, Ginny."

I arrived back home to, once again, face cheers at the Club and even from neighbours. There were congratulatory cards in the post but one envelope stood out. I rarely received anything official, a tax code or the occasional bank statement maybe but this was not one of those. I looked at it for some time wondering why there was a symbol of a golfer in the corner. Had I done something wrong? Had the powers that be disqualified me from one of my tournaments after the event? Could they do that? I didn't think so but why the letter?

When I did open the envelope, it left me even more bemused. It was from a clothing company requesting me to give them my agent's contact details. Agent? I didn't have an agent. In any case why would they want to talk to them? I decided to talk to Alan. Perhaps he knew what the reason might be.

The next day, I was back at the club in the pro shop with a queue. James had joked that I had had enough holiday but I'm certain he did not consider that almost everyone coming into the shop wanted to talk about the Championship. "Was I not disappointed at missing out by a shot?" was a common question. I thought, were they joking? Second place in my first pro Major? Of course,

I wasn't disappointed, though, deep down, I would have loved the chance of going head-to-head in a play-off with Ingrid, win or lose. The onslaught of members gradually eased before a golf society turned up. They didn't initially recognise me for which I was grateful, then the guy organising it came back in to sort out a few things, checking that the nearest-the-pin and longest drive cards were in place. As I reassured him, he suddenly gave a gasp.

"Oh my god. It's you, Sophie Jordan! What on earth are you doing in here?"

It was my turn to grin. "Trying to earn some money, sir. Now, if I might nudge you. You only have a few minutes to make your tee-time."

"Blimey, I've got the best amateur in the country telling me I'm going to be late on the tee, oh my! Thanks, Sophie, we'll see you later." He went out the door and then came back in. "Sorry. Well done."

With the society out on the course the shop quietened down for the first time, just as James came in.

"I have a bone to pick with you, young lady."

"Oh dear. What have I done now, sir?"

"My workload has trebled since last week! Societies by the dozen trying to book days at the home course of some Amateur who just won the Silver Medal. And." He paused. "I have had calls from three different businesses looking to talk to you or your agent. Do you have an agent?"

I looked at him with my mouth gaping. "Me, an agent? James, sorry sir, why would I have one?"

"Sophie, you are headline news. You can get some sponsorship without affecting your amateur status and there are people who value your name, but are you ready to deal with them direct? I don't think you are, no offence."

"No, she isn't." Neither of us had noticed the shop door open or seen Ginny stop there, listening. "But I am."

James smiled. "I guess you are, I will leave you both to negotiate a deal. Careful, Sophie, don't get your fingers burnt. I know this lady well." And he left us, laughing his head off.

It was obviously not appropriate to carry on the conversation in the shop but, with Alan back from giving a lesson, we were able to retire to the club bar and get coffee.

James had left what details he had with me and I passed this to Ginny along with the letter I had got in the post.

She was to the point. "You do need an agent. In the longer run you are likely to be snapped up by one of the larger management consultancies but, for the time being anyway, I'd be happy to take that role."

I looked at her for a moment. "Agents charge for their services, don't they? How much, Ginny?"

Ginny smiled. "Not going to burn your fingers, am I? Look, it does have to be on a business footing otherwise there could be problems, not that I expect any. Five percent plus reasonable expenses."

I thought for a moment. "Agreed, but I have final say on any deals. Nothing gets done without me knowing."

Ginny laughed. "Agreed. I'll run up a simple agreement which will allow you to move on when the big boys come after you."

"God, Ginny, you sound so sure. Can we just work on the next few months? I mean and worry about what comes next?"

"Leave it with me. I suspect the clothing company may be looking for you to wear their golf gear and model it."

"Model it! Look, let's get this clear. Ordinary golf gear yes but not if it shows any part of my body."

Ginny looked surprised and then frowned. "There's something I don't know about, why are you so concerned?"

"Didn't you notice when we shared my bed? Ginny, I have two scars that run from my neck down to my thighs. They're where the car scraped across me. One on my back, the other across the front. They're hideous. No way are they going to be exposed."

Ginny thought. "So, no swimsuits, no shorts. What about skirts? And what about your prosthetic?"

"Skirts might be ok, depends on how long?" I grinned. "Not mini-skirts anyway. Look I don't mind my leg being seen, I do wear the occasional dress. Let's say, depends on why."

"Good. Now I will find out just who else wants you."

"Ginny, do you think we can get enough to pay for the US trips? For both of us?"

She chuckled. "If I can't manage that I may just have wasted several years of my life at uni and then PR. You concentrate on your golf. Leave the pennies to me."

The Ladies Amateur at Augusta is one of the big amateur tournaments and, although relatively new, has a special place in golf. Not that long ago the idea of a female competition at the home of the US Masters would have been a pipe-dream. Now there were two, a professional and an amateur. The amateur takes place on two courses with the last round over the Masters course itself, just a week before the main attraction. And let's be real, the Masters is one of the top events on the world stage and I intended to be there to watch all four rounds. Assuming Ginny did her job!

And she did. Though there would be an incident that left me wishing she hadn't been so successful.

A Photoshoot goes wrong.

"Right, Sophie, you know where you are going?"

I nodded. Ginny was fussing around me like a mother hen. She had gotten me a contract with the clothes company which had arranged a photoshoot at one of the local TV studios. Enough cash to pay for the first trip to the States.

Why they wanted me instead of one of the pros still eluded me but, as Ginny put it, never look a gift horse in the mouth. She had had to explain the term, I had heard of it but never really understood it. The deal was simple, a single shoot for the summer collection with a second later in the year for their winter clothes, payment ten thousand pounds per shoot with half the second shoot payment upfront. Riches!

Ginny continued. "Now, I will not be able to be there for the start but I will join you. Need to see a man about a dog. Don't worry. There will be a chaperone so you won't be on your own with the photographer and another thing I did check on. You will have a private changing room."

I duly arrived at the studios to a warm welcome and was given an escort to my changing room which had a second door opening on to the studio itself and a hanging rail with several items of clothing on it.

The photographer was already there setting up her equipment. What happened during the next hour or so became increasingly uncomfortable for me. Firstly, the chaperone Ginny had promised me, wasn't there and then the photographer became quite irritable when I asked where she was.

"Look, young woman, I'm not male so you don't need anyone. I'm sure she'll be here soon enough. Can we not just start?"

Perhaps, I was naïve. My excuse, I made to myself later, was two-fold. I had never done a shoot before and she was obviously right about not being male.

I went into the changing room and put the first top and trousers on. For a while it seemed to go smoothly until I reached the fifth set, which looked completely different from the previous clothes. The two pieces lacked the brand imprint and consisted of a mini-skirt and a very low-cut top, not golf attire at all. A quick look at the following clothes disclosed a bikini swimsuit and some underwear. To say I was unhappy was inaccurate, I was furious. Going back into the studio I confronted the other woman.

"I'm not modelling non-golf attire. No swimwear. No underwear. Just what are they doing in the changing room?"

She laughed at me. "You should check the contract, love. No photos. No money. I suggest you get back in there and change."

"Forget it, I don't know your name, but I'm leaving. Contract was quite clear. Nothing other than golf wear and they aren't that."

She moved across the room, "Now look here, Miss Up-your-nose, I've already got film of your so-called undies. You get that swimsuit on or else. I'll be paid good money, more than the pittance they pay me for taking the photos." With that she grabbed me and pushed me against the door. "Do you understand me?"

I looked at her with a mix of hate and fear. "Leave me alone!"

She opened the door and shoved me through. "Now change!"

I stood there after she had, mercifully, shut the door. As it closed, I caught a flash of light and looking up saw a lens, a camera lens! She had been spying on me as I changed! Before I could react, the outer door opened and the young woman, who had escorted me, came in with Ginny.

My fury was still in full cry but I took a deep breath and asked calmly. "Is it normal to have spy cameras in your changing rooms?"

"What? No, of course not. What do you mean?"

I pointed and her expression of horror was enough to know who had placed it there. Even as I recognised it the young woman was talking on a radio/pager. "Security, lockdown the building. Code red. You see the photographer visitor, hold her. Don't let her take anything off the site. Nothing!"

Ginny was in shock. "Where's the chaperone? Sophie, where?"

"She hasn't arrived yet. I don't think she's coming. The photographer's a woman."

The door to the studio opened. "Get a bloody move-on, you tart, I haven't got all day. Oh shit!" Her voice died away as she saw I was not alone and she tried to shut the door.

Ginny reacted first, smashing it open with her foot into the other woman's face. "What the hell are you doing here, Meredith? Up to your old games again?"

The woman reacted with a snarl. "Well, if it isn't the ice maiden? Watch yourself youngster, she'll tie you in knots. And you're too late, it's all on the web already!"

"Then you're facing a jail sentence, Meredith, and not before time." Ginny was amazingly calm. Turning to the security team that had arrived in response. "That laptop and any mobiles, they contain illegally obtained images."

They looked to the young woman, who clearly had more clout than I might have realised. "Do it, my responsibility. Jurgen will confirm."

Ginny was still worrying. "It might be difficult. If she has been sending it via her mobile datalink, we may be too late."

The young woman, Jill, I learned later, laughed. "They won't have gone anywhere, Ms. Donald. This building has multiple areas that are blocked from mobile signals and these rooms are two of those. We can't have free data signals, too much risk of broadcasts being interrupted by phones going off."

Meredith screamed with rage and, I think, would have hit one or more of us except that the security guards stepped in. Jill continued. "Now, Mrs Wilson. Your choice, we retain all electronics until you see a lawyer and try to get them back or we delete all content from them. That's your camera, mobile and laptop, reset to factory setting. And any other recording devices. You're taking nothing from here that might be used against Ms Jordan."

"You can't do that."

"I think we can. You should have read the terms and conditions under which you were using the studio, Mrs Wilson. They provide for you trying to take material from the building that might bring our business into disrepute. It's my judgement that such photos would do just that and that is covered by our absolute discretion. My discretion as it happens as Head of Security and Deputy Head of Productions. Your choice, madam." The latter word was uttered with a level of contempt that dripped with distain.

"You'll hear from my lawyers, bastard." Meredith was clearly raging desperate to avoid the loss of her material before she started to try and leave.

Jill stopped her. "Security will need to search you before you go. Two of our female staff will be here in a moment. Then you will be escorted out of the premises. I will make you aware, now. You will be blocked from using our buildings in the future."

Meredith's temper was not improving and she tried to stop the search taking place. I was not too surprised when the security team discovered two memory sticks, one in her pocket, the second in her bra. A third stick was in her handbag.

Furious, she flounced away between the security guards with a parting shot. "I'll be back with my lawyer."

Jill looked at the laptop and her mobile. "I need to get someone down from IT. We need to break the passwords."

Ginny was looking thoughtful. "I wonder." She said moving to the computer and leaning over the keyboard, before typing. A moment later we were in.

"How did you manage that?" Jill was startled. "That password must have had, what, eleven characters and you got it first time."

Ginny looked up. "That piece of garbage is my ex. If there was one thing, I learned it was that she is quite lazy regarding security of her files. Try 152433 for the pin on her mobile."

Now excited, Jill took the phone and entered that number. "We're in. Now, we must to be careful to only extract photos of Miss Jordan. Both the legitimate ones and the others. We might be in a difficult position if we remove any others, I'll want to talk to our legal team, before we do."

Ginny was flicking down the picture files with increasing anger. "I've found Sophie's and will transfer them to my mobile. Then you can call the police."

I looked at her. "Why?"

Jill had moved to look over Ginny's shoulder. "My god! They. They." She stuttered. "They are awful. Turning to one of her colleagues. "Get a call out to the local CID. I need to speak to someone responsible for dealing with child abuse. Move it! Everyone. This stays with us until the police have this lot. We may need to allow that worm back in the building with her lawyer tomorrow and I don't want her spooked. Understood?"

Everyone nodded. There was an underlying sense of muted anger even amongst those that had not seen the photos.

"Ms. Donald, you said she is your ex. You were married?"

Ginny gazed at the backdrop of the studio before replying. "I was. We were. Biggest mistake of my life. I did learn what a control freak she is but I never saw anything to suggest that she had sunk or would sink to that level of depravity. Jill, I will give you the password for the record. Would you change it before giving everything to the law? You will understand why, I think, when you see it." She passed a piece of paper over with a hastily scrawled note. Jill slowly nodded. "That's you?"

"Yes. It was supposed to be a joke between us at the beginning. Sour and bitter now."

I asked about the memory sticks. "Will those just be of me? Do you think?"

"We'll check and I will, personally, delete any of you, it's Sophie, yes? If they are just of you, they will simply be destroyed."

"You are comfortable about doing that? She might use their destruction as a lever for damages." Even then I had not fully taken in what it was that had upset them.

"She is going to have a lot of very difficult questions to answer tomorrow and in the coming days. I rather doubt these bits will feature high in her thoughts, unless they have more of this," Jill paused, "subject matter. If they do, she will end up wishing they had been binned. Jim, Sean, you both search this room. Make sure that there are no more cameras hidden. Find any, destroy them."

The two men nodded and started stripping the room.

We all left the room and moved the electronics to Jill's office. As we got there her phone rang. She listened for a moment and then nodded. "Thanks, Steph. I hoped it might be you at first, at least. How soon can you be here? Sorry, you are here? How?" She listened for a moment. "She is unbelievable. We need a few minutes before we have this meeting with her. Find an excuse to leave her in reception. You know where my office is. Good, see you in a few minutes."

We looked at her. "Your ex, Ms Donald, Ginny, is back. She has accused us of stealing her mobile and laptop!"

Ginny looked aghast. "I told you she is a control freak and she knows what is on that hard drive. She's trying to get the laptop back before anyone can break her password. How do we stop her?"

"We can do that. We will show Steph, what we found. She's a DI and capable, I've dealt with her before. We have a mini-crime-stopper programme for the area and she's a regular on it. I wouldn't want to be Mrs Wilson facing her."

A few moments later, a smart woman came into the room. "Jill, good to see you. Now what the hell is happening?"

"First, I must introduce these ladies."

Steph looked over at us and then laughed. "You mean Sophie Jordan and, Ginny, I think."

Jill gaped, almost as surprised as I was.

"I play a little golf and watch the top players on the box. How could I not know Miss Jordan? And she named Ginny at the Open. How can I help, ladies?"

Ginny recovered first. "Detective Inspector, you need to see some of the images we found on Mrs Wilson's laptop. I am sorry, I think I should warn you that they show a level of depravity that is terrifying."

A few minutes later, Laura was speaking on her radio, leaning through the window to ensure that she had a signal. "Boss, I need backup. I intend to arrest a suspect. This is a case of serious child abuse."

Now I was shaking, the woman was a paedophile?

"Jill, how did you crack the password so quickly? Who else knows?"

Ginny intervened. "I guessed it. Mrs Wilson was my wife. We divorced eight years ago. I hadn't seen her since, until today. She is still using the same password, daft as it may seem."

"That's crazy but useful." Steph said, she was still, I think, struggling with the horror we had been exposed to, well that they had. Ginny had made serious efforts to ensure I did not see any of the pictures.

Jill's voice interrupted the conversation. "That was reception, she is demanding her equipment. She is causing something of a scene. There is another police car at the entrance. Your backup, Steph?"

"Yes, it will be. Now, Jill, I need to remind you to be very careful as to how this is reported. I'll make sure you are kept in the loop ahead of the rest of the press but that needs you to be, well you know what I mean."

Jill nodded. "We won't be able to avoid acknowledging that someone has been arrested here but I think we can avoid anything that might jeopardise any case. Now, let me come back with you. I'll bring her laptop and mobile. If we let her have them, you can arrest her in possession of the evidence."

Steph smiled. "Good idea. Let's go."

"Sophie, Ginny. I suggest you wait here. Stay out of sight." Jill said, as she left the room.

I am told that the arrest was relatively straightforward, Meredith was faced by three police officers and could do no more than argue loudly that they should be arresting Jill and her colleagues, not her. She had signed her own downfall by accepting back her computer and phone confirming, after she had signed into the former, that they were hers and not copies. That was when the Detective Inspector had produced handcuffs and carried out the arrest while quoting her rights. The other officers had to almost drag her to their car. The words of arrest triggered the realisation that her computer had already been hacked and she tried to throw it under a passing car. The swift action of Steph in catching it proved the last straw and Meredith, sullen to the end, stopped resisting.

I am glad to say that that was the last time Ginny and I ever came across that woman. I believe she managed to do a deal which meant that she only got a short prison sentence by selling out other abusers. It did her little good, five years in solitary, for her own protection, took its toll. When she left prison, she apparently committed suicide. Ginny was more sceptical believing that someone had taken revenge. There was little interest in her death, a short column noting that a sex offender had died.

I would like to say that her death saddened me but I felt only relief that such a person could do no more harm to innocents. Ginny and I had both moved on by then. We were never involved in the immediate events for which I was grateful, I needed to focus on the coming months and the lead up to Augusta.

Thanks to Ginny rescuing the initial photos, we were able to complete the first stage of the clothing contract. She also encouraged them to pay more due to the trauma I had suffered from "their" photographer. There needed to be a second shoot as not all the range had been covered but that was handled better and went smoothly. That time we used my Club as background and the resultant photos were much better.

What hurt most in that late autumn, was Richard's absence. He had headed off to the States to take part in the Korn Ferry Tour Qualifying School. If he was successful, he would be playing that side of the Atlantic all the time. Should he have failed he would be back home, at least for a few months before he went to join his parents and prepare to try again in a year.

To my shame, I had a little hope that he might fail. I knew I was being selfish but I really wanted him with me, not four thousand miles away.

As we moved into the winter I suffered, as all golfers do, by not being able to get out on the course as often and practice was centred on the range as Alan tweaked aspects of my swing. I also made several trips to the hospital as they worked on my leg to improve the linkage to my nervous system. I resisted the idea of a completely new leg then. I was happy with the existing one and did not wish to change until it became essential.

November came and went quickly for me. By then I was becoming more used to not having my evenings occupied with Richard. Once the school began, I followed it with dogged interest and mixed feelings. At first it looked as if my hopes would be fulfilled, Richard's first rounds left him well down the list, and I suddenly felt as guilty as if I was kicking his balls into the rough. We exchanged texts the evening after his third round and I found myself berating him for not playing to the standard I knew he was capable of. I think the last text was something like, "Get off your backside and smash it. I love you."

Three days later and he was in the top ten with exemptions on the Tour for the following year. At the same time, I was over the moon, because he would be able to do what he had always hoped for, and, I hate to say it, down in the dumps for the same reason. Apart from a few days around Christmas, it might be years before we could be together again.

I think he knew how I was feeling but what really upset him and drove him into a rage was my suggestion that I give up my golf and move to be with him. Some of his words as he reacted to that idea were unrepeatable but could be summed up as, "Stop talking rot, Sophie Jordan. Grow up. We knew that this might happen, even if I were on one of the European tours. You said it yourself. You give up your career and I'll never speak to you again!"

I cried myself to sleep, that night, in a way I hadn't done for years. He was right and I hadn't expected to be with him forever but how I wished that that was wrong. For days, after we had argued, I remained depressed. I desperately needed to talk to someone but I couldn't discuss it with any of my family nor did it seem right to talk to Ginny.

It took more than a week before I bumped into Fiona at the Club and finally spilled all my emotion on her. How unfair was that? That evening, after I had closed-up the pro-shop, she reappeared and dragged me off to a pub close to the golf course but with almost no risk of being seen by anyone we knew.

It took time but, over a couple of drinks, neither of us was driving, I let it all out.

"Fiona, I mean, I know I wasn't his first girlfriend and I'm pretty sure he liked me but I keep feeling like I was just another tick in a box. You know, have a relationship with someone with one leg, tick, and I hate myself for thinking that way."

Fiona looked at me in astonishment. "Oh, Sophie, you are a mess, aren't you? How do I put it kindly? Yes, Richard had other lovers, well at least one and, yes, you weren't the first. But you couldn't be more wrong about him and how he feels about you."

"You can't know that, Fiona." I responded miserably.

"Oh, but I can. I know he told you about the older woman, didn't he? Well, that was me and we still talk. We are still on good terms even though our relationship ended, the physical bit anyway and, I probably shouldn't tell you this, you are the only girl he has really loved."

I laughed. "You mean you were the woman I gave thanks for, for him being such a good lover, especially that first time."

"Yes, you should know, as he does, that it was only a physical thing. I'd just broken up with my lying little toe-rag of a husband. I found I needed bedding and Richard was pleasant, ready, and willing! You know why he decided on the States rather than pro-school here and the European tour qualifier, don't you?"

"Because his parents are out there now, they just got new jobs at MIT."

Fiona smiled gently. "It didn't occur to you to question why he never took you back to meet them? They've been out there for at least four years. Richard decided when they went that he wanted to stay in England. He felt it would be the best way to improve his golf and build his experience here before choosing how to go forward."

"And he chose the States to get away from hop-a-long." I was sure now that that was why.

"Lord, Sophie! Ginny has told me often enough how you underrate yourself. Richard went to the States because he feared, fears, that if he stayed, he would stop you reaching your best. That your golf would eventually be hit by the distraction of, well, all the side things you enjoyed together. He told me of those concerns the day before he left and he was about as low as you are now. The difference is that he gritted his teeth because he wants to see you winning. Keeping you was something he could not live with if you didn't manage to reach your potential. And to be quite clear, we all see that as the professional world top ten!"

I looked back at her. "I don't understand you or the rest. I'm an amateur who's had a run of good luck. I know it means I've got some opportunities next year but even if I do well enough to think about turning professional - world top ten? Come on."

"Sophie, please don't listen to that daft voice in your head that seems to constantly tell you that you aren't good enough. Being big headed is one thing that's not good but nor is being modest to an extreme." She sighed. "I guess you won't believe you are any good until you are number one or you've won all the majors or both. Just carry on playing like you do and work on the little bits, Alan points out. Then watch us congratulate ourselves when you are there."

I was shaking my head when she continued. "You may feel a little lonely at the moment but that will pass and you'll probably find someone else before long, don't forget you have all the looks you need."

No matter how much I disagreed with Fiona, I had to admit that talking with her had helped me make it through the rest of the year. Richard came back for Christmas and to arrange the sale of his flat. We had several outings to restaurants and the local pubs but, possibly surprisingly, we didn't end up in bed together. I don't know quite why but it just didn't seem right for either of us. Until New Year's Eve that is. We had enjoyed a meal and, I'm not sure why, as he walked me home, I dragged him back to his flat stripping off as we crossed the living room and pulling him into bed.

Perhaps I just wanted to remember a one-night stand with him, daft wasn't it, given the time we had been together or to remind him of what he would be missing. Whatever, bed was good enough that I spent the whole night there.

If I had wanted that to act as a reminder of what he would be missing and stop him heading back across the Atlantic. Well, it failed and I don't think I really expected or wanted it to work. We did at least part as good friends and I guess that that was for the best.

All too soon, Richard was back on a plane heading for his new life on the US golf courses. There was a little emotion, I can't say that I didn't shed a few tears after we parted at Heathrow, but I wished him good fortune.

By January, I needed some better weather. Ginny, again, came to the rescue. A second sponsorship deal was struck with a hotel chain. They had a series of hotels around the Mediterranean and wanted film of me on one or more of the twenty odd golf courses.

Checks with the R&A confirmed that appearing on a golf course to advertise it was fine but I should not actually be playing unless in an Elite competition and hotel and travel expenses were fine. I know that the rules were intended to make it easier for amateurs to fund such expenses and so on. I am still not that sure they are as clear as the authorities intended.

Anyway, I found myself, with Ginny in tow, spending a few weeks in warmer climes. Playing in local events. Ginny was quick to point out who I was which meant that I was welcomed with open arms. Perhaps that encouraged me to relax and enjoy myself on the courses without the focus needed when playing the bigger competitions. The welcomes became even warmer when I didn't win, giving some of the locals the kudos of beating me.

All too soon, my holiday was over and we returned, back to the cold damp weather of England. All I could do was think and practice. Refining the weaker parts of my game, and there were a lot, took practice and time with Alan. His frequent laughs, when I moaned that I'd never get it right, did take away some of the stress as my thoughts started to turn towards Augusta.

Ginny, in her agent's role, was focused on sorting out our travel arrangements but startled me when she told me that she would not be travelling out with me.

"I'll be there in time for the tournament but that won't be before the Tuesday. And before you ask, I'm taking a few days away with a friend." Her grin almost made me dissolve, I knew exactly who the friend was.

"Have fun, Ginny." Was all I could say at first and then I couldn't resist. "Give Steven a hug for me!"

I am still unsure as to why she blushes so easily but her red face confirmed my guess. I would just have to take the trip out by myself, that's life, I thought. I didn't know then that Ginny's absence would lead to a meeting that would change my life.

Chrissie Breaks Some News!

Mid-March and I'm almost packed. Then comes a call from, of all people, Chrissie.

"Sophie, it's me. Can I come round?"

"Of course, when? I'm at the golf club." I felt a little guilty as I had hardly seen my friend since the trial. I had not returned to school after my sixteenth birthday using my training as an "Apprenticeship" which allowed me to escape full time education. I was not exactly academic while Chrissie tended towards A-star grades and had headed off to uni as soon as she could.

"I'll come there. I've got news and I want you to be the first to know. See you in the bar."

Now I was intrigued. We had been good friends at school, two parts of the trio with Dawn. My heart hiccupped, I hadn't thought as much about my dearest friend in months, how could I have forgotten? Was this the reality of time passing and memories fading? It was wrong. I made a pact with myself. I would visit both her grave and her parents before I left for the States.

A little over an hour later, Chrissie burst, there was no other way of describing her entrance, into the bar rushing to the table I had nabbed near the window.

"Gosh, Sophie, you look great! All this fresh air is doing you wonders!"

I stared back at her, before pouring a glass of wine from the bottle I had acquired. She looked radiant but then she always had looked far better than me, or Dawn for that matter.

I decided to take the bull by the horns, she wasn't here for chitchat.

"You look good yourself, Chrissie. In fact, you are glowing. Spill the beans, what is your news?"

"This is." she replied, pointing to the door.

To say I was startled understates my shock. Chrissie had always been the most forward of my friends, there were various rumours, that she did nothing to quash, that she had lost her virginity, or given it away, long before she was sixteen. Boyfriends had come and gone, seemingly worn out. The person coming through the door was not who I was expecting.

Chrissie was, I knew, studying medicine, it had always been her dream, for as long as I had known her. Now someone I knew, was crossing the floor. Kate, the paramedic. The first responder that fateful night who had, in all probability, kept me alive by slowing the blood loss. She had, later, visited my bedside to see how I was doing.

"Sophie, you are a wonder!"

I sat back. "Mostly because you knew what you were doing, Kate."

It was Chrissie's turn to look nervous. "You know each other?"

Kate and I both laughed together, which had Chrissie looking even more on edge. I decided that I had to put her back at ease.

"Chrissie, we do know each other. Your friend is the paramedic that saved me after the car hit us. She stopped the blood flow such that I am still here. Kate, I know you visited me on the ward but I'm not sure I ever thanked you."

Kate smiled gently. "You did Sophie. Right after you had screamed at me for not letting you die with your friend."

The memories came flooding back. "I am so sorry, Kate."

Chrissie decided to try and get a word in edgeways. "Look, this is supposed to be my chance to reveal all, you two. May I speak?"

I looked at Kate, there was something about the way that Chrissie was looking at her that suddenly jelled. "Go on."

"Sophie, will you be my bridesmaid?"

"Uuh?"

"Kate and I are getting married. In August."

Now I was out of kilter, Chrissie, the teenager that had had boys for breakfast, for elevenses and other meals for that matter, was about to marry her girlfriend? I mean, wow!

"Of course, I will." I stuttered. "If I can."

"Oh, Lord, I didn't think. Where are you playing?"

I thought it out. "I should be back in England, if all goes well. I'll be in France for the Evian Championship in July but back for the Open at the beginning of August."

"So, when do we need to set the date? Second half of August?"

"I'm not that important but I can certainly clear my diary after the second weekend."

Now it was Kate's turn to grin. "There you go, Chrissie, love. I was sure all the big golf was over by then. Sophie, it's so good to see you again."

We spent the next few hours catching up with each other's progress. Not that I needed to say much about mine except to tell them about my leg and how it was better than ever. They had both been following the news of my golfing, prowess they called it! They had not realised that I had invites to play in so many of the majors and told me I should be on Facebook updating everyone. Me on Facebook! Not a chance, I thought.

Chrissie had, naturally, left school with top A-levels, Kate told me, not Chrissie herself, and started a degree course in medicine linked with the local University Hospital where Kate was a part of the A&E team.

"You've made it to Doctor then?" I asked.

"I have, I always wanted to be one but, for me, paramedic was the only route, it took a little longer but I made it in September. We've been working together on and off as Chrissie does her placements. She'll make doctor quicker, in two years at the most."

Chrissie admitted that they had got together more than a year before, after a student party that the paramedics had been invited to. The rest, she said, was history.

Towards the end of the evening, I managed to corner Chrissie in the Ladies. Conscious of Ginny's experience and that my friend was barely twenty, I expressed my concerns. After I had explained why I was worried and Chrissie had calmed down, she laughed. "Sophie, I thought you knew me better. It's Kate, you should be worried about. I don't think I have given her much room to stop loving me. And I'm not looking to let her escape!"

"But you bedded every boy you could get hold of. How come you've changed?"

Chrissie smiled. "And wasn't that fun! But when I met Kate, something did change. There is something about her that transcended everything I thought I knew about love. Sophie, haven't you got anyone?"

"It's a long story but not now. I have had one love but he's not with me anymore."

"Oh, Sophie. What's happened to people? They should be falling over themselves."

"Chrissie, have you forgotten? I'm a hop-a-long. Not the best choice, am I?"

"That is daft. God knows I wish I had your looks. You be patient, you'll find your Kate, as it were."

Back in the bar, I sent them on home, wherever that was, and returned to my parents, wondering how I could tell them about that terrible teen, they had known back when I was still at school.

Heading to Augusta.

A few days later and I was ready to start out for my first trip to North America. Although the Augusta event would be first, I was booked to stay over through the Masters before travelling on to Texas and the Chevron. My second major after the Open.

In late March, my Mum and Dad drove me down to Heathrow; to Terminal Four, crowded with holidaymakers and other travellers. I had only flown to Spain on that one holiday. Now I was going long-haul and on my own! My parents had parked and walked with me to the check-in where the queue was long and hardly moving. It seemed everyone had decided to arrive early for my flight, not to Augusta but to Atlanta. I would then need to take a domestic flight on to finish the trip.

After we had stood unmoving for almost half an hour, I made the decision that we should make our farewells there. I still had four hours before my flight and there was no point in Mum standing there tiring by the minute, Dad was almost as tired and he would be driving back.

Having told them to go and completed hugs, I watched them slowly walking away. Come on, Sophie Jordan, you're a big girl now, you can hack this.

As the queue slowly edged forward and I wheeled my golf bag in front of me there were a few quizzical looks and I could imagine the question on those minds. "What on earth is she doing with golf clubs? This isn't a flight to the Algarve."

That brought on a burst of nervousness, I mean it really wasn't a flight to the Algarve. Should I back out now and try and avoid the ignominy of missing both cuts thus proving that I really didn't have the game to play at these levels?

While I had been losing myself in those thoughts, check-in attendants had been working their way down the long lines checking people were in the right place. Eventually they had reached me and there was a gentle nudge. "Excuse me, Miss. Could I check your ticket please?"

I pulled out my mobile and showed my electronic version. "I am in the right place, aren't I? I've never flown from Heathrow."

The attendant smiled broadly. "Well, Miss Jordan, you are in the right place but not the right place, as it were."

I looked at him in horror, could I have got it that wrong?

"This is a queue for your flight but you should be over there." He said pointing to the first-class check-in desk.

"I can't be. I couldn't afford that. I'm in economy."

"Not today, Miss. Word came down from on high. The best amateur golfer in the country does not fly economy. Not with this airline! Now, let me help you with your bags, Miss."

There was something of a buzz in the crowd as I was being escorted across the floor and I overheard one conversation which, despite being somewhat embarrassed by the attention, made me smile to myself.

"Told you, silly girl is in the wrong terminal."

"You know, Colin, you really need new glasses. She is being taken over to the First-Class desk."

"All right for some, gets an upgrade by a flash of her eyelids!"

"I give up. When we get back you are going to the optician. That's Sophie Jordan, that brilliant young golfer!"

"Don't be ridiculous. She wouldn't be flying economy. She'd be first class anyway."

"Maybe not. She's only an amateur. She isn't earning the big money. Not yet anyway."

Completing my check-in was as smooth as it could be. The only delay being the need to provide a dozen autographs to the staff. I still don't understand why. I mean it wasn't as if I was Tiger Woods or Georgia Hall for that matter, but they insisted.

I then got an escort to the security check although there was something of a ruckus when the gate lit up like a beacon. The electronics in my leg had triggered every alarm going. In my nervousness I had forgotten to switch them off and, even though I had a letter from the hospital explaining my condition and how to allow for the intricacies, I still had to undergo an additional search before they were satisfied.

The lounge for first class was another eye-opener and I relaxed for the first time that day with a drink.

Shortly after I started my walk to the gate, I realised that I needed a comfort break before I boarded, and headed to the nearest Ladies. To my horror there was an unbelievably long queue. I knew that I could use the disabled section although in practice I tried to avoid doing so. A hop-a-long I might be but I had always felt that there would be someone else left waiting who had a greater need than mine. This time I had no real choice. Wait and maybe miss the flight? I also did not think I would be able to last until I could use the facilities on the aircraft. Maybe that was being too unsure of myself but I wasn't about to take any risks.

As I went in through the door, I felt the pressure of a few pairs of eyes. Couldn't they see I was really disabled?

It took me a few minutes before I was done and quickly made my exit, only to find a perfectly fit looking young man waiting to use the same facility. I think I glared at him, how dare he?

Then, as I headed down to the gate, I suddenly felt guilty. He looked familiar but I had no idea why. Anyway, how did I know he wasn't disabled? I knew that my leg wasn't real but I had been told that the prosthetic was such a match that you had to know it was there to see it. Sorry, I whispered.

As I reached the gate. I found two aircraft doors and I was guided through a shorter file of waiting passengers to the left entrance. I guessed that this was the route to the first-class section, at the front of the plane and that proved true. I found myself looking around in amazement. That one trip to Spain had been in a smaller aircraft and I don't think there was a first class. This plane was a Dreamliner, and huge. My seat must have been as big as two or three economy seats – wow! Well, it took up as much room. How the other half live, I thought before realising that was me, for this flight anyway.

An attendant came over to me with a glass. Of champagne! "Need any help, Miss Jordan? Just call me."

I found the baggage locker and, having dumped my bag, settled back into my seat, and relaxed with a few sips of the alcohol. At first the next seat was empty and then a young man came into the area led by another of the flight attendants.

It was the same individual I had crossed at the disabled loos! And, oh that's crazy, how did I not recognise him. He's the guy who won best amateur at the Open. Heck, what's his name? Robert Ward, that's it! He is seriously good. Beat the US Amateur Champion into second.

I decided to take the bull by the horn.

As he sat down, I turned to look at him. "You're Ward, aren't you? Rob Ward? You won the Amateur Championship, didn't you? And the Silver Medal at the Open."

PART TWO – ROB BEFORE.

The Dreaded C-word.

"That's got to be wrong, I'm only eighteen!" I shouted at the surgeon. "I can't have cancer! I'm fit. I play golf every day. I walk miles. I'm not overweight. I don't even drink much, not as much as my friends do, anyway."

"I'm sorry, Robert, but the test results are clear. You have cancer. At your age fitness has little to do with it."

Growing Up before the Worst.

When I look back to my childhood I realise now that I was very lucky. My parents both had well paid jobs, Dad as a dental surgeon and Mum as a Chartered Accountant. As a result, I and my twin sisters had the freedom to try all sorts of sports and other activities. At least, so long as we kept up at school.

Despite being twins my sisters found themselves attracted to quite different pastimes. Rachel studied piano while Susie chose to try football at which, as she demonstrated to the rest of the family, she was quite good.

It was just as well that we were encouraged by my parents to try whatever we wanted. I first joined the local cricket club playing in the juniors for two years before realising that I just did not enjoy being hit by a red ball, travelling at speed.

Dad was irritated by my, apparently, not continuing his own sporting pedigree, he had been a good distance runner and a fast bowler. Running was never my idea of fun so having given up cricket, I was under a little pressure or, to put it another way, a lot of encouragement, to find another out-of-school sports interest.

As I said being hit by a small red ball coming the other way fast was not my scene, so the idea of hitting an even smaller white ball which was not moving had attractions. It started as a bit of fun on the local par three course but soon became quite an obsession.

From lessons in groups, moving on to one-on-one sessions with the local professional, I found that I had some natural talent. Competing at my local club by the time I was twelve I had been given the chance to take part in the monthly medals and other senior competitions. My handicap fell rapidly until I was playing off better than scratch at fourteen.

For the first time I entered one of the bigger junior national competitions. I confess that I was no different to most teenagers;

full of confidence and expectation. The reality of discovering that I wasn't good enough to even make the top twenty and get invited to the next tournament, brought me to a sudden and, for a time, depressing halt. If there were so many better golfers, what chance did I really have?

To this day I remember the words of my professional.

"Robert, that was your first venture into the great big world. You still have much to learn and much work to do. But I have watched you long enough to be confident that you have what it takes. If you work at every element of your game. Remember, some of those in that competition have far more experience and they are older. That makes a difference. Now get back on the range!"

Peter was, I am glad to say, right and over the next few years, I found even just working on my game enjoyable. By seventeen I was playing all over the country, usually chauffeured by my father!

County Opens finally led to my first attempt at the Amateur Championship. I was preparing to play in the pre-qualifying rounds when it happened.

I had put the occasional stomach pains down to tension. Too much practice, competitions plus A-level examinations on the close horizon. Blood was a very different matter. My doctor's reaction was almost unbelievable. Within a week I was undergoing tests in the local hospital. Even then it took my mum's panic-stricken face when she learned that I was headed for the oncology department to drive home to me that this was serious.

At my first consultation the surgeon warned me that my one hope was that they had caught the cancer, if that was what it was, early enough. The MRI scan was crucial. Five days later I was back for the results. "You have bowel cancer."

My initial reaction was of disbelief. "But I'm only eighteen!" Then, I fear, I lost it. Screaming that it wasn't possible. The specialist waited patiently until I calmed down.

"Yes, Robert. You are very young and it is unusual. Few people fall victim at your age or even before they are thirty. The good news is that everything indicates that it has not penetrated the sides of your large intestine. I am arranging for you to be on my list on Monday. The sooner we act the better. Now, come on, you must have questions."

Of course, I had questions, though and perhaps to her surprise, they were about golf. Could I delay until after the Amateur Championship in five weeks' time? How would an operation affect my future career? I was already dreaming of turning professional.

"Delay?" She gasped. "At the moment you have been lucky. If you delay there is a high chance that the cancer will break out of the bowel. If it does that, you will almost certainly be terminally ill within weeks, even with an operation."

"And my future golf?"

"If all goes well and you approach your return to playing sensibly there is no reason why you should not be back competing by next year."

"Next year!" To say I was hurting would have been to understate the emotions flooding through me.

"I am afraid so. Take that time and there is no reason why you wouldn't be able to play again."

"Professionally?" I was still struggling with losing almost a year of my life.

"I can't say. I understand that you are currently an amateur. Turning professional is more about your ability than the loss of time. Being able to play following a full recovery is, I am sure, probable." She continued. "Now, do you understand what a stoma is and why it is needed?"

I sat and listened, still with a degree of disbelief at what I was hearing. My large intestine, the bowel, would be removed and a part of my small intestine, the end, would be moved and be fixed so that it would protrude through my stomach. The surgical team would add a plastic bag but I would have to learn to manage its operation every day for the rest of my life. She called it an ileostomy.

I know it sounds self-centred but my last question was, would it affect my sex life. It was with some relief that the answer was that that part of my anatomy would be unlikely to suffer any side effects. I did not, at that time, think about how other changes might affect my girlfriend. That was for the future.

For me the next few days were and remain misty. Pre-op checks and other procedures. To be frank, I really did not and do not want to remember. By the Monday everything was ready for me and I was taken down to theatre, still a little numb even before the anaesthetic.

My first memories afterwards were of pain and discomfort as I lay in a hospital bed finally properly awake on the Tuesday morning – wishing I wasn't, if I'm honest. Mid-morning the surgeon appeared and looked as happy as I had seen her.

"Robert, we got it in time. No evidence that the cancer had escaped. The operation was successful and, for me, as routine as they get. Not for you, I know." She smiled before giving the stoma a swift look and nodding in approval.

That evening my parents appeared. Desperately trying to hide their relief even as Mum looked aghast at the tubes and cables attached to me, but there again I had wondered why so many. They spent an hour before giving up the battle to keep me awake as the painkillers left me drowsy.

There was no sign of Annie, my constant companion of the past few years, but I heard Dad saying the hospital were only allowing two visitors at a time. I only learned later that she had come that evening while I was asleep and had fled the ward in tears.

They say that the passage of time is a personal thing. Until now I had not really understood what they meant. Days in the hospital dragged like months even though I had my laptop and could still study. After the first forty-eight hours at least.

Eventually my specialist was happy that my recovery could continue at home and discharged me with a simple warning.

"I will see you again in a month's time. Until then, no golf. Not even putting practice. You should recuperate quickly. You have youth on your side but don't make the mistake that just feeling a bit better is a green light to start swinging a club. Get it wrong and you could put back returning to the sport by months, if not years."

I gritted my teeth fully intending to be back on the putting green as soon as I could walk without too much discomfort. That was until I found out that Peter had banned me from the club and spread the word amongst the other club pros in the area. He was adamant. No golf until he had word from the hospital that I was fit enough.

My opinion in that didn't count, he said. He wanted me back competing as soon as possible but not at the risk of my damaging myself such that I never played again. I resigned myself to a long boring summer. My exam studies would benefit, my dad said, with an extra couple of hours available to revise each day.

What hurt most was the absence of Annie. We had been together for nearly four years first as schoolmates, then friends and companions and, more recently, as lovers. Whenever we could find time alone, anyway. I tried to talk to her but all my calls went straight to her voicemail and she wasn't returning them.

Eventually, a letter arrived. Annie had seen me in hospital on the day after the operation. Upset by all the medical equipment attached to me, she could not stay. With everything suddenly very real and alive she had done what she had avoided beforehand. She googled my cancer and found as much information as she could handle but it was the photographs of stomas that terrified her. At that moment fate intervened and Annie decided that she would never be able to cope with the changes to my body. It was better, she had written, to split now rather than live a lie.

I sat there stunned, my first reaction being to run to her home, a couple of miles away, a ridiculous notion given that I was still struggling to walk without some support. Then I unashamedly wept. Annie had been the love of my life for so long that the idea of not having her support and comfort drove home how my life had been changed by that damn cancer.

Perhaps it would have been better if the medical people could not have saved me. Was I doomed to spend the rest of my life alone? If the girl who loved me, had loved me, couldn't face being with a partner with no bowel, why would anyone I met in the future want to be with me, to see me naked?

I admit that I fell into deep depression, locking myself in my bedroom coming out only for food and other necessities. I refused to talk to my parents and avoided video calls with my sisters who had returned to university once I was home.

My parents were becoming desperate as they tried and failed to lift me from my malaise. Then someone from the stoma support group called on me.

"Rob, you need to come down." My mother called. "You have a visitor."

My heart leapt, could Annie have changed her mind? I dragged some clothes on and stumbled down the stairs. Then I realised that the visitor was dressed in a nurse's uniform. What? Why?

"Rob, good to meet you. My name is Cathy Doyle and I'm part of the stoma support group. We'll be available from now on. Even when you are fully discharged by the surgical team."

"Hello." I said dully. "Why are you here now?"

"To introduce you to the support group and see both how you are and if you need any help."

"Help! Can you get my girlfriend back? She can't stand this bloody thing. Won't even meet me." All my misery came tumbling out in a blast of anger.

"Oh!" Cathy frowned. "Of course, everything happened so quickly I guess you didn't have time to talk about what was going to happen to you, did you?"

I nodded. "She was away visiting relatives. We had one call which wasn't great. I guess I shouldn't have expected her to stay. She can have any man she wants but it doesn't make it any easier."

"No, and it seems an emotional decision without much thought. I'd say it is unusual but then most patients are, as you know, older and are married or at least in long term relationships. I suggest that, once you are off the surgeon's follow-up programme, you come to one of the self-help groups. That will give you the chance to talk to other people in the same place. It may help you approach the future in a more positive way. Remember, without it there would be no future at all."

After having examined my stoma, which she confirmed looked good, she left promising another visit in a month. Looks good, I thought, only a medical person could possibly believe that rubbish. The remaining weeks, until I saw the surgeon again, dragged. My exam studies didn't help even if they improved my chances of getting better results. I can't say that I was that worried. Being successful at golf did not need A-levels in the sciences but I had to concede that they might provide a backup should my sporting plans fail. Failure is a terrible word and until then I had refused to consider it as applying to me. Now I fretted continually.

A Slow Return before the Amateur Championship.

Four weeks after my operation I arrived at the hospital feeling as good as I had since our first meeting. My first words after she had carried out an examination, with more depth than that of the nurse, was as you might expect.

"Ms Green, please tell me everything is well and I can start playing again."

She smiled. "You can start playing again, though I recommend you work with your coach carefully. If you like I will talk to him with my thoughts. You may need to adjust your swing to reduce the strain on your tummy muscles, at least at first. Here are some exercises. They should help strengthen your stomach."

I gave her Peter's number and headed home where I had quickly changed into some golf gear before realising that lifting my golf bag might not be a good idea. With no-one else at home to give me a lift I resigned myself to walking to the club with just an iron and my putter.

Even that was a waste of energy, Peter had been watching for my arrival and intercepted me before I could even get a bucket of balls. "Now, Rob, let's take this one day at a time. Putting practice today. We'll look at a few exercises to improve that part of your game."

For an hour he devised various formulaic routines before sending me home.

"Rob, you know how important putting is. That last exercise, you could do at home but, when here, set up that circle of twelve balls at five feet from the hole and then try to hole all twelve. Then move out a foot at a time and repeat the process."

I looked at him. "Why that way? Surely my practice green routine before a round works."

Peter stared back. "And how many three putts do you make? This is a process that the likes of Jack Nicklaus, Lee Trevino, recommended. It is all about embedding a routine of stroke making. Most players miss more straight putts than they do ones that aren't straight. Keep the balls at the same distance until you make all the putts. Miss one and repeat. Get them all and replace a further foot away from the hole and so on."

"And how far away should I end up?"

"Set your target at ten feet but don't expect to get that far. Remember at ten feet even the pros only have a success rate of around forty per cent."

"That's a joke, yes?"

"No, that's a stat from the PGA Tour. I dare say we're no better."

I buckled down, it was clear that I wasn't going to be allowed to swing a club for some time and, I reminded myself that if I was honest, I did miss more than my share of shortish putts for a plus handicapper.

Two months after the operation, Peter finally agreed to let me back on the range. I had had the all-clear from the hospital a couple of weeks before but he was as cautious as ever.

"Now just a gentle eight-iron, Rob."

I tried my usual swing and caught my breath. It was crazy, the pain I had been getting, before the problem was diagnosed, had vanished to be replaced by an immediate pull on my chest and lower abdomen. I gasped. Peter nodded trying, I suspect, not to laugh and I glared at him.

"Now you know why I wanted you to wait, Rob. The medical people have a tendency, to under estimate the long-term impact of an operation. You can expect to feel some muscle pulls, you won't have been expecting. On the other hand, the other stomach ache you were getting should have vanished. One other point," and now he did grin, "you haven't swung a club for more than two months.

You are going to have to take it steady and build up your range practice piece by piece."

I knew he was right but it was already late August and I hadn't been able to play at all that summer. I really did want to get back out on the course competing but, in the end, I had to go along with the exercise regime that Peter set up. I gathered he had had multiple conversations with the hospital physiotherapists on how to return me to top form and had adapted their suggestions for getting me back to my old self, as far as he could.

It took the rest of August but by the second week in September, I was able to take my first foray on to the golf course. When I eventually came off the eighteenth green my whole body seemed to be aching but the big positive was that I had completed the round and had, surprisingly, scored well. Fewer putts did help!

The work on my swing had generated a smoothness that, I admit, compensated for the loss in distance, as I had had to focus on the swing and less on the power. I had attempted a few drives using my old power swing only to find myself rapidly holding my stomach. Peter, as always, had been right when he had guided my development during that boring summer.

Despite the obvious progress, I was lacking competition and with winter rapidly approaching the chance of any serious play was receding into the spring. Then came news I had not expected. Mum and Dad had decided to take their winter holiday, not on the ski slopes of the Alps but on the Costa del Sol.

My sisters had already declined to go. They were in their second years with their degrees and couldn't spare time away. In any case, Susie said, she was in the busiest part of her football season. Our parents had decided that to holiday in the warmer climate of southern Spain would be good for them and me. I didn't have any sensible argument against as long as I could take my clubs and get some play on the local courses.

That was, of course, the idea and just after Christmas we flew to Malaga. Three weeks of golf in warmer weather was exactly what I needed. By the time we were due to return to the UK, I was managing to play a full round of golf without any noticeable pain. Fatigue was more of an issue but even that had become less obvious as the holiday progressed.

Back in England, I was limited to off-course practice for most of February. Fortunately, March dawned bright and cheerful and by the second week I was back on the course and looking forward to the competitions in April. As these got underway it became obvious, to me if not to everyone else, that I was no longer the longest driver at the club. I had lost thirty plus yards in distance to the mixed joy of my friends and the more competitive golfers. On the other hand, my drives and fairway shots were far more accurate. Losing balls in the trees or rough was far less frequent and my scores dropped rapidly. Two county competitions towards the end of April gave me the confidence that I was on my way back. I had won one and had a top-five finish in the other and Peter agreed that I was ready to try for the Amateur Open for the second time.

Back home I went on-line to find out the entry requirements only to discover that I should have entered by the end of the previous October! I had lost another year and I wasn't happy.

I know I should have remembered. After all that had been the rule when I had entered last year. The truth was that my focus had been lost with the operation and the slow, all too slow, recovery.

It didn't stop me heading back to the club and berating Peter. Somehow, I think, he was ready for me and after I had finished my tirade of abuse, he simply smiled, walked back to his desk and after a moment opened a file and then passed me a sheet of paper.

"Oh shit!" My reaction was short and to the point. The paper was a print out of my entry. Peter hadn't forgotten, he had simply not looked to put added pressure on me.

My abject apology was accepted.

"Rob, if you had not created hell, I wouldn't have given you that. I wanted to know that you still had the drive in you to carry on. The emotional drive. That which should never appear on the course but which must be there inside."

When I look back at that period of my life it sounds, even to me, that I was focused only on my golf to the exclusion of all else. I did, of course, sit my A-levels coming out with decent grades later that summer.

And I did try to convince Annie that I was the same old me. We finally met in the early autumn. It was to no avail. She admitted that she felt ashamed at not having faced me sooner but she was adamant that she would not be able to maintain the relationship. She was sure I would find someone better than her, I deserved that, she said and my repeated assertions that I didn't want anyone else fell on deaf ears. She wanted to remain friends but nothing more than that. In the end we did at least part on good terms.

My sisters were far from happy with Annie but, at my request, they did not take any of the actions they suggested she deserved. They just set me up with a couple of dates which, in truth, would have been unlikely to go anywhere even before my op.

I did try calling one of the girls who had, when we were still at school, tried to date me. Then she had had no chance and now, I found out she was engaged and expecting. No fun that way either. I resigned myself to the life of bachelor and turned to trying to make the best of it.

I had two months to prepare for the biggest test of my game, the Pre-Qualifying Round on the Friday before the tournament.

Those two months passed quickly, very quickly. Over those eight weeks I played in seven Elite competitions, doing my best to lift my world ranking status. I was certainly not going to make any of the other championships around Europe unless I could play well enough to gain an occasional wildcard. The Amateur Championship would be that entry card if, and I knew it was a big if, I won then I would have the chance to play in some of the biggest tournaments, the Open, the Masters and those entries to other Championships would be assured.

But it was the **IF** that bothered my parents. Not the **IF** I didn't win but, was I prepared for that possibility and the need to wait another year. In the end I had to convince them that I did realise that winning was/would be against the odds. Let's face it some of the best golfers in the amateur world would be there. Former winners, the US Amateur Champion, last year's winner who had chosen not to turn professional yet. And me, with only a few months of competitive golf in the past year.

It took a conversation between Peter and my Dad to settle their nerves.

"Rob has the ability. He has the drive. The only thing that might hold him back is that if he goes the whole way then he's going to have to play ten rounds of golf in six days. That's hard work for the fittest of golfers and we won't know if his recovery is far enough advanced until then. Only time will tell." Peter's understanding of why they were worried helped plus the fact that he agreed to act as my caddy and his promise that, if it did prove to be too much, he would pull me out of the competition.

"Over my dead body." I thought, gritting my teeth at the idea, while conscious that it was a possibility.

It didn't help to know that, as far as anyone knew, no person with my disability had been successful at the top of the game. Truth was, we didn't know if anyone had managed to play golf at all after getting any form of stomach related cancer. There again, it would be rare for such players to broadcast the issue, I wasn't about to start telling strangers or even other club members who didn't know me.

One day I hope it will be possible to find a way to encourage other sufferers to take the leap, not just into golf but other physical activities they might otherwise fear but, for now, I wasn't yet in a place to spearhead such a drive.

June arrived and we headed west. Pre-qualifying would take place on the Friday on two courses close to Porthcawl and I would be playing at Pyle and Kenfig Club. The main event would be played at Royal Porthcawl itself. That club had hosted the event on several occasions as well as the Senior Open Championship.

Thursday dawned bright and sunny and I found conditions helpful to playing golf which was good but possibly not useful for understanding how the course would play on the Friday with rain and wind forecast. Still, I could at least get a feel for the greens.

It was an enjoyable day, playing partners were friendly and we offered each other help in various aspects, lost balls and so on. I knew, as did they, that the next day would be different. We would all help with wayward shots if we could but that would be that. The top ten best scores from our venue and the Grove Club a few miles away would qualify. Miss that cut-off and I would have to wait to learn whether any of the reserve list players obtained an entry.

I woke the next morning to dark skies and the news that play had been suspended due to an electrical storm approaching the area. My original tee-time had not been until late in the morning, in fact I was in the last but one trio due off at just after noon, now it looked as if we would be lucky to get started before three o'clock, if then.

When I arrived at the course, we were told that, although play was now expected to start by eleven, it had been decided that half the field should start from the tenth hole and that included my group. As a typical links course, it shouldn't have mattered but I did have the sense of a sudden disadvantage. Of course, those playing on the other course would face the same issues and conditions would be the same for us all, it still felt wrong though.

Peter would have none of my gripes. "This is how the big comps go. The one thing neither you nor they can control is the weather. Starting on the tenth is the least of your problems, Rob! That wind is at least a two-club strength and you will need to adjust for it."

I nodded gloomily. "I can't remember playing in this strong a wind."

"You probably haven't but you are usually playing on courses inland. Parkland locations. The guys with the advantage today will be those who live on the coasts, you played with one yesterday." Peter grinned.

I had and Julian had been helpful to me and another of the players, passing on a little of his knowledge. I guessed then that, once the results were in, he would be up there in the top group and I would be proved right, just.

This was pre-Qualifying for the Championship, it should have been exciting. It wasn't. To be truthful it was a hard slog. All we could do was to try and avoid mistakes. The idea of making lots of birdies rapidly took a back seat and when the odd red score came to any of us there were mutual congratulations. I was lucky and managed three with only two bogeys to offset them. Would one under be enough? History suggested not but the conditions had been as tough as most had faced.

I bumped into Julian as I dragged myself into the clubhouse. How had he done?

"Not great, Robert. Level par. It's a case of wait and see how they did at the Grove. I'm fifth here or was? You?"

I had to admit that I had managed one under. "Sorry, Julian."

"Don't be sorry," he laughed, "it's how things go and we can still hope."

With the disruption caused by the weather and the earlier delays the results from the other course were still outstanding and we wouldn't know for nearly an hour how they compared. As they came in Julian and I sweated it out until it became apparent that the scores at the Grove were worse than ours. Julian finished ninth and I was tied seventh. With the first ten guaranteed a place we were in.

With Friday done and dusted, I could focus on more practice over the weekend. Specifically, at least one round on the Grove course. Weather both days was warm but blustery winds kept us focused. My own feelings could be summed up in a comment to Peter on Sunday evening.

"I think that the guys who had to play the Grove on Friday were unlucky. It isn't that long but you can't afford to be less than accurate off the tee. Those fairways are tight, Peter."

"All the more reason to play within yourself, Rob. The good thing is that your work during the winter has improved exactly that part of your game."

"True but putting will win or lose it. The greens are lightning quick despite the rain we have had."

Peter laughed. "And that is links golf for you!"

I still struggled with the sheer size of the field that plays the qualifying rounds. For two days, two hundred and eighty-eight golfers would compete over two courses with just sixty-four places available for the matchplay stages. Together with any ties, that is. Hard work for them, I thought, as they would be playing a preliminary round on the Wednesday morning. If they won, they would be straight back on the course to play someone who would have had a restful start to the day.

That problem was for two days' time, first I had to deal with the Grove. Conditions were good, if not ideal, and the early starters were doing well. By mid-morning the leaders were five under par. For me the start was not good as I found a greenside bunker and could not get up and down to save par but, from that point, I found myself coping well with the breeze and, guided by Peter, I contrived to hit every fairway off the tee. At the same time, I also hit all the par three greens. Birdies came at a steady rate and I also finished at five under.

It is difficult to admit that I was both happy with how I had played but depressed by the other scores. Despite my sixty-seven, I was not challenging the top scores. More than a dozen players on the Grove had posted better numbers and, I think, another fifteen or sixteen were tied with me. Tomorrow would need another good score or a slide down the standings was inevitable and this became even more apparent when the scores from Pyle came in. One player had shot sixty! Twelve under!

Peter settled me down over dinner with his own interpretation of the way the day had gone. "We already knew that the Grove was the tougher course, that was apparent during the pre-qualifying. Tomorrow you'll be on Pyle. Your turn to shoot low!"

"But I shot low today, at least I thought I had. You think I will need to shoot in the low sixties, I mean lower than today?"

"I rather think that another sixty-seven will be ample to qualify, though it may not get you the easiest of draws, we can only wait on that. For the moment, you are tied around forty-fifth and there are another forty within two shots. That means that around eighty-five are seriously in the mix. Just remember that, if we ignore that sixty, you are only three shots back. Tomorrow, it's all to play for."

I nodded, as ever he was right. His analytical mind guiding me.

As had become a ritual, he asked after Ken, and how I felt generally. I should say that Ken was the name I had adopted for my stoma. The nurses had suggested naming it. Their advice being that it would allow me to talk to family and friends about it without sounding medical. Ken became my alter-ego and, daft as it seems, using a name did reduce the risk of unintended embarrassment.

"He's fine and so am I, Peter. Better than I thought I might be."

"OK, Rob. Just remember. I'm carrying your bag but I don't want to have to carry you, off the course."

Day two, crunch time.

We were one of the earlier groups with a ten-twenty tee time.

"Just remember, Rob. Look for accuracy off the tee and forget the others. You can't do anything about them, all you can do is play your game."

I often wondered about the relationship between the pros and their caddies. Now Peter was showing me a little of that, or should that be a lot? I knew that the final choice of club and shots would be for me to decide but, I reminded myself, listen to your guiding light.

With Peter's considered backing the round went well and I did in the end match my score of the previous day. In fact, I went one better. In the clubhouse at eleven under par, I fidgeted. At least a dozen players from Pyle had already posted better scores, had the course played that easy?

With half the field still out on the course I could do no more than wait and, as I said, I fidgeted. Slowly a few scores started filtering through from Grove and they were not good. Only a few players appeared to have matched their day one scores with some scoring particularly badly. Even the overnight leader had finished only two shots better than myself, posting one under for the day.

Time seemed to slow. For a long time, or so it seemed, nothing was happening, no more scores from the Grove and only a few from Pyle. Then an official walked into the room.

"Sorry, everyone. I know you are all waiting on the results, unfortunately we have had a tech meltdown and are having to process cards manually. Most of the players are either in the clubhouses or have only a few holes left to play. For your information, the indicative cut will be at seven or eight under. It is possible that that will change but, in my opinion, it is unlikely to be worse than six. Thanks for your patience. We are working on the draw for tomorrow but that may not be finished, now, until after eleven o'clock."

One voice spoke up, asking the question on the minds of most of us. "How will we know our tee-times for tomorrow?"

"We are working on a tech solution which will be available and you will receive a text and an email as soon as the process is complete. I am sorry for the delay but rest assured you will learn your fate tonight."

There were a few light-hearted grumbles but that was only amongst those of us who were now sure we had made it. Quite a few of the players made their farewells, they clearly now knew they would not make the cut and would be on their way to their hotels or possibly homeward bound. It was hard not to feel for them, so near and yet so far.

As they left the room there was something of an uproar. One of the golfers, a particularly young looking individual, was on his feet looking across the room at those leaving and shouting. "That's it, you losers, slink off home! Don't stay on to watch me win the lot!" One of the older men turned back. "Win? You will have made the cut by a shot at most! No chance, you pathetic moron! Most of these guys will destroy you at matchplay. The rest might take a few extra holes. If I were you, I'd wait and see if you can play good golf. And two things. Firstly, I saw you play and if that is your best, well hard luck. Secondly, we aren't all losers. I finished six shots ahead of you and that makes me a loser? Time to grow up, young man."

The youngster went to respond but a second player grabbed him and forced him back into his seat. He clearly had some strength of mind which allowed him to control the outburst but the damage was done. The atmosphere around the room seemed to have darkened, mostly with anger which was being suppressed by the rest of the players successful or not.

Peter and I looked at each other and shook our heads.

"How to make friends and influence people? Let's hope you avoid him, Rob." Peter's words summed up my own feelings, that person was clearly not going to be fun to play.

I had scored well enough in the strokeplay to be one of those that avoided the Preliminary Round. I must admit that I almost wished that I had been in that round. That was when I walked on to the first tee and met my opponent. The over-the-top young man was in conversation with one of the local caddies before turning to grin at me. "The lamb to the slaughter, hello."

As he immediately turned his back on me, Peter touched my shoulder and said quietly. "There's only one way to shut this twit up. Beat him."

The match official called us together and we tossed for start. I lost and the other player, announced as Daniel Fatuna, decided to go first. "Might as well start as I expect to continue!"

I looked back at him and simply laughed, which seemed to irritate him. Clearly, I was supposed to get angry but, just for once, I realised that all I needed to do was to let my golf answer his attitude.

And answer it did. In spades.

More rude comments, when I took my three-wood off the tee, were quietened by my second shot which finished just three feet from the pin. Despite his drive having finished a good sixty yards further than mine he could only find the edge of the green and his first putt finished a good couple of feet past the hole. It was then that we almost had the first falling out as he walked to his ball and promptly picked up even though I hadn't conceded the second putt.

The referee looked towards me as if to ask but a nudge from Peter and I simply replaced my own ball, my shorter putt had not been conceded, and I carefully holed out for birdie. One-up!

We arrived at the second tee with Daniel already teeing up and reacting badly when it was pointed out that he had lost the first and it was no longer his honour. For a moment I thought he was going to throw a tantrum before he backed away.

If his demeanour was bad at the start, it would not get any better with repeated unforced errors and a couple of thrown clubs. On the second occasion he broke his eight-iron against a tree and then argued, with the official, that he was entitled to get a replacement. When the official, correctly, told him he couldn't, his response was consistent. "I'm reporting you! You're done!"

The official smiled in my direction in apology, though he owed me nothing. In amongst those tantrums, I continued to play, to be honest, nothing more than steady golf. The main thing was that I was making no mistakes and I was winning with birdies or pars to which Daniel had no answer. We reached the ninth green and I was again close, perhaps two feet below the hole. I had given up expecting Daniel to concede any putt and walked up to mark the ball. He headed to his ball just off the green before chipping it four or five feet past.

This time he went forward and was looking to pick the ball up. "Daniel, I'd like to see you putt that." I'm afraid my temper was gradually shortening.

He turned around. "You are joking! That's a clear gimme!"

The official intervened, again. "Mr Fatuna, the putt has not been conceded."

Daniel snatched his putter back and duly stood over the putt before missing it, by quite a margin. His putter flew, just missing his caddy.

It hadn't made any difference, as I tapped home my own putt for birdie and moved to six up at the turn. An astonishing score as far as I was concerned. The tenth and eleventh holes followed a similar pattern although he managed to get halves at these. My approach at the twelfth found me closer to the hole than my opponent. Daniel's first putt ran past the hole by a few feet but this time I told him to pick it up. Peter's suggestion, I would admit. "Allows you to focus on your putt."

Despite it being a difficult eight feet or so I sank my own putt to win the match. I turned to shake Daniel's hand only to find that he had marched away, smashing his putter as he went. His caddy, who turned out to be a local, came over. "Sorry about that." he said, "I should be commiserating with my player but to be honest he got everything he deserved. Good luck, Rob, well played."

I had made the last thirty-two which meant a guaranteed invite back the next year, assuming I was still an amateur. I am still not sure whether that eased my own mental approach or just made me more determined not to need that exemption. Whatever, the hard work really began. The final days of the Championship each involved players completing as much as thirty-six holes in a day and I admitted to myself that this was a step beyond my recent competitive strain. Would fatigue begin to hit home?

With an early start for my third-round match, Thursday promised to be a long day. Peter suggested that I change my diet to reinforce my energy levels. "Think of it as being faced with the requirements of a marathon."

"I never was any good at running. Hated it." I complained.

"Thing is the stamina requirements and associated fitness for golf, particularly when two rounds are required in a day, are not that dissimilar. And I do know that we need to take account of Ken's needs."

I walked on to the first tee that morning to be greeted by an old adversary. "Gordon, I didn't realise we were going head-to-head. This is going to be a lot more fun than yesterday, Peter."

"From what I heard, that would not be that difficult." Gordon grinned. "Need revenge for that last club game we met in, though."

His reminder that I had beaten him once before did nothing to ease my tension. That match had been an inter-club meeting and I had been lucky to win on the eighteenth. That's in the past, Rob, I told myself. This is another day.

It was more fun, although I suspect our caddies might have disagreed. The lead, when there was one, went back and forth but I walked off the sixteenth with a one-hole lead with but one thought in my mind. Could I play the par-five seventeenth well enough to hold Gordon off. He had been comfortably out driving me and was perfectly capable of reaching the green in two, would I be able to get close enough to challenge him?

Following my own shot finding the fairway, as far as we could tell, the tee-shot was a blind one, Gordon unleashed a huge drive and I gritted my teeth as we walked up the fairway. As the landing area came into view, we were faced with one marshal pointing to a ball on the right side while a second marshal could be seen almost a hundred yards further on.

"This will be my ball, I guess, Peter."

He grinned, "If it isn't, we may well have problems, Rob. I doubt your drive would have reached anywhere near that distance. You are near enough to go for the green, just, but I wonder if you would be better off looking to leave a wedge in. You'll reduce the risk of going in one of those pot bunkers."

"But if Gordon's ball is where the marshal is, he will only need a nine-iron or even a wedge from there."

Peter laughed, quietly, he was never one to rejoice in others misfortunes. "If I have read the signal correct his next shot is not going to be easy."

I looked at him. "Why?"

"I think he caught the downslope and he's found the bunker. It's a huge drive, three-hundred and sixty yards perhaps, but that is why that bunker is there. Play it safe, Rob."

Peter was right. I laid up to about seventy yards finishing close to the last fairway bunker. Luckily my ball had a little fade on it and bounced away from that trap. Gordon had not been that lucky. His ball had finished tucked up under the lip of the bunker. By the time we had reached them, after I had played my second, it was clear that he would even struggle to land a shot on to the fairway.

I really felt for Gordon, even as I sensed I might be able to win the match at that hole. Finally, he stood over the front of the bunker and played a shot that I would have been proud of. He flicked the ball with a wedge sideways across the bunker and contrived to keep the ball in play, albeit in the rough on the other side of the fairway. From there he struck another good shot which hit the green. Unfortunately, he could not generate the spin to stop the ball close to the hole.

From my position in the fairway, I was able to launch a wedge shot high enough to stop on the green, perhaps ten feet away. In the end the result was a formality and I was through to the last sixteen, winning two and one.

The end was so different from the previous day. Gordon's well done jelled with my commiserations over his misfortune. "Rob, you played well enough to deserve to win and, well, next time it might be you in the sand. Good luck this afternoon."

Round four and this time I knew I would be in for a tough game with my Japanese opponent being the Asia-Pacific Amateur Champion. He had also been runner-up in the Japan Amateur Championship. A seasoned competitor in the world top ten, Haru was one of the favourites.

Favourite he may have been but he was a pleasure to share the course with. I am not sure I was as good as him when he raced into a three-hole lead after six holes but it was difficult not to admire his play, while vaguely hoping he might break his driver or putter!

I dug in, reminding myself that there were still twelve holes to go and Haru was, in theory, human and thus could make mistakes. Finally at the eighth, a chink in his armour showed when he missed the green with his second shot finding a deep bunker. I hadn't tried to reach the par-five in two, it was far too long for that but I, rather as I had in the morning, managed to leave my approach a matter of a dozen feet away. Haru's sand shot left him too much to do to get down in four and I was left with that putt. I recall suddenly realising that all the training back in that dismal August was paying off and I sent the ball rolling around and into the hole. Only two-down!

We halved nine and ten but I hit a great tee-shot on the par three eleventh close to the hole. Haru graciously conceded the hole after his own shot missed the green and he could not get close enough with the resultant chip and we went to the twelfth. Here, and I was starting to like this hole, Haru found a fairway bunker well beyond my three-wood's range. Minutes later the match was all-square.

"All for you now, Rob. Keep playing within yourself, Haru's lost his way, for the moment." Peter's quiet encouragement was an essential edge to keeping me from trying anything silly. The next five holes were halved meaning that we went to the eighteenth still all-square. "Sudden death now, Rob." Haru smiled and offered his hand which I shook warmly.

I'm not sure if that friendly move might have disrupted my focus but my drive missed the fairway landing in the light rough. Not a big miss but it would make my second shot more difficult, I thought as I made way for my opponent who took his driver out and struck a superb shot straight down the middle. That would prove to be a mistake from which he would not recover. He had outdriven the fairway landing in the rough that splits the hole around two hundred and sixty yards from the tee. I think he had expected to reach the other side and finish with a wedge into a difficult green.

I still had almost two hundred yards to go for my second shot but had no difficulty in reaching the green or at least the apron leaving me with a chip or putt, I wasn't sure which at first, of perhaps forty feet. Haru had little choice but to try and hack his ball from deep gorse type growth with the ball ending up in one of the fairway bunkers still well short. He did hit the green with his sand shot but, with little spin, could only watch as the ball ran to the back edge. A short while later my two putts were enough to win the hole and the match.

Haru was gracious, wishing me good luck in the quarter final the next day before, I suspect, heading off to gnash his teeth.

Peter simply said "Well done, Rob. Now we prepare for tomorrow."

My next match, my quarter-final was the match that didn't happen. We arrived at the course in good time to practice before we were due off, only to learn that my opponent had been forced to withdraw with a damaged wrist. He had, it seemed struck the top of a bunker lip with his follow through when playing out of the sand the day before and had not recovered.

Shortly after one thirty I was walking on to the first tee to meet another of the favourites. This time it was the US Amateur champion, Jason Walker. With the pleasantries over he got us under way with a mammoth drive down the middle. Only the wind stopped him reaching the green but he finished in the greenside sand. My three wood was more than enough on the short hole and I was able to use a wedge to find the centre of the green and follow up with a single putt. Jason was shaking his head as we walked to the second having been unable to match my birdie.

Peter quietly commented. "Didn't allow for the wind and didn't play the course. Surprising. He's a good player and he must know that you beat another favourite yesterday."

"You think that he was trying to put pressure on me? Trying to make me react? Didn't know I have you, Peter." My grin was infectious as we walked on to the second tee.

This time I used my driver and Jason made the same choice but his drive was too far left. Out of bounds and I was two-up after just two. Things carried on with a little less drama and I reached the turn still two ahead. I lost the tenth when the American drove the green and was able to sink his putt for an eagle but he was unable to put enough pressure over the following holes to pull level.

Eighteen and I needed a half for the win. Jason hit an almost perfect drive but he had, on this occasion, only used a fairway wood as did I and, with a lucky bounce on the fairway I finished closer to the green. Forced to attack the flag to have any chance Jason saw his approach fail to spin enough and a few moments later he conceded. "Well played. I do hope to see you again at the Open, Rob. If not, then back home next year."

Afterwards, I turned to Peter. "I am in the final? Am I dreaming?"

"No, Rob. You've played well and totally justify being on the tee tomorrow. Now back to the hotel, food, and rest."

Saturday dawned and the fair weather, we had benefitted from all week, had vanished. The sky was dark with storm clouds and the wind had picked up, to very strong if not gale force. I grimaced as I looked out from my hotel. Still, it was the same for both me and my opponent, I told myself, provided he doesn't live on the coast.

I would like to say that I found my first big final memorable but for most of the time we both struggled with the conditions. By mid-afternoon, as a little sunshine started to break through the cloud, the final was all-square at the turn. Nine holes to go and nothing to show for the first twenty-seven.

The tenth and fourteenth holes, both par threes would prove critical and I won both. The first with my best putt of the day for a birdie and the second with a par, though I did feel for my opponent who missed a short putt for the half. Those two holes in the end were the difference and, without playing my best, we shook hands on the seventeenth. Like myself the other finalist had been a qualifier. But Germany, it seems, has few links courses and he had, he told me, exceeded his expectations by a long way. Runner-up meant he would be back.

For me the biggest prizes were the invitations to play in the US Masters and our own Open.

Before that I was left with my acceptance speech at the prize giving. It was not difficult to thank the greenkeeping staff and the organisers but finding the words to compliment my opponents and all the players who had taken part and made the tournament a success was more difficult. In the end I decided that I would have to ignore the tantrums of Daniel and simply thanked everyone.

Preparing for the Big One.

There was just about a month before the Open, time for a couple of local Elite competitions. As the new Amateur Champion, I found myself facing close attention, sometimes, it felt, too close. Nice to be occasionally asked for my autograph, but the downside was the commentary, I could hear, about how my shots lacked finesse or were not typical of a golfer of my supposed ability.

Apart from ignoring the critics there was little I could do. I am pleased to say, I did win one of them. without playing particularly well. Save it for Hoylake, I thought, before the reality broke through. Was I really going up against the likes of Rory McIlroy and John Rahm to name but two? Perhaps it was a step too far.

I struggled with those thoughts for days before I was able to meet up with Peter, who had taken the opportunity to have a few days away. He was as upbeat as ever.

"Rob, when you walk on to that first tee you will be no different to any other player in the field. Play to your best and you should make the cut and after that keep going. Will you beat any of those top players? Probably not, but they have off days and you never know. At the end of the tournament there is the Silver Medal awarded to the top amateur, now that is a prize worth aiming for."

"But am I ready? I don't think I'm playing that well and Ken has been irritating me, especially when I try for a full drive."

Peter looked back at me with concern. "You haven't mentioned that to me for a long time. How do you mean "irritates"?"

"My stomach seems to pull against it."

"Rob, I think you should give one of the nurses a ring and get some advice. You don't want to find yourself having to pull out halfway through a round."

I nodded, wearily. I had been having quarterly meetings with the hospital team until the end of the previous summer when I had been discharged subject to annual scans to check that the cancer had not returned. Having to call Cathy felt as if I was failing, stupid I know but that was how the changes to my body had left me feeling. I was different and, with Annie gone, I was lonely, in a way I had never expected to be.

I made the call and, after quizzing me, Cathy arranged for an out patients' appointment with her colleagues for the next week. Rather quick, I thought nervously. Eight days later I was at the hospital where two of the nurses examined both my stoma and the area that had caused my concern. They were on the edge of a conclusion, when Ms Green, my specialist appeared. I hadn't expected to see her and it was clear she wasn't there to see me. A short conversation between the professionals ensued before she also took a moment to examine my stomach.

"No real problems, Robert. You have, we think, I think, simply pulled a muscle, maybe two. I suggest you use some ibuprofen cream and tablets. When you play golf, consider a back support, the nurses will arrange a prescription so that you can get an appropriate version. Good luck with the Open. No real reason not to take part."

Back home, I had to explain to the family as well as to Peter that all was well and I could head up to Southport on schedule.

Monday of Open week! I'm here, can I do anything to learn more? Striking balls on the practice range, I wondered if I could find playing partners. As far as I could find out no other amateur had arrived, perhaps playing a round solo might not be a bad idea, I thought.

"Young man, it is Robert isn't?"

I looked around stunned to be addressed by someone I knew only too well, from the television coverage of golf.

"Er, yes, Mr Fleetwood."

Tommy laughed with joyous amusement. "Rob, that's Tommy. I can't remember the last time anyone, apart from my bank manager called me Mister! Now, I'm about to go out on the course. Coming?"

Coming? That was a wasted question, I was dropping my club back into the bag and Peter was grinning his head off as he moved into his caddy role, picking up the bag and heading off to the first tee. Where we found a second pro. "Hello, Rob." Tyrell Hatton was getting ready and I was suffering from nerves without being on the tee. Two top pros were happy to include a mere amateur in the practice! And it got worse!

Tyrell asked a question or. to be honest, suggested. "What do you think, Tommy? Our Amateur Champion should lead us off?"

Tommy's friendly nod of agreement was accompanied by a gesture. "Lead the way, Rob."

Perhaps that was what I needed. After all, on Thursday I would be teeing off with other professionals for real. That round was probably unique as both pros took turns to provide help and advice. Peter took a back seat, though I suspect I caught him making notes more than once.

As we finished and walked back to the clubhouse, both Tyrell and Tommy wished me well. One of their caddies made the best comment. "Son, you'll do okay on Thursday. Just stay relaxed like today."

And Now We Play.

Thursday morning and I was in an early group. The weather started gentle and we got away to good starts. That is to say, the pros were both three under as we reached the turn while I had had nine pars. I lost my way a little on the second nine and finished two over par walking off downcast despite the compliments of my playing partners.

By the end of the day, I knew I would need to be much better the next day. Had there been a cut after eighteen holes I would not have been playing the second day at all.

I needed a good kicking and Peter provided that. "Not your best today, should have had a couple of birdies in the first nine and maybe no bogeys on the back nine. So! Rob, get your head up. You're not out yet and you showed enough to re-enforce the idea that you can shoot an under-par score on the course, weather permitting, tomorrow. Now eat, get some sleep and we go again tomorrow." And he was right.

By the afternoon of the second day, as I walked on to the tee, the predicted cut was at two under par. I needed a four under par round to have a chance. Oh Lord, I thought, six fewer than yesterday, what chance do I have of that?

As ever Peter gave me the encouragement I needed. "Just play your game, conditions are better today. That sort of score is well within your capabilities."

Of course, we were starting on the tenth tee for the second round, the nine holes I had really struggled on the day before. But, as Peter had said, the weather had eased over the day and was as good as we could expect.

I still started slowly with pars until the par-three twelfth. Then my best tee shot of the day gave me a ten-foot putt for birdie which I duly sank. It was just the lift I needed and by the turn I was back to level par for the tournament.

There was no way of knowing if the cut line had moved but I had a target, two birdies and I had a chance. The first came at my eleventh hole, the second. My drive found the fairway and was just long enough to catch a slope which left me with a much shorter approach. I took full advantage drilling the ball to the heart of the green despite the breeze into my face. The first putt looked long and difficult at first but I finally decided on the line and struck my best stroke of the day. I had read the turn just right and the ball finally dropped, after a heart stopping moment when it teetered on the edge. Another birdie at a par-three, the fourth, moved me to two-under and I started to believe that I might make the cut.

The short fifth provided an opportunity and I started to enjoy myself with another birdie. Perhaps I relaxed to far, with a disastrous double bogey at the par-three seventh where my tee shot found the infamous donut bunker. Two holes to go and I was now under the cut line unless there had been a lot of other disasters out on the course.

Again, I needed a birdie and the eighth provided the best opportunity. Good drive and I had a chance. My second shot was as good as, I think, I have ever struck and landed on the green short of the pin. It was the roar from the crowd that told me that the improbable had happened. That approach had not only hit the green but the ball had rolled on after its bounce and dropped in for an eagle two!

That buffer was, in the end, more essential than I had realised. A par at the last and I had reason to be upbeat. I had done enough to make the final rounds, or had I?

I made my way to the scorers' tent to hear a voice I really did not want to hear berating the scorer whose only offence is usually to remind a player that he had to sign his card, I thought. As I entered the room that player pushed past me almost knocking me over. "Damn spies, that's all you are!" he cried as he went down the path. I had recognised him, though I hadn't realised he had qualified. Daniel was in his usual form.

I completed the formalities alongside my fellow competitors and learned then that the cut line was now expected to be at three-under, which was indicative that the conditions had been conducive to low scoring on the second day. It would mean that I had a few hours to wait before I would know if I had been successful, though Peter did say it looked unlikely that there would be any further change.

"Rob, what was all that about?" He then asked me.

I had asked the scorer who would only say that they had called Daniel back to warn him that officials were studying video of him taking relief without checking if it was allowed. If they decided that he was not so entitled and had gained an advantage then he would, of course, be disqualified for signing a wrong card.

"That young man acts as if the world owes him everything. If he carries on like this, he risks a permanent ban from the game. What a waste!"

"I feel sorry for those who had to play with him these past two days. I hope I'm not with him, tomorrow. Assuming I have made it."

Onward, you've two rounds to show you deserve to be here. I guess I am not that different to other amateurs playing in a pro tournament, there is a sense of disbelief even when you have made the cut when others both amateur and, of course, professional have missed it.

As I practiced on the range and the putting green, I must admit to dreaming of being in the mix on Sunday afternoon.

Then I looked at the leader board as I moved from the putting surface and reality came home to roost. My three-under had been enough to make the cut but that meant I was only, **only**, eleven shots back from the joint leaders and the top five on the board were all former major winners.

Back to the real world, Robbie, I said to myself. Now let's see if you can catch the top amateur, who is? In the end it took a little research to find out that my semi-final opponent at the Amateur Championship, Jason, was in pole position at six-under. Only three amateurs had made the cut. Incredibly, Daniel was on four-under par and seemed to have escaped any punishment from yesterday's round. Word had it that he was threatening action if anyone got in his way in his quest for the Silver Medal.

We were down to two-balls and I was playing with an American, one I had admired over the years, Tony Finau. He greeted me warmly with a well done for making the cut. "Not my best form, I'm afraid, so just ignore me out there."

Ignore him? Well, I had played with two other pros, one of whom had not made the cut. If he said ignore him, I would try but ......!

Of all the four rounds this proved the most enjoyable. Tony, despite his comments, was clearly relaxed enough to chat with me as we walked off the tees. His warmth and encouragement were just what I needed and, I believe, helped me to shoot another five under round, one shot fewer than Daniel as it turned out and two less than Jason. Tony had also scored five under. The Silver Medal was in reach and I was damned if I would let Daniel lift it. Jason – maybe. Daniel – no.

Sunday morning and Peter was adamant and annoyed. Someone, somewhere, had decided to pair me with Daniel!

"Rob, first if you keep playing this way you can win the Silver Medal. I do not know why they have paired you with that childish idiot, probably had moans from the pros. You will just have to remember the last time you met. And outplay him again. One small point, I had a quiet word with the officials and there will be a referee following your group. If he steps out of line, I want him stamped on."

I would like to report that Daniel had learned something from his previous issues but that he had not done so rapidly became obvious. As we walked up to the tee the starter began his announcement. "On the tee, the Amateur Champion, Robert Ward."

I started on to the tee itself, there was an objection. "Hey, you've got it wrong. It must be my honour not his." Daniel was pushing his way on to the tee swinging his driver in such a way that it had me and Peter ducking out of the way.

"Mr Fatuna, the status of the leader board has Mr Ward to play first. You will withdraw." The referee's words were voiced with such force the words "or else" were not needed and Daniel, muttering, backed away.

On the other hand, I moved back and forced myself to go through my usual routine a second time. My drive was everything I hoped for, drawing down the left side of the fairway the ideal finish.

Daniel almost ran from where he was standing and seemed to take no preparation. It made no real difference except that his drive, good as it was, and longer than mine, would finish in the right rough.

His triumphant snarl was typical but I just ignored him. Peter and I knew that the green sloped away from us and the need to get some spin on the ball was essential. With a ball lying in the second cut of rough Daniel, who had crowed at his extra distance, could not manage to do that and his ball finished in the fringe at the back of the very deep green. Oh, I should have said, the pin was right at the front, the toughest position. As we reached the green Daniel threw one of his clubs in anger. Several minutes later he had had to settle for a bogey five while I had the simplest of putts for a birdie.

As his attitude worsened, if that were possible, his play deteriorated with bogey after bogey moving him out of contention for the Best

Amateur. By the turn he was only one under par for the tournament while I was twelve under still just one behind Jason, who was three groups behind us.

Those scores sound good but I must admit that neither Jason nor I were in the mix. The leaders, still to go out, were all eighteen under or better, and the weather had been kind which always leads to low scoring. By the professionals anyway.

The back nine dragged, the pressure of constant foul language emanating from the other party did not make for enjoyment. It was necessary for me to simply focus on my own game and try as best I could to ignore him. Even today I struggle to understand how he remains playing the game.

By the time we reached the eighteenth, I think I would have been trying to hide, if I had scored as badly as Daniel did. He was fourteen over par and heading for an eighty-six, but hiding was clearly not in his makeup and as we reached the tee, he demanded and took, almost by force, the honour, which he had never actually had. The referee looked to warn him off but Peter raised a hand indicating to let him be.

It did not help as his drive headed far right into trouble. Another club hit the woodwork on the side of the tee and I could see the referee making a note. In my turn I hit a reasonable drive, not my best, but into the fairway and I ended up with a final hole par. Daniel ended with a triple bogey for an eighty-nine. Shaking hands was not on his agenda for which I confess I was grateful.

In the end I had had a great scoring round finishing with a sixty-five, seven under par and I had won the Best Amateur, the Silver Medal!

When I look back, I am proud of how I handled the difficulties of that final round. I must admit that my Best Amateur win would be of much lower impact than that of Sophie Jordan's performance a few weeks later. But for an English golfer to win the Silver Medal did generate a few inches in some of the newspapers.

Looking Ahead and Maybe Love Again?

August and September were generally low profile for me. I had already entered competitions around the country but the highlight was an invitation to the Italian Amateur Championship.

The financial support of my parents was invaluable and without it certainly the overseas events would have been beyond me. I had two part-time jobs, one in my club's pro-shop and a second at a local gardening centre. They did help with the day-to-day expenses but were never going to provide enough for trips to mainland Europe or, when I thought about it, to the USA the next year. Perhaps, those were a bridge too far, there would be other chances, I felt, if I could complete pro-school and get on one of the tours.

And that was a question that I was almost scared to answer. I had been certain that I could reach that level before the operation, now I struggled to carry my bag. The strain on my stomach muscles was a constant background ache. At some of the bigger competitions I had the option of hiring a caddy and I could manage that cost, just about.

In the end, I was forced to ask my parents if they could really afford the cost of supporting my golfing needs. The answer was full and to the point. They could afford reasonable amounts and they would do as much as they were able to. Mum reminded me that they were helping my sisters through university. By now Susie was in her last year at Loughborough studying for a Sports degree and playing football. Rachel was at the Liverpool Institute of Performing Arts studying Music. Dad summed it up. "This is your degree course. Might not be quite the same but you are on track to make a living from it. Of course, we'll help and," he paused, "we have already booked a holiday for the week of the Masters, so you'd better be on form!"

I took the chance to ask why no-one had been at Hoylake to watch me play there, after all Mum and Dad had been at the Amateur Championship. There had been a plan to attend without telling me but the girls had made the point that it might have put me off my game. Now they were all regretting staying in the background. They did not intend to make that mistake with Augusta!

Behind the scenes my sisters were making plans. They were still pretty fed up with Annie's attitude, more so than I was, and determined that they would find me a replacement, despite their previous failures. That's the trouble with family. Once they had decided, nothing was going to stop their efforts unless I decided to emigrate and even that might not have been enough.

Both had boyfriends and took it in turns to organise blind dates for me as part of a foursome. In fairness they had good taste but I found it very difficult to respond in a positive way. There was one young woman who had been at school with me, who had been warned off by Annie in the good old days. I got on well with her and decided that another date away from Rachel and her partner was worth pursuing.

There was a couple of weeks gap, I was in Cardiff playing in the local open, before we could get together but the second date was just as friendly. Teri was the opposite of Annie, who had been quite reserved and when I told her that I would be away for another competition the next week she took the bull by the horns.

"I'll come and join you. Just make sure it's a double bed in the room!" She had an infectious grin and I agreed, a little reluctantly I will admit. There had only ever been Annie and after her reaction, I was extremely nervous as to how Teri would react when she did see me undressed. I was perhaps overly cautious, my sisters had explained everything and I am sure that Teri would have done her own research, so in that sense she was as ready as she could be.

Five days later I returned to my hotel from my practice round to find Teri in the hotel reception waiting. "Come on, Rob. Let's go up, we can have dinner later."

In the room, I made her wait while I cleaned up after the round, I didn't want her put off by my sweaty body, it had been a hot day and, of course, I needed to change Ken's bag. As I went to leave the bathroom I was suddenly hit by nerves. It almost felt like I had never been to bed with a girl before, what if I couldn't hack it, I thought.

As I entered the room there was Teri lying on the bed, looking like a Bond girl, with a grin wider than a typical fairway. "Come on, Rob. I've been hoping for this for years! You just weren't available." She said and I dropped on to the bed next to her.

For what seemed a long time I forgot about Ken and enjoyed being with a girl again. Afterwards, before we went in search of dinner, we showered together and Teri's reaction to the difference in my anatomy was, to me, both surprising and exciting.

"You know, Rachel and Susie were both very clear about what had happened to you. They warned me that I might not like it and asked me to be understanding about how I might end things, if I couldn't cope. I don't know why, you a real man and how! Can we go again later?"

I gave her the biggest hug I could before we went down for food. "We can try."

My trip to Italy was difficult but rewarding. Thanks to the help of a local caddy, whose English was rather better than my non-existent Italian, I played as well as I have ever over seventy-two holes finishing at nineteen under par and winning by five shots.

Ever tried to take a large trophy on board an aircraft? I am not sure what would have happened if the pilot had not seen me arguing with check-in staff. It turned out that he was an avid golf follower and recognised me from my exploits in the Open. A quiet word from him and I was treated like royalty.

Teri was always waiting when I got back from the weekly trips around the country. The necessities of her own job, as manager of a local garden centre, not where I had my part-time job, involved long hours, and often required her to work weekends. When we could be together, she was insatiable in bed and provided me with a boost to my self-confidence that I needed, in a way that I had never expected to experience. Not since the surgery, anyway.

The winter weather arrived early with heavy downpours, howling gales and freezing frosts. Golf courses across the country were closed rather more than usual and I was forced to retreat to the driving range and an indoor putting surface for what seemed like weeks on end. Teri was not unhappy, the weather meant that she could entertain me at her apartment almost as often as she liked.

Christmas came and had a family feel that I had been missing in a way I still did not understand. Susie explained it to me when she and I were despatched to prepare Boxing Day tea. "Rob, do you not realise that we knew how empty you have been feeling? This Christmas is the first time you have had your own girlfriend for years. That was the gap, not us, not Mum or Dad. Annie wasn't here, now you've got Teri and you owe me!"

"Sis, I do but don't hold your breath if you are waiting for payment!"

It was a good festive season topped off by Rachel announcing her engagement to her long-term boyfriend, Colin, who was a fellow student at LIPA. Susie and I, I must admit, collared him later that evening and left him in no doubt what would happen to him if he did her twin any harm.

Rachel happened in on us and was not happy. "Let him alone, you bullies! He is mine and he is staying mine. You stop trying to frighten him off!"

We were forced to make shamefaced apologies before the four of us headed out to the local pub. Teri had gone back home to be with her mother who was on her own and had asked that she and her three sisters spend some time together without partners. I would learn later from Teri that her Mum had explained that she was not well and had wanted tell her daughters without others being there. "Sorry, Rob. It was just too sensitive for her to tell us with our other halves being there. Can we go and see her tomorrow? I'd like her to meet you and once the New Year gets here you are going to be travelling more and more."

We did go to see her Mum who greeted me like an old friend. She was delightful but, I learned to my cost, she had a mind like an iron rod. What she wanted she got.

By the end of January Teri and I were no longer together. Teri's sisters were already married and she was the only one, not yet attached, as her mother had emphasised and that meant looking after her was Teri's responsibility. Or else.

It hurt me, how it hurt. But it was seeing Teri's distress that really hurt. She faced an indeterminate period as a servant, as I saw it, looking after her mother and, our relationship had, I thought, moved beyond the purely physical side.

The last time we were together, she explained. She could not live with herself if her mother was left alone in her final days. Not that she was being given much choice. Nor could she expect me to wait. Her mother was unwell but not, by any means, terminal. "Which means I might be tied to her for years yet. That wouldn't be fair to you, my love. Better you go and find someone who can give you what you need. Can just love you without any sideshows."

I would wait, I told her. But she was having none of it. Annie had been a painful separation but this was even worse because we were neither being given a choice.

When I explained to my mother later, she was livid. "I know I have your father but even so, if I ever try that on you or your sisters feel free to dump me in a home. That is so selfish. No mother should deliver such a guilt trip on one of their own!"

Susie was bereft, she had really believed that Teri would be the love of my life but this time, unlike Annie, Teri got only sympathy. "That's not fair, it really isn't. Not fair to either of you, what a selfish bitch!"

March arrived with a slight lessening of the wet weather but it remained difficult to play any sensible golf. My home course was no different to the others within easy reach and while not totally waterlogged was very wet and muddy. I had always intended to fly out to Augusta a full week before the Masters began. Adjusting to the jetlag and warmer weather seemed a good idea. Now I brought forward my plans. I would fly a week sooner and look to play some golf in the area before finally settling in the immediate vicinity of the course. My family would be flying the weekend before the tournament and I decided to make the trip on my own.

Heathrow.

Airside at Heathrow was less exciting than I had expected. So many shops, bars and eateries seemed to smother the buzz of anticipation that, as a first-time flier from Terminal Four, I had been expecting. Not that I hadn't flown before but only within Europe and never from London until now. With over an hour to go before my flight was due to board there was no time pressure so I took the time to browse the books on sale at a newsagent in the vain hope that there would be something to soothe my nerves during the nine hours crossing the Atlantic.

The bookshelves did their usual job and I became engrossed. Moving from one book to the next before, to my delight, finding a copy of "Miracle at Augusta," a seemingly appropriate book I had never read. As I paid for it, I heard, to my horror, the announcement of the final call for passengers travelling to Atlanta. I needed to move fast but a visit to the toilet was a necessary first call.

Having reached the conveniences, I found long queues not just for the ladies, hardly unusual, but for the men's as well. The only answer was the disabled section with no-one waiting.

As I reached the door a tall, slender and, frankly gorgeous, young woman came out. I stood aside to allow her to pass but there was no thank you, merely a glare at the idea that an apparently fit young man might be using the specialist area. I said nothing. If only she knew. Perhaps better she didn't, I thought, as I shut the door. In any case, she didn't look as if she needed that part of the set-up either. As her figure disappeared into the distance, I suddenly thought I recognised her. Don't be daft, I thought. She's just another model, you've seen her in an ad somewhere.

Having readied myself for the trip, I raced down to the gate to find that there was still a crowd of passengers waiting. I wasn't as late as

I had feared and I joined the back of the queue. Things were not happening that quickly but, eventually, I reached the final boarding check. From there to the aircraft was only a few minutes' walk away. As I reached the aircraft door, I was stopped by a flight attendant who was checking seat numbers to help us take the best aisle.

"Mr. Ward, I don't think your seat allocation is correct."

As she looked more closely at my boarding pass, she called over to one of her colleagues.

"Tony, this is Mr Ward. Isn't he one of the two passengers we were told had been upgraded. Shouldn't front desk have re-assigned him?"

Tony was openly irritated. "Yes, they should have but they are useless, they leave everything to us. Sorry, Mr. Ward, just my rant. You are, sir, going the wrong way." Scanning a tablet, he continued. "Our compliments. Our head office team has indicated that the Amateur Champion does not fly economy. Not on this trip, anyway."

I found myself being guided all the way forward into the first-class section! Certainly not economy!

"This is your seat, Mr Ward, my colleagues will be with you shortly." And Tony vanished before I could thank him.

I looked around for somewhere to put my cabin bag and then noticed the seat next to mine was occupied by the beauty from the disabled loo. Talk about a shock. Suddenly I realised where I had seen her before. Not in an ad but on Sky's golf programme.

Oh my, I thought, she's the Ladies Amateur Champion, Susie Jordan. I had seen enough of her golf to wonder if I could ever be as good as her. And I'd upset her in the terminal!

As I sat down, she turned to look at me. "You're Rob Ward, aren't you? You won the Silver Medal at the Open."

She'd recognised me, how had she done that? There had been far less coverage of my success. I mean after all, I had won the Silver

Medal at the Open, but in the overall scheme of things had finished well down the leader board. This super golfer had almost won the Ladies Open. Robbed by the World Number Two with a last hole birdie!

PART THREE – MEETING

"We've already met, I think, outside the loos?" Rob said.

"You're right, sorry if I was a bit harsh. Not used to using them myself and, to be honest, you didn't look as if you need them either." Sophie found herself smiling, he seemed a nice guy and he plays good golf!

"I know. It's a hidden one. I had cancer which led to changes. Got to be honest, yours isn't obvious either."

"Really? I think that might be a back-handed compliment. Didn't look at my legs that closely then?" I know I'm not going to win a beauty contest but he might have said he admired me, even if he's only being polite. Sophie felt rather down at that idea.

"Sorry, Susie. I can call you, Susie?"

Sophie laughed out loud, in a way she hadn't since Richard left for the States. "Oh, Rob. Of course, you can but, how can I put it? It isn't Susie."

Rob's face reddened. "Oh, God. I've got it wrong, haven't I?"

Sophie smiled warmly. "I'm sorry, yes, its Sophie. I haven't laughed like that for months. So whichever, Rob, Susie or Sophie is fine."

"You look so good, you make me think of my twin sisters, Rachel, and Susie, and, don't ever tell them, I do think they are beautiful. I'm sorry, Sophie. And I mean it, I don't understand what you mean about your legs, they're great."

Sophie looked at him. Was he being honest, did he really think she looked good? I'd better admit it, he knows me but not that I have a false leg, that I'm a hop-a-long.

"Rob, don't worry. I mentioned my legs because one of them isn't real. I mean it's a prosthetic. From the knee down. I lost it when I was fifteen. I thought it must be obvious."

Rob looked at her in amazement. "I didn't know. How can you play golf with an artificial leg? Oh my god, I knew you were good but that takes your golfing to another level. I mean how?"

Sophie, or Susie, she thought, almost giggling, considered her response carefully before answering. "I don't know about a different level; you did great at the Open. Did you really have to play with Daniel Fatuna in the last round?"

Rob looked at her. "I did and a brainless idiot, he was. Oh, sorry, not a boyfriend, is he?" Oh heck, he thought, am I treading where I shouldn't. Sophie's laughter eased his worry.

"Boyfriend? I only asked because he was a member of my Club, the powers that be kicked him out. Worst attitude I ever came across." She grinned. "Rob, you are going to have to tell me. What he is like to play with or against. I mean, I hope that idea isn't too painful a memory.

Rob groaned. "Two experiences I would like to forget but maybe later?"

Oh dear, my turn to put my foot in my mouth, Sophie thought. He does look good, though. Oh, Richard! Am I really that ready to go for someone else? No, I'm not. But the next few hours look as if they could be more fun than I expected, I guess.

The flight attendant came through checking seat belts before asking them. "Miss Jordan, Mr Ward. Any chance of a few autographs? We don't often get two top golfers on the same flight and you two are going to the very top, we're sure."

Rob looked startled at the idea while Sophie grinned at his apparent discomfort. "Yes, Harriet. It is Harriet isn't it, your badge is trying to hide!" She laughed.

"Ooops! Don't let the boss know! It is Harriet." She looked nervously around but no-one else appeared to have spotted or overheard the conversation.

"That is a lovely name. Quite an old one, too." Rob responded. "Can't remember where I first heard it."

Harriet laughed. "I was named after the character in the Lord Peter Wimsey novels. My Dad thought she was the perfect example of a strong-minded female, a bit like my Mum!"

Time passed quickly for the two golfers as they talked shop for most of the flight. At least that was how Rob saw it when looking back. Sophie had proved an engaging acquaintance with as many golf anecdotes and jokes as he could remember but it had been his recollection of the times, he had found himself facing Daniel that surprisingly proved the most interesting. And she seems to find me good company and wow those model good looks, a real beauty.

"You know, Sophie. What bemuses me is how he has escaped a lengthy ban and why he seems to act as if his surname is either a weight or, maybe, provides him with the right to act as if he is owed the world."

"I can't help but feel sorry for him in a way. He has the potential to be a good golfer, if not a great one, but he blows it almost every time. I mean he made the cut at the Amateur and at the Open but then acts as if everyone else should step aside and let him win. The last words I heard him speak at our club was that he was going to win the Amateur!"

"Really?"

"Well, almost. He included a shout that I was just a flash-in-the-pan. I'd only won one tournament of any scale and was pushed into telling how, to the other juniors."

"And that was the Amateur?"

"No, nothing that big, well not as big but important. I was given a wildcard. It was the French International Lady Juniors' Amateur Championship, so not at the same level but I did enjoy that trip."

"You got a wildcard and then just went and won it. Not surprising given what you have done since but it must have been a nerve-wracking time for you. On your own in a different country. Anybody go with you?"

"Only a dozen Club members! And there were fights over who was going to caddy for me!"

"Wow. And Daniel couldn't accept that."

Sophie suddenly looked bemused. "That's true and now I'm wondering why. He ranted that he or another of the juniors should have got the wildcard and not me which was stupid. It was for a Ladies event."

Rob looked nonplussed at the idea that Sophie could have been called anything that didn't reflect how good she was.

"You know. I rather think that that brainless idiot probably considers Tiger a flash-in-the-pan. It is frightening what goes on in his mind to cause him to act to his own detriment. Is his handicap better than yours?"

Sophie laughed.

Oh, how she laughs, Rob thought.

"Before he left my Club, he was playing off two, I think." She looked at Rob before deciding that he did want to know her handicap. "At the time my own handicap was recovering to plus four. I haven't looked lately. I'm only playing in scratch comps but I guess it's a bit better now probably plus five, maybe six."

"That good! Puts me in the shade." As Sophie raised an eyebrow. "Plus four."

Sophie looked at him. "Shade? Do you realise Sergio Garcia turned pro with a similar number, don't underrate yourself, Rob."

"But, Sophie, why did you say recovering?"

Sophie clenched a fist hidden from Rob. "I was at plus five and a half before I lost my leg. It took two years to get back into positive numbers after my first year back playing. Look, Rob, let's be honest, I've just had a run of good luck. I'm here for two tournaments and

I'll be surprised if I make either of the cuts. I've just got to give it a shot."

Rob would not have been surprised, if he had talked to Ginny, to find his mental shock matched her view of Sophie's lack of self-confidence.

"That's daft, you don't get runs of the sort of success you've managed just with luck."

Sophie looked pensive. "You sound just like my coach, my caddy, and my Ladies captain. I do sort of, sometimes, think I might do okay, but then reality hits home and I look at how good the top players are."

"Oh boy, I've only known you a few hours but, look Susie, I mean Sophie, I saw that putt at the Open and you led the field at the end. It took a sensational shot from Ingrid what's-her-name to beat you. She knew what she would have been up against, if it had gone to a play-off. She's now the number one and, frankly, she fears you. It was clear from that Sky chat the two of you had afterwards."

"Don't be ridiculous, Rob. She also saw how bad I was at the start of the Open. That was a crazy result."

"Yeah, just like Justin Rose's first Open. Fourth! Now he's won a Major and had multiple tour wins over the years. Jeepers, if you ever become more self-confident the rest of the girls might just as well go home."

Sophie's laughter disturbed the rest of first-class and there were several murmurs of irritation, she looked around. "Sorry, everyone. I couldn't help it."

Turning back to Rob. "And you Rob. How's your self-confidence before the Masters?"

"It is sort of okay. I just wish I could play at your level. My game is far more erratic."

"Oh dear. You won the Amateur, during which you destroyed Daniel, despite his shenanigans, and, as I recall it, you finished tied tenth at the Open. That was reported as the best performance by an amateur since Justin. If that's erratic, please can I have some of your consistency because that must be phenomenal."

"Excuse me both. Might I have your autographs and a few moments of your time?" A smartly dressed woman had crossed from the other side of the plane.

Both Rob and Sophie nodded and happily signed the autograph book that she provided, before.

"Now, I should first apologise for interrupting. I wonder if I could have some contact details."

Rob looked at her with a little suspicion. "Why?"

The woman chuckled. "Sensible, Mr Ward. I suspect, no I know, that my employers will wish to talk to both of you. My name is Louise Dalton. I work for Global Sports. We act as management consultants and agents for top sportsmen and women and I believe that you will both qualify within the near future, if not already."

Rob looked amazed. "But I'm only an amateur. I haven't won anything apart from the Amateur Championship. I'm not even sure if I'm good enough to turn professional, yet anyway."

Sophie's response might have been a little more of a surprise. "Louise, I already have an agent and I don't think I want to change."

Louise looked surprised. "Would you mind if I asked who that might be?"

Sophie thought for a moment before deciding that it did no harm. "I doubt you will have heard of her. She's Ginny Donald. She is my caddy most of the time as well."

It was Louise's turn to disturb the equilibrium of the deck with a shriek of amazement. "Ginny Donald! My word, you have done well, Sophie."

Sophie looked at her with a questioning look.

"Ginny Donald was, or is, one of the best. She built a cracking little business. Global bought it and we haven't regretted it, even if she wouldn't join us personally. Sophie, please give her my best wishes and tell her, we may well be looking to acquire her latest addition!" As she finished talking there was an announcement requesting that passengers prepare for landing. "Best of luck, both of you. No doubt we will be talking again."

Rob and Sophie looked at each other. "Did that really happen?" Rob asked. "Is your caddy that good?"

"I had no idea, though she's been doing pretty well raising sponsorship for me." Sophie replied, thinking, I do need to talk to Ginny and soon.

After the plane had landed and the immigration process completed, the two parted company as they were booked on different flights to Augusta.

"Give me a call when you've settled in. We could practice together if that works for you, Sophie." Rob waved and headed away to his own flight desk leaving Sophie wondering if she should.

PART FOUR – TOGETHER

Sophie.

As I watched Rob disappear into the crowd, I decided to make the most of my stopover wait and call Ginny.

"Ginny, you didn't tell me you were a big success with your PR business."

There was a pause, then. "Sophie, why do you ask?"

"I was upgraded by the airline and sat next to Rob Ward. You know - the Amateur Champion. We were asked for contact details by a Louise Dalton? She said that she knows you and sends best wishes!"

Ginny's silence could be felt, before. "I knew they'd be looking for you. Thought I might be able to enjoy working with you a bit longer, Sophie."

I laughed, sometimes Ginny sounded far more nervous than I did. "Don't you worry, Ginny. I've no intention of going anywhere. They won't be looking to sign some amateur who's just been lucky."

"Sophie, I give up. Go and get your flight and we'll see you in a week's time. Going to see more of Rob?"

I wasn't sure I had heard her right and was a little slow to respond and Ginny laughed. "Good for you, lass. Take care." The phone went dead and I never did have the chance to say "only on the golf course."

Truth was, I wasn't certain I did want to see more of Rob. My feelings on the flight and the unexpected sense of missing him even as he vanished across the airport lounge. My split from Richard was still too raw. I wasn't ready for another relationship, was I? For the first time since he had set off back to the States, I found myself wondering if I could make a new friendship like that.

It was perhaps a good thing that my flight to Augusta was called a few minutes later. My confused mind had concrete things to think about and I headed for the gate.

This time I remembered to switch my leg's electronics off and the security system merely bleeped as it sensed the metal innards. I did have to suffer an additional search and prove that the sensors had identified my prosthetic as that and I was able to board the aircraft with no more than a short delay.

No first class on this flight but I was able to get a seat with additional legroom thanks to the flight crew and the generosity of another passenger who switched seats.

With the plane airborne, I found myself chatting with the woman next to me who seemed quite knowledgeable about the upcoming tournaments, although she admitted that it was the Masters that was bringing her home to Augusta, from her work in New York.

Then, halfway through the flight, she took a closer look at me and I twitched, realising that she might have recognised me. I was still not aware of how much of the Ladies Open had been covered in the States and had assumed that there would have been very little. After all it was not The Open.

"Young lady, I am sorry. You are Sophie Jordan, are you not?"

I nodded, a little wearily. Was this what it was like for the professionals, unable to go anywhere without being accosted by strangers?

"And, I sense, you find it difficult when busybodies like me recognise you. Try not to worry too much, Sophie. It will happen less as time passes. I doubt anyone else on this flight would realise who you are but it's my job, you see. I work for the New York Times and I cover golf for the sports section. I should have recognised you immediately but I was a little lost in my column for tomorrow's paper. And please, this chat is off the record."

I smiled. "Really?"

She looked shocked that I might question her statement, then she laughed. "You are very sensible, Sophie. Look this will not be in my column but, please, would you give me an interview after the

Augusta Amateur? You'll be playing there and, I guess, in the Chevron, won't you? Please, it would be a scoop for me ahead of the locals."

And when I miss the cut, I thought. "I doubt you'll still want one but if you do, then yes."

She looked quizzically at me. "Why wouldn't I? You almost won the British Open and I know the top pros all speak well of you. Future world number one has been suggested by more than one of them. Here's my details. Get your agent to ring me and we will sort out your fee for the interview."

Now it was my turn to look surprised. "I'll do that once I get to my hotel or, as she is back in England, tomorrow morning anyway."

"Thanks, Sophie. Look, good luck next week. See you after the competitions. I'll leave you in peace."

I was feeling tired and gratefully closed my eyes for the last half hour of the flight. It was only as we left the plane after landing, that I realised that I had left her business card behind! Then to my relief a flight attendant caught up with me with not only the card but also my bag! I went red with embarrassment but, as I thanked her, she grinned. "Not a problem. You're not the first to forget a bag. Just lucky I spotted it before you were through the exit doors."

Reunited with my carry-on and, a little while later, my clubs and case, I set off for the taxi rank. Only to find that there was a shuttle bus for the hotel.

Having reached the hotel, I found part of the check-in being dominated by a family group of four or five arguing with two of the staff. I wasn't sure but it appeared that they were demanding an upgrade because the rooms they had booked were inadequate. At the same time the staff were adamant that there were no other rooms available.

I knew that with the Masters imminent most of the hotels in the area would soon be full even though the Major was still almost two weeks away. It was only later that I realised that my own competition had had an impact. After I had waited for a little time a third member of staff appeared and called me over to another part of the large check-in desks.

"That's fine, Miss Jordan, I will take you up to your suite. If you'd like to follow me."

"Oy, she's on her own she doesn't need a suite. You can switch us round. One of the rabbit hutches you've allocated us will be big enough for a single. You'll do that won't you, Miss Whoever-you-are." The older woman in the family turned and, aggressively, poked me in the stomach. The implied "or else" made me step backwards away from her before I looked at my escort.

"Mrs Terteron, this lady will not be changing her room for anyone else. If you and your partner are not happy with your rooms, I suggest you find another hotel. If you can. Now, madam, if you will excuse us."

For a moment I thought the woman was going to attack him but she saw some sense, he was built like a rugby front row, although I had a feeling that that might be an American football quarterback, and she backed away.

At the desk I could still hear the other adult angrily denouncing the staff, with threats of contacting their chief executive and having them all fired, but it was clear that he was not going to have his demands agreed to.

As we entered the elevator, must remember that, I thought, not lift, I asked if that sort of thing was common place.

"Not usually, Miss, but that family try it on every time they stay. They have two family interconnecting rooms capable of sleeping eight people, comfortably. Most of our suites are booked out throughout this month usually by golfers or the media and all of them are filled this and next week for the Ladies Amateur. As for their getting us fired? Well, we'd be at bigger risk of that if we downgraded you."

I looked up at him. I might be almost six feet tall but he towered over me. "I don't understand. I'm sure my agent," gosh, I suddenly thought, I'm calling Ginny that now, "would have simply booked us two standard rooms."

He chuckled. "And she did that. But Miss, you are the face of the hotel chain. We couldn't have you in anything less than a suite. Ms Donald has also been upgraded to another room although, I admit, not to a suite."

"I sometimes want to throttle her. She never told me we were able to book into one of your hotels here in the States." As the elevator came to a halt and its doors opened, we stepped into a hallway with stunning views through windows on either side of the building.

Scott, I'd finally spotted his name tag, led me over to one of two doors leading off the room. "This way, Miss Jordan."

He opened the door and led me into a large beautifully furnished room with panoramic views across the city. There was a bar, a huge television screen and sumptuous chairs and couches. Then it sank home. There wasn't a bed in sight!

My expression must have shown my uncertainty as Scott opened a door into another part of the suite. Two bedrooms. One double and one twin-bedded, both with en-suite facilities and how! The walk-in showers were huge. It was clear that this room would happily sleep at least four, if not six, people. What did he call it? A junior suite?! And, finally, there was a small kitchenette with fridge and microwave.

Scott smiled at me. "I guess you aren't yet used to this luxury, Miss." After I shook my head, he continued. "Don't worry, if you can't get something to work just press the call button and your butler will be in like a shot."

It was already late afternoon and I could feel the jetlag starting to hit. I decided that quick calls home and to Ginny should be my initial priority before getting a meal. You must try and stay awake until ten o'clock here, I told myself, best way to start overcoming the time difference.

Scott promised me that a table in the hotel restaurant would be reserved. A quiet corner placing to minimise the chance of my being identified. As I was on their website posing around different hotels in Europe it was, Scott told me, very possible that I would be seen as the model and not as the golfer! He and his colleagues would do their best to protect my privacy during my stay.

My parents were as amazed as I was at my description of the suite and the service. Ginny just purred with approval, at least that was how it sounded over the mobile.

A little while later I sat down in a relatively quiet restaurant, probably because I was early, and tucked into a very large, to me anyway, Caesar salad with chicken. I was halfway through that enjoyable course when my mobile rang.

I almost ignored it but then decided that if it was a call from back home it must be urgent.

"Sophie, is that you?"

It was Rob and he sounded somewhat distressed. "Yes, Rob, of course it is. What's the matter?"

There was a brief pause and I guessed that he was calming himself down before. "They've messed up my hotel reservation. They don't have a room for me. Are there any rooms at your hotel?"

I thought for a moment. "Look, Rob. I'm pretty sure they are full but you could share mine."

"I couldn't do that. That would be totally unfair for you to have to share."

His response confirmed my decision. "They upgraded me and I have a two-bedroom suite – more than enough room for you to have your own room and en-suite. Now get yourself over here before the restaurant closes and you go hungry."

I gave him the hotel address, and my room number, and settled back to finish my meal, wondering if I had made the right decision. Oh, Sophie, I do hope he understands that this only to help him out and not an invite to anything else, I thought. I mean we haven't had the chance to really get to know each other. The flight was just a conversation, it was fun, but nothing more than that was it?

As my thoughts drifted onwards, it did occur to me that he had, at first, refused the idea of sharing my room. Only after I told him of the facilities did he, a little grudgingly, accept. Ah well, I decided, I can always hide in my bedroom.

Now what did he say? Half an hour to reach the hotel? He should be here quite soon then. I'd better finish up and find a seat in reception. No point in leaving him wondering how to get to the suite.

For once I got my timing right. As I crossed the hotel foyer, I could see Rob pulling his golf bag and luggage out of a limo. His face lit up when he saw me waiting and I felt my heart flutter, he was not lacking in good looks and maybe in another time....

Calm yourself, Sophie Jordan, you are just helping a friend in need, nothing else. I was not sure if my brain and heart were completely in synch but I had made the step and would have to see what happened. Just not yet, I kept telling myself.

"Sophie, you are a lifesaver. I'm not sure what I would have done. There doesn't seem to be a vacant room in the city." His voice did not help but at least he hadn't made a move to kiss me as a part of his thanks, damn him!

"Come on, Rob. Let's get those bags up to my rooms." Even as I spoke, I could see Scott heading towards us.

"Miss Jordan, can I help?"

I explained the situation and within a moment Rob's belongings were being despatched to the suite. We were able to find a seat in the bar, Rob had eaten, it turned out, and over a drink, I managed to get him to explain exactly what had happened.

"I really don't know," he said, "it was the right hotel and the website's confirmation was recognised by the receptionist but, they claimed, they must have double booked the room and there were no other rooms. They did try to find me a room elsewhere, there is a mutual set-up apparently, but all their contacts were also full. At that point they washed their hands of me."

As the evening wore on, I found myself starting to drift off, trying not to fall asleep. "Sorry, Rob, jetlag. I do need to get some sleep; it has been a long day."

"Susie, oh Lord there I go again, sorry. Sophie, of course, we should go up."

Once in the suite, I showed Rob round the rooms. I had already set up in the double bedroom so he got the twin. It didn't seem to bother him. Like me he was quite taken aback by the sheer size of the facility.

I was on the edge of sleep and left him to sort out his own room, clothes and so on, before making my own preparations for sleep. I remember getting ready and lying down. The next minute, it seemed I woke to the bright light of a rising sun. It was still early. Just as Ginny had warned me. That I would find it difficult to get a full night's sleep. Back home it was just after nine o'clock and I had a little way to go to adjust. I rolled over and tried to go back to sleep without success. I did push myself to rest for another hour before finally giving up.

That hour was restless, I was awake but my mind was drifting again between thoughts of Richard, who was playing later that week out in Hawaii and Rob, who would, I guessed, be struggling with the jetlag too.

It was with these thoughts that I remembered that I hadn't sent Richard my weekly "Good Luck" message. Eight tournaments into his professional playing career and he wasn't doing too bad. No wins but five top-ten finishes, and nothing worse than twentieth meant that he was slowly adjusting to his new life and keeping himself in line for the end of season challenge that might, just might, get him a full PGA Tour card.

Most of the time, I missed him like mad. Then there were times when I found myself getting on with life without thinking about him. The early lows after he had left England were becoming less harsh in their effect. It was just that when I did think about him and our time together it still hurt that those good times were behind us.

Having finally got up and sent the message, I decided that a session in the gym would be wise. The day before had, I reminded myself, not involved a lot of exercise. To my surprise when I did get down to the exercise area there were already several people working out. The supervisor still insisted on checking me out before allowing me to carry out my normal routine and it took a little persuasion before he accepted that my leg did not preclude me from using the various pieces of equipment.

It was not a particularly comfortable session. Back home I used a gym close to the golf club where I was known and, generally ignored by the other patrons. Here, I sensed constant looks from both the men and the women and they were not all friendly. I persevered and focused on my own routine. It was only as I finished that I realised that all but one man had left the exercise room.

His accent reminded me of the family at reception when I had arrived. "You're the one who got our room. Just who do you think you are? I think you owe me big time." As he spoke, he approached me with a leer and I backed away from him, suddenly frightened that he was about to assault me.

Just before he reached me there were two voices and to my relief the supervisor and Rob entered the room together. Rob moved quickly towards the individual with clearly serious intent and he retreated towards the exit. "Just a misunderstanding. Thought she needed help."

"Rob, it's okay. Leave him." I cried out before sitting down on the nearby bench shaking.

The supervisor had followed the man out of the gym and we heard him speaking to the man with a degree of his own venom. "You, and your family, are banned from the gym and the pool. Your actions are unacceptable. We have you on video. The hotel will not allow other guests to be intimidated or left fearing for their safety."

He came back into the exercise room. "Miss Jordan, my apologies. If I had realised that you were alone with that pervert, I would have been here more quickly. When I saw his actions over the video link, we came as fast as possible."

"You watch us exercise via a video link?" I asked him, slightly uneasy about that.

"We do. Just to ensure that, if anyone gets into trouble with the equipment or is taken ill, we can respond quickly. He won't know it but the links are just for monitoring. I mean they do not record. To be truthful that is the first time I have been happy that we have them. Always thought it was a pain having to keep an eye open. Maybe we have been lucky, I've never had to respond until today."

Rob intervened. "Sophie, I think you need to get back to your room. You look badly shaken up. Come on." He took my arm and helped me to my feet before slipping his arm around me and walking me to the elevator. "Jon, thanks for your help. We'll be back later or perhaps tomorrow."

"Not quite my pleasure, Mr Ward, but I am glad we were in time."

Back in the suite, Rob made me sit while he prepared coffee from the storage cupboard he had found. The next half an hour went quickly as I emptied my mug before deciding that a shower was the best way forward, before we went down to breakfast.

Rob followed me to my bedroom door.

"Sophie, I think you should leave your door a little open. I won't come in unless you call but I'd feel more comfortable knowing I can hear you if you have a reaction to that episode."

I looked at him and decided this was a good man. For the first time since Richard, I leaned forward and gave him a kiss. "Thanks, Rob. You were wonderful down there. I'll leave the door. Are you not going to get a shower?"

He looked a little embarrassed by the kiss but kept his cool.

"Once you are finished, not before, Sophie."

"You are special, you know."

I realised I was falling for him far too quickly. Did it matter? Is this the infamous love on the bounce? Do I care? I need to think about this, don't make a mistake. Rob could be a good friend but will he be more? I don't really know and he might not want more. Be steady my beating heart. No more advances, Sophie Jordan. Unless, unless, he responds positively.

I managed to complete my shower without incident, just the usual grimace when I saw my body in the mirror, full length of course. The idea of food was starting to drive my thoughts and, donning the hotel dressing gown, I went to my bedroom door to let Rob know he could get his own shower before we went down to eat.

He looked startled when he saw me and I smiled. Not the best view I suspected but at least the gown was decent. Quite quickly we were sitting down for breakfast. With the comforting feeling of food improving my general ability to cope, I explained how the event earlier had been a terrible reminder of the evening when Dawn died.

Rob's reaction was unsurprising, a mix of incredulity and concern. Did I still suffer from post-traumatic stress disorder?

I hadn't thought of it in that way for a long time but, as I told him, the occasional nightmare seemed to be the only indication that there were still harsh emotional effects. I told Rob of my promise to Dawn and her family. That I would make her sacrifice worthwhile, which had been my driver ever since and that seemed to be overriding more than the odd backflash.

After breakfast, I made my excuses and, leaving Rob to his own practice, headed for a local course where I had booked a tee time before leaving England. I did not expect to play well but Ginny had agreed that it would help in pushing my jetlag into the distance, as she put it.

An hour on the range and practice green loosened me up before I aimed for the first tee via the pro-shop. The professional gave me a warm welcome before asking if I would like a competitive round.

I had not been looking for one but she told me that if I delayed my tee-off for twenty minutes I would be able to play in the ladies' medal. As we talked an older woman came in to the shop and was introduced as Clair McGregor, the Ladies' Captain. My reputation had preceded me it seemed and she and her fellows would be delighted if I would honour them by taking part.

Lord, I thought, my reputation? Is that going to be repeated wherever? It wasn't easy to agree, but I guessed it would have been harder to convince them that I wasn't ready to play serious golf only one day after crossing the Atlantic. I duly accepted the invitation having confirmed that I could take a trolley out. In fact, it turned out that the whole field planned to use buggies as there were steep slopes to contend with.

If I had realised what my playing handicap would be, I suspect I might well have refused. My handicap index had moved further than I had thought and I had to play off plus six.

Not sure if I can play to that on a course I have never seen, I thought, and so it proved. I did break par, to my surprise, with a score of sixty-nine but the net score of seventy-five was never going to be good enough to win and perhaps that was not a bad thing.

Playing helped me to relax after the trip and the morning event. I could allow my mind to drift towards Rob, when not focused on the actual shots. Lunch followed the round and I gratefully accepted the invite to join the other ladies. The golf had been enjoyable and the company, so important, friendly from the off.

After we had eaten, the results were announced and I had come fifth. I was still applauded for my gross score and they wished me well when the real game began the following week, as their Captain put it, while thanking me for taking part.

Fatigue was beginning to hit me, a mix of the golf and residual jetlag, and I headed back to the hotel and some rest before dinner.

Rob wasn't around for which I admit I was quite happy and that allowed me to settle back and doze for what turned out to be a couple of hours, much longer than I intended. It was Rob's return that disturbed me.

"Sorry, Susie. Oh god, there I go again! Sophie! I didn't mean to wake you."

"Not a problem, Rob, I've dozed far too long. Let's have a coffee and I intend to have a shower before dinner. A good day?"

"Yes. Time practising after I walked a local course, just for the exercise. One you will be getting acquainted with; Champions Retreat."

My heart skipped a beat. The first two rounds of the Augusta Ladies Amateur! Why had Rob taken the time to visit the course?

"I couldn't resist seeing the challenge you will face next week. Challenge it certainly will be but you'll feel quite at home." Rob grinned. "And I will be following you!"

He suddenly sounded unsure. "Is that okay? Sophie. I mean if you'd rather that I didn't, I'd understand, I think."

I looked at him and realised that he really wanted to stay close to me but was nervous that he was overdoing it. Did I want him to? I wasn't sure myself but I certainly was not about to stop him being at Champions Reach.

"Rob, of course you can. Just don't expect to be watching me at The National. The practice round which everyone can play is behind closed doors, so you won't be able to be there."

He looked askance. "There is a round in public and you will be in it, I have no doubt, Sophie."

I groaned inwardly. Sooner or later and probably sooner I was going to start missing cuts, I knew it, why did no-one else? "I hope you are right, Rob, but don't get your hopes up."

He shook his head. "I'm not listening, Sophie. You are brilliant and you'll prove it."

We went down to dinner with that mild disagreement in the air but it was still an enjoyable evening. The night would start out badly and the next morning would be, well, different.

Once in bed, I found that I could not get to sleep. Overtired from the golf and the remaining jetlag, I tossed and turned before finally drifting into a fitful doze. Then the nightmare came back.

I knew it had because I could hear the voice of my brother gently calming me before cuddling me. I can remember clutching on to him as the fear of another man replaced the original monster. As he held me, I, at last, fell into a deep prolonged sleep; only waking to daylight and the shock of still being held by, or was that holding, Rob.

Now I really knew that I had had another nightmare episode but how Rob managed to hold on to me was still a mystery. It was obvious that he had, himself, fallen asleep and now I needed to wake him. My left leg was being pinned and I did not have the strength, without my prosthetic, to use the other leg to pull myself free.

As I tried to nudge him and ask him to wake up, I saw his gown had
come undone during the night and a stoma bag was partly visible.
I knew of them as my aunt had one. How on earth had Rob got
cancer at such a young age?

His pants, a good thing he had them on, had a bulge which I
recognised as the morning effect. One doesn't have two brothers, I
thought, without being aware. Knowing that to be the case, didn't
help my self-esteem but I don't have much of that anyway and, oh
dear, I'll bet he can see my thighs. The scars!

My quiet calls to him to wake up eventually succeeded and Rob
stirred. As he woke, I could see he was embarrassed by the situation,
why I don't really know. He had been my knight in shining armour
for the second time!

"It's okay, Rob, I think I know why you are here. I had that dream,
didn't I?"

He nodded, as he carefully disentangled himself. I decided to take
the bull by the horns and told him I knew what had happened to
him, explaining about my friend's Mum.

You could say it was his turn, as he, too, talked about my scars. For a
moment I wanted to run away and hide. Then I could see in his face
the misery that he might have upset me and I took a deep breath
before explaining that what he had seen was only a part and that I
wasn't that beauty he had suggested I might be.

He looked at me thoughtfully and I sensed, to my inner turmoil,
that he was thinking that they were not the negative I knew they
were. Then without a word he made the excuse of needing the loo.
Not quite what he said and I couldn't resist a small, complimentary,
dig.

As he vanished out of the room and I headed for the shower. I
was, suddenly, struck by the idea that what I had seen might be a
little more than I had assumed, that he still found me physically

attractive. I mean, I said to myself, why else would he be embarrassed?

A little while later, after a breakfast at which there was not a lot of conversation, we decided to go back to the golf course I had played the day before. The club professional was pleased to see me back and that another Amateur Champion considered it worth playing there. They were probably also happy to take our green fees, of course!

The morning passed all too quickly. For once, we were both playing a friendly round of golf and could enjoy the course. It wasn't entirely non-competitive, we had a small side bet, but it was an enjoyable morning. I had intended to go back to the hotel for lunch but Rob suggested we try one of the local fast-food outlets to see how different it was from a similar chain back home. He admitted that it wasn't the same but the food was good to eat, bigger portions and better cooked.

It was a good thing that we had eaten well, as dinner would be late, at least for me. Ginny was due to land early evening but she wouldn't reach the hotel until after eight o'clock. Back in our room, I did suggest to Rob that he might want to eat earlier and I think he got the underlying hint that I wanted time alone with her.

When he left to go down to the restaurant, or possibly the bar, he stopped and gave me a kiss on the cheek which startled me a little. Only after the door had closed did I react. Too late! Why, oh why, didn't I return his display of affection with a real kiss? Sophie, you must get your act together! He's good looking and doesn't seem to have been put off by your scars, or has he? I worried myself. Perhaps that was what the kiss really was. Just a show of friendship not one of underlying passion. I settled back and decided to surf the TV channels. There didn't seem much else to do while I waited for Ginny to arrive and before I knew it, I was dozing off. I jerked awake to the sound of the room's telephone ringing.

"Sophie, it's me. Fancy a drink? Before we eat, I mean?" Ginny sounded as eager as ever to exchange news and surprisingly fresh, given the journey. She did make me smile.

"Five minutes and I'll be down."

And five minutes later I was stood at the entrance to the bar stopped by the sight of a person I had not expected to see – Steven. But Ginny had only booked two rooms, was she anticipating sharing with me? She didn't know about Rob, there'd been no reason to tell her before she reached Augusta. Then I noticed the bottle of champagne on their table. Ginny and Steven were clearly not expecting to need another room, that was transparent but even so, champagne? I had seen the prices of the various sparkling wines and gulped. This was no ordinary drink.

Ginny's first words were just as surprising. "No, Rob then, Sophie?" I looked at her. "What makes you think he is around? He wasn't booked into the same hotel."

Ginny purred like the cat that had got the cream. "So that isn't him sitting over there, then?"

I looked across the bar to see Rob at a small corner table trying to hide. "Ginny, there's nothing going on between us apart from my helping him out. His hotel messed up his booking and there aren't any hotel rooms left in the city. My suite has two separate rooms both with ensuite and he's been staying in it. In any case you've got questions to answer as far as I can see."

Ginny laughed as did Steven, who responded. "I guess we have, Sophie. You are looking well. Call Rob over, we might as well meet him now rather than over breakfast and Ginny will tell all."

I went over to Rob and invited him to join us explaining that Ginny was not on her own. After the mutual introductions, I turned to Ginny with a raised eyebrow. She nodded and grinned. "You guessed it, Sophie. We are now an item, as you youngsters would call it. Have been for a few months but didn't want to tell anyone before you, Sophie. It is because of you that we met. We've no plans for a wedding yet but eventually...." She looked at Steven who looked rather uncomfortable at this but, at the same time, rather proud.

I was very happy for Ginny and, I guess, for Steven but I still needed to explain more about Rob and that took a little time before we went in for a meal. Rob had not eaten so he joined us and he and Steven spent most of that time talking golf, while Ginny and I talked about other things.

Eventually, Ginny was forced to give into the jetlag and dragged Steven away to bed. Rob and I also headed back to the suite. That night I did sleep well, partly because I knew Rob was next door and there was his good night kiss too, as far from a brotherly peck as I could imagine. That was all but I went to sleep with an unexpected tremor in my heart.

The next morning, Ginny and I were up early. It was the first day of practice and I wanted a full session on the driving range and bunkers. Putting came last but, in some ways, I felt that my play from the sand could always do with improving more than the other aspects of my game. Ginny put it another way. "You don't go in many but, when you do, getting out cleanly is top of the priorities." My warm-up duly completed I headed to the starter's hut to confirm my allocated start time. While waiting there was a tap on my back. "Miss Jordan, may I speak with you?"

I turned round to find Aiku, the Japanese player I had beaten at the Amateur. "Of course, Aiku. I am sorry, I am terrible with names and cannot remember your surname."

"No apology from you is required." She said with a formal tone in her voice. "I must and wish to apologise for my behaviour and that of my sister on that day in England. It was inexcusable. I hope we can meet again on a better occasion."

I paused before responding. "Thank you. Accepted but I feel the apology should be to my caddy who was hurt but I, too, hope we can meet in better circumstances."

While we were speaking, I suddenly realised that Aiku's sister was having a similar conversation with Ginny. With that covered I asked Aiku if she would like to practice alongside me. It seemed the best way that we could ensure that bygones were bygones and Aiku's smile at that idea confirmed that I was correct.

After a chat with the starter, our mutual start times were adjusted and a quarter of an hour later we set out on the course. As we walked up the first, after our tee shots, Ginny was able to tell me what had caused the ruction back home. "Aiku's sister has explained that Aiku suffers from severe migraines and dizzy spells. That day when they argued she was trying to convince Aiku to withdraw. She is worried that there is an underlying reason that has not been found and Aiku's vision was and is being affected, hence her incorrect choice of clubs so often that day."

Having done the necessary notes in her yardage book and after I had played my second shot, to the back of the green as it happened, I looked towards Aiku who was some way in front. "That is a shame. I feel for her, and her sister. At least, I know what my problems are."

I could see Rob and Steven in amongst the small crowd that was watching us and thought about how lucky Ginny was. Was I as lucky? I wasn't that sure but I could hope.

The round continued in good spirit, as practice rounds tend to, until we reached the fifteenth, a short par four with water alongside the green and across the fairway. I took my three-wood to try and leave a sensible second shot while Aiku looked to her driver. After two good shots that met our respective needs, we started down the path to the fairway together, having another chat. Then Aiku suddenly stopped with a cry of pain. She stumbled and collapsed to the ground. Even as I went to her aid, I could see Steven racing towards us, yelling for medics to be called urgently.

Within a matter of seconds, he was next to Aiku rolling her over and starting resuscitation. A medic was quickly next to him and they continued work until a second medic, on a buggy with a defibrillator, arrived. As the full medical team took over, I could hear Steven telling them that he believed Aiku was suffering from a brain tumour or growth. One medic demanded how Steven could know, clearly questioning his knowledge. His response had me gasping. Even Ginny seemed taken aback

"I trained as a doctor and then joined the army as a battlefield surgeon in various locations around the world. I have seen this before. She will need hospital treatment urgently but then you already know that."

The mention of the army stopped the medic in his tracks. His stance changed as he came to attention before saluting Steven. "Sir, Doctor. Captain Hill. A privilege to meet a former member of our allies."

Steven stiffened himself to return the salute. "My privilege too, Sir."

The two men agreed to meet later for a drink after Aiku had been transferred to an ambulance accompanied by her sister who was in a terrible state. One of the course officials took charge of Aiku's clubs and we were left to finish the round alone. I cannot claim the last four holes were brilliant but that is why we have practice and, if it is a valid excuse, my mind was more on how Aiku was. It had looked serious even before Steven's diagnosis. All I could do was hope she would recover and, maybe, one day return to golf.

Back in the hotel, I dragged Ginny into the lounge for a coffee, leaving Rob to his own devices. Steven had gone elsewhere.

"Ginny, did you know he was a doctor?"

"No and yes. I knew he was medically trained and in the army. I didn't realise he is a doctor. I mean he isn't practising or anything."

"I do hope Aiku is okay, I guess it will take scans before an operation. The question is, will the tumour be operable?"

Ginny nodded. "We are assuming that Steven's diagnosis is correct. It does put into perspective the events of last year. Steven always felt that their behaviour was inconsistent with their background."

There was no news by the next morning as we headed back to the course for our last practice session. I would have left a message for Rob to try and find out but he had already gone to bed by the time I finished talking with Ginny and had gone out before I was up.

I did find it a little disconcerting that I didn't even see him that night or before I left that morning. I didn't think we had had a falling out, just not seen much of each other that day. Sophie, he's just a friend. You can't start expecting him to be at your beck and call, you know. Telling myself that, I found quite hard, I realised that I wanted more. For the first time since we met, I really did want more than the occasional kiss. But did he? I needed to clarify that and decided on a plan for that evening.

For the moment, golf took precedence and I focused on my game ahead of the first round the next day. The day went well, although we got a sense of the potential for bad weather to intervene. The downpour mid-afternoon caused a degree of upset for those who had chosen for whatever reasons to play later in the day. I was fortunate to be playing the eighteenth when the heavens opened and we only got slightly wet. As the rain continued and the greens started holding water it was apparent that some of the field would not be able to complete a full round. Had we inadvertently gained an advantage? It seemed unlikely but we did at least have the chance to finish early.

After reaching the hotel I decided that I needed a shower and fresh clothing before acting on the plan I had hatched earlier that day.

Rob was in his room also, I assumed, showering. He and Steven had been following us around the course and had ended up wetter than

Ginny and I. Having dried off I donned fresh underwear. Both bra and pants were flesh coloured and showed my figure off well. What they didn't do was hide the scar crossing my chest.

Taking a deep breath, I went to the door to Rob's room and knocked. There was a pause before Rob appeared dressed in his gown, I think he had just grabbed it before answering my knock.

"Sophie? What?" He was startled which is what I had intended, I wanted his instinctive reaction to how I looked not a considered thoughtful response. Then he smiled. "Lord, you look stupendous!"

I started breathing again. "Really? How can I Rob? They are horrible, the scars, and there is no hiding them unless I'm fully clothed." I turned round. "There's a second across my back too."

Now he looked serious. "I can understand why you say that and if I had really thought about it before seeing you like this. I might have agreed with you." My heart fell until he continued. "But you are truly beautiful. Now I understand what your old boyfriend saw in you and why you are so attractive. Thank you, Sophie, for trusting me."

I leant forward and pulled him toward me. "Thank you, Rob. That means the world to me." I kissed him, giggling as he had not had the chance to dry off after his own shower and was still wet. "I think you should get dried off and then I'll buy you a drink in the bar."

I retreated to my own room with a buzzing in my head. Rob's words were almost unbelievable but, as I thought about it, matched Richard's own reaction the first time he had seen me naked. You won't ever be able to look at them without feeling depressed, Sophie Jordan, but at least you know that others do not always see you in the same light, I told myself. Then I caught sight of myself in the mirror and groaned, perhaps they just needed an eye test, how can they not see how disfigured I am?

We had just enough time for that drink before the others joined us for dinner. With the tournament due to start the next morning, we stayed in the hotel for the meal. I had drawn a tee-time of eight-thirty and that encouraged me to retire early leaving the others to chat over the last of the wine.

I really hoped that Rob would try to join me in my bedroom but, at the same time realised that such activity as we might get up to was not wise, ahead of the need to focus the next morning. With a rueful thought I closed my room door, leaving the do not disturb sign on.

It wasn't long before Rob came up and I did hear him gently push my door before leaving me to sleep. I did feel good. I sensed that our friendship might well become a little more than that.

Rob.

As I headed off to catch my flight from Atlanta, I took a brief look back at Susie. Oh, my life, I have got to get her name right! To my surprise, she looked a little downcast at my leaving her.

We hadn't talked about our exes all that much but I gathered her boyfriend had taken the opportunity to qualify for the Korn Ferry Tour, successfully, and that she was still emotionally raw from their breakup.

On my side, I reminded myself, Teri had been there for me until only a matter of a few weeks before and I wasn't ready yet to replace her as it were. What I hadn't been prepared for was to find myself enjoying the company of a drop-dead gorgeous woman who knew as much, if not more, about our sport than I did. And that ignored the fact that she was clearly a far better golfer.

Those thoughts kept rambling through my brain for the entire flight down to Augusta and in the cab to the hotel. That part of my trip had gone smoothly but the wheels came off when I reached the hotel reception.

"I don't understand. I have the reservation here. That's your confirmation email. Why have you not got a room for me?" I was trying, very hard, not to lose my temper.

"I am sorry, Mr Ward. There has been a system malfunction and we have double booked several rooms including yours and the other guest has already checked in. My colleagues are trying to find you a room at one of our other hotels or other local establishments."

I was forced to wait for almost an hour before I was told that there were no rooms within the city, although they had found one at a motel twenty miles away. I had already searched the internet for rooms without success and it seemed that they were at a premium or, to put it another way, non-existent.

What the hell was I to do? Twenty miles would be too far, it wasn't as if I had a car. Maybe, just maybe, the hotel Susie was staying at might have a room. Dare I call her and ask? Was it fair to put my problem on her?

The hotel offered me the option of having a meal while they continued their efforts, even though they had already insisted that they could not find another room. I decided to accept.

An hour later, no room, nowhere to go, no change. I finally decided to make that call.

"Sophie, sorry. Do you know if your hotel has any rooms available? My booking has been messed up."

She seemed to think about it before she told me to come to her hotel. I could share her room. That was not what I was looking for. I felt Teri looking over my shoulder. It's two bedrooms, she was saying in my head, you don't have to share the bed but, my love, if that's what it takes, you should take it. We can't be together but that shouldn't mean you need be lonely for ever.

Having agreed to get a taxi to Sophie's hotel, I told the reception team that they could at least get me that cab and pay for it. To my surprise they agreed to transport me using a hotel limo. Half an hour later, I was in the reception of Sophie's hotel being greeted by her.

Boy, did she look good. There ought to be a queue of males looking to date her, I thought, or even women. But then she had told me about, what was his name? Richard, so it does look as if she prefers men.

As we greeted each other, a member of staff came over. He confirmed that they also had no empty rooms but, if Miss Jordan was happy, they were too. In moments my bags and clubs had been taken away for delivery to Sophie's suite while we headed into the bar for a drink.

For almost an hour we chatted about the rest of our journeys and Sophie's talk with a reporter. That was a reminder, not that I needed one, of her standing in the sport.

It was a good time but it was obvious towards the end that Sophie was struggling against the jetlag and, if I'm honest, I was feeling tired as well. We decided that bed was the right place for both of us, just not the same one!

When we entered the suite, I was shaken. The sheer size of the main room and then a kitchenette to one side and through a second door two ensuite bedrooms. I have friends whose homes are no bigger and I had to ask. "Sophie, how can you afford this?"

She chuckled. "I can't. It turns out that this hotel is a part of a chain with properties around Europe. I got, or rather Ginny got me, a sponsorship deal with them. I had to be photographed at various locations on the Mediterranean coast. On their golf courses. It seems I am now the face of the chain and was automatically upgraded. Now, sorry, but you get the twin room. I'm already settled in the other."

She's apologising for my only getting the twin! I'd be on the streets but for her generosity!

"I'll be fine, Sophie. I'd have slept on the couch if necessary. And you don't need to apologise, please. I'm in your debt not the other way round."

She nodded with a wry smile before wishing me good night. As the door to her room closed, I wondered, for a moment, had I missed an opportunity? Before mentally berating myself. Rob, you are an idiot. She's a great girl and will soon have hosts of admirers and in any case Teri's still back home. Or I wish she was, I growled to myself.

Having sorted out my room, I headed into bed and was asleep almost before I had hit the pillow.

Although I had fallen asleep quickly, I cannot say that I had the best of nights and, as I expected, I found myself awake at only just past five o'clock. I knew I should probably stay and at least rest but once awake I find it difficult to remain in bed. Well, not when Teri was next to me, of course, but apart from on those occasions I would be up and heading for the course, or to the gym, before work.

I forced myself to relax for a while before giving in and deciding to dress and slip down to the hotel exercise area, which turned out to be a full gym with several men and women already working out.

There was a supervisor, Jon, who insisted on a check-up before he would let me start exercising on any of the machines. This took a few minutes during which time most of those people finished.

As Jon completed his checks, he noticed that only two persons were left. He looked at a video screen, one of four, which showed a man and a woman, Sophie. We could see the man approaching her and, as Jon turned up a volume control, we heard him talking in a threatening manner.

"Quick." I said. "Fastest way to them!"

Jon responded, instantly. "Follow me."

He led me through the back door, a staff only sign was on it, and we needed only a few yards before we were in the room. I pushed past Jon. No-one was going to hurt my friend, not if I had anything to do with it.

The man backed away with a sneering. "Just a misunderstanding. Thought she needed help."

Sophie had sat down on a nearby bench, visibly shaking. As I went to comfort her, I could hear Jon giving the man a clear message as he banned him from the facilities for good. That individual vanished, carrying his clothing change with him and Jon came back in, clearly worried.

Sophie was quick to reassure us that we had been in time to avoid what she admitted was an unpleasant experience going any further and that she was fine. I was pretty sure she was more upset than she was letting on and insisted on taking her back to the suite. Jon had explained the purpose of the CCTV and that it didn't record but he hadn't told the cretin, who we hoped would be worrying about any comeback.

Sophie seemed a little unsure of her footing and I gently put my arm around her waist guiding her to the elevator. She appeared to be glad of the support and leant on me all the way to the room. Back there I made her sit down while I used the kitchenette to prepare a couple of mugs of coffee. After that was finished, she decided that a shower was the next thing to do before breakfast.

I convinced her to leave her bedroom door ajar, promising not to go in unless she called me. I was worried that she might have a delayed rection and said so. That was when she suddenly kissed me, thanking me for that and for my reaction in the gym.

I wasn't expecting the kiss and didn't react. Sophie didn't seem to be pushy or forward, not like Teri, but was that a suggestion that she wanted more than a simple friendship? The idea was certainly attractive and I hated to think it might be nothing more than a sisterly show of friendship rather than that of a would-be girlfriend. Boy, was I falling for her in a romantic way? I didn't know. Was it too soon after Teri?

Sophie finished her shower a lot quicker than I remembered my sisters doing, they always took ages, and came to the door wrapped in a hotel gown. She looked fantastic, which was amazing. After all hotel dressing gowns are not exactly designed to be sexy.

Her smile at my reaction suggested that she knew how she looked but all she said was. "Thanks, Rob. I'm fine. Get yourself a shower and we can go for breakfast. I don't know about you but I could eat a horse."

I nodded and went, as instructed, to my own room. That wasn't the easiest departure from Sophie's presence but I did need the shower.

Within a short time, we were sitting down to breakfast and a further chat about the event in the gym. For the first time Sophie gave me some rather graphic details of that infamous evening when she had lost her leg. She explained that the way that the idiot in the gym had approached her was a horrible reminder of the way that her friend had been assaulted in the ten-pin alley. I found it hard to listen, how had Sophie recovered from that trauma?

After breakfast she headed out to a local golf club where she had booked a round even before leaving for the States. Her advance planning was amazing.

I had had no plans as such. My first week was intended as a time to, largely, deal with the jetlag. I would be looking for a club where I could play and practice, after a few days.

Meeting Sophie had affected me more than I could have expected and I changed my mind about an easy day. The Ladies Augusta Amateur doesn't start on the Masters course, I knew. Question was where did it start. I learned from the concierge that the first two days, before the cut, would be played at a location called Champions Retreat. I got a cab and went there.

When I arrived, there was some difficulty about allowing me to walk the course until, to be honest, I lied. They were happy enough to let someone who would be caddying to do so and I did not dissuade them from that belief. It was a thoroughly fun few hours as I walked around what is a very attractive golf course. Having obtained a yardage book, I made copious notes as I walked.

Afterwards I headed back to the hotel's own golf set-up and spent time on the range before returning to the suite where I found Sophie asleep on the couch. She stirred as the door closed and I was quick to apologise for disturbing her.

She said it wasn't a problem. She had dozed for longer than planned and now needed a coffee.

Over the drinks, we exchanged news about our day, so far. I told about visiting the golf course but not about the notes in the yardage book, I'd give that to her caddy as her starter. I knew she would want to make her own notes but maybe, just maybe, mine would help.

When I told her that I wanted to follow her while she played, she looked shocked. Had I overstepped the mark? I backed up as fast as possible leaving it up to her. It took her a moment to tell me that I could do that, if I really wanted to. Surely, though, I would enjoy watching the others more.

She does down play her chances, I thought. I would learn that that was how she saw herself, as she warned me that I shouldn't expect to be able to do so at The National itself.

"Why not?" I asked, anticipating the answer but needing to hear it for myself.

"Everyone gets the chance to play a practice round on the Masters course on the Sunday but that's behind closed doors and only the top thirty will play the final round on the Monday. So, forty-two of us are going home after the Sunday round."

"And you are convinced you won't make the cut, is that it?"

Sophie's frown spoke volumes. "Rob, everyone seems to think that cuts in competitions are for other players, not me. Everyone except me, I should say. I'll try, of course I will. Just be prepared to have the day off on Monday. I mean, you can still go and follow some of the other players."

I found it difficult to listen and insisted she would be in that final thirty. Dinner was pleasant but that minor disagreement seemed to rankle me more than I would have thought possible. I knew she was brilliant and so did others, why not her? And the more I was with her the more beautiful she became.

We both managed to keep going until after ten o'clock that evening before tiredness claimed us and we both retreated to our beds. I fell asleep almost immediately only to be woken a few hours later to the sound of screams coming from Sophie's room.

Grabbing my hotel dressing gown, I hurtled from my room into hers looking for the guy who had threatened her in the gym or anyone else for that matter. There was no-one! Then I saw Sophie threshing around in her bed and realised that she must be having the nightmare she had told me about.

What could I do? What should I do? I had to do something and, in the end, went to her bedside whispering. "Sophie, you're okay, you're okay. Just a dream."

My words seemed to calm her but not to quieten her cries all that much. I put my arms out and wrapped her in them, sitting next to her, allowing her to cuddle up to me. I had no idea who she thought was there but, whatever, it seemed to work and she slowly settled back into a calm sleep.

After a few minutes I tried to slip away, only for Sophie, now well asleep, to roll over and grab on to me even more firmly. I gave up and resigned myself to having a lot of questions to answer the next morning.

As I tried to relax, I realised that, in her more frenzied moments, she had thrown the bedding off. Then I caught sight of her legs in the faint light of the passageway. They were gorgeous but there was something not quite right. A line or a mark on both. What was I seeing? Dear God, what had he done to her?

Thinking about that kept me awake for quite a while but eventually, despite the uncomfortable position, fatigue won out and I slipped into a deep sleep.

"Rob, Rob, wake up, wake up. I can't move."

I stirred suddenly alert and conscious that I was still in Sophie's bed. Oh, I thought, am I glad I had kept my pants on, I hope that bulge is not too obvious. I slowly disentangled myself, stretching carefully to avoid catching Sophie by accident.

She was looking at me with some concern. "I had a nightmare, didn't I? Sorry, Rob, it is terrifying when it happens. Was I very noisy?"

I told the story of how I came to be asleep in her bed. "I'm sorry, Sophie, I didn't plan to be here all night."

She smiled. "I'm glad you did though. I find it difficult to sleep after I have that dream. Sorry if I grabbed hold of you." Her expression turned sombre. "You said you had a hidden disability. I think I know what it is. Sorry, I couldn't help but see the bag."

I growled inside. Obviously, my gown had slid open in the night. Sophie was being kind, since Ken was not the only thing on show.

"I had cancer when I was eighteen, lost my large intestine. Sorry, it's not the prettiest sight. How did you recognise it so easily?"

"My friend's Mum had the same issue when she was in her forties. My mum warned me and my brothers that she had been very ill and had to have surgery. That was in case I saw anything odd when I stayed with her. I never did but I asked her one day what the doctors had done to her to make her well. I was fifteen at the time and just recovering from the loss of my leg. She explained it all and how she had called it Lizzie. I had to promise not to tell anyone else. Rob, have you got a name for yours?"

I looked at her and decided to be honest. "Ken. The nurses suggested it. You told me about your leg but what about your thighs? Sophie, I couldn't miss the scars on them. From the same event?"

To my horror I thought she was going to cry. Should I not have said? She would surely have realised that without the duvet covering her I could not have missed them. Oh lord, Sophie don't cry. It doesn't change how you look, at least not to me and clearly not to your previous boyfriend, did it?

To my relief, Sophie gathered herself together. "Rob, they are from the car scraping across me, twice, and you haven't seen the whole of it. They run almost to my neck, one on the front and one on my back, and the surgeons can't repair them more than they have. So, you know now that I'm not the beauty you and others keep talking about." She smiled ruefully.

I gazed at her trying to imagine how the rest of her would look without her clothes on. Logically, scarring like that should have made me nervous but, and it was odd, I felt that in some strange way they would add to her beauty. Though I rather doubted that Sophie would ever expose her body to me.

What am I thinking? I've hardly left Teri and I'm looking at another woman as more than a friend, a very lovely woman but so soon. Now I need to control myself and make a careful exit without showing anything else.

"Sorry, Sophie, but I do need the little boy's room. Will you be all right?"

She suddenly grinned. "I'll be fine. Not that little a boy, though, as far as I can see."

I coloured and made a swift exit, heading for my ensuite and the shower, before breakfast.

After we had eaten, we both went to a local club for a friendly round of golf. Did I say friendly? Sophie decided that whoever lost should pay for lunch. And I did – on the eighteenth hole!

It did give me the freedom to opt for a place that Sophie might not have chosen. Chinese fast food is my favourite and there was a local chain outlet like one I knew back home. Sophie, to do her justice, took to the idea with a resounding positivity.

Afterwards she did suggest that I might want to dine on my own in the evening. Not because she didn't want me at the table but because she expected to be eating very late. Her caddy was arriving but wouldn't be at the hotel much before nine, Sophie thought. It didn't take long for me to concur with her suggestion, not due to the lateness of eating but because I felt she would want to have time with her friend without me getting in the way. Breakfast, I thought, would be soon enough to meet her.

"I'll try not to wake you tonight." Sophie said. "Not when I come back from the restaurant nor later."

"Don't worry about that. Enjoy the company." And I gave her a kiss, which I think startled her, in a positive manner. As I stood in the elevator heading down to eat, I was kicking myself. If I was going to kiss Sophie, it should be a proper kiss, not a peck on the cheek!

When I did get down to the restaurant, I decided that I wasn't yet ready to eat. Lunch had been quite filling, so I decided to take another walk before returning to the bar.

To be truthful, I really needed to clear my mind and try and come to some form of understanding exactly how I felt for Sophie. On the one hand I still had feelings for Teri but it was true that that romance was over. The question was, was I being fair to Sophie if I attempted to move our relationship in the direction my heart was asking me to. Should I take the risk of her rejecting my advances?

After an hour or so strolling around the local area I returned to the hotel, still not hungry, and settled for a beer in the bar dropping into a chair in a quiet corner. I was relaxing, people watching, when a couple came into the bar and claimed a table on the other side of the room. I couldn't help but notice that they looked in my direction and were having a quiet word. Surely, they hadn't recognised me. I was in semi-darkness, just some minimal lighting, and I'm not exactly front-page material, am I? Am I?

It took a few minutes from their sitting down but then a bottle arrived at their table. They appeared to have something to celebrate, I thought, with champagne at the hotel prices. The woman was looking towards the bar entrance clearly waiting for someone to arrive and join them. That someone appeared and I gasped. It was Sophie, but she was expecting to meet up with her caddy, Ginny, not a couple. Just what was going on?

Sophie did hesitate when she saw the couple before breaking into a beaming smile and greeting them both like old friends. After a few words during which the others both looked in my direction, Sophie came over and invited me to join them.

It turned out that the two were Ginny and her new partner Steven. They had met during the Amateur Championship when Steven took over the role of Sophie's caddy after Ginny had fallen and damaged her shoulder. The rest, as Ginny put it, was history.

The evening was great and I was very glad that I had not eaten. The ladies chatted away together while Steven and I talked about The National and the Masters.

Eventually we could see the jetlag catching up with both Sophie's friends and they retired to bed leaving us to finish before going up to bed ourselves. That sounds a bit more than it was but I did give Sophie a proper kiss which she returned, before we went to our separate rooms.

The next day was the first of two practice days at the Champions Retreat and Sophie and Ginny were up early travelling to the course ahead of Steven and I.

We had agreed to join them at around the time Sophie was due to go out on the course and left just over an hour later. We reached the first tee to find that she was going to play alongside a competitor from Japan called Aiku. Steven was somewhat taken aback by this chance as, he told me, Sophie had beaten Aiku in the quarter-final of the Amateur and there had been a degree of bad blood which had been responsible for Ginny being hurt. Bad blood, he admitted, that he had not understood.

Whatever had happened before, it seemed that the girls were content to play together and we had an enjoyable time watching them working the course as well as they could.

It was on the fifteenth that it happened. After they played their first shots, Sophie and Aiku walked up the fairway chatting. It was sudden in the extreme. Aiku cried out and collapsed clutching her head before becoming very still. Even as an official could be heard calling for medics, Steven pushed his way through the crowd and reached Aiku, starting resuscitation. Medics were on the scene quickly and started work on restarting her breathing and, I assumed, her heart. Just what had happened. Steven could be seen talking at length with the senior medic who, after a moment, straightened himself and gave Steven a salute which was returned. I decided that the mystery would have to wait as Aiku was taken away on a medical buggy, clearly en-route to hospital.

The next day required some concentration as the news from the hospital was mixed. Aiku was in an induced coma while investigations continued. Word was that Steven had been correct in his initial diagnosis, it seemed that he had been an army medic and was a qualified doctor. I found myself thinking that Ginny had landed a star.

Ginny might have done well with her partner but later that afternoon Sophie gave me a shock. I had just finished my shower, we had all got wet in a sudden downpour, when there was a tap on my door. I grabbed the dressing gown and with a desperate tug tied it in place before opening the door to a sight that I do not believe I will ever forget. Sophie was stood there, dressed only in bra and pants and clearly nervous as to how I might react. Oh my god, she is a beauty.

We spoke briefly, she felt that the scars which as she had told me crossed her body from her thigh to just below her neck would be so unbearable that I could not possibly want to be with her. It seemed my first reaction had put her at her ease. She thanked me and gave me a kiss, laughing as she realised that I was still very wet from my shower.

"I'll see you in the bar, Rob. I owe you a drink."

As she vanished to get dressed properly, I retreated to my own room in a little confusion. Did Sophie want a full relationship? Did I? My mind was twisting. Teri, I suspected would be saying, through gritted teeth, don't be a fool, Rob, she is gorgeous and it looks as if she wants you. Don't lose her. Even so, Teri was still a raw emotion.

I headed down for the drink and we enjoyed a chat about anything but us.

Sophie, I suspected, was still unsure of her feelings and so was I. When I finally went up to bed her door was closed with the do not disturb sign lit. I still gently pushed but it did not give and when I thought about it, before sleep caught up with me, she was being sensible. Tomorrow was too important to divert Sophie's attention from her focus on the golf.

Champions Retreat.

"On the tee, the British Amateur Champion, Sophie Jordan." And we were underway. I was partnered up with two players from Korea who were polite but not forthcoming. Like me they knew we would need to concentrate. Of the seventy-two starters only thirty would make the cut after the two rounds on the Champions Retreat course and a good start was imperative.

The next four hours were a time of focused intent and passed quickly. For me it was a very good round and the practice paid off. Without too much excitement I contrived to post a score of sixty-eight, four under par, and, by the end of the day, found myself in third place two shots back from the leader. My playing partners were not so lucky, both found the water on the fifteenth and ended up with double bogeys which meant that they both finished at level par, not out of it by any means but it would be harder for them to challenge for the lead the next day.

It was a quiet evening, a good part of which I spent talking to Ginny. Rob and Steven had gone out for a drink with the medic from the course. We had not had much time together since Ginny had arrived and I took the opportunity to quiz her about the reaction of men to my disfigurement. She was considered in her answer.

"Sophie, first you must accept that you have the sort of looks that most men love and a lot of women would kill for. I am sure that I have told you that before. The thing is that the most good-looking people, both men and women, have imperfections and it is often those imperfections that add character."

"But, Ginny, you are talking about little things, perky nose, small birth marks. My scars aren't little, are they?" I just couldn't get how Rob could have reacted as he had. "I just don't understand how Rob, and Richard for that matter, could call me beautiful even when I am naked or nearly so."

Ginny grinned. "It is counter-intuitive isn't it. But beauty is in the eye of the beholder and they obviously disagree with your view of the mirror images you see. Ride with them, for once they know better."

I wasn't sure that Ginny was right but I resigned myself to never being sure about me or my body. Bed was a necessary next step although I was off later the next day, just after midday. For once, I felt that I had a real chance of making the cut and sleep came swiftly and soundly.

Day two and I, again, find the course favouring my game. There is one blotch on the score card. On the par three eighth, I misjudge the wind and my tee shot finds the back bunker. Left with a bad lie, I make the mistake of not playing safe and accepting a likely bogey. My sand shot races away over the green and hangs just above the water leaving a difficult chip, I walk off with a five to offset the birdies from earlier in the round.

Ginny is again my saviour, encouraging me to ignore that, as we walk toward the next tee. I know that these things happen and it is essential to focus on the next hole, what is done is done, but it is not always easy.

The ninth, a shortish par five, would prove the answer. On the first day I had played the hole conservatively finishing with a par, today Ginny suggests that I should be aggressive. With wind assistance I take driver and find the fairway only just short of two-hundred-and-seventy yards downslope. The ball finishes close to the right edge, ideally placed to allow a direct shot to the green. This time I judge my approach shot to perfection, finishing only a matter of ten feet or so away. The resultant putt drops and my double bogey has been countered by an eagle!

The back nine holes are without drama, just one birdie at the par five eighteenth means that I finish at seven under par and tied third, only one shot back. Now I face The National and, I could scarcely believe it, I was in with a chance!

From the side lines

Those two days were as enjoyable as I could recall for many long months. Sophie steadily made her way up the leader board finishing the first day in third place. She came off the course buzzing.

Ginny explained that for once Sophie was thinking positively about the next day. "You won't believe, Rob, just how negative she can be. To see her looking ahead with some confidence about the cut is the best feeling I can remember."

We didn't see much of each other that evening, mostly because I went out with Steven and listened to him and that medic exchange experiences of their times in the armed forces and especially the demands that they had faced on the battlefields. It was both educational and my respect for these brave men would be difficult to describe. I could only say to myself. "Don't ever moan again about difficulties on the golf course, Rob. Win or lose."

The second round saw just one moment of danger. Sophie did something that I know she must have regretted. Playing a difficult shot when she could have taken much less risk, I watched with my heart in my mouth as she ended with a double bogey, undoing her earlier efforts in one moment of madness.

When watching the professionals on television I have always admired the relationship demonstrated by both players and their caddies. Now I watched a caddy provide the support her boss needed.

Whatever Ginny said to Sophie as they walked to the next tee must have been inspirational. The par five she faced was not long but was a double dog-leg. As I watched, Ginny handed Sophie her driver and I gasped. The first dog leg was left to right and I already knew that Sophie's preferred shot was a draw, this drive really needed a fade. And, boy, did she find a fade! Minutes later she completed a remarkable eagle and by the end of the day we were joyously applauding her as she not only made the cut but was well placed, one shot off the lead.

Sophie - The Night Before The National

Back at the hotel, I felt I could relax a little. The next day would only be practice. On the Masters course.

What was I thinking! **ONLY** practice on **AUGUSTA NATIONAL**? Perhaps relaxing was not the way to go. I would need that chance to understand the course from being on it, not just from television coverage.

Ginny organised a meal at a high-class steakhouse near the hotel and all four of us took the chance to forget about the golf for an hour or two.

Later, as we are being whisked to the suite by the elevator, I look at Rob and find him looking back at me. He doesn't look that sure about what to do, if anything. He seems to be mirroring my own thoughts. Did I want to get closer? Was it too soon? Was he having doubts about a scarred hop-a-long? I wouldn't blame him, I thought, but I do wish I knew how he really felt.

As we reached the door to our rooms, I took a deep breath. "Coffee, Rob?"

He nodded. "That would be nice, Susie. I'll be back in a minute."

He swiftly disappeared into his own room and I could only chuckle, he clearly was not operating on four cylinders at that moment. Just as confused or just worried about telling me he didn't want a relationship with me?

I set about making the coffee and took the mugs back into the suite's lounge area. I was just in time, putting them down on a table when Rob appeared. If I had been even a few seconds later I think I might well have dropped them. Although he had donned his dressing gown it was open and, apart from his briefs, he was wearing nothing at all. I could clearly see his stoma bag. Was he worrying that I would be put off by that? Oh, Rob, I thought, that is as daft as it gets but does it mean you do want more?

"Sophie, oh lord, I called you Susie again didn't I, sorry. Look I wanted to be as open as you were about your body. You can't avoid Ken, it's too obvious and it wouldn't be fair on you to face it, if you wanted more than we have now. If you do. I mean." He stuttered. "Am I making too much of it, Sophie. I mean tell me if you want me to get lost, I'd understand."

Tell him to get lost? There I was worrying, that he didn't want me, and he's scared I'll throw him out, as it were. Are we two mixed up people or what?

"Rob, I think I might want more but can we take our time? Step by step?"

He nodded and, I think, was about to head back into his room for clothes. I couldn't have that I wanted to feast on his taut physique. I took my mug and leant back cuddling up. It wasn't any more than that and, well, a few kisses.

The next day we parted, Ginny and I for The National while Rob looked for another club with practice facilities. Steven went off on one of his mystery errands for Ginny.

It was a busy day and, in its way, enthralling. Remember, I told myself, there isn't a golfer in the world who wouldn't pay a fortune to play here. Practice itself went well and I had a few laughs with others who had made the cut. The greens were lightning quick even though we were told they were not as fast as they would be later in the week for the Major.

We were on the last hole of our round, my round as Ginny reminded me, when the heavens opened. In a few seconds we were soaked through. Not sure I had ever been caught by such an instant weather event. To be honest I was certainly glad that we had started when we did. I wouldn't have enjoyed continuing in those circumstances.

We made the decision to simply take the available transport back to the hotel where we found the guys in the bar, where else, having coffees. They had not experienced any adverse weather, which was surprising, but that's life.

Ginny and I certainly needed to freshen up and to dry out for that matter and headed for our rooms. Steven was quick to follow Ginny but Rob remained sitting. I went back to ask why and he moved like a shot to join me.

Back in the room I went towards the shower before, turning back. "I'll only be a minute but...."

I left it in the air, if he wanted to, he could watch me but he might be wary, was this step a bit too quick for him? Was it too quick for me? I wasn't certain but I was increasingly feeling that I wanted to move faster. Within a couple of weeks, it was likely that we would be separated by an ocean. After the Masters I would be moving south to Texas while Rob would be heading home to England.

He did and, to my hidden delight, swiftly undressed and joined me in the shower. We took it in turns to soap each other and gradually other activities took us from the shower into the bedroom. I couldn't help but wonder in my mind. Was this right? Somehow, we managed to stop short at kisses and cuddles. It should have been frustrating but oddly seemed more satisfying that there were still other bridges to cross. At least it did for me and, I felt, Rob was in the same place.

Rob – that Night and After.

That evening we all had dinner at a nearby top-quality steakhouse. How Ginny had managed to get a table I have no idea, but the food was excellent and golf was relegated to a sideshow for a couple of hours.

Later, as Sophie and I reached the outer door to the suite she broke through my thoughts with the suggestion of coffee. An offer I gratefully accepted.

In the closeness of the elevator, I could not avoid her perfume or, for that matter her looks. I sensed that she was uncertain about things and to be honest I was trying to come to a decision as to whether I should try and take things forward. And I realised that I wanted to? Oh lord, what if she didn't? Was it too soon after her breakup from Richard? Was I wrong about how she felt? What if she really hated the idea of a Ken?

Sophie headed off to get the coffee while I went into my room. Even as I pushed the door to, I was stripping off and into the en-suite before I could change my mind. A few minutes later with Ken sorted and my gown loosely on me I went back into the lounge just as Sophie was putting the drinks down. She jumped and I smiled, if I'd been a moment or two quicker, I suspect she might have dropped them.

Then I realised that I had called her Susie again. She grinned at my apology. I think she knew I was confused. With a sense of inevitability, I told her that it was okay if she couldn't stand Ken. Then I thought, was I expecting too much, perhaps she really did just want to be a friend and nothing else. I stuttered over a few words before stopping and looking at her in desperation.

"Rob, you are daft. You look at me and say I look great and then you are scared I couldn't cope with you not having all your tummy. I think you have a gorgeous body and good looks and you look as if you'd make a good lover." She paused. "I think I would like something more than just a friendship but can we take it one step at a time?"

I think my heart missed several beats. You just need to be patient, Rob, don't rush things. I nodded and then got up to go to put some more clothes on. "Don't, Rob, you've nothing to hide. Let's just have our coffee before sleep takes over. Oh, you can kiss me, if you want."

If I want, oh yes please, I thought, as I leaned over.

I had had many kisses by Teri and, before her, Annie. That first real kiss with Sophie seemed far more special and, as she cuddled up against me with her coffee in her hand, the day was one to remember.

For me the Sunday was just a time to visit the local golf club's practice facilities, I had to remind myself that the Masters was less than a week away but practice there would not start until Tuesday. And Sunday practice for Sophie and the other competitors was behind closed doors.

Despite occupying myself with practice I had one worry about later in the week. I still hadn't found a caddy.

Back at the hotel the afternoon dragged until the return of Sophie and Ginny both looking a little bedraggled. "We managed to get hit by another of the local downpours, too late for waterproofs so we stayed wet!"

Ginny's explanation had Steven, who had only just returned himself, looking bemused. "I saw a few dark clouds earlier but not a drop of rain. Local must really mean local here."

"Well, we two need to freshen up, then dinner, then an early night." Sophie nodded. "The weather forecast is not good, so they have brought forward the tee times. I was expecting to be off just before eleven but they've decided to split the field between first and tenth tees and start an hour earlier. I'm off at around eight. From the first, I'm glad to say."

With that the two headed up to their rooms, Steven followed Ginny but, at first, I stayed in the bar. A moment after she had vanished Sophie reappeared. "Aren't you coming up, Rob?"

I was on my feet and almost chasing her to the elevators before it hit. One step at a time? What happened during the next hour was wonderful.

The Ladies Amateur at The National.

The weather forecast and radar warned of storms in the afternoon and the organisers had, the night before, decided to split the field with the bottom half starting on the tenth. Was I glad that I was starting on the first and would have the time to adjust before we reached Amen Corner.

The round started steadily, for me, with four pars before I made the move, as the commentators would put it, two birdies at the fifth and sixth and I was up to the top. More pars followed and thanks to Ginny's input I managed to avoid a bogey before the twelfth, Golden Ball. That dangerous par three over the water has finished many a round over the years and it is not difficult to understand why.

During my practice round I had managed to hit and stay on the green but now it was for real and there was a strong gusting wind. I watched as my playing partner struck what looked like a six-iron. The shot was good but it became clear she had over clubbed and she found the back bunker. Horrible.

After some thought, at least as much as was allowed, I took my seven-iron and hit a delightful shot, delightful that is until it hit the green and I watched, in horror, as the ball spun back down the slope and dropped into the front bunker. With a bogey looking likely, I was not happy. Ginny had to remind me that my sand shot was at least on to a green that sloped upwards and made my shot easier.

She was, as ever, correct. Jenny played a great sand shot but could only watch the ball finish in the fringe over twenty foot from the pin. I was able to look at trying to hole my sand shot without too much risk. I didn't, of course, but left a putt of only five or six feet for par. Five or six feet, Ginny reminded me, is no gimme at

Augusta but I kept my cool and sank it. Jenny was not that lucky and three-putted to drop out of the lead.

Steady play brought me one more birdie and by the time I reached the eighteenth tee I was feeling as positive as I can remember. If I was right, I was leading! Then I saw a leader board. Someone called Bull had set a clubhouse score one better than my own current score. Ginny saw that as well and her remark would remind me of her approach. "Nothing to lose, Sophie. Go for it."

A birdie three, ten minutes later, and I was into a play-off with, and now I realised who it was, Anna!

Anna had naturally had time to adjust to the idea of playing me in a sudden death and was ready and waiting. I had barely time to take a comfort break after the usual routine of scorecard checking and signing before we were being driven back to the seventeenth for the first extra hole.

For the first time I found the crowd more partisan than ever with the cheers for Anna being muted for me. Good tee shots set us off and the play-off was underway and continued hole after hole. We halved the seventeenth and eighteenth – twice. After that we went to the sixteenth, another famous par three. Anna struck her best shot of the day leaving her ball only a couple of feet from the hole. Mine was almost twenty feet away.

Faced with an almost certain birdie, I hit what seemed to be the perfect putt. For an age the ball rolled end-over-end. Then, as it started to drop into the hole, to the disbelief of all watching, it rolled round the back of the hole before climbing up and out again to stop hanging on the edge.

A few moments later Anna completed her birdie and I had lost.

I know I had finished as runner-up in one of the biggest amateur tournaments but, somehow, not winning hurt more, even with Anna's commiserations as I congratulated her. Her admission that she had been lucky didn't help either.

I was down when I got back to the hotel and went to my room to try and come to terms with the sense of so-near-yet-so-far. I knew others considered my finish as unlucky but I couldn't help but feel that that was the problem. My lucky run was over. I knew I wasn't as good as they kept telling me but just maybe I had had a tinge of hope that I could make it.

I must have spent an hour wallowing in self-pity and hating myself for it. Why do we have such inconsistent emotions? Why couldn't I just feel good about finishing second?

Eventually, there was a knock on my door and Rob appeared, clearly concerned that I had not joined them in the bar.

"Sophie, you should be proud of what you did. You know that no golfer wins every week. Now buck up. Quick now, freshen up then we can go and celebrate."

I looked at him. I hadn't seen him in that sort of mood and it shook me that he could care enough to risk my anger at being told off when all I really wanted was to be held. By him.

"Oh, Sophie. Come on, you'll win again. Now, we can spend some time together later but we can't leave Ginny and Steven to finish all the wine that's awaiting you." He leaned forward and kissed me. He still wanted me – even after I had lost!

From the side lines again.

Monday had dawned warm and sunny but the forecast did suggest isolated storms in the afternoon and it looked as if the organisers would be proved wise.

The morning remained fine as Steven and I followed Sophie and Ginny round the course. It was, though, a day of tenterhooks. At the start it was clear that any one of six or seven players might win, including Sophie, of course, but as time passed no-one could break away from the pack.

Finally, the game reached the eighteenth tee. By this point Bull had finished and had posted a superb score, one ahead of Sophie. "Come on, Sophie!" I shouted, unable to suppress my nerves. As we watched it became obvious that she and Ginny had seen the nearby score board and knew what was needed. Out came the driver, no playing safe now, and the ball flew down the centre of the fairway setting up her second shot perfectly. She needed a birdie and, my new love, got just that.

What was I thinking about at that moment? I do not in all truth know. My emotional charge from seeing her respond to the challenge just said it. I was in love again.

Sophie and Anna had clearly gained mutual respect at the Amateur Championship in that enthralling final. I hadn't seen it but had heard enough tributes to understand that their golf had been of the highest standard. Now they had to go head-to-head in a sudden death play-off.

Well death there was but it wasn't sudden. Four holes shared before the officials took the two teams back to the sixteenth tee, for the first time. Both the girls hit excellent tee shots but Anna's finished only a few feet from the hole, while Sophie faced a twenty foot plus putt across the slope.

Steven and I had managed to reach a point on the opposite side of the water opposite the pin. We could see that in true matchplay Anna's putt would have been conceded. Not in a play-off, though. I could barely watch as Sophie walked back and forth across the green trying to get the right line for her effort. This had to go in. I am not sure that I have been so tense watching a golf shot in my life. After what seemed to me to be a lifetime Sophie finally stroked the ball over the green and into the hole .... and out again!

"I don't believe it, that ball went into the hole and somehow climbed back!" Steven's shock was also apparent. For me it all came down to the fact that a cruel reaction of ball and hole meant that Sophie had been beaten after a storming effort by Anna.

Anna still had to sink her two-footer for the title but duly did that before the two girls embraced.

We were all a little miserable as we made our separate ways back to the hotel. I guess to say miserable is to overstate it, Sophie had finished runner-up in one of the biggest amateur tournaments. We should have been pleased for her but when the gap between first and second proves so small, it isn't easy. More importantly it was clear that Sophie had taken it badly, muttering that she had told everyone she had just been having a run of good luck and now that run was over. It was ridiculous, of course, no-one performs like she does just by luck but I was finding it hard to pick her up.

After we got back to the hotel, we split up agreeing to meet back in the bar in an hour. In the suite Sophie shut herself in her room and I bowed to the inevitable wait. If she needed space then that was fine.

An hour and a half later, I decided enough was enough. Sophie needed a gentle kicking. If she took exception and wanted to kick me out. Oh shit, dare I risk that? I must. Sophie must realise that we all care about her and that we all know how good she is. Damn it, if we had offered her runner-up before the start, I am sure she would have bitten our hands off. She's done great, but Ginny has said it. She has no confidence in herself.

Deep breaths, Rob. Here we go.

And I tapped on the door, opening it without waiting for an answer. Sophie was curled up on the single chair in her room and was clearly in a real downer. I had a go at her and told her she needed to freshen up before Steven and Ginny drank all the wine or whatever they had on the table. She didn't look happy but nor did she lose her rag with me. I lifted her up and kissed her, before she went into the ensuite, with, I thought, a little more bounce in her walk.

We went down to join the others with Sophie in a somewhat better frame of mind and, in the end, it was a good evening. Later was better.

Disaster.

My first proper practice session for the Masters went well though Sophie's warning that the greens really were as fast as everyone claimed proved more than true. The next day, when the rest of the professionals arrived would be busier and probably more difficult and, of course, the paying public would be present for the first day. I would be there mixing with the top players for the second time, though, how could I complain!

Steven and I got back to the hotel to find builders working to repair damage to the roof over the hotel entrance and, in the suite, a totally distraught Sophie. Ginny had had to return home. I wasn't sure that she was very happy that Steven had wanted to stay and caddy for me. Steven had said she would be back for the Chevron in two weeks' time but I knew that Sophie would be missing her. I didn't think it would be that bad.

"Sophie, what's up?" I couldn't think of anything else to say.

"It's my clubs!"

"Your clubs?"

She crossed the room and pulled her golf bag from behind a table. I gasped. The bag must have been crushed in some way and the clubs, well the clubs looked as if someone had taken a hammer to them.

Speechless, I looked at Sophie who answered my unspoken question.

"I was waiting for a cab when a tourist coach backed into the building. It brought down a part of the entrance and then, I think, it ran over my clubs. They're wrecked. Every shaft snapped except for my putter. What am I going to do?"

I had to simply hold her as her tears flowed. What could she do? How could I help? Replacing the shafts was certainly possible but we couldn't go home and I doubted that they would be worth repairing in any of the nearby golf shops, I had seen the prices charged for other items. A second-hand set might have been possible for an average golfer but I was looking at a seriously top player, however much Sophie might disagree. Then it sank in - top player - and I knew what we had to try.

"Come on, Sophie. We are going back to the golf course; I have an idea."

She looked at me wondering if I had lost my marbles or something similar and maybe I had but, as much as it might have been a crazy idea, there was one possibility that could save the day.

Rescue.

With Rob off to his first practice session, with Steven. I wanted to be active so I started out to the golf club we had played at before. Outside the hotel I waited for a cab to arrive when to my astonishment a coach reversed into the canopy over the entrance area bringing down a part of the roofing. I managed to jump clear but my clubs and the bag were hit by falling concrete. When I reached the bag, after the dust had settled, I found to my horror that it had been ripped in half and every one of the club shafts snapped in two. Only my putter had, by some miracle, survived.

My initial reaction was to scream. Then I started trying to find a local golf shop that might be able to replace the shafts. With the help of Scott, I found two but neither reckoned they would be able to get replacements immediately. One offered to provide replacement clubs but the price was so far from my ability to pay that it was impossible, even if my travel insurance covered it and I wasn't sure about that. With no hope of replacing the clubs, so far as I could see, I crept back to my room and curled up in misery.

I was still there when Rob returned clearly happy with how his first practice session had gone. Happy that is until he saw me.

The first thing he did was to pick me up and cuddle me, Lord I must have looked a mess. Then he demanded to know what the problem was. To say he was shaken probably understates his reaction. Was I okay? Had anything hit me? After I had eased his worries in that sphere, I showed him my clubs. He nodded as I told him how I was struggling to find anywhere to repair them.

He sat there thinking for what seemed forever, although it probably wasn't more than a few minutes before he stood up. His next words confused me but he made it clear. We were going back to the National. He wouldn't explain beyond the fact that he had had an idea.

The cab to the course did not take too long, most of the traffic was going the other way, leaving as the day's practice was coming to an end. It took a few minutes for Rob to convince the gate staff to let us in but his players pass finally did the trick and he carried my bag, as carefully as he could, leading me towards the commercial area.

It took another few minutes before he found the marquee that was advertising the wares of the manufacturer of my clubs. What was he thinking about?

With the crowds slowly dispersing there was no-one occupying the salesmen and Rob went up to one, explaining the events of the morning and my problem – could they fit new shafts? Before the Chevron Championship?

"Let me see, Miss Jordan." He took one of the irons and studied what was left of the shaft and clubhead for several minutes. "Miss, these are a very old set are they not?"

"I have had them for five years and I think they were end of range at the time."

"You aren't serious, Sophie, if I may call you that? You took Anna Bull to a play-off using a design that old? That is amazing. The trouble is that they are so old I am not sure we can easily refit them. Even here I will have to order the older fittings."

He went to a computer and started doing a search when, of all people, Rory McIlroy came out of a back section.

To my surprise he noticed us and turned with a beaming smile. "If it isn't Sophie Jordan! Young lady, very well done! And you, too, Rob."

To say I was stunned is to say the least. This was a multi-major winner congratulating me. Oh wow, Sophie, he's one of your heroes and he's saying well done. Has he just confused me with someone else?

As I stood there speechless, Rory noticed my bag of clubs and we had to explain again what had happened. Rob interceded to say that we had been hoping the team could help but they were struggling to find an answer. Rory turned to the salesman and quietly asked if they could do anything? And if not why not?

When he got the same answer, that we had, he looked astonished. "Eight-year-old clubs and still plays like a world number one?" I heard him gasp before having another quiet word the end of which I did hear. "... anyone moans put it on my account. You have the chance to pick up a future top player and sponsor her clubs in a year or so."

Turning to me he asked. "When are you going to turn professional, Sophie?"

"I'm, I'm not sure I'm good enough but if I do, well, it might be after the Open at Birkdale." I think I said as I stuttered at the idea.

"Good. Now you sit down with Tony here and he will fit you out with new clubs, compliments of our team. Fitted and ready by the end of the week. That'll give you a couple of weeks to get used to them."

I think I was about to collapse. He was arranging for me to have the most up to date clubs! And paying for them, in some way. I tried to control my tears.

"That. That. That. I can't take that. I couldn't repay you."

"Repay me? Sophie, these guys will be rushing to join the queue when you turn pro. Just let them have first chance to add you to their list of top players. They'll treat this as an investment in you. Won't you Tony?"

Tony nodded with a smile. "He has a habit of seeing the big picture and, yes, let's get to work."

The next hour or so was quite unbelievable. Modern ball tracking technology and other equipment, I couldn't put a name to, was used to build a picture of my ideal clubs. As the sky darkened with sunset, Tony finally decided that they had got everything as right as it could be.

"Right, Sophie, come back Friday morning and we will complete the process. Cheer up, these will take your game to another level." He paused. "If that is possible. I googled your career and wow. Do we know how to build clubs that last." He grinned, before turning to Rob. "You're Rob Ward aren't you. Sophie's opposite number. British Amateur Champion, as she is. Think of us if you are looking to change your clubs, Rob, when you turn pro and good luck this week."

We left the marquee still in a state of slight disbelief. What am I saying? Rob believed when I could never have. I really owed him for that idea and his support, didn't I. Yet I suspected he wasn't looking at it that way. It didn't matter, I did.

Back at the hotel, we found Steven wondering where we had been and still intrigued by the damage to the hotel front. Explanations followed over beers and, in my case, a large glass of wine. His response was definitive. "Bloody hell, you got Rory to help out!"

We had to explain that it wasn't really that way but I did wonder if anything would or could have happened without his intervention. At the same time, I realised that I would need to call Ginny the next morning and then, Alan. He had always provided my clubs and I hoped he would be able to accept that that part of our relationship might be over. I know it sounds crazy. That he might object to my getting such clubs. But he was family and it mattered. Ginny might be concerned that this would impact her role as agent, I wasn't sure in what way, but this was all new to me.

After waking early, again, I made those phone calls. Alan was, I think, a little sad that his clubs had not survived, but over the moon that I was getting the latest model. At the last moment I decided that I would not let Ginny know yet, unless I was asked to enter any sort of deal.

I had tickets to the par three competition, a day of fun for the pros, serious fun but nevertheless they were out to enjoy themselves.

Before heading to the course, I spent some time practicing on a local putting green. I found myself surrounded by a group of girls fascinated by what I was doing and I enjoyed showing them. Maybe one day one or more might become pro golfers and I hope that then they might remember that hour. Oh, and there were the selfies and autographs! It had only taken one to recognise me and all piled in with pens and paper and mobiles!

Joining the crowds, I was able to wander the course unrecognised for hours absorbing the atmosphere. Then I bumped into Anna, like me she had stayed on to watch the tournament, and we had a little more fun talking and discussing the various players before I invited her to join us for dinner. Her delight made it worthwhile as I sensed a friendship growing that might last for a long time to come.

Friday and this would be a crucial day both for Rob and me. Overnight he was the leading amateur and in the top forty overall. He didn't expect to repeat that performance and it was my turn to tell him that all he needed to do was play sensibly and he would make the cut. His tee time was mid-afternoon and he was not planning to leave until later that morning. I decided to go ahead as I really wanted to find out if I had a new set of clubs or if I still needed to wait.

This time I had to join the queues as I did not have access to a player's pass but it was fun. Everyone was in good spirits looking forward to a day's memorable golf. Of course, play had been underway for almost two hours but that didn't appear to dampen the enthusiasm. The threat of rain was the subject of a few conversations that I could overhear. Augusta does seem to suffer from bad weather most years.

Although I tried to keep a low profile, I guess it was inevitable that someone would recognise me and programmes and other writing materials were soon out looking for an autograph. The best of this was that many of those asking were young children eager to record their meeting with a "real" golfer, pointed out by their parents. Me, a real golfer?

Once in the grounds I made my way through to the marquee area and went in, to be greeted not only by the sales guy, but by a director from head office. My initial sense of nervousness was soon settled by his warm, even effusive, welcome.

"Delighted to be of assistance, Miss Jordan. Amazing that you have been able to perform so well with such old clubs. I take that as a compliment to the quality of our manufacturing process. Tony tells me you expect to turn pro later this year. When that happens, we will be delighted to talk to you, or your agent, about a future relationship. In the meantime, good luck at the Chevron. Tony will check out the new clubs with you. Don't worry, Tony, I'll cover for you until Becky gets back."

Tony took me into a different segment of the set-up and unveiled a new bag full of clubs. I had been so upset that day that I hadn't even thought about the need for a bag and this came as a welcome bonus. But how would I find the new clubs?

In short, the answer was – fantastic! The back area's tracker technology was brought into use and it was soon clear that I would need to adjust my club choices in future. The extra yardage and increased accuracy were clear even after only a few shots. I couldn't fault the equipment and said so. Tony's response.

"Good. Now go and play the Chevron like the pro you will be. Good luck, Sophie."

I left the clubs in the care of Tony and his team and went in search of lunch. By the time I had finished, Rob was on the practice range and having wished him good luck, I made my way down to the first green to watch the players coming through.

The Masters

The first day of competition had proved difficult. Gusting winds made scoring hard. In the end I managed to handle it well enough to avoid any real disasters finishing just the one-over-par. Surprising, to me at least, was that that score kept me in the top forty. Maybe I had a chance of making the cut. I had to remember that it was not an easy task for an amateur to achieve that target. Sophie, I knew, thought I was more than good enough but she didn't realise that I don't have that level of confidence in myself.

Friday – and I got a great start with a first hole birdie. The rest of the round was a bit up and down but I managed to move into the red with more birdies than bogeys. For me the highlight was the sixteenth where I almost holed my tee shot at that famous par-three. That the ball appeared to replicate that of Anna when she had beaten Sophie on the Monday added a sense of déjà vu but even if I didn't get my first ace it helped me to finish at two under the card, well above the cut line.

We had a good evening but I remember being concerned that I had to keep my focus. Top twenty-five would guarantee me an invite back next year, as an amateur or professional, if I could brace myself and make that jump.

We had been lucky with the weather but the forecast for Saturday was not good. Clear skies that morning heralded hope and I spent plenty of time on the practice green. Augusta greens are the most treacherous in the game and I wanted to try and maintain what had been a decent performance.

As the day developed the clouds had arrived and it was very dull as I reached the first tee. My playing partner went first and I followed with a good middle of the fairway drive. As we walked off the tee, the heavens opened and I mean that. Within a couple of minutes, quicker than we could get our waterproofs on, the torrent of water was flooding the greens and some fairways. It was inevitable and before I could play my second shot the siren went, stopping play. All that we could do was to go and mark our balls before retreating to the clubhouse.

Three hours later we returned to play in some of the worst conditions I can remember and scores suffered. I managed to avoid any terrible disasters but neither could I recover from the bogeys and I posted a seventy-six. Depressed by what I thought was a game killer, I was surprised to find that my round was far from the worst. Unfortunately, nor did it move me up the leader board. My dream of a top twenty-five finish was dead.

Back at our room, Sophie did her best to try and perk me up, pointing out that, whatever tomorrow brought, I had already won the prize for leading amateur but it wasn't enough. Sophie would, I had no doubt, be playing all the Majors all the time but I doubted that I would be good enough. Club professional, yes, but tour pro? That was a different kettle of fish.

I fear I was not good company that evening and left the others for an early night, not even waiting for Sophie. Back in my bed I cursed myself, you must stop being a self-pitying wretch, Rob. Just show them what you can do tomorrow. I tried but I cannot say that I had a good night.

Sunday dawned and what a change. Fantastic spring sunshine with nothing more than a breeze. I find it difficult to understand such extremes of weather but like most of the field took advantage. Scoring on this final day was better, almost across the board, which would have been depressing enough except that I was taking full advantage myself.

Back in the clubhouse, I found that I had posted one of the best rounds of the day if not the best. I could see that it wouldn't be sufficient and I felt my spirits drop. Only Sophie grabbing me for a hug helped, as she and Steven, well pleased with how I had played, dragged me off for some food. That was good in as much as I had to wait for the leaders to finish and the prize giving. Something of a boost to my emotions as the pros themselves added their congratulations on my winning best amateur and on my final round score – second best of the day.

I think Steven summed the day up with, what I had to admit, was a pointed comment. "Rob, you showed today that you are not out of place on the course among the world's best players. You'll be back one day."

Dinner was a mixture of emotions as the others tried to lift me until eventually, with apologies to Steven for leaving him, Sophie pulled me to the elevator and back to the suite. Once in the room, she pulled me into an embrace with a kiss and then pointed me in the direction of my ensuite with words that almost stopped me in my tracks. "Rob, go freshen up and then I want to see that little boy of yours!"

She had vanished into her bedroom, before I could say anything, but left her door ajar. The invitation was transparent and I was ready and back there as quick as I could move. As I went to enter Sophie's room I hesitated. I knew what she wanted, I thought. Was I ready though? Then the truth sank in. Sophie had been the one to ask that we take our time, now she wanted to move on before, I thought, we both left Augusta for different destinations. I opened the door to see her coming out of her own ensuite. I still had my underwear and gown on which meant that I was rather overdressed, to say the least, and, oh boy, did she look wonderful.

I will remember the rest of that evening and night for a very long time. If Teri was driven and insatiable, well Sophie was gentle and as good a lover and when I finally fell asleep with her in my arms it was as deep and restful a night as I had had in months.

We did get down to breakfast the next morning but we were not exactly early and Sophie, god bless her, looked a bit windswept!

I was lucky that my flight home was the next day, most of the other golfers would be heading out for home or the next tour event that Monday and I had decided not to leave until the Tuesday which meant that, after Sophie had finished on the range, we were able to enjoy the afternoon together.

Tuesday came far too soon and we had to make our farewells as Steven and I both headed for home. Sophie would be flying south later and looked a little lost as she waved us off. I found myself texting her even before we had reached the airport. And missing her.

Au Revoir, Rob. Now for Houston and The Woodlands

As I had intended, after dinner, I apologised to Steven and practically dragged Rob to our rooms. Once in the main room I gave him a full-on kiss before telling him.

"Go get freshened up, Rob, then ......"

I dived into my room and, after stripping off, headed into the ensuite. I came back out as Rob, carefully opened my door before coming in. He stopped and, for a moment I feared he was having second thoughts, then he moved and we seemed to merge as one. What a night!

Thankfully Rob was not due to fly home until the Tuesday which gave us that day together before I was forced to wave him and Steven off to the airport.

I wasn't over the moon and I think that Rob realised it. His first text arrived before their flight was due to take off, in fact it might have been sent before they reached the airport. Truth was I was missing him far more than I could bear and we had only been together a few weeks! Why is it that love can hurt like that? And that was despite knowing that we would be together again in only three weeks' time, after I returned to England.

I had another couple of days before I was due to fly to Houston and I spent time on the hotel's driving range getting a better feel for my new clubs. I knew, intellectually at least, that the more modern clubs provide extra distance, while also being more forgiving of the errant swing. What I wasn't prepared for was the actual difference compared to my old clubs.

Tony had explained that there had been six updated versions released to the retail trade over the years since mine were first sold.

What he hadn't said, that was for his boss to tell me, was that these clubs I now had would not be released until later in the year.

Only their sponsored professionals had these and it had been Rory's suggestion, on the quiet, that I warranted getting them. Now I started worrying. What if I didn't manage to handle them? Would the difference be a negative? I mean, I know I'm only an amateur with some luck and there was Rory talking me into saying that I would turn professional after the Open. I should have told him differently, shouldn't I?

Two days later, I reached Houston, landing in a storm. Hotel and a rest, I told myself. No golf in this weather that was clear and, in any case, I had almost a week before the tournament got under way. Ginny was not arriving until the beginning of that week which left me to my own devices.

The hotel turned out to be another in the chain and I found myself enjoying another upgrade, this time to a senior suite! The downside, according to reception was that they did not have a separate room for Ginny. They hoped we would be prepared to share an even larger arrangement of rooms than in Augusta. Personally, I had no problem and I doubted that Ginny would.

Attached to the hotel was another golf course and practice area and, as a guest, I had free access to those facilities. The week passed, occupied by practice and more practice and I rarely left the hotel grounds. There were texts and calls with Rob, both video and ordinary calls. We did boost each other's spirits – Rob had confirmed he would be at home the week I got back and the fact that we only lived some thirty miles apart promised some good times together.

Other calls to my parents and from my brothers made me feel uneasy. Something was not quite right and no-one was telling me what. In the end I called Ginny and asked her to find out if anything was wrong. She couldn't help and I had to just keep nudging when I was talking to any of them. I didn't manage to talk much to my Dad but that wasn't unusual – he often left calls of any length to Mum.

A week on and Ginny arrived looking as well as I could remember her. She did moan a bit over dinner at my allowing Steven to stay and caddy for Rob and now he was stopping back in England. I do wonder why she feels I can control anyone, let alone a man as besotted with her, as I rather imagine Steven is.

I kept my little secret until the next morning when, before we went down to breakfast, I pulled my new bag out of the bedroom. Ginny looked at it in astonishment.

"What! Where? How? Why?" She stuttered. It made for an interesting discussion over the food, following which she summed it up in her inimitable fashion.

"Sophie, is there any chance that you will start believing in yourself? Do you imagine that someone like Rory McIlroy would pull those sorts of strings for any two-bit amateur? He must have seen enough of you to recognise your potential and your ability. Now, my friend, believe!"

Oh, Ginny, I thought, you don't change and I know you are probably right, but how can I prove it to myself?

We had one day around the hotel which helped Ginny adjust to the jetlag. Then two days of serious practice before the Chevron got underway. During this time, I became increasingly enamoured with my new clubs. Ginny, on the other hand, was struggling to adjust for the increased distances I could now achieve. She found it straightforward understanding my woods, which were allowing me to send the ball twenty-five yards or more further than before but my irons almost upset her.

Having demonstrated how the clubs were helping me, using tracker technology, I convinced her that I had built my confidence in their consistency to a point that meant that I was starting to feel far more positive about my game.

It took that first day for Ginny to suddenly understand how I felt. I smiled to myself. For me to be confident was so far from her view of me that she was finding it difficult to believe what she was seeing and hearing.

The Chevron.

First Ladies Major of the year and the weather supported the superb course and its surroundings. I had bumped into a few of the pros, I had played with at St Andrews during the practice rounds, playing one round with Ingrid who claimed to be enjoying seeing me play. Ginny commented later that Ingrid's caddy had muttered that that enjoyment was likely to be being spoken, through gritted teeth. He told Ginny that I had really given Ingrid a fright that she had not completely got over. I had not realised that the British Open was her first Major title and to come so close to losing it, well......

On the first day I played with two locals who had not qualified for the Open and had only seen highlights on television. They were very much up for the challenge on home territory and, I felt, seemed to consider that being drawn to play with an amateur was rather inappropriate and an English amateur at that. Eighteen holes later and they were, I think, gnashing their own teeth. Both had scored well, one finishing three under par and the other also in the red at one-under. Where they had difficulty was that **that** amateur had shot six-under without a bogey on the card. For the first time in my life, I walked from a course, during a tournament, feeling on cloud nine. The clubs had performed and so had my swing.

Back at dinner, with the golf channel broadcasting highlights, Ginny told me that she had heard a caddy comment, that metronomic was the only way to describe my swing that day. "I doubt that, Ginny, I think that they had other swings on their minds."

"Typical American television though," she commented, "no coverage of your round nor, it seems that of Ingrid or any other Europeans."

Day two was not quite as good. The weather had deteriorated with strong winds but I still avoided a bogey and there were two birdies. That was good enough to enable me to tie the lead. The overnight leader had had a bad second round. Ingrid was two back but I knew that she would remain a threat to anyone at or near the top of the leader board.

Even American TV couldn't ignore me now and I spent time being interviewed live. A second spell at the Sky cart followed and proved a much more relaxing session.

Saturday. Somehow things felt different. Everyone back home was exhilarated by my performance but I was becoming increasingly aware that I hadn't been able to talk with my Dad for nearly a week. He was always out or tied up at work and Mum didn't sound her usual good-natured self. Something was wrong and I knew it, I just didn't know what.

Ginny felt my unhappiness at the mystery and sought to reassure me. "Focus on the golf. That's what they want you to do. Do it for them and all will be well."

Despite having won several amateur tournaments, I had never actually played in the last group in a four-day competition. Now I learned that there is a little more pressure. To be honest, a lot more. With Ginny's help, I looked to filter out the crowd, a very partisan crowd at that. The others in the group, we were still playing in three balls, were both Americans and there was no doubt who the locals were supporting. In fairness, there was applause for my good shots, just a little muted and formal rather than the exuberant cheers when the others hit reasonable ones.

If you need to quieten a crowd then the best way is to play well or at least outplay the locals and I did just that. By the end of the round, I was twelve under par and three shots ahead of the field. Neither of the others would be in the final group on Sunday. That would be Ingrid, myself and a Canadian, Joanne. Oh, wow, I thought to myself. You are leading a Major after fifty-four holes. What is going on?

Sunday and I get off to the perfect start with a birdie at the first. I sense a feeling that the others are wondering what they will have to do to catch me and I freeze. Only Ginny can do what Ginny does, I thought, as she calms me down and I recover from my errant tee shot at the second to manage a par. That shock over, I continue to register par scores. Joanne, from Vancouver, I understand, and Ingrid manage birdies to reduce my lead to two by the turn but the back nine have been my favourite part of the course and I find the nerve to achieve two more birdies. Ingrid does close the gap but I go to the last hole knowing that, unless she manages an eagle, a par will be good enough. I had birdied the par-five three times already and went to the tee as confident as I have ever been.

This is for you, Alan, and everyone back home, I am thinking, as I launch a huge drive down the middle of the fairway. Ginny wants me to play safe and lay-up but, for once, I overrule her. Taking my three wood I drill my second to the back of the green. Ten minutes later and I can sink a short putt for my own eagle to win my first Major.

Joanne is gracious but withdrawn, having finished third. Ingrid hugs me. "There you go youngster, I knew you'd make it and I'm glad you are still an amateur, I'd be the poorer if you weren't. See you in France."

I knew my emotions would get the better of me and I almost collapse into Ginny's arms in tears. "Thank you, Ginny, I couldn't have done it without you."

From Elation to Despair - in moments.

Ginny hugs me hard before taking me to one side and to my shock produces her mobile. "Love, you will need to hold yourself together. There is someone on the phone who needs to talk to you. **Now.**"

"Sophie, you were wonderful. You have made me so proud of you, thank you." The voice was faint and the words spoken slowly, as if through a fog.

It is my Dad but I have never heard him talk that way, struggling to breathe and quiet. That wasn't him he was always happy, bright, and strong in his speech. He continued before I could talk.

"I am so sorry, love, the doctors tell me that I will not be able to last much longer. Look after your Mum and remember I love you – you are the star in my life."

"Dad, Daddy!" I can't control myself. "I love you. I'm coming home now. I didn't know. I would have been back if they'd told me. Oh God, don't die, Dad, I need you."

My Mum comes on the phone, I can almost feel her tears. "I'm sorry, Sophie. He wouldn't let us bring you back. He wanted to see you play one last time. You made him so happy. All your work over the years paying off with today's result." She stopped for a moment. "He's gone, my darling. Now, go and get your trophy. We'll see you later this week." She puts the phone down, as I slowly collapse to the ground, sobbing.

Amid my grief, I can hear voices asking if I am okay. Was it just the shock of winning the Major. Ginny explaining that I have only just learned that my father was dying. The tournament's organiser was left gasping.

"That is the worst news. If she wants to miss the award ceremony that will be perfectly all right. We can explain."

It is my turn to grit my teeth. That was not an option. Dad would be furious, if I missed it. I force my tears back and climb to my feet. "Sir, I need to freshen up but I will be there, if you can give me a few minutes. My father passed away a few moments ago. I can only give him credit for today."

He looks askance but nods. "I am truly sorry for your loss, Miss Jordan. Is there anything we can do?"

"Just get things ready. I am not sure how long I can keep strong."

He nods again and I have a sudden thought. "Sir, the best amateur award. Could that be given to whoever came second amateur?"

"Of course, that is most kind of you. I do not know if she is still here but it can be arranged."

Ginny took me into the changing rooms, making sure I was able to continue. In the privacy of the empty room, I fear I turned on her.

"How long, Ginny? How long have you known? Why didn't you at least tell me my father was so ill? I thought you were my friend." Even as I said it, I wished I hadn't. I knew she was only doing what my family had asked but it still hurt.

"I am sorry, honestly but your Dad told me himself, after he was told he didn't have long, that it was his dying wish to see you play in another Major. He knew that you would have dropped everything and gone home and that would have cost him the chance to see you win. You see, he always believed you would hit the top. You gave him that, Sophie."

I slowly nod and then hug her. "I'm sorry, Ginny, I know you did what he wanted. I didn't mean to blame you." I was back on the verge of tears but forced them back. "Let's go."

As we returned to the spot where the trophy was waiting, the sponsor's representative came over to congratulate me privately and to ask how I wanted to handle any announcement. "That is for me, Sir."

The first part of the ceremony involved the award to the best amateur, as I had asked, and that turned out to be Anna, I hadn't known but was really pleased. Then it came to me and my post-acceptance speech. I started by listing all those who should be thanked. The sponsor, the greenkeepers, the club, the volunteers, and finally the other players for their part. I finished with a final thank you.

"Everyone, I am sure you saw my tears at the end of my round and I am sorry for that. I want to dedicate this trophy to my father, who passed away shortly after I finished. He wanted to see me play and wouldn't let anyone tell me he was ill. He was my guide, my friend, as well as my Dad. I know he will be looking down on me from now on, but he won't be at home when I get back. There will be a big gap left in my life. All I can do now is to prove him right in how he saw me. Dad, this is for you. Thank you."

As I finish the tears return but I just let them pour down my face, as I raise the trophy for the cameras and the fans, whose applause is now deafening.

With everything over, Ginny and I headed back to our hotel where I received an ovation from the staff.

That evening I gave an interview to the New York Times as I had promised. It was more difficult but she left happy promising Ginny a copy before publication.

There was also a phone call, which I had not expected. Richard. I knew he would have been watching how I did but calls were not a part of it. The loss of my Dad pushed him, he said, to call. A text was not the way to offer support. He knew my parents and had admired my father. There were more tears but I just prayed that he would continue to challenge on the tour.

PART FIVE – ONWARDS.

Rob back home and watching Sophie.

I landed back at Heathrow to be met by Rachel and Colin. I had been expecting Susie and was initially worried that there was something wrong. That worry was not immediately reduced when Rachel said.

"Hi, Rob. Susie's sorry but she has had to go for a medical." She grinned, as only a wicked sister can, as she saw my face drop before putting my mind to rest. "Nothing to worry about. She's being signed up by one of the Women's Super League teams."

It took a moment for me to realise how good that was. Susie had always been sporty and had taken up football even before she was ten. She tended to underplay her sport but I knew she had been playing for one of the smaller teams in their Championship. Now she was moving into the WSL! That was a big step and would mean she would no longer be a part-timer. That move was the football equivalent of my turning pro and getting a Tour card – wow, was my secretive sister hitting the big time!

Colin, having congratulated me on winning best amateur, turned to Rachel. "We should be heading back home, love. Or do you want to give Rob, our news first?"

Now I found myself looking from one to the other in consternation. Was it good news or not so good. I found myself thinking that one possibility would be that I was going to become an uncle and I wasn't sure that would be good, for Rachel anyway.

Rachel repeated her wicked grin. "No, Rob, I can see you thinking you're going to be an uncle, but the truth is we aren't looking for children, not yet anyway. Our news is that we've both got jobs, working together!"

Now I was buzzing. "Where? You couldn't have hoped for better, could you?"

"On board one of the Caribbean cruise ships, that's where!" Her smile gave me a big boost at a time when I had been thinking about my Susie. Lord, there I go again.

As Colin drove us north towards home, Rachel quizzed me about that other golfer, Jordan.

"Look, Rob, you weren't very open about your time in the States before the Masters. You went to the Ladies Amateur, didn't you?"

I was startled. I hadn't told the family much about Sophie's competition but Rachel seemed to find that important, I wondered why. Before I could ask, Rachel smiled with a warmth that only my big sisters could get away with.

"I spotted you in the crowd during a highlights programme. There you were yelling at Sophie Jordan just before she teed off at the last hole. You seemed very excited and, dare I say, emotional. Then you were in the background when she lost and you did not look at all happy then. Come on, Rob. How come you know her?"

I spent a good part of the remaining journey telling of my amazing Sophie. About Rory's reaction. About her brilliance and how she had stolen my heart and how I was missing her.

Colin looked as if he was having trouble understanding how that could happen. He had met Teri, at Christmas, but was not, I thought, aware of the breakdown of that relationship. Rachel was, on the other hand, looking as pleased as punch.

By the time we got home I had already called Susie, only to get her voicemail, I left a message and settled back, waiting for Sophie. Oh my, now I'm confusing Susie with Sophie, not the other way round. The family had prepared a celebration for me and it was a few days before I was back to work on the range readying myself for the next amateur open in Scotland. Susie and I had a few hours of enjoyable chat about her success which gave me a sense of pride and I did manage to avoid calling her Sophie!

Sophie and I kept in close contact. Well, as close as you can over thousands of miles. Truth was the warmth of her smiles when on a video call was just not the same as when we were next to each other. Despite that I still found it hard to understand, myself, how I could have fallen for her in such a short time? It was even more difficult wondering. Why did she bother with me, at all. She could have anyone!

A fortnight later and the Chevron started. I was soon glued to the TV watching for any sign of that future superstar and rapidly becoming irritated by the failure of American coverage, which the UK TV channels relied on. There seemed to be no interest in non-Americans other than the top Koreans and Japanese. I was surprised that not even the Open champion was being shown.

Then, on the second day, Ingrid made a move to the top five which could not be ignored and some amateur had grabbed a share of the lead – my Sophie was up and kicking some butt, as the Americans would say!

By the end of the third day, Sophie had a three-shot lead and was playing golf without errors. Fifty-four holes without a bogey, this was brilliant golf.

We had limited ourselves to one call at the end of each day during the competition and in our call that night, Sophie sounded about as upbeat as I had ever heard her. She was going into that final round looking at how she could win it, not how she might blow it. I could only tell her to go for it, that I would be watching every minute until she picked up that trophy! She laughed at that but, this time, she didn't pooh-pooh the idea, just thanked me for the clubs!

The final day. And Sophie was playing with Ingrid and a Canadian in the final group! She started with a birdie to increase her lead to four shots then, on the second tee, something went wrong. Over the previous three days, the statisticians had recorded her as having hit forty of the forty-two fairways and the two misses had finished in the first cut, a quite amazing feat. This time her swing looked, well wrong, and her ball missed the fairway finishing in the trees. How Ginny did it I will never know but from those trees Sophie still contrived to hit the green in three, close enough for a par. I suspect her playing partners must have been inwardly cursing as what looked to be a certain bogey vanished into the distance.

By the turn, Ingrid had reduced Sophie's lead to just two and I began to fear that the experience of the World number one would put too much pressure on my love. I should not have feared for her. She held Ingrid off, matching birdies with birdies until the last hole.

With her lead still at two shots, if she kept her head, Ingrid would need an eagle. Kept her head? Ingrid would get a birdie but Sophie just blew the hole apart and finished with her own eagle to win the Major, and to do it as an Amateur!!

Truth was that I needn't have worried. Despite everything Ingrid could throw at her Sophie had remained almost icily calm for most of the round before that brilliant finish.

Then things went pear shaped.

With the mutual handshakes and hugs finished, I saw Ginny pass her mobile to Sophie. What on earth was she doing? That wasn't the place for a phone call! Then I could see Sophie shaking and starting to cry and as, I assumed, the call ended, she crumpled to the ground sobbing.

Fortunately, someone controlling the coverage switched to other scenes but it didn't help me. I found myself on the edge of tears, myself. What had happened to cause such distress?

The television commentators were also at a loss. A few tears, of happiness, were to be expected but this reaction to winning was clearly not that.

There was a lull of several minutes, covered by the usual talk while the experts waited for something to happen. Then the cameras switched back to the presentation ceremony. For some reason, best amateur was being awarded to Anna Bull, then it was time for Sophie. She looked ashen faced but resolute. Having been given the trophy in front of the crowd, which was uncharacteristically quiet, Sophie appeared to brace herself before making the usual speech of thanks to everyone involved. At the end of that, she paused, before dedicating the win to her father. The call had been with him and he had died just after she spoke to him.

I felt like collapsing in a heap. Of all the things that had happened to Sophie this must be the worst.

The next morning, we talked for some time. The previous night she had missed my call, being unable to talk to anyone, apart from her Mum. Ginny came on the phone to tell me that Steven would be collecting them from Heathrow and I was welcome to join him.

The meeting at the airport was subdued. Hugs and a kiss but little else. Sophie was still, I thought, in shock and grieving at a level that I could not reach. The only thing was that she appeared to find being able to cuddle up to me while Steven drove us home something of a relief.

Together Again but not for long enough.

By the next day, we were back in England. Steven was there to collect us from the airport and, wonder of wonders, so was Rob. The journey home was subdued but the comfort of Rob's strong arms, holding me, helped.

I entered the house to an almost silent room. Mum was sitting waiting while my brothers were both there as well. I felt that they might be expecting me to be angry but that emotion had drained out of me on the long flight back. My Dad would have been the force that protected me, as he would have seen it. How could I blame the rest of the family.

Unlike my earlier wins there was no celebration and we simply helped each other as much as we could while we prepared for the funeral. Even when I went to the club the congratulations were muted with many hugs but no loud cheers. Alan and James had been in touch with the family and followed that up with briefings to the staff. All the members had been informed of my loss and were asked to give me space.

During that time, I did not, for the first time in years, spend much time practicing. I could not focus on the game and Alan suggested that that would be the case until after Dad's funeral. I knew that he had been hit hard by the loss of someone who had become a close friend, from that time, almost thirteen years before, when he had first asked for permission to take me on as his protege and it seemed to hurt more when I saw my friend and mentor in such distress.

Funnily though, it was James who seemed hardest hit, even though he had only met my parents, at the Amateur Championship, the year before. It would be some time before I found out why.

The funeral took place on a Friday, three weeks after Dad had passed away. What astonished us all, were the numbers of people who attended. Dawn's parents were among them, unsurprisingly, as they and my parents had become quite close after that fateful night and it was good to see them, even on such a sad occasion.

That evening, Chrissie and I, spent some time together at her flat. Kate was on duty and had been unable to be at the church. Chrissie was excited to hear more about Rob, it seemed that someone had seen us together in Augusta and jumped to a conclusion, duly leaking it on Facebook to a group that Kate was a member of. I had to admit that the conclusion was not without substance and promised to introduce him once we had got together again.

I didn't tell her how much I was missing him. Rob and I had limited ourselves to calls and texts during the run up to the funeral. Perhaps, I should have invited him to the funeral but it seemed a little unfair as he would have known no-one except for Ginny and Steven. I had promised him that we would be able to meet up the day afterwards but the devil in him changed that. What I did not realise was that he had been at the church keeping a low profile and I had not been the best hostess at the wake afterwards.

Bernard, the elder of my protectors, as they sometimes liked to call themselves, had recognised him. I'm not sure, even now, just how much golf my brothers watch, on the quiet as it were, but it was enough for them to have seen Rob winning the Silver Medal.

While I was off with Mum and William, my other sibling, Bernard had got Rob a drink and grilled him. What was he doing at the funeral? How did he know me? Bernard, reasonably, assumed that it had to me that Rob knew and wanted to understand what that meant. I wish I had been there to defend him but it seemed that he did a good enough job on his own, to the extent that when I got home, from Chrissie's, there was Rob waiting for me, flanked by my brothers, and talking with my Mum.

My initial reaction was anger. He should have told me! Then it sank in. He was missing me as much as I was him and all I wanted was to feel his arms around me. I crossed the room pulled him out of his chair and kissed him long and hard. I am not sure who was more startled, my brothers or my Mum.

In the next few minutes, I made it clear that Rob was staying the night – with me. There was some banter between me and my brothers who warned Rob, if he were to make me unhappy. My Mum looked happier than she had since I got back from the States and nodded in support of me.

I let Rob fetch his case. Sensible fellow, I thought, and took him up to my room. I was lucky, in that I had the larger of those rooms in our house. Bernard had moved out after uni and was living with his boyfriend. Sometimes things work out in unexpected ways.

I had had a small double bed since I lost my leg, the idea was that I would be less likely to fall without my prosthetic on, if there was more room. Now I could use it as most doubles are used! We did try to be as quiet as possible and, to be fair, no-one complained the next morning.

After breakfast, Rob told me that he was hoping I would travel back with him to his home so that he could introduce me to his family. Being the weekend, he was expecting both of his sisters and his parents to be there and he had already had to explain to them, how we had met.

We set off after lunch taking the journey slowly so that we had a little more time to ourselves.

When we arrived, I was welcomed with a warmth as good as I might have expected back home. Rob introduced Rachel and her fiancé, Colin, who were packing before flying to their new jobs in the Caribbean. Then he turned to Susie, my alter ego in a way, and announced that she had just been signed by a leading Women's Super League team.

Susie, he said, would be a Lioness before we could blink an eye and I am afraid that the rest of the family suffered a degree of neglect as the two of us lost ourselves in sport. Susie was in awe of my success and played down hers, but then don't we all. She and her twin are real beauties and I still don't see why Rob thought I reminded him of them. It didn't matter, they were both good fun.

Rob's parents were also welcoming but a little concerned, I thought, at the speed of our romance. We both had to explain that things were as they are for reasons that even we could not wholly understand but that it felt more than right to both of us.

They did point out that we would need the strength to handle periods of absence. Even without being experts on how the tours operated they identified that we would be likely to be in different parts of the country or even in different countries a lot of the time. I saw Rob smile as he looked at me and my heart fluttered again. Distance was not good but I did not think it would be the fatal aspect I had feared. I hoped.

Monday morning came too soon and Rob took me home. He was off to Scotland and I was heading to Portugal for a tournament on the Algarve. The thought of going to that part of the world brought a wry smile to my face as I remembered the Heathrow check-in.

And our first real separation began.

Meeting the Families.

The next few weeks were tough. Sophie was tied up with the rest of her family preparing for the funeral and we were forced to limit ourselves to a video call and a few texts each day. She didn't want me to go but, at the last minute, I decided that I would slip into the back of the church, unannounced, and then keep a low profile at the wake.

In my innocence, I thought I could remain out of the picture. Only Steven and Ginny would recognise me and they could be trusted to ignore me. Then, afterwards, I would try and comfort Sophie.

All went well at the church. The family were, naturally, pre-occupied and that continued at the wake. Sophie hardly left her mother's side and much of the work chatting to guests fell to two men, a little older than me, whom I guessed were her brothers. Then disaster hit.

Bernard, as I found out, looked across to the corner where I was trying to be invisible and after a moment walked over to my table. "Don't I know you? Wait a minute, Silver Medal at the Open and best amateur at The Masters? Rob Ward, that is you, isn't it?"

I could hardly deny it and he started to dig a bit further, to my chagrin. "You know our Sophie then? She hasn't mentioned you but then things haven't been normal."

I was forced to explain, over another drink, about how we came to know each other. At the same time, I admit to limiting how much detail I provided.

"You came to see our Sophie?" Bernard sounded more appreciative than accusing. "You'd better come back home and meet the rest of the family. Sophie's gone. Spending some time with her best friend, Chrissie, but she won't be late."

The next couple of hours were surprisingly pleasant. When I look back, did it help Sophie's mother to have a stranger to talk to about her Dad? I don't know but I was certainly made welcome.

We heard her come through the front door with a call of. "I'm home! Sorry, Mum, I didn't mean to be ...." She stopped talking as she came into the room to find me sitting between her brothers who both had grins a mile wide.

Bernard spoke first. "Hi, sis. This guy claims he knows you. We thought we should keep him here until you were back. Now, what should we do? Kick him out? Lead him to door, nicely, and then kick him out? Or should we make up the spare room?"

Sophie looked at her brother and very quietly replied. "Bernie, you want to live a long and prosperous life? Then you'd better let Rob alone or else!"

She crossed the room and pulled me to my feet which made her hug and long kiss much easier. I rather think that that sent a clearer message to the family that she wanted me to stay and not in the spare room! She turned to her mother. "Mum, this is Rob. He is special. He's going to be around a lot."

Her Mum smiled gently. I think that my appearance gave her an emotional boost on what I knew had been a difficult day for her and everyone else. "Rob, you clearly make Sophie happy and that means you can come here, whenever."

"But, Rob." William injected, with a smile. "If you make her unhappy.... start running!"

For a moment, I thought Sophie was going to hit him. "Will, shut it. Please. You frighten Rob off; you'll answer to me! Mum, sorry but Rob is coming upstairs with me."

Her Mum smiled and then chuckled, happier, I suspect than she had been since they had lost Sophie's Dad. "See you in the morning, both of you."

Sophie left me for a moment and went to give her Mum a hug and a kiss and I heard her whisper. "Thanks, Mum. Love you."

That night was special on a different scale, but I did get a right telling off in private. Sophie was adamant I should have warned her. Sophie agreed to let me take her back home to meet my family. Although we only lived some thirty miles apart, we managed to take most of the day to reach my home.

The evening was great, I had warned my parents and they, and the girls, gave Sophie as warm a welcome as they could. Not too surprising, I guess, was that Susie and Sophie, got on like a house on fire – a case of top sports people having things in common. Not that Susie considered herself at Sophie's level but clearly Sophie was more than impressed that she might be talking to a future international footballer!

Rachel, and Colin, were equally impressed though I fancy they were a little bemused that we had fallen for each other in the way we had.

The rest of the weekend passed all too quickly before I had to deliver Sophie back home on Monday morning. She would be preparing for a trip to Portugal for a tournament there while I was heading north for the Scottish Amateur Championship.

She was also a little upbeat for another reason which niggled me. Her ex, Richard, had won his first Korn Ferry Tour event and that success had her on a high. I knew that they were no longer in a relationship but that she felt so pleased for his success seemed a little wrong.

Portugal and then the Amateur.

The following weeks passed quickly. Portugal was warm and the golf superb even before the Championship held at Vilamoura.

The Old Course is called that as it is the second oldest course on the Algarve. A mature course it lends itself to a challenging three rounds of golf. Unlike many amateur championships this was a stroke-play competition throughout, which played, I believe, to my strengths. It is not the biggest competition and I found that none of those players I would have recognised were there.

Warming up on the first day, I suddenly stopped. Was I really feeling confident about my chances? That wasn't me but then this was a competition more in my comfort zone, I told myself.

Despite that positive feeling, I did not have it all my own way, there were, of course, very good golfers as demonstrated by the leader after day one. She shot eight-under-par on, it turned out, her home course. Three shots back, I was in a pack of players on five-under.

It was funny but, for once, I seemed to be under the radar of the field. No-one apparently had linked me with my win at the Chevron and I was able to enjoy playing with less pressure.

Day two and I hit the front! This time it was my turn to shoot sixty-four and take the overnight lead at thirteen-under. Now my past caught up with me. Both my playing partners on that day had recognised me and they made it clear that they weren't happy that I was playing in **their** little competition. Little? I still find that hard to understand. I mean it was the Portuguese Amateur Open!

A year before, that attitude might have caused me a problem but now, I found, it simply made me more determined. Within three holes my two-shot lead was up to five, two birdies and an eagle did at least quieten their mutterings. I simply played steadily from then on finishing with a round of seven-under and the best three round total I had ever achieved – twenty-under-par. Sadly those two players decided that ignoring me, beyond the briefest of handshakes, was their only way of objecting.

Fortunately, the local sponsor was more than happy to have a Major winner competing and winning. No such thing, I recognised, as bad publicity.

I returned home just in time to see Rob, before he left for the continent himself. We had two days together, staying at his home. His parents were away for a long weekend and we had the house to ourselves. The trouble was that despite the joy of seeing him, I was struggling with the fact that he would be gone, again, and I wouldn't see him until after the Amateur Championship. I took the opportunity to spend every minute, I could, with him before we had to split. Me heading to a competition in Wales, while he headed for Germany.

Over that last breakfast we discussed our plans and Rob admitted he had decided to turn professional after The Open. He no longer felt able to keep living off his parents and had not been able, despite Ginny's help, to find a sponsor. I offered to help, I now had four sponsors which meant that I was able to even save some money despite the travelling costs.

"Sophie, you are putting off the inevitable." Rob smiled at me.

I groaned inwardly. He was right, as was Ginny. It made no sense to stay an amateur. Even I had begun to feel that I could at least make a living on the Tour.

June came and with it a trip to the Belfry for a chance to defend the Amateur Championship. As the defending champion I was not worried by the pre-qualifying which was just as well, The weather was foul to say the least and I was only too pleased to not have to play before the Monday.

It is rare for anyone to retain the Amateur title and I did not prove the exception. The two days of stroke-play went well and I finished in the top four. The early rounds of the matchplay were straight forward and, for me, finished with three or four holes to spare, The semi-final was different, Francine was back and playing better than I remembered. This time we ended up playing extra holes and it was the end of my defence. I could not match her birdie at the twenty-first hole and bowed out.

It did not hurt as much as I thought it might. A year before I would have just shrugged my shoulders and told Ginny, there you are, told you I wasn't that good. Now I just needed to get my head together and prepare for the trip back to the States for the US Open.

Two weeks later and Ginny dropped a bombshell.

"Sorry, Sophie but I won't be coming to the States with you and, even if I did, I wouldn't be able to caddy."

I just looked. What was wrong? Ginny chuckled, recognising my concern.

"Don't worry. It isn't bad news, not for me, anyway. I'm expecting!"

Now I was pleased and amazed in equal measures, "Ginny, that's fabulous news! It is, isn't it?"

"Let's say we are both pleased and excited. A little surprised. I didn't think I could have a baby so it wasn't planned. But I'm looking forward to being a Mum!"

I was over the moon for my friends but now I had to find a new caddy and eventually I asked Ginny how did I do it? She smiled.

"Look, Sophie, when you've finished the Open at Birkdale you will need to look for a permanent caddy anyway. Until then I'm going to loan you Steven, if you want him, of course."

Of course, I wanted him but what did Ginny mean? A permanent caddy? Then it dawned on me. Ginny expected me to turn professional after the Open! Not defending my title at the Amateur was, in her world, irrelevant.

Slowly, I began to think, was she right? Could I really make that leap? I had already won a Major, was it possible? Somehow, I felt that I was being backed into a corner, not by Ginny, but by my own game. Perhaps the US Open would provide me with a better idea. I decided to try and put the idea into the back of my mind. I had two Majors to play before then.

Rob, so near and yet ....

Sophie had not managed to win her Amateur Championship for a second time which did not increase my own confidence. I knew that such defences usually fail and I had almost decided to pass up the chance. Sophie had told me not to be so daft. Still, I told myself, give it your best shot and you never know. The first two rounds went well but then I had had plenty of practice of medal play.

Into the matchplay and my form reaches a high level. My first two matches are over very quickly, neither getting past the fourteenth hole. Now I am getting my hopes up and, while a longer match, I win my quarter-final without too much upset.

Semi-final, and I find myself playing Haru again, what a delight! Last time we went the distance but this time, I am playing better and despite his own improvement, as far as I can see, I manage to reach the final, winning on the seventeenth hole. His friendly reaction, as we shake hands, is to beg me to turn professional, so that he will have a chance next year!

Sophie is running with a smile as we chat on video. "Now you can go one better than me! Good luck, Rob."

And I do, nearly. My opponent in the final is an Irishman, Conor McGrath. From the first I lead until the seventeenth when I miss the fairway by a street, my worst drive of the day. Conor takes full advantage to level the match for the third time. This time I cannot bounce back and his birdie at the last is enough to take my title away.

I am depressed and moan at Sophie for not being there and I upset her. She is away in Spain competing and needs the competition before she heads to the States for the US Open. I knew only too well that she couldn't be watching, just as I couldn't be at her Amateur defence. I call her back later to beg forgiveness and although she is warmer and chatty, I worry that I shouldn't have shouted at her in the first place. Oh shit, I think, I really let my misery hurt her and I don't ever want to do that.

The US Open.

Medina has a magic for any European golfer after the amazing Ryder Cup finish all those years ago. For me and the other golfers it promised one of the hardest challenges of the game. Two days of practice took nothing away from that idea but it was, to me, noticeable that the American TV coverage was no longer ignoring Ingrid nor myself.

When I look back at the championship, I know that I should be happy with how I performed. Good rounds on the first two days ensured I was in the mix during the weekend. In the mix that is until the weather changed halfway through Saturday.

The leaders and I suffered the side effects of a storm that almost blew us away. By the end of the day, not one of us in the top ten at the start of the day remained on that first page of the leader board. I was not alone in seeing decent shots simply blown off course and we spent far too much time trying to recover from the deep unforgiving rough. My own personal score moved from five-under-par back to level with the card, while the new leader had set a target of five under before I had even started my third round.

Saturday night was dismal and only Steven's comment helped. "Sophie, you didn't play badly and you never know. Tomorrow might be different and you are only five back despite everything."

He wasn't wrong except that the weather did not improve at all. With no golf possible on the Sunday, the tournament faced a Monday finish or would have if the weather had permitted. By late Monday afternoon, we had still not been able to start and the agonising decision had to be made to call an end based on the fifty-four-hole scores.

I returned home deciding that I needed to focus. I had the Evian Championship only three weeks away and that course had a reputation which promised to favour my game.

A Summons and then: The Open.

Back home I was shocked to learn that White had contrived by some means to get the Court to hear an appeal against both his conviction and the sentence. The case was to be heard in three weeks' time and I was required to attend.

Despite this clashing with the Evian, lawyers for the Crown Prosecution Service were adamant that the court would not agree to an adjournment to allow me to play. I had mixed feelings. The loss of the chance to have another go at a Major had me raging at my continuing misfortune and then raging even more that that bastard had, somehow, contrived to get a hearing. It did not take me long to determine that White would regret it.

One saving grace was that The Open would complete before the court case started and that allowed me to travel down to Royal St George's to support Rob. Ginny had let Steven caddy for him but had decided not to go herself. She told me that she wasn't having an easy pregnancy and needed to rest more than usual.

It was a good week, as Rob played his socks off, repeating his previous performance, winning the Silver Medal, and finishing tenth for the second time.

This time he did not have to suffer playing with Daniel. That awkward individual had been banned by the golfing authorities for twelve months following more unsavoury actions at the Scottish Amateur Open. His ban from all golf, had been upheld on appeal and he had been warned that, should he return to the sport and offend again, a future ban would be for years. His threats of court action to overturn the decision had not materialised.

Rob had, as he warned me, decided to turn professional and would be travelling to Spain for the qualifying school later in the year. He had managed to get a few sponsors' invites but a tour card would be the best route to ensuring regular tournament play.

Rob turns professional.

Despite not retaining my Amateur title, my tenth place at the Open the previous year meant that I had qualified automatically for a second year. One of my friends had suggested that that made it easier – I had the experience of playing in three Majors and that was for the good. They weren't entirely wrong but the US Open remains an experience I want to forget.

For me, therefore, today is my chance to try and show I can compete, which after the debacle of my appearance at the US Open, needs reinforcing. I need that, I told myself, to counter the nightmares I still have, after my failure to cope with the conditions at Pinehurst. It wasn't just that I missed the cut but that I never looked like making it from early in the first round. Even though I didn't finish last and my playing partners were sympathetic, I still felt embarrassed by my score, easily the worst I had managed in many years.

Walking on to the first tee at Royal St George's was no more stressful than it always is when playing in an important competition and I was aware that I had proven that I could compete at the top level – just not win!

And I had Sophie there to support me! What on earth does she see in me? She may still be an amateur but she's already a Major winner. Me, well I hope to be a tour pro and I guess that means I harbour some hope of, one day, winning one of the big ones. That beautiful girl may not be thinking of winning Majors but everyone else in the game isn't talking so much about her ability, but more about just how many Majors she will win when she does turn professional!

I get off to a good start, shooting level par for the first day, which given the windy conditions, typical links golf weather, proves a decent score. Things are not so bad for me and my playing partners the next day, we get the better of the weather, and I manage to shoot four under and ensure that I won't be going home until Sunday evening. It is still very like last year though, I'm doing well but a long way back from the leaders, that's how it feels anyway.

Sophie decides that I need relaxing and drags me off for a meal and, back at our hotel, some afters. I do, eventually, get a good night's sleep and wake the next morning refreshed and ready to try for another high finish.

They call Saturday moving day and, I can understand why, as early starters make a charge up the leader board taking advantage of benign conditions. The forecast is for the winds to pick up later in the day and I am glad that I am back on the course by mid-morning. As my round progresses the breeze does get stronger but my early birdies are enough to compensate for the over-par finish of the last five holes. Seven under leaves me in twelfth, six shots back and that is better than the year before in terms of my score but worse for position.

Thank goodness for Sophie, she has a gift for lifting my spirits when I feel down on my golf, a gift she never seems able to use on herself! With her ready to track my every move on Sunday, I have another good start. Another sub-par round and I manage to replicate my finish of twelve months before – tenth.

I have already decided to turn professional immediately and look to Q-school in September and November. In the meantime, I will take advantage of any sponsor invites plus those events that a top-ten finish grants me entry. I will be busy over the coming months and that means I will be watching my girl from afar. We know that this is likely to be a regular thing but it doesn't make it any easier.

Before all that I must be in the public gallery at the Old Bailey supporting Sophie as she gives evidence at White's appeal.

A few days later and I am having difficulty controlling myself as White's counsel attacks Sophie repeatedly even implying that if she doesn't undress in front of the court and display her scars then she is lying about them.

Despite the rules, I swear at him loudly. It takes Chrissie, sitting next to me to calm me down as the call for silence in court rings out. I doubt I would have been able to take it quietly except that one of the Law Lords, Lady Justice Aires, interrupts the counsel and proposes that Sophie accompany her and the barrister's clerk into the privacy of her chambers. The barrister is forced with bad grace to agree and I ease back in my seat.

The session finally finishes with the judges deferring their decision for seven days. I do not think that Terrent, the barrister, is a happy man. The judges were clearly not impressed with his attitude.

The Court of Appeal

White's appeal would be heard at the Old Bailey and I was forced to travel down to London with Chrissie and Kate, who had both also been summonsed. We didn't know why but it did not auger well for the process we would be involved in.

Two days of expert evidence had been completed and Chrissie had also testified, when I was called to be questioned. The prosecution counsel was careful and quite gentle while asking some very pointed questions before the defence counsel started.

"Miss Jordan, we have heard the pack of lies you used in answering my learned friend's questions. Now perhaps you would engage the court with some honesty." I counted slowly to ten in my mind, understanding that he was trying to make me say anything to stop his challenges.

"You have claimed to have lost your leg and to have suffered extreme scarring from the accident. How is it that you can still play golf at such a level as you appear to be able to? Or is there a twin sister the court is unaware of?"

One of the judges intervened. "Mr Terrent, what has this line of questioning to do with your client's appeal?"

"My lords, there is no question that the sentence given my client would have been less if the Judge had been aware that Miss Jordan did not, in fact, lose a leg. Miss Jordan and her family are not wealthy and she would have had to rely on the NHS to provide her with a prosthetic, if she needed it. The most advanced leg approved for use by the NHS cannot provide the flexibility demonstrated by the witness in recent golf tournaments. It is clear, that while her leg may have been damaged in the accident, it cannot have been severed as suggested and surgery ensured it was reattached."

I stood in the witness box seething, what did this idiot know. Suddenly missing the Evian was brought into perspective, keeping that bastard behind bars for as long as possible was far more important, preferably with his barrister.

The judge sighed. "Miss Jordan, if you would answer the question."

"My lord, if I might sit down, I believe I can answer that by a demonstration."

White's counsel intervened, almost shouting it seemed. "Answer the question!"

I looked at him. "I have two scars caused by the car. They run from just below my neckline down to both of my thighs, one on my back the other to the front side of my body. I do play golf at a decent level. I do not have a twin sister. I do have an artificial leg, which I admit is a remarkable piece of engineering. If their lordships permit, I will show you." It must have been clear to everyone that I was becoming emotional and angry.

A different judge spoke. "Mr Terrent, that seems to us to be a reasonable response."

Terrent looked at me. I sensed that he felt on the edge of losing his most potent argument while wondering exactly what I intended to do. "How do you intend to demonstrate those injuries? Provide us with a strip tease?"

"Objection!" I thought for a moment that the prosecution counsel was going to strike Terrent before the judges intervened again. "Mr Terrent, that is enough! Miss Jordan, that specific reaction will not be necessary."

"My lady, my lords, I had intended to simply show the tops and bottoms of the scars but if it proves necessary to ensure that the defendant remains locked away for a very long time then I will undress." There were gasps from around the room. "I will also remove my false leg."

"Why should we believe you, Miss Jordan? Believe your claim that the scars cover your torso?"

I looked back at him with contempt. "I understand that photographs of my injuries before surgery were made available to you. I am sure you will be able to learn enough." With that I slowly undid my top until I had exposed both scars. Then I pulled my skirt up, again far enough to show the scars on my thighs. I also realised that White was present via a video link and could sense him salivating at the idea that he might see more.

"And the leg?" Terrent was speaking with scorn again as I sat down. Switching off the electronics, I unclipped the links to the thigh section and removed the leg, lifting it higher so that it could be seen by the judges as well as that nasty little man. "You still haven't proven that those scars are the same, Miss Jordan."

There was a cry from the public area. "You bastard!" Rob had finally had enough.

"Silence in court!" The clerk to the court responded to the shout and the rumble of discontent spreading across the gallery as he had to but I sensed that his words were being delivered in a sympathetic tone.

I looked at Terrent with the same look I might have used on finding that I had trodden in dog waste. Before I could respond one of the judges, clearly angry at the demands of the barrister, called him out. "Mr Terrent. I will not allow the witness to be forced to undress in front of the whole court. That is as distasteful a demand as I can ever recall."

"My lady! She must demonstrate that she tells the truth!"

The judge's tone suggested that Mr Terrent might well be in real trouble, before. "If you really feel that that is essential to your case then I would suggest that your clerk, it is Miss Hain I think, and I go to my chambers with the witness. If Miss Jordan is prepared to show two other females that should be enough."

Terrent seemed to growl before indicating to his clerk that she should accompany the judge and myself out of the court room.

We entered the judge's chambers. Once in, she turned to me and apologised. "Miss Jordan, I find the defence counsel's attitude indefensible but, if you would be so kind. Miss Hain, I expect an honest response to what we are about to see."

"My lady. Miss Jordan, my apologies as well. I must do as I am required by my principal."

I nodded. It wasn't her fault and at least we had privacy. As I undressed, I made one comment. "Both of you. This is what I must see every morning."

There were mutual gasps from the two of them. "The doctors couldn't do better?" The judge asked.

"No. They did a wonderful job when you consider what they were working with." I had to grit my teeth. Having to expose myself in this way was humiliating, even if those witnessing the damage to my body were both professional and sympathetic.

As we finished and I prepared to return to the court room, I could hear the defence clerk asking the judge if she would help her find different chambers. "I cannot work with him anymore but, if I just leave, he won't give me a reference."

"Complete this case, Miss Hain. I will have words."

"Thank you, my lady."

We re-entered the court room which had been held while we were absent. Once the judge had sat down with her fellow judges, she had a quiet word, before. "Mr Terrent, I suggest, strongly, that you finish your cross examination of Miss Jordan and then call your clerk to give evidence."

"My lady, my lords. That is hardly appropriate, Miss Hain is not a witness."

"Mr. Terrent, you demanded that evidence be provided and part of that evidence can only be provided by your clerk. Or should we suggest that the prosecution call her?"

Terrent, who had been briefed by his clerk, looked up at the bench. "I would suggest the latter, my lord."

"In that case, continue. Carefully, we would suggest."

"Miss Jordan, I would remind you that you are still under oath. How did you raise the money to purchase that prosthetic?"

I looked back at him. This was a question that had never occurred to me.

"I didn't. The specialist team at my local hospital provided me with four artificial legs over the five years since I lost my leg. Each has been better and this one is the best."

"That leg is as far beyond the best the NHS can provide and yet you did not pay for it. That is probably the biggest falsehood in your evidence."

"Mr Terrent, sometimes the truth is more unbelievable than fiction. I am sorry that you cannot differentiate between the two."

I thought, for a moment, he was going to explode mostly because I had failed to lose my temper and, I admit, I would have liked nothing more than to thump him with my leg.

"No further questions."

Counsel for the prosecution requested that the judges permit Miss Hain be called as a witness for the prosecution and a few minutes later she stood in the witness box.

"Miss Hain, please describe what Miss Jordan demonstrated in the judge's chambers."

The clerk held her breath for a moment.

"Miss Jordan bears two scars that start at her neck and finish at the top of her thighs, one down her back, the other to the side of her chest. They must have been worse; the surgical corrections are obvious."

She then added without prompting. "I have the greatest admiration for Miss Jordan, a weaker person would, I suspect, have curled into a corner and given up. She has done far better than anyone could reasonably expect."

I glanced across to see Terrent, flushed with anger. Miss Hain had said more than she needed to and I wondered how she might suffer when they returned to chambers after the case had ended.

Once he had refused the opportunity to cross-examine her, the judge raised her voice. "For the record, I concur with the witness's words. They accurately describe the life-changing injuries that Miss Jordan suffered."

The next witness called by Terrent was Kate. Terrent was as abusive in his approach with her as he had been with me.

"Miss Williams, you were the first medic on the scene, yes?"

Kate went on the attack. "It's Dr Williams, thank you. Yes, I was the first responder and arrived a few minutes ahead of the first ambulance."

"But you weren't a doctor then, just a paramedic with basic training?"

"That depends on what you mean by basic training. I had been a qualified paramedic for four years and was already in advanced training to become a doctor."

"So, the court needs to be aware that the initial medical support was by a semi-qualified individual. Why did you not assist the other female injured in the accident?"

"Sadly, the other girl was clearly already dead."

"And you are/were an expert on that?"

"Her head had been crushed by the car wheel. There were other injuries that would have been fatal but that was the most obvious."

"And Miss Jordan?"

"Miss Jordan was breathing although she had heavy cuts to her body and her leg had been severed."

"But you could save her?"

"I did what I could to reduce the bleeding by using a tourniquet on her upper leg and then strapping her torso to pull the cuts together. I managed to buy the trauma team at the hospital the time to carry out surgery."

"Very clever, I am sure. And for the record, how long was Miss Jordan in surgery?"

"I was told later that the operations, to stabilise her and repair as much damage as possible, took about six hours."

"And her leg? What happened to that?"

"I placed it in a surgical bag but it was obvious that nothing could be done with it."

"So, you, a partially trained paramedic decided that the leg should be discarded. On what basis?"

"Two answers to that. I didn't decide. That was left to the surgeons. Secondly, the upper part of the severed limb had been crushed. The surgeons confirmed that the damage was beyond repair."

I sat watching this piece of theatre, as I saw it, while wanting to be anywhere but the court room, as Terrent went back and forth trying to get Kate to make a false statement. He failed and in due course was forced to end his behaviour. Kate was his last witness.

The judges ended the session. Advising those present that they would deliver a verdict in seven days.

I returned to the court, a week later, to hear the decision of the judges. This was formally delivered by one of the male justices, I suspect because of White's misogyny which had clearly not improved over the years since his imprisonment.

The written judgement took some time to deliver but it was summed up at the end.

"We find that the original verdict was correct. The judge's summing up was accurate and fair. We confirm that the defendant was guilty of deliberate murder, no other outcome was reasonably possible."

I could see that Terrent was not happy and White was swearing and shouting at the screen in the prison room.

"As to the sentence of life with a minimum of thirty years. We find that the judge was not fully aware of the injuries suffered by the surviving victim and her sentence was, therefore, not correctly constructed."

White let out a shriek of triumph, at least that was how it appeared. The judges had had to cut the audio feed, almost to silent, due to his repeated interruptions.

The judge continued. "We have decided that the original sentence did not reflect those facts. In view of the incomplete knowledge of Justice Armitage, the sentence was, in our unanimous view, too lenient. Mr White, your sentence of life imprisonment remains. You will, however, serve a minimum of forty years before you may be considered for parole."

I could not help but continue to gaze at the video screen. For a moment, it looked as if White was going to have a fit as he swung fists at the prison officers, clearly condemning everyone in the court room.

There was one further comment from the Judges. "Mr Terrent, we find your approach to this case to have been unacceptable and will refer your actions to the bar council. Court rise."

Terrent went pale but made no response, seeking to leave as quickly as he could.

Afterwards, Rob, Chrissie, Kate, and I got together for a drink. Celebration seemed the wrong reason, the appeal had opened old wounds, but a degree of satisfaction that White had failed in his attempt.

It was the first time that the others had met and, I thought, both were impressed with the other. Rob took the opportunity to thank Kate for her work that fateful night. Without her he would not have me at all and for that he would always be grateful.

Fortunately, for me, the court hearings were over and there was still a week before the Women's Open, at Birkdale. Steven would be my caddy, for the last time, after that I would be on my own. And that was quite scary.

A Case of Fighting Back!

I arrive to find myself suddenly the centre of attention and I realise that my second place the previous year has not been forgotten nor my win in Texas. When am I turning professional is a repeated question and I am forced to avoid a direct answer each time. After that first day of practice, I decide that I must discuss my options with Ginny and Steven.

We have a long enjoyable evening before I drop the cat among the pigeons. I am considering turning pro now, before the tournament. Ginny looks startled, before she nods with a smile.

Steven is not quite as positive. "Have you thought it through, Sophie? This seems to be a sudden decision rather than a considered one."

I take a moment to answer him. "In a way it is sudden but I have been forced to accept that I am good enough to, at least, give it a shot. I lacked the confidence to make that change before but the Chevron really hit home. I'm a Major winner and everyone expects me to turn professional after the Open. I just wonder. If I keep putting it off, will I ever have the nerve?"

Ginny looked at Steven. "You have more experience, love. What would you advise?"

He thought about it. "Sophie, you need to consider whether you want to enjoy this week still as an amateur or are you prepared for the stress that playing for money will add."

"I'm not that certain. How do you mean?"

"It isn't about how competitive you are. Look, as an amateur, you stand over a five-foot putt. If you miss it, well that's life. As a professional that missed putt might cost you a thousand pounds, possibly more. It is inevitable that your game will be affected."

I nod slowly. Steven wasn't saying I wasn't good enough but warning me that playing wouldn't be the same. I resolve to sleep on it and talk to them in the morning after a chat with Rob, who is now away in France.

The chat with Rob, to be honest, doesn't help. He has a view about my golf which means that he has assumed I would make the change sooner rather than later.

Breakfast and we have another early start. I have decided. After my final practice round, I will advise the powers-that-be that I will be playing as a professional. No sense in waiting, I need to go for it. Ginny is excited and so is my family. Alan cannot be found and is not answering his mobile. I leave him a voicemail.

Steven is more down to earth. "Now the real work begins, Sophie. Let's get at it."

Twenty past nine and I walk on to the first tee. My normal nerves have been elevated by the sports headlines. "Chevron winner turns professional!"

First shot and I manage to hit the fairway with a good if not great start. Then I start to understand Steven's advice, my second shot misses the green right, my normal draw vanishing as the ball heads in a straight-line past the green and a few minutes later I three-putt for a double bogey. This is not a good start and I find my body tensing.

The rest of the round is a constant struggle against that tension and almost five hours later I finish with a seventy-seven, seven-over. I rush from the course as fast as I can, distraught. Damning myself for listening to everyone telling me I was a great player, when I wasn't.

I spend time on the range afterwards before leaving for our hotel. It still takes most of the evening for me to recover some semblance of calm and my leg is aching like never before.

Steven looks to calm me down.

"Tomorrow you can play relaxed, Sophie. A best estimate is that the cut will be around four-over. Which means..." he smiled, "you'll need to shoot sixty-seven or better to make it and that is a big ask even for the experienced players."

"So, we'll be going home Friday then." My grin is forced but at that moment I can't see any other possibility.

Only Ginny sees a glimmer of light. "There is hope, Sophie. You played the back nine holes in just the one over, that means you were getting used to things and already playing more relaxed. And, hell, what's eleven shots. You've three days to catch that Canadian."

I hadn't bothered to look at the overnight leader board but Ginny was right. Joanne had shot sixty-six for the lead while Ingrid was nowhere to be seen. Ah well, Steven is right, let's just go and enjoy it tomorrow, what will be will be."

Friday and I am a late starter. Steven is remarkably relaxed but then I guess that is what his role is. He is right though. The nerves of the day before have all but vanished and I get underway with a better drive. My playing partners are flirting with the predicted cut line which is now at three-over and a long way for me.

But if the first on day one was a disaster today it is brilliant. They say it is the toughest opening hole of any of the Open venues and I can believe that. Still, I tell myself, hit that green and you have a chance and I do. With Steven's help I judge the putt perfectly and that's one back.

Steven is, in many ways, a steadier influence on my game than Ginny. Right from the outset, that day, he counselled me to be patient. "Pars are good, birdies better, but you need to avoid the bogeys early on." He told me. Easier said than done but I listen and try my hardest and it works. By the turn I am two under for the round and that elusive cut line suddenly looks as if it might be achievable after all. If my luck holds, I tell myself.

Apart from that first hole putt, though, single putts have largely been missing. My birdie on the ninth only requires a tap-in. Then a fifteen-footer drops on the eleventh, for a par.

"Now that was a great clutch putt, Sophie." Steven is grinning at me. "Those are the ones that really count. Let's push on."

Something has happened with my putting and approach shots and, in the next four holes, I get three birdies. I'm five under for the round and, unless things change, I will make the cut. Now I really am relaxed. Birdies at the two par-five holes, mean I finish with the best round of the day. A, to me anyway, stunning sixty-three and I am level-par for the competition. Tomorrow I can play my normal game, I tell myself. I'm nine shots back and there isn't the same pressure to perform in my rookie event.

Ginny sees it differently. "You need to understand how much is at stake, love."

I look at her. "Go on."

"You don't need to do anything exceptional. A level-par finish last year was worth around thirty thousand pounds."

"Sorry, how much?"

"One day, Sophie, you will have done some homework and I will be redundant. Those players that finished level with the card won about thirty thousand pounds. One under was worth an extra four thousand. Even one-over-par was worth twenty-four thousand."

"Oh god!" I whisper. "What did the winner get?"

"A bit under eight hundred thousand. Worst case, you'll win about twelve thousand for finishing last."

"Eight hundred thousand! Oh lord." I was having difficulty breathing. That sort of money was the subject of dreams and I know I should have known but I hadn't ever thought about the big money. Now even the money I could win by being no more than average over the next two days was more than I had ever had.

She grinned at me. "Don't forget though. Steven gets ten per cent and the tax guys will be looking for their wedge too."

That evening was better than the day before, by a street, and I was able to watch the highlights in the hotel bar with the others.

No alcohol for me, I had determined to remain teetotal during competitions, nor for Ginny who had developed a small bump, but Steven was free to get a beer!

I hadn't really focussed that much on the programme but suddenly I heard my name. The commentators were talking about me. "How do you see the rookie, Sophie Jordan's chances, Laura?"

"Look, we are talking about a prodigy. Her first day score was, I believe, the worst round she has had in years. I did wonder if she might have decided to turn pro too soon. Maybe she wasn't ready, despite last year and the Chevron.

But look it, she is a Major winner and she won't be twenty-one until later this year. Today she showed the sort of spirit such a player needs. Nine shots back. It should be too many but I'm not sure I would bet against her being up on the first page of the leader board."

Ginny is nodding in agreement and I try to shrink into the shadows around the table.

Saturday sees a decent first hole with my approach finishing some eight or nine feet from the pin. The first putt rims out and I feel a different irritation. Suddenly I begin to understand Steven's warning on Wednesday. Perhaps he sees something in my demeanour but, as we walk to the next tee, he gently nudges me. "Nothing wrong with a par and not every putt drops for anyone."

Trouble is that I don't seem able to hole a birdie putt and that is the only part of my game that misfires. Ginny will tell me later that over the first dozen holes I hit every fairway and every green in regulation but not once did I sink a putt over seven feet. I still have twelve pars to my name but the leaders are up and running early doors with birdies galore.

All change at the thirteenth. I miss the fairway, then the green. Bogey on the cards and I am looking at a difficult chip. Get it wrong and I could be faced with dropping two shots. I pace back and forth before Steven suggests my Texas wedge, as he put it! "My putter?" I ask.

He nods, "Less risk, Sophie," and hands it to me.

I have already worked out a line for the chip and decide to use that as a guide. Inside I am almost laughing at the audacity of the play. A few moments later and I am laughing out loud. Forty odd feet and the putt hits the hole dead centre and drops. It feels like an eagle, as the potential bogey turns into a birdie.

Now I feel elated and Steven must calm me down! I birdie the two par-fives for the second time to finish at three-under-par. Not in that top ten, Laura referred to, but respectably placed. Joanne has built a bigger lead and at thirteen-under is two shots clear of the pack.

I can look to the final day with the confidence that I won't disgrace myself.

And I, again, shoot the best round in much more difficult conditions. The first three days had been warm with gentle breezes. Sunday sees strong winds and it is dull, if dry. My sixty-five lifts me to eight-under-par and I finish ninth.

For the second time I must face the gauntlet of the Sky cart and realise that I was lucky to have avoided being interviewed on the Thursday. It is fun and looking back at some of the holes where I had gained on the field was pleasant, if embarrassing when you consider how lucky I had been.

Of course, I'm not in contention and Joanne holds on to her lead to win her first Major. Which starts a chat on the television later as to whether women's golf was entering a new era. Seven first timers in the last eight Majors!

The end of the discussion focuses on prize money. As Laura had pointed out before, even though it is the richest Major, the Open had a prize fund that was little more than an average PGA tour event and paled when compared with the men's Majors.

It was something that I am not sure I was bothering about that evening. My ninth place had earned me a hundred and forty thousand pounds; a fortune.

Throughout this period, I have kept an eye on Richard's form which had sadly plummeted after his win. I could not work out why but he had missed six of the next seven cuts and was now in danger of losing his tour card.

I continue sending him my weekly good luck messages which, I confess, Rob finds hard to understand and, unreasonably I think, is a little jealous. He has nothing to worry about but, maybe, I worry that the periods when we aren't even in the same country drag at his wish to be with me. I doubt he has had any contact with his previous girlfriend, Teri, given the circumstances of their split but I still find myself worrying that he might be in touch when I am away.

Was this confirmation of the problems that Richard had addressed by heading to the States? It was like an itch that I couldn't scratch and even Rob himself struggled to handle my nervous approach to life.

Press Exposé but who?

I arrive home to find a journalist waiting outside my home and it isn't to interview me about the golf.

"Miss Jordan, my paper is preparing an exposure of the mismanagement of the local hospital. I need to warn you that you will be the subject of a specific attack on how they have been spending taxpayers' money."

"Look, I am only just back from Birkdale, Mr.? Can this not wait?"

"Jonny Felton, apologies, my card." He gave me a business card which appeared to confirm his claim to be a journalist. "This article is due to be published on Wednesday, if not tomorrow. I would recommend that you allow me to explain and let me have your response."

Something told me that he was trying to be reasonable, even though I didn't have the slightest idea what he was talking about.

"You'd better come in, but I will need a moment, it has been a long journey home."

I lead him into the house. My brothers are both away and only my Mum is there. Having explained who Mr Felton is, I leave him with her while I freshen up.

Twenty minutes later I sit in shock. "Miss Jordan, you will remember that you were attacked in court by counsel for White over the cost of your leg. That is an important aspect of the article. You may not be aware that the hospital has run up excess spending over the last four years to the tune of around ten million pounds. Now most of that is caused by individual things that on their own are immaterial. Your prosthetics are not in the same category."

I look at him in dismay, Terrent's attack had left me cold and I had not really taken in the implications of his words at the time. Now they were being used to attack my friends in the prosthetics team but how and why?

"I don't understand. The legs were each nothing more than improvements on the previous ones why is that so important."

"Miss Jordan, you had no idea how expensive they are?" My expression must have said it all, because he continued. "We understand that that last leg cost over a million pounds. The four legs totalled almost two million."

"I don't understand. I never asked for special treatment. I assumed that they were standard."

He looked at me. "You didn't realise you had been selected for such treatment."

"No. That sort of money. I can't understand why. I wasn't anyone special."

"Unlike now. Top golfer likely to make a fortune but possible only because taxpayers' money was spent on you. I will talk to my editor but I cannot promise you an easy ride, Miss Jordan. The hospital has repeatedly refused to speak to us. They quote patient confidentiality. Stupidly, in my view, they deny spending that money on you. I had hoped you would be able to provide an explanation. I am sorry to have taken your time."

After he has gone, I decide to call the hospital. It takes some time to find Anita and explain what has happened. She is reluctant to answer my questions and quite evasive. Eventually, she gives up and explains.

"Shortly after you left hospital with that first temporary leg, we received a message from a solicitor. She told us that a client of hers wished to provide you with the most up to date and advanced prosthetics and their client undertook to supply and pay for them. It was done on the express basis that the client would remain anonymous. Even you were not to be told. That person kept to their promise. In fact, they provided more than the base cost. They paid for me and the team to be trained in the use of the electronics and I understand that they are also funding research into how these prosthetics might be mass produced so that we can provide them to amputees as a norm."

"Anita, you need to tell the press about this otherwise they are going to crucify you. If you need me to write to you, I will send you an email as soon as we finish."

I was completely stunned by what she had told me and I intended to find out who my benefactor was and why. First, though was the need to protect the people who had over the years become friends. The article was published and there was reference to the mystery individual's donations but, even then, the paper questioned the truth of it. Although they conceded that they couldn't prove that it was a lie.

I tried to find out more about the mystery person but ran into a brick wall. The only thing that came out was that the reason was because of my then nascent ability as a golfer. My benefactor had joined the band believing that I was a future Tiger, their words not mine. No-one could emulate his ability and success, could they?

It seemed to be impossible to identify who had spent all that money on me, money I would probably never be able to repay no matter how successful I might be. It was Rob who made the breakthrough, one morning as the sun flooded into the bedroom.

"Sophie, you know. Whoever organised those legs must have known you or one of the people at your club. Who else would have known about your capabilities and was close enough to want to help."

"You mean a member?"

"It's possible but what about Alan or the club committee itself?"

I thought about it, for long enough that Rob was forced to nudge me. "Sophie, we haven't got much time before we need to get up."

I grinned and rolled over. Benefactors and golf slipped into the background for a while.

At breakfast I finally came up with an answer to his last question. "Not Alan, he's generous and lovely but he doesn't have money. I think he is comfortable but not rich. It couldn't be the Club. I've seen their annual accounts and they don't have that sort of money. Whoever it is must be wealthy beyond my knowledge. Oh! Wait a moment, Rob. Keep this to yourself, but I wonder?"

Rob looked at me without a word, waiting, before I decided that he would have to wait.

"Sorry, Rob. I need to talk to someone and it wouldn't be fair on them to have told anyone else, if I am wrong."

"But you have an idea, Sophie?"

"Yes, but I could be totally wrong, so patience, my love."

Leaving Rob to complete his packing before he headed for home and then to Italy, I did a search on the web before I took a walk over to the Club. Alan was away and I had promised to fill-in in the pro-shop for a few hours. I knew I didn't need the work now but these were friends and it gave me an excuse to be there.

When I arrived, I found that Fiona was there helping Richard's replacement with the new systems and generally handling the steady flow of members. As ever she was a little or, perhaps I should say a lot, over the top.

"Sophie, you wonder woman! Come and meet Alan's new assistant pro. John, this is our star."

John laughed. "Sophie, an honour. Looking to book a lesson?"

I almost said "No" before his humour struck. That was why Alan had given him the job, I suspected. Having chatted for a few minutes, broken up by those members, who knew me, demanding to shake my hand, I asked Fiona if I was needed or if could I leave them for an hour or so.

She chuckled. "Haven't you resigned yet, Sophie? We're fine, come back at eleven and you and I can have a coffee. John will be okay.

He's learning all the idiosyncrasies of the shop's systems a lot faster than you did!"

I smiled; Fiona was quite correct. It had taken me what seemed like forever to understand the way the computer worked on tee-times and so on. "See you later, folks. Good to meet you, John."

Now I was free to take the step I was close to freaking out about but take it I had to. Entering the main clubhouse, I headed for the Secretary's office. James was at the filing cabinet with his back to me but turned to my tap on the door.

"Sophie, how wonderful to see you." He hesitated as he caught sight of my frown.

"Mr. Caunter, I think that I have a bone to pick with you."

He looked at me with some concern showing. "I don't understand, what have I done?"

"You didn't tell me that you were paying for my prosthetics. I mean you did, didn't you?"

Now he looked angry. "That damn newspaper!" He sighed. "Yes, Sophie, I did but you were never supposed to know. How did you find out it was me? Who told you?"

I smiled. "Nobody told me. Once I knew that I had a secret benefactor. It wasn't long before I realised it had to be someone who knew me and my golf. No-one else has that sort of money but you, you were, I suddenly thought someone I didn't really know. So, I Googled you and ...... well you will know what I found."

"Go on."

"You are or were one of the leading scientists in cyber-electronics. Formed a company to develop artificial-intelligence controlled prosthetics. Sold most of it to one of the Silicon Valley giants. You are a self-made multi-millionaire and you also retain a share of the business you created. James, you have the contacts and the money but why me?"

"Sophie, it is a long story. To be truthful, your golf had little or nothing to do with it. I would have done the same for you," I could hear the emphasis on "for you" but let him continue. "no matter what you did, even if I had never met you."

Now I was struggling to understand the implications of what he was saying. "I don't understand. That doesn't make sense, I know I can play golf but I'm nothing special."

He smiled as gently as I can remember. "Sophie, you are to me. Look I will need to explain, it is a long story. Will you have dinner with me? Just the two of us?"

I thought about that, Rob would be back at his home preparing to fly to Italy. And Bernard was at home for the night with Mum. This man had changed my life in a positive way. I could at least accept his invitation.

"Okay, James. Please, I do need to understand."

He nodded. "I will book a table and let you know where. Please can we keep this between us, at least for the moment?"

It was my turn to nod.

Back home I had to field Rob's questions. I promised that I would tell him either later or possibly in the morning. I don't think he was that keen on my having dinner with a Mr X. It took a little physical effort on my part to get him feeling rather more relaxed about my plans.

After Rob left, the day dragged until, midway through the afternoon, I had a text from James. He was sending a car to collect me and we would dine at a rather upmarket eatery. Not one I would ever have thought of, at least not in the past. I searched my wardrobe to find my best clothes.

"You need to think about a bigger wardrobe, love." It was my Mum. "Now you're hitting the big time, you can and should get yourself some clothes other than the golf tops! I think you are going to need them."

I grimaced, Mum was right, but I had never been one for fancy clothes. She laughed at my discomfort and I hugged her. "I know, Mum, it's just not me, is it?"

"Wasn't, Sophie darling, but now ...... and tonight is special?"

"I think so, Mum. I promised not to say more, not yet anyway."

"Be careful, darling."

James' car duly arrived and took me to the restaurant where he was ready and waiting for me. We sat down with some wine, my choice of drink, and James explained. To my incredulity the story had started long before I was born.

"I was adopted. My parents would have adopted my brother, as well, but he had already been moved to another home and, in those days, adoptive parents weren't allowed to contact other adopted children or their adoptive parents. I should say that I was only a few months old, my brother was, I learnt later, a year older. We had no memories of each other. When I was five my parents tried to find my brother but the adoption agency told them that the other parents had refused contact. At that time, we or they couldn't do anything else but, when they told me that I was adopted, they also told me that I had a brother. From then on, I wanted to find him."

I broke in. "Are you saying my Dad was your brother? Why didn't he tell us?"

"Sophie, he didn't know, not until a week or so before he died. You are right, I have made a lot of money and that can do many things. I paid a researcher to find your Dad, but not to tell him. When we tracked him down, we found a close-knit loving family. It took a lot of thought but I decided not to announce myself. I feared I might disrupt your parents and you and your brothers and for that I could never have forgiven myself."

"But why your job at the golf club? You don't need the money."

"That is true but I had time for idle hands and I do enjoy golf. And, of course, you were the rising star. I could be close and keep an eye on you all and be there if you ever needed help. That night in town struck me hard until I realised that that was the time to help but I couldn't let you know. That is why I used subterfuge."

"So, Dad never knew you existed."

"Not until you were in the States. He knew he was dying and he had always wondered about me, after we met watching you. There was an itch, as he put it. Something about me reminded him of himself. He called me at the Club and we met. I have always had the greatest admiration for him, and your Mum, they did such a job building your family despite having little money. They made up for that by providing a loving upbringing to you and your brothers while instilling in you all those positive aptitudes."

"Does my Mum know?"

"I don't know. I believe that your father was going to tell her but I am not sure if he managed to. His health deteriorated rapidly. All that kept him going that last week was that determination to see you complete another Major. Winning it was beyond his wildest dreams. For what it is worth, my dear, he died a very happy man."

I sat listening to this remarkable man, wishing that we had known of our relationship before. I felt sad that he had felt unable to contact my parents sooner. I disagreed with his idea that our family would have been hurt by learning of his existence. Now I needed to convince him to meet with my brothers and my Mum.

Outside of our home we had no other relatives, my grandparents on both sides of the family had died a long time ago. To have an uncle or an aunt for that matter, was a part of family life that we had missed, not consciously but our friends all seemed to have extensive families. Perhaps it had drawn us closer as a family, I thought, and that was why James had stood back from contacting us. He knew all about us but I didn't know much about him outside of his business exploits and, to be honest, his money.

"James, what about you? Your family?"

He smiled, a little ruefully. "My parents died when I was in my twenties and I lost my wife not long after that. I'm just a single, now. No other family. Looking after you made everything worthwhile but I have never met anyone else."

So, the man, who had found a way to repair my leg, was alone. That wasn't right and I made that clear. I would speak with my Mum and then he had to come and meet the family as a relative, not just as a friend. For a moment I wondered if I had overstepped the mark, then he nodded. "I wish now that I had made the effort before. Let me know when would be best. Now, shall we eat?"

After some wonderful food, I must bring Mum here, I thought, we headed for the car, James had arranged, to collect me and, now, take me home. As we parted, I gave him a hug and a kiss. "Good night, uncle. Thank you for this evening."

I felt that his eyes were a little moist but he held himself in control and turned to his own car.

I was not aware that someone was watching us, wide eyed, and that explanations would be required the next morning. Even if I had seen them, it would have made no difference. The journey home was short and I was bubbling with excitement.

In so many ways my arrival back home with my news was a bit of a damp squib. Mum already knew about James, Dad had told her of his long-lost brother but, as it happened, hadn't managed to explain who he was, only his name. She had told my brothers and would have told me except that there had not been a good time. On the other hand, they all wanted to meet him now that they knew his identity.

I promised to invite him home as soon as he could come.

The following morning, I leave early for the Club looking for some practice on the range and, possibly, enjoying a social round of golf. It will be my last week off for some time as sponsor invites to play in the upcoming tour events are, amazingly, piling up. My real problem is finding a caddy. Alan and Steven had offered to try and find a suitably qualified individual whom they felt would be a good fit but had not succeeded yet.

I walk into the changing room to be accosted by, of all people, Ginny. Her bump is growing steadily and she has had to resign herself to not being able to play until after the birth, so for her to be there, is surprising.

"Sophie, have you fallen out of love with Rob?"

"Sorry, Ginny, I don't understand. We're fine, although he's off to Italy today."

"He went home yesterday, you told me. Half a day, and you are canoodling with another man. I thought more of you than that, Sophie." She sounds, no she is, angry with me and I don't help her temper when I laugh with more gaiety than is, in her view, appropriate.

"Oh, Ginny. I'm sorry. You were at the restaurant last night, yes? And you saw me in the car park? Kissing someone, who wasn't Rob?"

She nods, with a little growl.

"What you saw wasn't what you think."

"I saw you and James Caunter. You embraced and then kissed him. I know that much." Ginny sounds disappointed now, rather than angry.

"Ginny. Look. You need to keep this to yourself. James is my uncle. I only found out yesterday. Please. I am not sure he is ready for that to be known outside of my family and me."

Ginny's face is a picture. "Uncle?"

"Yes, but there were reasons why I didn't know until now. He is very special to me. One day I will be able to tell you why, but not yet. Now, as you are here, let's talk sponsors."

She slowly nods. "It would be good to hear sooner but I can keep my mouth shut for the moment. Now, my telephone has hardly stopped ringing. We are going to need to consider which offers are the best. Only one, I suspect, is a slam dunk for the other side. Your clubs?"

Now it is my turn to nod but I decide to show Ginny that I am not that simple in negotiations. "What are the offers?"

Ginny grins. "Their offer is at least as good as any other and it has an added benefit, an increase when you reach top ten."

I see the numbers she is talking about and gulp. "They mean.... I mean that much a year! Oh my!"

"Now, we need to talk clothing. Your current sponsor has increased their deal. You could get a bit more but there is a benefit in getting a reputation for loyalty."

The discussion continues for nearly an hour by which time I am overwhelmed by the scale of money on offer. I ask Ginny one thing. Is it normal for a new professional to be as popular amongst the brands as I seem to be, or is it just that I'm not used to handling such sums.

Ginny thinks long and hard before. "I don't think it is but .... most new professionals are not already Major winners and that is what has encouraged them to try and get in at the bottom. Win another Major and these will look rather miserable compared with new offers."

"I need someone to help with the financial aspect, Ginny. Do you know anyone?"

"Let me have a word with my own advisor. If he can find space then he would be a good one."

"Thanks, Ginny. Now I need...." My mobile went off. "Chrissie, hi. Oh! Sorry, I'll be there in fifteen minutes."

Ginny looked at me questioningly.

"My best friend. Apart from Dawn, that is or was. She's getting married and I am supposed to be at a dress fitting. I'm a bridesmaid. Ginny, I'm going to have to run."

A Wedding.

Ever since my return from the States I have, amid the funeral preparations and the Open, been trying to get to dress fittings on time, not always successfully and this one, I had forgotten. Still, I told myself, it is the last one with the wedding on the coming Saturday. I just didn't know what to get my friends as a wedding present.

Until the Open, I would have settled for one of the presents from their wedding list, they had a list that I could cope with then, not having much money and knowing they would not expect one of the more expensive gifts. Now I could afford something extra special but what? I mean I could manage to pay for the whole wedding but I rather suspected that that would not be wise.

I decide to talk to Chrissie's parents. As I explain to them, Chrissie has been my friend since primary school, Kate saved my life as the first responder. They deserve something special. Kate's parents are not happy about their daughter being gay and while they were not trying to get in the way they are refusing to help with the costs. Sadly, they will not be attending the wedding either.

Chrissie's mother looks at her father before telling me that the best present, wedding related, would be to contribute towards a honeymoon.

That's when I remember Chrissie talking about one day being able to go whale watching in Alaska. I think Kate would enjoy it as well and head off to the travel agents after the fitting.

It takes a little explaining that I want to give a voucher that covers the flights, cruise and possibly a trip into the Rockies and I want the voucher to be such that it is not obvious that I am booking the best cabin and business class flights. The team in the agency is tickled pink at being charged with that task.

Saturday comes but Rob is missing. Against his expectancy he has made the cut in the Italian Open, only his second pro competition. I am both pleased for him and at the same time fed-up.

Now I am going to be on my own, on a day which should have been a happy one together. Of course, it is a happy day but I do miss him. It is another reminder that our relationship is going to have to cope with periods of absence. I know that others must face similar separations, I just wish I wasn't one of them.

The ceremony is amazing and loving and I feel proud to be a part of it. At the reception afterwards it is clear that both Kate and Chrissie are full of thanks to all those who are there especially Kate's parents! They had made the decision that they did wish to be a part of their daughter's life after all.

I had slipped the envelope with my gift voucher into the pile of cards and other gifts and watched on as the pile was opened, with a certain level of nervousness. Would they see me as showing off?

I need not have worried. Kate's face as she saw it is matched by Chrissie's a moment later before they both turn to me, sat a few seats away.

"Sophie, how can you afford this? It's too much." Kate voices their initial response to the scale of the holiday booking. Chrissie would tell me later that it was the most wonderful gift I could have found for them.

"Trust me, Kate. I can afford it now and I am so glad that I can give you something to say a small thank you to both of you."

She looked back at me with a raised eyebrow.

"Kate, remember that Dawn's sacrifice would have been for nothing if you hadn't turned up and been brilliant. The tourniquet I understand was normal but tying belts around my body to hold me together? That action was what gave the surgeons a chance to save me. I can never thank you enough and since I turned pro, I do have the money. More than I could ever have dreamed of. Chrissie stood

by me throughout the aftermath and was steadfast in her support.
Now, enjoy the trip and the scenery."

Q-School.

I don't believe that many people outside of those who look to earn a living from my sport realise just how hard it is to gain a tour card for either of the two main tours. The European tour requires a total of ten rounds of golf from the one hundred and fifty-six who make the final and even then, the majority will not succeed.

The first four rounds would take place at a variety of courses around the Globe, except for the Americas, in September with twenty-three plus ties qualifying from each group. To say I was nervous can be summed up by my realisation that I would probably need to shoot at least sixteen under-par.

Four days later and I managed to do better than that. Sometimes I surprise myself but Peter was remarkably upbeat. "I always knew you had it in you, Rob. Now you just need to repeat that in Spain."

Spain in November is not that warm. The Costa Dorada is beautiful but not that far from Barcelona and does not get as hot as the Costa del Sol. Despite that I was determined to enjoy myself. Peter has often told me that I play better when relaxed and enjoying the course, or in this case both the courses. His last words to me before I leave are.

"Remember, Rob, you don't need to win it to get your card. Yes, there's more prize money at stake but that pales against what you can earn on tour. Don't chance missing out on a top twenty finish by risking everything just to win."

"That's easier said than done." I mumble. "I've always aimed to win; without that drive I'll probably miss the cut let alone the top twenty!"

Peter grins. "You'll do okay. Good luck and I'll see you in a few weeks' time."

And I do do okay. In fact, I do better than that, shooting twenty-four under par over the rounds and that is good enough for fifth of the twenty-eight who gain their Tour cards. Now I can play tour events without relying on sponsor invites and I am on the road again, looking for a caddy.

Sophie is all smiles when we talk on a video call later. "Told you, you could do it, Rob!"

A New Caddy and a return to The Woodlands.

Rob went on to finish in the top-ten in Italy, an impressive success but he can't get back before I head to Spain for my own tour event. He will be competing in the qualifying stage of Q-school before the end of September with the aim of reaching the final qualifying rounds which take place in November.

This first year I will be relying on invites from the sponsors of events. I will need to perform well enough to get a tour card for future years.

I arrive in Andalucia to be met by Carlos, a middle-aged good-looking individual. Steven had suggested him as a caddy whose approach would fit well with my style of play. I had a style?

He is, Alan told me, a former pro who had one tour victory on his record but he had not been consistent enough to stay on the tour. He had switched to caddying some ten years before but was currently unattached. They hoped we might fit together to form a winning team.

That week is not bad, although I don't win, finishing fourth. Carlos is happy enough to commit to stay with me and I am, to say the least, also pleased to have a caddy who knows about the pressures of the tour.

The following months are not easy. The need to play at the top of my game, all the time, is something that I find draining. Carlos tells me that that is not unusual at first. I wonder if I can ever get used to it.

There are no wins but, at the same time, I finish in the top-ten every time. Carlos is a superb guiding light and, in the same way that Ginny did, keeps me focused when I finish second, two events on the trot.

With no tour events in December, I return home to spend time with my family and with Rob, who I had only seen for a couple of days in three months. He has won his tour card finishing fifth at the Q-school finals.

All too soon, I am on the road again and now I have an aim. April will see me back at The Woodlands to defend the Chevron, this time as a professional.

February. I win my first tour event, in Morocco. Carlos is ecstatic and I sense that it is not just because of the money. He admits that this is the first time he has caddied for a tour winner and he is over the moon.

In March I find myself in South Africa for two competitions. Two top-five finishes mean that these last weeks before Houston, prove positive preparation for the first of the year's Majors.

Another brief trip home for both Carlos and me, before we head for the US but Rob is now in the Far East. We still talk each day but the distances and long periods between being physically close, grate on me.

I arrive in Texas two days before the practice sessions start to find Carlos ahead of me. He has already walked the course and worked on his notes. The practice rounds go well and, possibly for the first time, I head for the first tee on Thursday with a degree of confidence that I am playing as well as I can.

I am, of course, aware that only Annika Sorenstam has won the championship two years running and that was back at the turn of the century.

"I can do my homework, sometimes, Ginny!" I chuckle to myself.

That first day sees some very good scoring and Ingrid sets the pace, in the early rounds, shooting six under. I am late out and conditions are not quite as easy but I manage to stay in touch, two shots back. It is only on the second day that I suddenly appreciate how much I enjoy the course. Last year was good but this year is better and my golf is exceptional, as I see it anyway, over the second and third rounds with the result that I start the final eighteen holes with a four-shot lead over an equally young golfer, a Korean, Ko Song. Ingrid has fallen back and is out of real contention, as is Joanne.

Maybe I am too relaxed and by the tenth hole my lead has evaporated. Ko is playing some brilliant golf and is five under for the nine holes. Carlos keeps nudging me to focus but by the thirteenth I am two behind and struggling.

My opponent is concentrating so hard she might be on another planet as she tries to outplay me and maybe that works against her. I finally respond with a couple of my own out-of-this-world approaches and the resulting tap-in birdies get me back level with her by the sixteenth and we match pars at the seventeenth.

The last hole and we both reach the par five green in two. Ko's approach finishes some five or six feet from the hole but mine catches the wrong side of a hump that crosses the green and I have a long putt starting uphill before it will turn downhill towards the hole.

Suddenly Ko is smiling and chatting away to her caddy. That she was distant and silent throughout the round did not concern me but her change of attitude irritates me. Clearly, she believes that she will have that putt to win, or possibly even two putts, and that annoys me. This is my championship and you're not getting it that easily, I think.

Having studied the putt extensively, I decide on the line and I move to make my stroke. Despite this Ko has not quietened and an official must call for silence. She is abashed, I think, and apologises. My putter has been my saviour all day and it does not let me down. The ball crawls to the top of the rise, almost stopping, before it catches the downslope and trickles downwards, moving faster. I hold my breath, is it too fast? Then as it reaches the hole it catches the top edge and drops for an eagle.

Now Ko's demeanour changes. What, I suspect, felt like a free putt to win is now a necessity just for a play-off and the focus, that had allowed her to reach a winning position has, for the first time, gone. She and her caddy spend an age trying to get the line. The putt is across the slope and even if she gets the line right it will all be about the pace. Intellectually I can sympathise, emotionally I am in a turmoil. Twelve months ago, I spoke to my Dad as he was dying, now I just want to finish and hide away for a few minutes.

Ko, eventually, stands over the ball and strikes her putt. The line is good and the ball turns towards the hole but she has misjudged the pace and misses. The resultant second putt is almost as far away but she manages to compose herself and sink that, guaranteeing her second place, on her own.

As we shake hands and exchange congratulations and commiserations it finally sinks in. I have won my second Major and this time: there is prize money! Dad, you were surely looking down on me today.

By Tuesday, I am back home and the family have me watching a recording of the Sky coverage after the finish. I had, naturally, been through the interview process but had not seen any of the post-championship analysis.

I can understand that my performance is a highlight but then there is the question of, whisper it, the Solheim Cup. There is a discussion about team selection and the consensus is that, assuming I don't get an automatic place, I should be one of the Captain's picks! I wonder if I could go into hiding. I am not ready for that, not yet anyway.

Rob is still travelling, and he is doing well. Of course, he was unable to play the Masters again but as I told him – always next year. Problem is that with the time differences we are not even talking every day now and he seems further away. I miss him and worry that there might be another woman. I wonder if he is having the same worries about me.

I call on Ginny and Steven and little Ellie, who was born while I was in the States. She is a tiny, healthy baby, which is the most important thing.

I have a few weeks before the next European tour event and use them to have my leg checked over. It seems important, as on two occasions the leg has frozen, fortunately not when I have been playing but it provides for a reason to worry. The hospital team take a download of the memory bank and check the physical leg itself. There is nothing apparently wrong with that side and they send the results off to James' operation.

At the same time, I head back to the Club. I want time with Alan. He has been my coach for almost fifteen years. Now it is time to put things on a professional level. I still want access to his advice and guidance on improving my game. I find it difficult to trust anyone else and now I have the chance to return his love and generosity.

"Sophie, you owe me nothing. You repaid my trust with your hard work."

I bang my head against an imaginary wall. "Alan, I owe you everything. You saw what might have been nothing and helped me turn it into a half-decent golfer."

"No, you did that, Sophie." There are dents in the wall.

"Okay. Okay. That's the past, Alan. I will still need a coach in the future and I want you to be that person. That means we put the arrangement on a professional footing. I'll get Ginny to talk to you about a retainer and I don't want any arguments, Alan."

"If you must, Sophie. You know you have made my life worthwhile. Your family are great and treat me as one of them, before that I had no-one. So, remember, I owe you as much."

I run into James and stumble to a stop. He looks transformed. I don't mean he is any less smartly dressed but his whole look strikes me as someone who lost a penny and then won the Lottery. I am careful how I treat him. I'm not sure that our relationship is known about and I haven't been able to see Ginny, in private, since I got back from the States.

I wait until we are in his office, before I give him a hug, and ask if I can spill the beans to my friend.

"Of course, you can Sophie. Ginny has already pinned me in a corner, when she brought the baby in. Checking I wasn't taking advantage of you! Now you are back for a few days, we can be open about it. I gather you have had a few problems with the leg?"

I gasp, something about patient confidentiality comes to mind, before I grin. "Not sure how serious but, I guess, you know what has happened?"

"Yes. I think the team understand why and they are working on a software fix. I got a copy and found it rather interesting, analysing the output. It is a long-standing problem with all cutting-edge technology, the designer of the software can't identify every possible outcome. If I am right, the problem is to do with the links to the nerves in the thigh, there is a glitch in the process which has, on those occasions caused the links to operate outside the parameters they are designed to work under. How did you fix it?"

I laughed. "Just what you do when a computer seizes. I hit the off switch and then turned it on again after a few minutes."

"Good for you. I hope that the answer will be found and installed before you head for France."

That trip is only just over a week away and I find myself spending more time at the hospital. Nice though it is renewing the friendships developed over the years – I would have preferred to be with Rob or back at the Club practising. By the end of the week my leg has been refined and the software answer, hopefully, uploaded.

I spend an evening with Ginny and the baby and take the chance to explain about James. She is dumbfounded, as much because she never saw him as any form of computer nerd, as for his generosity. Of spirit, as she puts it.

The next week, I head to France for a tour event before a move on to the Belgian Open, two weeks later. I am aware that a top-ten finish in the latter might be my entry to the Scandinavian Mixed, one of the biggest non-Majors in Europe. A win provides a certain entry!

My performance is not good. For some reason, I cannot lift my focus to the levels needed and duly finish well down the field in both events. I head home depressed. Missing out on the Scandinavian and Rob still being away, combine to leave me fed-up with myself, and him. Not for the first time I realise how lonely being away can be.

Back home I find myself trying to understand why my game has suddenly taken a downward spiral and get my team, as I call them, together for a brain storming session. There are several ideas floated but the one that strikes home hardest goes against how I had been feeling before the Christmas break. Carlos's comment reflects how he has seen me play.

"Sophie, you are rarely the fastest starter in a tournament. That hasn't mattered as you are usually "in the mix," as you, English, call it. Those last two starts were poor, by your standards anyway, and I think it may be because you are not playing enough competitions."

"But there haven't been any more. Only every two weeks for the most part." I muttered.

Alan was frowning. "You are both right. There are fewer European tour events at the start of the year, probably to do with seasonal constraints but you, Sophie, have been used to playing every week as an amateur other than in the depths of winter. We need to look at your schedule next year but at least the events from June are weekly."

Ginny raised her hand to attract attention. "Should we look to change Sophie's schedule now then? Perhaps taking a break before the LPGA isn't that good an idea?"

"I wasn't planning on going to Sweden except for the Scandinavian and I'm not in that but there is the Helsingborg Open next week, and the German Masters two weeks later. Only thing is, that would mean flying from Germany direct to the States; it's only a week before the LPGA."

"That might be a good idea. Jetlag shouldn't be any worse." Alan was quietly thoughtful, as ever. He had beaten Ginny down further than I had wanted when negotiating his retainer but I could work on that, I was thinking.

"Why aren't you planning on the Scandinavian, Sophie?" Steven was looking at his tablet, checking on the schedules involved, I thought.

"I needed a top ten finish in Belgium, at least. I'm not sure but I might have had to win it. Why?"

"But you qualified before you left for France, your World Ranking gets you in, if you want." Steven was checking.

Ginny chuckles. "Sophie doesn't tend to follow such mundane things, love. Sophie, your World Ranking is in the nineties and rising. I rather think your performances in the Majors as an amateur must have contributed to that and, don't forget, the last two competitions are only bad from your viewpoint."

"So, I could play every week between now and the LPGA? Are you up for that Carlos?"

"That is my job, boss." He grins.

"Ginny, can you sort flights for tomorrow?"

It is her turn to smile. "I'll get my assistant on it!"

"No peace for the wicked." Steven laughs.

Afterwards, Alan and I discuss how I might improve my game. His input strikes home.

"I've been chatting to all three of your caddies and we think we have identified one area where you could improve your game."
I look at him waiting.
"It's how you approach the first round. Looking back at the record, you have never led the field after eighteen holes. That isn't a major issue but they all, with hindsight, suggest you are more conservative at the beginning of a competition. Sophie, is that because you don't feel that you know the course well enough?"
Now it is my turn to think, how do I approach the start of a competition?
After a few minutes, I respond. "I'm not sure that that is right, after all I have usually had two days of practice. I don't think it is a conscious thing but, now you have talked about it, I wonder if I am thinking that I mustn't mess up. What do they say? "You can't win it on the first day but you can lose it." Could that be driving me?"
Alan looks startled. "I don't think we looked at it from that viewpoint but it is a fair thought. I suggest that you ask Carlos to encourage you to take more risk, that is to be more aggressive in your shot choice. Now that doesn't mean playing daft shots around trees or suchlike."
I look askance at him. "I couldn't do that, Alan. You taught me early on to accept the cost of a poor shot. If it needs a safety shot out of trouble then so be it." And I laugh. "Look out, Helsingborg!"

Sweden and a Misfiring Leg.

I arrive in Sweden, buzzing with anticipation. Can I deliver? Or will I sink? Thursday morning and I walk on to the first tee at Helsingborg, I am an early starter. Carlos has been briefed by Alan and myself. Practice has been good and I am ready to attack this delightful course.

First tee and I am presented with my driver. Ah well, I think. Here goes. I must hit the fairway and carry the bunkers. Over them and I will have to decide how to negotiate the approach which, like most of the front nine holes, is next to water. And hit the fairway I do. I know the dangers of the approach but Carlos shows his trust in me, giving me my three-wood. He reminds me. Play my normal draw but aim at the water's edge.

I look at him, must I take such a risk? Then I realise that, if I do hit my usual shape, the worst that can happen is that I find the greenside sand. A few minutes later and I hold my breath as the ball draws but only slowly, has the wind caught it? No, it hasn't. The result is wonderful and I complete an eagle.

From that point, I hit the course at a run. I take no unnecessary risks but, where I can, I attack. There are no more eagles but seven birdies leave me with the overnight lead having finished at nine-under par. Two days later and I have my second tour win. Two more sub-par rounds and only two bogeys.

Now for the Scandinavian Mixed, one of the biggest non-Majors on the tour. Faced with competing alongside and with the men for the first time, I find it more fun than I expected. I can hope, I say to Carlos, that I don't find the water too often. He laughs.

Continuing my new first-round strategy, I start in good fashion with birdies at the second, and fourth holes but the highlight of the round is at the par three fifth. Another good shot and I have my second ever hole-in-one.

As we walk through to the sixth tee, Carlos tells me the good news. I can give my little run-around away. Volvo are the sponsors and there is a new car awaiting me! Unless someone else matches my ace, of course. Fortunately, there is a delay on the tee and that allows me to catch my breath.

After that the rest of the round is quiet, three birdies on the back nine are only offset by a bogey at the seventeenth where I find the trees with my drive. That'll teach me, I think, before finishing with the clubhouse lead. Leaving my two playing partners, both Tour members, behind. There are no bad feelings though, just determination to outplay me tomorrow!

Days two and three are, somehow, more enjoyable, perhaps because I am grouped with another of the ladies and just the one male, but probably because my good form continues and I build a big lead. Television coverage back home makes the comment that come Sunday the tournament is mine to lose!

Not something I wanted to hear but I do, for the first time in days, manage to chat with Rob. He is back in Europe but did not qualify for the Scandi. He sounds fed-up. There seems little chance of our meeting up as my next tournament is in Germany a week before the BMW International, also in Germany, which he bemoans as bad timing since I will be in the States. I suggest that he travel to Germany a week earlier and we could have some time together, he perks up and decides that he will do that.

Sunday comes with good warm weather and my three ball gets off to a good start, all three of us birdieing the first. Not sure that they were too happy with mine but that's life. Four pars follow while my lead is cut to seven. Then as I walk to the sixth my leg freezes and I stumble. My initial response to the concern expressed is to say that I'll be okay. I switch the electronics off and wait the necessary time before turning them back on. Nothing. I try again, and again the leg remains dead.

It is not as if I can take a medical time out and I decide to continue, limping on to the tee. I know that my swing is going to be impeded. I can only move my body to a limited extent and my next decision is how to approach the shot.

This is going to be a time for experimentation and Carlos suggests that I try a three-quarter swing. His idea is that I will have to give up distance to retain accuracy, at least until I can adjust. For once I really am playing one-legged and it feels harsh. Just what is going on, I think. Wish you were here, James.

My playing partners play their shots and are asking what the problem is. When I explain there is unrestrained amazement and sympathy, at least up to a point. I sense thoughts that they might yet have a chance and I make the decision that whatever, they will need to play well to pull me back. Those thoughts give me a mental boost. Odd isn't it how things that should be negative can also be positive.

From that point I use my understanding of my game and, despite a reduced swing, send my drive down the fairway. I know that I will almost certainly not be able to reach the green in regulation so I aim to leave the right distance for a full wedge shot and that shot finishes close to the hole. I save my par. From then on, I choose care over risk and continue to make pars. As we continue, the others manage the odd birdie but also make mistakes. We reach the twelfth and my lead is still five.

Carlos suggests I try my leg again, we are approaching the more difficult part of the course and I do. He doesn't realise I have tried it several times, but this time there is a response and the leg quivers, vibrating. This feels worse than no leg, I switch it off again.

Despite having to change my approach on every hole, Carlos is cleverly guiding me and I avoid any disasters, just the one bogey, which is enough. Everything comes down to my wedges and putter and no-one can find enough birdies to catch me.

The television interviewer afterwards finds it difficult to focus on my golf. I am left trying to explain that there is a problem with my leg without sounding as if it is serious.

After we finish, my first call is home. My Mum answers and we chat. She is worried that I no longer have a good leg and I must tell her that the leg itself is fine, that it is the electronics that are misfiring. Once she is satisfied, she asks if I want to speak to my uncle! I say yes and will ring him later only to find the voice at the other end changing as he comes on the line.

"Sophie, what happened?"

It takes some time to explain that I really don't know and, in the end, I agree that I will be heading home on the first flight. I won't be playing Germany after all. The experts are going to need the week to work out just what went wrong and to find an answer.

The most difficult conversation is with Rob. He has not yet been able to see any coverage, having already left for Germany, and finds it difficult to discover that we are not going to be able to spend time together unless he simply flies back. He is not happy, fearing that I will have already had to leave for the States. He asks if I am trying to avoid him. I seem unable to convince him otherwise.

Back in England, I am met at the airport by James who takes me, not to the hospital but direct to his company. When I ask why, his words strike fear into me.

"I have been talking to my people. They tell me that what happened in Sweden cannot have been an accident. Sophie, has anyone else had access to your leg in recent days? I mean the electronics not the external parts."

"No. I haven't been with anyone who could have tampered with it. That is what you are thinking isn't it? Last people to have that sort of contact would be members of the prosthetic team at the hospital. Oh, James, is that why we are not going there?"

He nods, frowning. "Someone leaked the information about the hospital providing you with the various prosthetics and made that claim of a million pounds or more. That must be either an administrator or one of Anita's team. I don't understand why but now it looks as if they want to sabotage the whole process. That suggests it must be one of the latter."

I look at him. I know those people and can't believe that they would act in that way. "What do you think they have done, James?"

"It looks as if a virus has infected the software. A time bomb, which would only trigger on Sunday when you would be out on the course. Why? I don't know. The timing is suspect though and there is a lot of work going on to see if there were any suspicious betting patterns."

"People bet on me?"

"On the morning of Sunday, the odds against you being caught, by any of the other golfers, were hundreds to one. A relatively small bet would be worth a lot if, for some reason, you failed to complete the round or your game couldn't cope with the leg freezing. You carried on and won and that means there may be some very unhappy gamblers. It is all surmise now but, as I said, there is work going on to prove it one way or the other."

We are approaching the research unit where James' team have been working to simplify the workings of prosthetics such as my leg. James has explained that the leg, and its predecessors never cost the monies claimed by the press. Expensive, yes, but only if you allocate all the research costs to a single limb and, truth is, that while my leg might be the first one developed to the level it is, other limbs, mostly arms and hands, had been produced in the USA over a period of several years before mine was made. But the team still need to find a way to mass produce such limbs and reduce the cost before the NHS can approve them.

Once we have arrived, my leg is disconnected from the thigh section. The team leader keeps it in sight as she, and James, work together to upload the software into a desktop that he explains is isolated from the rest of their network. The software is run through a programme which will identify any changes when compared with a copy of the original version uploaded to my leg, a few weeks earlier.

The check seems to take forever before Charlotte exclaims. "There it is. Ouch," she studies the output, "that is more than a simple time bomb."

James looks over her shoulder. "Yes, I agree. It is a software bomb but it would need to be triggered externally. Charlotte, I didn't think we designed the electronics with any remote access capability. The team considered that too risky."

"We didn't and that begs the question. Has the leg's hardware been tampered with? Sophie, we're going to need to run a lengthy examination of both parts of the leg. We can handle the thigh element quite easily and quickly but you'll have to cope with the next version of the lower leg, at least for a few days."

"And that will fit me?"

"Oh, yes!" She smiles. "This has been designed especially for you, Sophie. You wouldn't have known but you have been our guinea pig in this development and we couldn't have asked for a better subject!"

I've been a guinea pig! I decide that my uncle will face the third degree later.

As Charlotte said, the examination of my thigh fitting is quickly finished and nothing untoward is found. She and James then bring out the new leg.

At first look it is identical to the other but then they allow me feel its skin. It has a much better texture. The links seem better but it is only when it is fitted that I understand the real changes. If my old leg felt good this was first class. Could I keep it?

The answer is yes but given what had happened, Charlotte wants to make certain any other crooks would fail in trying to sabotage the leg.

"I need to understand what was done and then the design will be changed to block any future attempts to damage it. You've got it for a few days anyway, Sophie."

"How soon do you think it will take?" I am conscious that I will need to head for the States by the end of the week.

"Three days at the most, maybe less. You are going somewhere?"

I nod. "Maryland."

James chuckles. "Nothing important, Charlotte. Some two-bit comp called the LPGA Championship!"

"James, I'm not that daft. It's a Major and we need to have Sophie ready and firing on all cylinders. Don't worry, Sophie, you'll be ready."

As James drives me home, I am afraid I do berate him. "Using me as a guinea pig, Uncle. Not sure that I like that."

He grins. "Charlotte was a bit unfair on herself and the rest of the team. Yes, you were the first person to have a leg but at one level it was simply an adaptation of one of the prosthetic arms we had already developed. The main problem they faced was the constant pressure of your weight on the leg and that wasn't fully solved until the third version. Even now we are still looking for improvements."

I look at him and smile. "I'm not really complaining, James. I'm just amazed at the whole operation and the work just to give me a chance on the golf course."

"Sophie, it's not just for you. You might be the most important, to me, but this is a long-term project that we hope will mean, in time, that every amputee can have a fully operational prosthetic. You are leading the way, others will follow."

We arrive at my home and James helps me unload before departing. "I'll see you soon, Sophie. Best you have time with your Mum and brothers, if they are here, of course."

I give him a kiss, though I am a little surprised at his unwillingness to come in. Inside Mum seems nervous, wanting to know that I am alright. I had called her to tell her that I would be delayed but that doesn't seem to be the issue.

William comes out of the kitchen and grabs me in a brotherly hug. "How's my baby sis?"

I look at him in amazement. Will is not the most outgoing of my brothers and this is unusual behaviour. "What's up? Mum acts as if I'm about to explode. You give me a hug!"

"Oh, Sophie. Mum has been worried that your leg is broken. Me, I'm just pleased to see my brilliant sister."

I'm not that sure but decide to head for my bedroom and call Rob. I am really wishing he had stayed in England but I can't blame him, much! The call isn't very long, for once we are both fed-up with each other and can only promise to talk tomorrow. I wonder if even that might prove wrong.

Later that night, my Mum calls me down to the lounge, she wants to talk to me, on my own. The conversation centres on me and Rob. Are we okay? How are things? She knows we haven't seen each other for weeks and even then, only for a day or two.

For the first time I am unsure of my answer. Mum's question has caused me to look at our relationship in a way I hadn't before and now I am uncertain. I promise Mum that I will think about it.

The next day is, frankly, weird. My new, temporary, leg works fine but, despite it being apparently an improved version, it feels rather uncomfortable and when I try it out on the range there is some resistance to my swing movement.

Finally, before I hit the putting green, I call Charlotte to alert her to the problem with the new leg and to ask her when my "old" leg will be ready. She doesn't sound happy and promises to get back to me.

A little while later, just as I am finishing my putting routine, James appears, "Sophie, do you have any commitments today?" I shake my head. "Come on, then. Let's go see your updated leg."

"I only spoke to Charlotte an hour ago. She hasn't come back to me, James, and she didn't sound all that certain about it."

"We've spoken. I think that your comments about the new leg left her disconcerted. Let's go. They have the answers to the problems with the old leg, that I do know."

He drives us across the county to the operations centre where we are greeted by Charlotte and someone, I didn't meet the first time there but who looks familiar, at least I have a feeling that I have seen her before.

"This is Gina, Sophie, she's been working on the leg's security and we are certain that that problem is solved. James, any progress on finding out who we are looking for, or why the leg was interfered with?"

James shakes his head. "There were some unusual betting activities but not enough to warrant any formal investigation. The only plus will be, that the industry will be alert, if there is anything odd involving Sophie in the future."

Charlotte brings out my leg and carefully fits it before turning the system on. I walk around and immediately feel good. This is the one I am used to and a few practice swing actions confirm that it is back to its best.

"What did you find?"

"A very clever, tiny attachment to the USB port. It worked as an aerial. That won't be possible with the new charging point and there is a cut-off button which will isolate the link to the central processors."

We head back to the Club and I am trying to work out where I have seen Gina before, it is a niggling itch in my mind. Finally, I ask James.

"How long has Gina worked for the team, James, do you know?"

"I'm not sure, Sophie. Why?"

"I'm sure I have met her or seen her, somewhere, recently." Then it sinks in. "Got it. She was in Sweden, in the crowd watching me play! Hell! James, could she be our saboteur?"

He looks across before he decides to stop the car. "Charlotte and I have been trying to check the background of everyone. Once we knew the way the link worked it had to be someone who worked on the hardware but knew enough about the software. That might have included the team at the hospital, of course. We had assumed that whoever did this was working with others."

He called Charlotte, she had worked with him from the beginning and owned almost as much of the company as he did, he explained, so was above suspicion. Once she had confirmed that she was alone and could not be overheard, James asked if Gina had taken any leave to allow her to travel to Sweden.

"No, she hasn't. The only time she has taken off was last Friday afternoon. She was going to Oslo, I think, flying out that evening. She was late in on Monday but nothing odd about that, she had warned us. Why?"

"Sophie saw her at the golf."

"What? She hates sport! Oh...." There was apparent realisation. "How do you want to handle this, James?"

"Talk to the lawyers. I do not want her to get anything for wrongful dismissal. Pending their advice, suspend her on full pay pending an investigation. Make sure she takes nothing in the way of intellectual property or equipment off-site. You need to ensure she gets no warning. You know what to do, Charlotte."

"Leave it with me, James. Apologies, Sophie, our recruitment checks were clearly not good enough."

"Charlotte, no need to apologise but it would be good to understand why."

And, in due course, we do learn that it was this hatred for sport, dating back to school PE lessons that was the driver, plus jealousy that a mere golfer was getting the fruits of her work.

It wasn't really her work, of course. She had only arrived on the scene two years before and her main contribution had been improving the new skin for my leg. She had added the aerial implant to the leg as far back as then but had only been able to develop the software bug later, inserting it when the program was being corrected for the earlier failures.

With the increased security, I am confident that the leg will perform as it has in the past and I will fly to the States with no worries so far as that goes.

European Tour.

For the moment, I am focused on my need to earn some money and with Sophie away in Sweden for two tournaments I wonder if we can ever get together.

The Belfry, best known for its holding of the Ryder Cup, is a regular on both the men's tour and the ladies. Never an easy course to play, the Brabazon is, in my eyes, a remarkable challenge. I arrive with my new caddy, John, who has played golf on the Challenge Tour but didn't manage to make the leap to the European Tour. Recommended by a friend of Peter, we have decided to work together for a year, or maybe longer. I have warned him that he is unlikely to become rich on his share of my winnings but he has talked to Peter and has a more positive view of life.

And, of course, the Belfry proves him right or at least I manage to handle conditions better than on the few occasions I have played the course in the past. Two sub-par rounds move me into contention and that is the first obstacle cleared. Another good round on the Saturday and I am looking at a top-ten finish.

Sophie has been watching some of the golf on a cable channel and is dutifully over-the-moon during our daily call. At least that seems to be how she sounds but maybe, I tell myself, it is just the mobile signal.

Sunday. I play well but just not as well as the rest of the field. I do manage to finish tied eighth. John is happy, his share means he will earn as much as he ever did win in a single event.

Now I do miss Sophie and head back home depressed by her absence. Susie is at home with her own news: she has been called up to the England squad!

When I tell Sophie she almost sounds more excited at that than she was at my result and I realise that I am too. It is then that I learn that rather than being back in England, she will be playing on the Ladies Tour in Germany the week before I am due there. Is she avoiding me?

I admit I whinge at her for not being there. Then she suggests that I travel over the week before my tournament and join her. My spirits are up and I organise everything such that I will be there before she leaves Sweden.

That turns out to be a mistake!

As ever I had been watching some of the golf live and some via highlights but I missed much of the final round due to being in the air. Sophie had a comfortable lead going into the final round of the Scandi and I looked forward to seeing the highlights from my hotel room.

The programme was already underway when I reached the room and I settled down to find that the commentators were bemused by something that had happened to Sophie. She wasn't swinging right, only perhaps two thirds of a normal swing. I was as mystified as they were until I saw her limping along the fairway. Something was wrong with her leg! It didn't stop her though and despite whatever the problem was she held on to win. That's my Sophie!

Later that evening I was pulling my hair out. Oh, why hadn't I stayed in England? Sophie's leg wasn't working and she was catching the first flight home the next morning. I know she had little choice but after our call I was angry. With myself and Sophie. Me, because I had been angry with her for not coming to Germany at all, and with Sophie for the same reason. Now I was faced with a lonely week doing no more than practice for the BMW. I felt guilty as well, she had the LPGA Championship the following week and must have been worried that she would not be able to rely on her leg.

In the end we make peace and put ourselves in the right frame of mind to focus on the upcoming tournaments. Sophie, of course is

faced with a Major and my own is one of the bigger Tour events; the BMW International.

A week later I tee off on the Thursday. I start well with a birdie at the first and by the time I reach the clubhouse I am five under and tied for fourth place.

I head for the lounge and a better screen which is showing the LPGA. Sophie has just teed off and I can see much of her round. And what a round. Almost five hours in awful conditions. As ever she plays steady golf and finishes in the red, just. Their leaderboard reinforces how good that is. Only six players finish under par and the low score is a seventy.

The next day I tee off early afternoon which means that Sophie and I are on our respective courses at the same time. I have another good round matching that of the day before and am now tied first. Sophie manages the continued difficult conditions well and has the overnight lead; in a Major, again! Now I expect her to be headline news and, of course, she is. Just not as big as a club pro who has matched her!

Saturday proves harder. I am not used to leading and by the end of the day have slipped back into a tie for third. John proves his worth keeping me focused after a bad start from which I mostly recover. Tomorrow I must try to make up the two-shot deficit I now face.

Things must have been easier for my Sophie. She has a three-shot lead but has a Joanne Fitzgerald in her pairing for Sunday – two Major winners going head-to-head.

The time difference works for me and I do not have to think about how Sophie might be doing. Perhaps that helps and, again with John's guidance I start well. By the time I reach the turn I am one of three players tied for the lead. A stunning start to the back nine, four birdies on the trot and I have the lead on my own. This is where John's experience proves invaluable. He knows that the adrenaline will be flowing as I reach the last few holes and he contrives, I am not sure how, to keep me in play and ensure that I avoid any serious errors.

Gradually we reach the final hole. My playing partner has dropped out of contention but the final pair are still only one-shot back. Now I begin to understand real pressure. The hole is a long par-five but has seen many birdies during the competition including, I admit, two by me. This is the moment I tell myself; you get another birdie and someone will need an eagle to catch you. After a heart-stopping moment, when my second shot catches the wrong slope on the apron, I face a chip over the green to a difficult flag position, are they ever easy?

After some thought I send the ball over the slope and leave myself a ten-foot putt. What was it that Peter once told me? Professionals only hole forty per cent of these? Now all those exercises need to deliver, I think, and deliver they do, as the putt drops. I have done all I can and now I must wait.

Oh Sophie, how I wish you were here! This could be my first Tour win. Twenty minutes later and it is confirmed I have won. Now I can only wait and see if Sophie can hold on to her lead.

The LPGA.

The Ladies' PGA Championship is being held at the Congressional Country Club in Maryland. This will be my first attempt at the Major. Carlos is travelling via his home in Spain and will meet me there. I wonder if this is how other golfer/caddy partnerships work.

What is hard to handle is the press coverage, I have been installed as joint favourite along with Ingrid and Joanne. That is crazy! Ko Song barely earns a mention despite her runner-up finish at The Woodlands.

The most sensible commentator, that I hear speaking on television, states that while my current form is good and no bad player wins the Scandi, he suggests that my lack of experience will work against me when playing in the biggest of the Majors.

He gets short thrift from the golfers, who are part of the team covering the event. The LPGA might be a Major but the US and our Open are older and carry more prestige, he is told in no uncertain terms. By this time, I have switched off, mentally anyway, and focus on the practice rounds.

Rob is also warming up ahead of his event in Germany and we do manage a longer and less stressed video call. The time difference means that he will have finished his first round before I start mine. I finish the call feeling more positive about our relationship than I have for some time.

I am a late starter on the Thursday and Joanne has finished, before I tee off. Her score, level par, is indicative that this is not going to be an easy day and the current leader in the clubhouse is only two under par. I say to Carlos. "Need to stay out of the rough today!"

He agrees. We tried a few practice shots from the second cut of rough the day before and confirmed that it is penal. Despite the success I have found by being more aggressive on day one, I decide that that needs to be tempered. Keep on the fairways otherwise I will be dropping shots, I remind myself.

"On the tee, from England, Sophie Jordan." The announcement is simple and assumes that the crowd are aware of my winning the Chevron, we are underway and I find the fairway off the first tee, always a relief.

Five hours later, and I almost stagger into the clubhouse, exhausted. Play was unbelievably slow and the need to retain focus harder than ever. My leg, the thigh anyway, is aching and I am praying that tomorrow will be less stressful. Some chance! Despite fatigue setting in over the last few holes, I have managed to avoid the deep rough except on the shorter of the par fives. There is no pleasure in being proven right. Hit the rough and you drop a shot. A bogey six on a hole, where a birdie was not difficult, feels worse than the single shot dropped. In the end I post a score of one under par. On a day when only a handful of the field shoot under par, I find I have reinforced my status as a favourite. Ko and Ingrid are well down the field and both may struggle to make the cut.

Rob has also had a good start and is buoyant that he has a chance. His optimism contrasts with my worry that fatigue may impact my play.

The second day and I am up with the lark. This time I am off in the fifth group and our hotel is not the closest to the course. Shortly before nine o'clock I am on the tenth tee, my first. I have never enjoyed playing courses back to front as it were but, on this occasion at least, seem to benefit. Play is much faster. I don't understand why, but I am not complaining. The course is not playing any easier but, just possibly, I find the pin positions more friendly. My conservative approach to how I play my tee-to-green element works and I make four birdies, this time with no bogeys. Five under par for the tournament leaves me leader in the clubhouse and, in the end, overnight as well.

My spell with the Sky team is as enjoyable as ever but my story is overshadowed by that of a Club Pro, Susan Trent, from Washington State who finishes at four under and will be playing with me the next day. "Shades of Michael Block." Carlos comments. "Should be fun, tomorrow."

As Carlos thought, the third round is the most enjoyable of the four. Susan proves a friendly and sensible player. We talk as we walk the fairways and she manages to stay in touch. A top-five finish would mean she earns more in one weekend then in her career to date but her target is no worse than top-ten and the chance to come back the next year. It reminds me that there are a great army of people around the world like Alan. People who teach and encourage golfers to play their best. The often-unsung heroes of the game.

By the time we walk off the eighteenth, I have, despite the round taking another five hours, shot a third under-par score and am three ahead of a group of players which, I am delighted to say, includes my playing partner. Tomorrow will be tough, I remind myself. Joanne, having had a poor second round, has recovered and will be with me in the final pairing.

Now my critic from a few days earlier is struggling to describe why he still thinks I will not win. "Look at the Chevron, she threw away a four-shot lead and trailed at the start of the back nine. Only won it because Ko Song missed a putt on the eighteenth. Now she has Joanne Fitzgerald to contend with and she knows how to win a Major. My money is on the Canadian."

Carlos tells me, later, I haven't bothered to watch the experts, talking about me or Joanne or Ingrid for that matter. "Nobody agreed with him. Just play your game, boss, and you'll prove him wrong and then it will be worth watching him wriggle."

As the last pair out, we start our round shortly after Rob has finished his and I get the boost of hearing that he has his first Tour victory and the BMW International is a big one!

And I do play my game. I match Joanne hole-by-hole as we both score well. Two others, from those three shots back, start better, cutting my lead to one shot, at one point, but as the round goes on, all of them, except for Susan, drop back, unable to match Joanne or myself. By the sixteenth, I sense that Joanne is now focused on not dropping any shots rather than trying to catch me and I lose my own concentration, pulling my wedge approach to the seventeenth wide into the dreaded rough. Carlos is distraught.

We walk up to the green before turning to where my ball has finished and I am lucky, oh so very lucky. The ball has carried over the virgin rough and landed in an area trodden down by spectators, only stopping against the grandstand. My free drop is still in a clear area and I can play a normal chip to the green. Stopping the ball anywhere near the pin would be remarkable and I focus on ensuring I do finish on the green itself. I can afford to drop one shot but not two. Joanne has a reasonable birdie putt.

An amazing thought flashes across my mind. Back home, they will be on the edge of their seats aghast at my error.

For once I am quite slow deciding just how to take my shot before looking to drop the ball on the fringe. Better short of the hole, is my thinking, and I contrive to manage just that. I can see an expression of dismay on Joanne's face before she holes her putt to close the gap to two and now my putt grows in importance. My focus is back though and I sink it, for my par. We match pars at the last and I have my third Major win and a second in the year. Afterwards I can watch Mr. Grump's, as I call him, final comments with a smile.

"Another case of luck." He growls. "That shot should have finished deep in the rough but it was so bad it flew the lot. Let's see how she handles things when the run of the ball is against her."

In fairness, most of his comments are focused more on the US Open in a few weeks' time. "She must be the favourite to win and she has the game. Even so it is a big ask for a twenty-one-year-old to handle the sort of pressure she will be under."

One of his colleagues commented. "I interviewed Sophie a couple of years ago just after she had missed out on the Open at St Andrews. She was still an amateur and worried about raising the money for the trips to the States as the British Amateur Champion. And even more worried that she wasn't good enough to make the cuts at Augusta or the Chevron! That she would let everyone back home down! You can be sure that she has her feet firmly on the ground and, of course, she has a good caddy. I'm not betting against her."

I head home on cloud nine. Rob will already be at home and I will be joining him for a few days before we are off again. Both families are delighted at our success and we are royally entertained at both homes during our brief break.

Seeing Ginny and the youngster is fun and I find myself baby-sitting for an evening. Rob is with his own friends and we are apart for the night, again.

Rob will be off to Celtic Manor for his next tour event but I have concluded that I will fly back to the States early for the US Open rather than going to Finland for my next tour event. That doesn't go down well with Rob.

I must explain. The repeated crossings over the Atlantic are having a cumulative impact on my body clock. Rob's response is typical, he hasn't noticed anything wrong with my body! I wonder sometimes about his sight but heigh-ho.

This will be my last trip to the States this year and I do want to prepare well. To add to the jetlag, the Open is to be played at Pebble Beach. Rob is still unhappy but grudgingly accepts that my decision is for the best.

Disappointment at Pebble Beach

I spend the first few days in California relaxing and limiting my practice to chipping and putting at a small course near to my hotel. Carlos enjoys the chance to be a tourist. All-too-soon we find ourselves at the Beach. Pebble Beach. The time has come to focus.

By Thursday I am as ready as I can be and walk on to the first tee alongside Francine. We had had an emotional re-union earlier in the week when we found out that we were to play together in the same group. She has no plans to turn professional, for now, but I suspect that will change in time.

Two days later, though, Francine has missed the cut and is on the way home. I have managed to survive but only just. My game has not been bad but neither have I reached the consistency I need to compete at the top. For the first time in months, I can play relaxed and by the end of the third round I have halved the gap between myself and the leaders.

From discussing my failure to make any birdies on the first day and only a few on the Friday the conversation on Saturday evening centres on whether I could repeat my third-round score of sixty-four, in the final round.

Of course, Sunday is another day and I don't manage a repeat performance. I do climb the leader board and finish fourth, a result I can hardly complain about. It is those first two rounds that leave me disappointed. Surprisingly, Mr Grump, as I call him, is sympathetic when reviewing the event on the highlights programme.

"She will have learned how difficult the Open is and that will be valuable in the future. I keep having to remind myself that she is still only twenty-one and has already won three Majors. When you think about that, the question becomes just how many will she win in the future?"

I head home. I need to work with Alan to try and identify what went wrong. My consistency has always been the base of my game and for those two days I lost it and I don't understand why. I do have a few weeks before I will travel to France for the Evian Championship. The other Major I missed the previous year.

Alan has already spent time analysing the statistics associated with each round and has several suggestions but his most potent comment is.

"I think you tried to do too much on the first day and your putting stats show that your wedge play was below par. You had almost no first putts of under twenty-five feet and had to settle for pars when your normal game would have given you plenty of birdie chances. Carlos supports that idea. On the second day you got more shots close for birdies but they were offset by some wayward approaches that cost shots."

"That doesn't explain why the third round was so good." I counter. "I didn't feel that stressed in the first two rounds not enough anyway to explain how bad I was."

"Sophie, you've been unbelievably successful. That doesn't mean that your game is infallible and it doesn't take much to cause you, or anyone for that matter, to become more tense mentally, with the result, you suffered. Saturday there was no real pressure on you and those two early birdies will have brought your normal game back. It's life and it will happen again. Hopefully you will understand what is happening and will be able to respond better."

The Open – so near yet so far.

Sophie calls me, just after I have reached my hotel, to wish me luck as I embark on my third effort to win The Open, which is at Carnoustie this year. There has been the usual fuss over the difficulties of accessing the course for the public and, to be honest, players are not all that happy either.

She is heading for the airport and promises to be with me by the weekend. Her result at the US Open was not what she wanted but she did finish fourth and that is hardly failure, I feel. It is the boost I need and I am now looking ahead with an upbeat view of my chances. Funny that just having an important person in the crowd can help your game and Susie will be there as well.

John reminds me, as we walk to the first tee on the Thursday, that the course is notorious for being difficult and for crazy decisions by past players! I turn to him and ask why he had waited until now. He just grins. "My job is to keep you grounded. You need to treat this course with real respect."

I knew he was right. Practice rounds had proved him correct and his reminder was exactly why we were getting on as a team.

Eighteen holes later and I have posted one of the best rounds of the day! The evening is fun, even if I can't drink. Like Sophie I never drink during a competition and Susie is virtually teetotal. That does not stop us enjoying each other's company and looking forward to Susie's future as a Lioness.

Sophie arrives late on Friday to the news that I am the overnight leader! Another good round means that I have a one stroke lead over Justin Thomas and two shots better than the rest of the field.

Three's a crowd they say but not that evening and as the girls work to ensure that I am more relaxed ahead of a big day.

Saturday dawns and the wait for my afternoon start drags. Did that affect me? I don't really know but my golf is certainly not as good as the first two days and I finish back in fifth place. The Sky cart interview is still positive, reminding me that I am still a rookie and only three shots back. It doesn't really help but Sophie and Susie are still upbeat, as are my parents and Peter, who have made the trip up that day to be watching on the Sunday.

Fourth round and I make a good start with birdies at both the first and second holes to rapidly eradicate the overnight leader's advantage after they bogey the first. From that point on though, it is hard work. The weather is tougher with strong gusting winds and no-one is scoring low. By the turn I am back into third and that is where I stay until the last hole. There I find the water off the tee, how I will never know, and finish with a bogey. Third place rapidly becomes fourth and winning becomes a next year maybe.

I am not the happiest person in our group but my mother does ask me how much I win for finishing fourth. She has a professional interest having taken on the mantle of my accountant and adviser. When John answers her question, she tells me to brighten up. Six hundred thousand gross is not to be sniffed at, she says.

She is good with figures, my Mum, but doesn't wholly understand the status of Major winner. She does quietly suggest that Sophie, despite her three Majors, has never won that sort of money in a single event. I do have to point out Sophie's prize money for winning the LPGA Championship had been over a million pounds. But, I think, my fourth place should improve my sponsorship deals and make me a more interesting target for one of the big management agencies.

Before dinner, I ask Sophie what is going wrong. "I dropped three shots in the back nine, Sophie. Could have won it! Or at least forced a play-off?" She smiles before explaining that she had similar problems in California. Talk to Peter, is her answer. Afterwards, Sophie makes the rest of the evening more pleasurable than most of those in the recent past.

Two days later I am proved correct. Louise Dalton calls me; Global Sports would like to talk and she will be in the UK later in the week.

The Aramco Team

By the time, I reach the Centurion Club I am back to feeling good again. The Aramco Series is unique not because it's a team event and includes amateur team members but because of the way teams are selected. I wouldn't know who I was playing with until the draw; part random and part picked by the team captains.

That day is just so much fun, meeting other golfers I already know and then I am selected! Joanne is a team captain and picks me. Having gone head-to-head more than once we know each other well. This is going to be fun, I think, and so it proves. The third professional in our team is Georgia Hull. I didn't understand why she wasn't a captain's selection but Joanne and I are ecstatic to have her as a team mate. Then we find out who our amateur will be and I am delighted to find she is someone I have played against and enjoyed her company. Denise O'Leary, the Irish girl I had beaten, just, in the Amateur Championship.

Three days of glorious golf. We fit together well as a team and finish in the runners-up spot before we complete the individual event which is won by Georgia. She has twice been beaten on the last day in the event but holds on to win by two.

It is my first real team event since junior better-balls at the Club and a revelation of the impact of supporting your team mates while, in the case of the professionals, working hard to outplay them!

All in all, it leaves me in good spirits before I head for Spain and the last European tour event before the Evian Championship. At Alicante, I get to meet Carlos' family for the first time. They are a joy although I feel I should apologise to Agata for taking her husband away from her. She just smiles, she is a real beauty and obviously doesn't consider me a threat!

The La Sella Open is a relatively new event on the tour but popular, not least because it is one event with a prize pot of over one million euros. My own form is much improved over the US Open, and even the Aramco, despite which I only finish fifth.

Is that a good omen for the Major, I ask Rob?

The next day Carlos and I are on the road again heading for the Evian Resort Club. For once it is my turn to be irritated with Rob. He now has no competition until August but has refused to come to France to watch. He will be spending more time trying to correct the weaknesses in his game. To my later concern I realise that my emotion is more anger that he refused to join me rather than that I was missing him. For the first time I wonder if we really do have a future.

The Evian and the Open.

The first day of practice goes well and it is quickly apparent that my original thoughts, twelve months ago, that the course might suit my game were accurate. By Thursday I head out to the first tee with a bounce in my stride.

Two rounds later without any significant hiccups I have moved into a two-shot lead. Not the most relaxing position as other top players are only two and three shots back and they include Ingrid, Joanne, and Ko Song. Still, as Carlos points out, better ahead than behind.

Saturday brings mixed reviews for me. I play well, shooting another sub-par round but I cannot match the two nine-under par rounds shot by Ko and Joanne and I will be playing with Ingrid in the penultimate pairing; two shots back.

Sky Golf are asking me how I see tomorrow. I grin and tell them that it is all to play for and ask me tomorrow afternoon. It sounds like bravado but I am wondering if I could outscore the leaders should they not match Saturday's superb rounds.

Ingrid and I get off to flyers with two birdies each at the first two holes and are joint leaders. We are doing what we must. Putting pressure on Ko and Joanne and it works. By the turn the lead has switched round and we now lead by two from Ko and three from Joanne. Funnily, Ingrid's performance is not my worry, I am happy to match her and bide my time. I am sure that a crack will appear and the whole tournament is, in the end, turned on its head at the sixteenth. Ingrid seems to lose her focus and sends her drive left into trouble. I hit the fairway and my follow up second shot leaves me an easy birdie. Ingrid's drive was out of bounds and she drops a shot. A two-shot swing and I finish with another birdie at the eighteenth to set a clubhouse lead, two ahead of Joanne and Ko, who are level with Ingrid.

351

In the end neither can do better than birdie the last and I have another Major.

In the after-tournament interviews, there is a question that almost terrifies me. "Do you believe that you could win more Majors than Annika Sorenstam?"

I gasp. "I have no idea! There are so many top golfers around. Can I win another Major? I hope so, but six more? I cannot look that far ahead."

"Well, Sophie, no-one has won four Majors before their twenty-second birthday. We wish you well, later this year, for number five."

I gulp and thank them.... Major number five? I might hope, but to win four in a year would be unprecedented, at least as far as I know. Ginny, you are going to have to check!

The schedule for the women's tour means that there is limited time between the Majors and I arrive back from the Evian with just a day to spare before I must head north for the Scottish Open which will be followed by the Open the following week back at Wentworth.

With no time to rest up I almost decide to miss the former once again but Carlos suggests, firmly, that he feels it would be better to play. We head north.

A week later we are on a domestic flight questioning why we bothered. Most of the other top players had decided to take the week off and the field, sadly for the Scots, was nowhere near as strong as they would have hoped. I end up in a fourth-round battle with a newly turned professional, Francine. At least that makes the company enjoyable or it would have been if she hadn't been in the group behind mine.

The two of us gradually pulled away from the others only to be caught ourselves by a South African, Amahle Biyela. She is a Zulu, unique on the tour and this is her best result. It is difficult not to feel happy for her, I have met her before and she has a delightfully free-spirited approach to the game. I must settle for tied second, which is not that bad a finish just a week before the big one. But I am questioning if taking part, and the additional travel required, was a sensible use of energy.

By Thursday evening my earlier question is being answered. The joint leaders after day one are six under par, seven shots ahead of me. My leg has been causing me a certain degree of irritation, as it does occasionally, but I refuse to blame it entirely. I am simply feeling the accumulated effect of playing and or practicing for two weeks without a break apart from the journey from Scotland down to Wentworth. Four birdies are offset by five bogeys, not my usual form.

Rob's call boosts me, he still expects me to win everything, and he reminds me that there is still a lot of golf to be played. Two days later and there is a lot less golf but the gap is down to one shot and guess who's ahead of me? Ingrid, of course.

Sunday is hard work; the greens are hard and unforgiving and everyone struggles. We reach the final hole joint leaders but I can only par it and for the second time Ingrid beats me with a birdie.

Mr Grump is bemused. Not with my play but by the fact that I had played in the Scottish Open. "Another learning experience for her, there is no doubt that fatigue hit her on Thursday. Perhaps next year she'll take the week off."

Three Years Later.

"And now we come to the Sports Personality of the Year."

I sit in the audience, still with a sense of disbelief. The last few years have been a mix of heartache and success. The success has been almost without precedent, I know, but it has a big hole in it. I still find it difficult to believe my luck over the years; four more Major wins in that time but not a single home win; the Open has eluded me, so why am I here at all, I think.

Looking back golf has been kind to me, romance less so. After a year of rarely even seeing each other, except on the television, Rob and I decided to split; it was just too hard keeping our relationship going. We remain friends and I stay in touch with Susie, especially. There were other surprises.

Just a year after I discovered who had paid for my legs, I arrived home to a bombshell from my Mum.

"Sophie, you know I loved your Dad as much as anyone could? Don't you?"

"Of course. You and Dad were the perfect couple. The best parents and, oh Mum, how I miss him. And you do too, don't you? That's not a real question, sorry. He wasn't old enough to leave us, was he?"

Even as I was speaking, I sensed that Mum needed my approval for something and I was not sure what that was. It was over a year since Dad had died and Mum was still only fifty-two. Had she found someone? Was that what had caused her nervousness? That I might object? But who could have got close enough to win her heart that quickly?

Then it slowly dawned on me. James, my uncle! My benefactor. Dad's brother. How dare he! He's taken advantage of my Mum's grief to wriggle his way into her life! Even as those thoughts swept across my mind, I gave myself a real mental kicking. That wasn't how James was and Mum was tough enough not to have fallen just because Dad wasn't there. In any case, I didn't know. Surely, though, there wasn't anyone else?

I finally asked her why she had asked the question and her answer was not quite what my whirling brain expected.

"Sophie, I have talked with your brothers about this. We didn't leave you out but I wanted to talk face-to-face, not on a video call. Your Dad told me, when he knew he was jumping ship, as he put it, that I should look for someone else. We had a wonderful time together but, he said, I have many years ahead of me. I didn't agree with him then and only now am I beginning to feel that I could be with someone else. If I do find that person, Sophie, will I have your blessing?"

"Mum, you shouldn't need to ask. If you find someone then, please, go with the flow. Is there anyone yet?" I was still wondering if James should be in my firing line or not.

Mum looked a little embarrassed. "Bernard and Will didn't ask. As you have asked, the answer is no, not yet." She seemed to hold her breath. "Sophie, please don't tell anyone and I mean no-one, not yet anyway. I would like to think that James might be willing. He has taken me out for dinner but much more like a brother might. Nothing more. I sense that for anything to happen, well, it needs me to make that move first."

"Oh, Mum. Go for it. He's a lovely person and the two of you would make a good couple." All I could do, then, was to hug her.

I did wonder if I should nudge James but realised that that was exactly what Mum really didn't want. Whatever, I decided, I could only be happy that Mum was recovering from her grief at the loss of Dad.

It would be a few weeks before James cornered me at the Club and asked my permission to date Mum! Having wound him up initially by expressing my horror at the idea, I laughed at his dismay and told him that if he was making my Mum happy then that was perfectly okay as far as I was concerned!

That change at home did make my decision a year later to move to the States and look to compete on the LPGA Tour easier; I am not sure I could have done that if Mum had still been on her own.

It took a lot of planning and talks with Alan, my family and Carlos. The hardest was with Carlos, who did not feel he could uproot his family. He didn't want to let me down but made the valid point that, if he moved to the States, he wouldn't be able to go home often enough. In the end we compromised and agreed that he would stay as my caddy for a year but no longer.

The move was made easier by the generosity of Anna and her family who offered to help us find a home big enough for us to use as a base during that first year. Anna had, I should add, turned professional, herself, six months earlier.

That first year was hard and there were no Tour wins as such and a couple of missed cuts. Yes, that's what I remember, two missed cuts! These were offset by two more Majors. Another US Open, followed up by an unprecedented third Evian in a row!

Even Mr Grump is more relaxed. Though he does wonder why I can't win my home Major. "She's still not yet twenty-six and has won ten Majors but the nearest she has come to the Women's Open is second; twice. I remind myself that she will have many more opportunities but the longer it takes the harder she may find it."

His comments are fair and I do wonder why, last year I missed the Scottish Open and ended up just barely making the top ten, a result worse than ever before.

I have continued to follow Rob and Richard, for that matter. Rob is managing to compete well enough to have lifted his ranking into the top fifty which means that he is beginning to qualify for all his Majors.

I wish the news was as good for Richard. After a second year on the Korn Ferry Tour, he finally did enough to get his PGA Tour Card but although he had had a reasonable rookie year, he had been unable to retain it in the second year. I understood he was giving the Korn Ferry a final try before looking for a Club pro job. I keep sending him good luck messages but do not get more than a Christmas card in return.

The announcers had been talking about the sports person who had won third place and it wasn't me. Then "And in second place, Sophie Jordan!"

There are a few hugs before I can join the throng around the trophy table. Warm applause and, crazily, I sense some disquiet that I haven't won. I didn't expect to get in the top three and attending the evening had seemed like a good excuse to give the family a night out. There is one individual there who I know and anticipate might, no not might but should win and now, like another family I knew, I was on tenterhooks.

"And the winner is ...." A long pause before. "the Lioness: Susie Ward!"

Now I was happy. Susie had been a mainstay of the England team, multiple goals and easily the biggest contribution to the team qualifying for the World Cup to be played the next year.

After the programme was over the two of us had a chance to chat. After she had disputed the result! Rob wasn't there as he was in the Far East. It would have been nice to see him again but perhaps it was for the best as Susie explained, gently, that he was back with Teri again. She worried that that would hurt me but to be honest I was pleased, if glad that I had learned it from a friend. Susie wouldn't say more about their being a couple again but I gathered it was partly to do with Teri's mother.

Back at home, I did find myself somewhat depressed. I was glad for Rob but now I knew that there was no chance of our ever getting together again and there had been times when I did dream about a reunion.

Mum hadn't returned home herself. She and James had decided to stay over for an extra couple of days; Christmas shopping, apparently. I wonder? I thought.

With no competition in the States or back in England I was able to take time off and get together with Ginny and Steven and young Ellie, now a bubbly four-year-old.

I saw Alan but only for a coffee. He was, I gathered from Ginny, a little tied up, with someone I knew quite well; Fiona.

"Fiona! How do you feel about that, Ginny?"

Ginny looked amused. "Jealous, Sophie? Or is it about the age difference? I mean how old do you think Alan is?"

I stuttered. "He must be well into his forties. He was the club pro here when I was seven and that's nineteen years ago."

Ginny smiled again. "He is forty-two. Fiona is thirty-eight. So, there's not that much difference, is there?"

I looked at her, slightly stunned and then I grinned. Alan had had no-one, apart from my family. That he was with another friend was good news.

What I hadn't told Ginny was that I was struggling to find a permanent replacement for Carlos. As we had agreed, he had headed back home after my first year in the States. Since then, I had tried out several caddies, there was no shortage of candidates looking to carry my bag, but I had not yet found one I felt I could trust in the same way.

It was Steven who broached the subject. He still took a close interest in my progress, as did all my friends, and had, unlike them, spotted the frequent change of bag carriers.

I was forced to explain that I had simply not been able to find someone I felt comfortable with, like Carlos.

Steven looked thoughtful. "I understand, Sophie. I have had similar experiences with golfers. Let me think about this, see if my contacts can find the right person."

I learned later that he had shared my problem with Alan and Alan was almost certain he had an answer. It would take a little work but a few days later, just as I was packing for the trip back to my home in California.

"Sophie, we have found the ideal caddy. He will be at your next event ready to start work. He does know who you are and we have given him a password, Tigris, so that you will know he is our suggestion."

I looked at Ginny, who was on the inside of the plan, but she shook her head.

"Give him a chance, we think he is ideal and you will be able to build a relationship that will last. Excuse our little bit of secrecy but he did ask that we not tell you until you meet. He has watched you a lot over the years and Fiona has done some research which supports our belief."

I am not going to suggest that I was other than intrigued. To be truthful I was angry that I could not be trusted by my friends. I caught the flight back with a burning desire to find out just who they believed would manage to fit the bill.

A week later, having got over the jetlag and days of fresh practice, I headed for the location of my next tour event. Having checked into my hotel, I made my way to the course for the first practice round.

"Miss Jordan, we have a person waiting who claims you are expecting him. He is on the driving range."

The official pointed me to the path I needed and I carefully lifted my bag. Despite having become more confident in my leg, bag carrying was still tough.

Fortunately, the range was only a short walk and I rounded a corner to find it quiet or to be honest, still empty as I was early. That was when I saw my future caddy and my heart almost stopped. How had I not guessed Alan's proposal?

"Richard, what are you doing here?"

"Tour golf proved too much for me and I was looking to get a club role, though I think you probably knew that, Sophie. Then Alan called me after he had spoken to Fiona. They wondered if I could stand being your bag carrier!"

"But Richard, you are a golfer and a good one. Don't you want to try for the Tour again?" I sort of knew why he didn't but I needed him to tell me that. My heart was fluttering about in a burst of nervousness.

"Sophie, I am a decent golfer but the Tours require more than just that and, well, I gave it my best shot. I had to do that but I know now that I don't have that extra piece to be able to survive."

"That doesn't mean you should want to be a caddy, does it?"

"You say that as though I should see it as a drop in status, Sophie. Most of the top caddies have played golf to a high level including on the tours. I do believe my experience would help you and well, we do get along, don't we?" His voice lifted in a sudden lack of confidence.

I looked at him in an equal level of doubt. Of course, I wanted him, and not just as a caddy. Okay, I thought, let's get down to business first.

"You know we did and, oh Richard, how I want what we had back!" I was stuttering and trembling with emotion. I gradually got myself back in control and continued. "But, before that, Sir. Business. Normal caddy rates, no arguments."

I could see him about to counter with a lesser demand, I did know him well enough to see a bit of Alan in him. "Agreed?"

He nodded slowly and for the second time in my life I stepped up to him and grabbed him in a bear hug and long kiss.

After he had disentangled himself, his response was just what I needed. "Now, time for some practice, boss!"

And that would be the start of a lifelong partnership both on the courses and off.

And for Rob – a new start.

"On the tee, Robert Ward."

I managed to launch a decent tee shot down the fairway and the final round of the competition was underway. Even though I was in with a chance of winning, I could only think about the evening back in England, the early hours tomorrow, here in Hong Kong. How I wished that I could have been in the studios with my family and my devilish and wonderful sister, Susie.

Sophie would also be there. I knew she had flown back from the States after learning of her nomination. My loyalties were split. Although Sophie and I had split up a couple of years earlier I continued to watch her golf with admiration. She should surely have won the Sports Personality at least once but this was her first nomination and it meant she was in a short list that included Susie. I felt sure that the audience vote would favour the Lioness which would reflect the team's success in the public eye. Despite Sophie's career emulating that of a certain Mr Woods, women's golf did not get the same profile as football.

For me, golf had become the driver that helped me over our split. Truth was that I believe that it had been coming for quite some time, even though neither of us had found anyone else. I felt that I could still count Sophie as a friend and we exchanged regular good luck texts.

My golf was allowing me to make a good living and John had proved an excellent caddy but it paled against my former lover. I was managing at least one tour win each year and was keeping my world ranking in the top forty but I was still hoping for that elusive Major.

Despite the steady and enjoyable, for the most part, golf, life felt very empty. I missed Sophie and on occasion Teri. There were times

362

when I found it depressing that I had no close female friends. Then things had changed, six months ago.

"Hi, Mum. How are you?" It was my daily call home.

"I'm fine and so is everyone else, love. I have some news that I'd rather have told you face-to-face. These video calls aren't quite the same."

I was intrigued. Mum was well up to the latest technology and not usually complaining. "Spill the beans, Mum."

"I had a visitor today. She called in my office, unannounced. Fortunately, I think, I was free."

What was she rambling about? "Go on, mother."

She realised I was wondering what was going on, I only call her mother when I'm not that happy.

"My visitor was Teri."

I gasped, what on earth?

"She had learned that you and Sophie weren't together any more. She was very quiet talking but wondered if I would let you know that, well that, if you wanted to get together again. If you could forgive her for kicking you out. Her words, Robbie."

I sat in my hotel room silent, shocked. Teri was stuck with her sick mother; had she died? Mum reassured me. As she understood it, Teri's mother had never been ill. Her story had simply been intended to tie Teri at home playing on the guilt Teri would feel if her mother had died alone.

Did I want to get together with Teri? Of course, I did. Sophie and I had broken up well over a year ago. It would have been impossible if we had been together, I knew that but I had managed that loss and Teri was no second choice.

I was due back home in a week and we duly met up at our local pub. Over a beer, Teri told me the story.

While she had been at work, her parent had been out socialising, not resting at home as she claimed. Teri had found out by accident when visiting another work site and spotted her getting out of a car. Suspicious, she took a few days off work and waited near their home to see if this was a one-off or a regular excursion. Every day that week she saw her mother being picked up by a man, she thought she knew. They would visit different restaurants and hotels before returning home in time to ensure that Teri would arrive there to find her ailing parent struggling with fatigue and unwilling to eat an evening meal.

The final straw was a discarded and used condom in the waste bin. The next day Teri left work early and waited at home for her mother's return. She had already packed and told her she was leaving. Teri told me that the reaction was incredible.

"You can't leave I need support and your sisters have their families. What will I do without you?"

Teri told her that she knew about her friend and about her findings. "Mother," she told her, "you have him. Use him but you aren't keeping me anymore. Goodbye."

"No-one will believe you. You'll cut yourself off from the family." Her mother raged at her. Then she quietened. Teri's sisters had been waiting in the next room, listening and it was then that they appeared.

"Won't believe what, mother?" Viv, Teri's oldest sister, asked, before. "If anyone is going to be cut off, it's you. You made us believe that you were ill and needed constant attention. You lied! Teri is going to stay with me until she can find her own place. You want help in the future you are going to have to apologise and make amends with her."

"We suggest that you think long and hard about how you want things to pan out. Come on, Teri." At that Angie, Teri's other sister, took her by the arm and guided her out to her car.

Sadly, Teri could hardly speak about her mother in the present tense. "I have got a flat now but I'm still not talking to her. Rob, I was a fool. Can you forgive me?"

Of course, I could. I did have to explain about Sophie, a case of no hidden secrets, I felt. Teri looked at me in amazement.

"Rob, you know I am nowhere near her to look at and her golf is brilliant."

I took a moment to respond. "Teri, you are almost as daft as Sophie. She never believed she could look good to me or anyone else. I know she had reasons but you are easily as good looking as her. Her golf is out of the world, far better than mine but that was the problem."

Teri looked at me with a look of astonishment. "Problem?"

"We were never together. We had a great time for two years but with us both playing, usually in different parts of the world, it just didn't work. We stay in touch with texts, mostly saying: Good Luck."

Teri grinned, a little uncertainly. "But how often are you home or in the UK?"

"Not as much as I would like." I hesitated. Was this too quick? Hell, I thought, we wouldn't have split up in other circumstances. "Teri, there is an answer to that. Travel with me."

"But I have a job, I do need to earn a living, Rob."

"Teri, I can't spend the money I am earning. I have prize money, most weeks, and sponsorship. You could help me. Be with me."

She grinned, a little uncertainly. "I need to think about that. Are you coming back to my place?"

I nodded, fortunately I had packed a few items and the night promised a great time.

We got back together a few days later. Teri's work had gotten in the way.

Teri had taken some time thinking about joining me on the Tour and, I admit, I had worried that I had overstated her wishes, to myself at least. In the end she decided to take the risk.

"What risk?" I asked.

"That you might find out that I don't live up to how you seem to see me."

I looked at her in astonishment. "I don't understand, Teri. You are what you are and you are everything any male would want. Bright, gorgeous, hard-working and, whisper it, sexy."

"Maybe, but you have had Sophie Jordan as a partner. How could I live up to her success? I have almost nothing. I'm no good at sport."

"Teri, that isn't relevant. Yes, I loved being with Sophie and we are still friends but when I look back, I am not sure we were really in love. Breaking up with her hurt, a lot, but not as much as when you and I parted. You know, Teri, I thought we had gone beyond the lust stage and I was falling in love when you were forced to shut me out. Now I know that I was and am in love with you on a level Sophie, god bless her, and I never reached."

Teri looked at me in silence, stunned, I think.

"Teri, I love you. I know this is probably too soon, so don't feel you have to answer me at all, now. Will you honour me by marrying me?"

If she was stunned into silence before, now she stuttered. "Robbie, oh Robbie. You can't mean that. You deserve more than I can give you. I know I'm good for you in some ways but marry you? That's scarily serious."

She stopped, as I looked back at her, nervous now that I had overstepped, again, and assumed too much. Then.

"Oh god. Robbie, I have loved you for as long as I can remember. Way back to when we started school together but Annie grabbed you then and wasn't letting go. I had to step away. You have always been totally loyal to your friends and I knew I hadn't got a chance.

Then we got together and all my dreams had come true until my mother, damn her, put her oar in. That's what I mean, Robbie. How can you trust me not to go running home again?"

"Teri, because I know you. You were given no choice and because your heart is bigger than most you reacted as you had to. Come with me on the Tour. When you are ready to answer my question then let me know. Let's enjoy the Tour locations and being together again; no commitment beyond enjoying yourself."

She slowly nodded and then stepped in close and kissed me. "Robbie, you know you are going to have to tell me how golf works. I've never had a clue about it."

Two days later, we were in the air heading for Italy and my next event. Another chapter in my life started.

A Time of Success on All Fronts.

The next eighteen months would bring me several Tour wins and two more majors but not the one I craved.

As time passed, Richard and I grew closer until he proposed on a flight back to England for the Open. As ever he reached out in a special way and left me with no option but to accept, not that I would have refused a proposal in the local takeaway!

We were married the following Christmas. It was a happy family time with Alan, Ginny, Fiona and, of course, James who had quietly talked my Mum into becoming his fiancée. I had caught her gently fingering a new ring on her hand and she admitted that the idea of marriage had been mooted. Just not yet. I told her not to delay; that Dad would approve.

Both of my brothers were there and I had the chance to meet Bernard's partner, Gordon, for the first time.

Kate and Chrissie were also there and that gave my Mum the chance to thank Kate again for her work that night which meant that that day could happen. Chrissie had qualified as a Doctor in my absence in the States and was already looking to move on to becoming a surgeon. Kate was adamant; she was not going that way; Doctor was fine for her!

Among the guests from the golfing world were fellow golfers including Ingrid, Anna, and Francine. And joining Susie and her twin, were Rob and his own fiancée, Teri.

That year was unforgettable for those reasons but also because it was the first time in five years that I did not win a Major.

Our first year married, saw me back on the Major trail. As I won the LPGA Championship for a fourth time.

By this time, my Mr Grump was calling me the Tigris!

"She must be considered in the same place as Tiger Woods. That's eleven Majors already and she is still in her twenties. I almost feel sorry for the others that must compete with her."

Things would change again, rapidly. By July I was in no place to compete. I was expecting and my early months were not good. I was forced to take the decision to stop playing until after the birth. Our daughter, Dawn Kathryn, would be born the following February. The birth was not easy and it took time for me to recover. I was not back on any golf course until late June.

Despite that interlude of almost a year I was determined to play in the Women's Open. For the first time since my debut as an amateur it was to be played at St. Andrews. This was the chance, I told Richard, to win the one Major that had eluded me.

Eventually, he accepted that I needed to have a go but only after we had had a real bust up over it. He did not believe that I was ready for the stresses of a Major, both the physical and the emotional. In the end, I managed to convince him that the chance, to play at the home of golf, was worth the risk.

The family were, naturally, delighted that we would be travelling from our home with the baby. Ginny pulled a lot of strings to find us two properties, not too far from St Andrews, which could cope with us and our family and those friends who were eager to follow me around the links.

I eased myself back into competition gently. Which is to say, I took the family to France and played in the Evian! I would not win but it was the right contest to prove that I was ready to play again and the chance to meet up with some of my friends made up for finishing well down the field.

We travelled back to England with me now confident that I would be ready in two weeks and Richard a little more relaxed.

My mother was stunned to hear that I was looking for a nanny for little Dawn. How my life had changed from that uncertain teenager scared of letting people down and not having a penny to her name.

That I needed someone to travel with us and look after the baby, while Richard and I were on the various golf courses, and that I could afford to do so, was a long way from my Mum's comfort zone. Those few weeks gave James and his team the chance to overhaul my leg, working with the hospital. I had had intermittent issues but nothing apparently major. The sixth leg had had those initial problems ironed out and I had switched a couple of years before. I still suffered fatigue in my thigh but had accepted that nothing could be done about that.

The real news was that the team had managed to develop a process that would allow, if not a production line, at least a way to provide similar prosthetics at a cost of a few thousands of pounds each; cheap enough for the NHS to be committing to using them in the future.

This gave me the chance to repay the hospital, to a small extent. I told Anita that I would provide the first twenty legs needed by under twenty-year-olds, anywhere in the UK.

As I told her, even if James had paid for my legs, the surgical teams had been the people who had supported me throughout. I made the offer with the same proviso he had insisted on. No publicity. I was not to be named in any way. She accepted that, provided she could tell the powers-to-be of the source of the funding. They would ensure, she said, that there would be enough additional medical support to ensure that other patients could benefit in the future.

The week of the Open duly arrived and, with Mum looking after Dawn, Richard and I were soon dealing with the pressures of practicing while I fielded questions from television and news reporters.

Thursday and I tee off just after midday. Conditions are good and early scoring has been low. Four hours later we walk off the eighteenth green and I get the summons to the Sky cart which brings back the memory of Ingrid being asked the same question. Of course, that had also been my first experience of the demands placed on professional golfers.

The round had been good but not exceptional; my four-under par sixty-eight meant that I was tied fourth and three back from the joint leaders.

Friday was again good; a faultless round of five birdies left me tied second but still three shots back from an old adversary, Anna. I think that the television team were not happy that I would not be in the final group with Anna but I wasn't worried about that. Final pairing on Sunday would be much more important I felt.

Moving day! And with Ingrid posting a superb round of sixty-three, she passed all of us. Just! Not for the first time she and I would be playing together in that last group and I would have to handle a two-shot deficit. Anna had not played well and was now three back.

I woke Sunday morning alone. Richard had moved into a second bedroom with Dawn. I am not sure I really slept any the better but I did feel more rested.

Somehow, though, I had the feeling that the day would prove the most important one in my golfing career; that I might not have the chance to win the Open, ever again. If I had admitted those feelings to anyone, I suspect they would have told me that that was how it was when you need a win to complete a career grand slam, but I had a niggly feeling that there was something going on that would interfere with my future.

As I headed down to breakfast, I gritted my teeth and reminded myself that I had outscored Ingrid on the final day the last time we were here in Scotland and I knew, now, that I was good enough to do that again.

Three holes into the final round and I was wondering if I was going to prove up to the challenge. Ingrid had had two birdies while I had only managed one offset by a bogey after I found a greenside bunker. I did pull one shot back by the turn but faced a mountain over the back nine.

Now it was Richard's time. His reminder of the way I had played the back nine, every round I had played on the Old Course, was what I needed. By the fifteenth Ingrid's lead had vanished. She had not played badly but her two birdies had been no match for my three birdies and an eagle which meant that we were level with three holes to play. The rest of the field had fallen back and it was now a two-horse race for the finish.

We both made pars at the sixteenth and seventeenth holes before we were faced with that hole, The Road Hole. Back when I had played the course as an amateur the eighteenth had been kind to me from the first round when I had almost driven the green to the fourth round when I had finished with a birdie to take the clubhouse lead only for Ingrid to match that score and win by a shot.

Those thoughts were flowing through my mind as I settled on the tee before almost repeating that drive. Ingrid followed but was thirty or so yards behind me and had to hit her approach first. Her shot wasn't bad but the ball spun away from the flag and rolled into the thicker rough just off the green. With some pressure taken off me my own wedge shot flew over the pin before spinning back to finish close to the hole.

Ten minutes later I rolled the putt in to win. That's right! I had finally won the one Major that meant the most to me!

My interviews with the various television teams were as enjoyable as I might have expected but there was one surprise. Mr Grump was at the Sky cart to congratulate me!

"Sophie, you've done it and proved me wrong again! You know I have often wondered exactly how you maintain your performance at such high levels and that I have said winning this was the one you might have struggled with. Now you do it only a few months after giving birth! I am delighted to have been proven wrong yet again. I'm going to be waiting now for the year you complete the grand slam of all five. Good luck, Tigris."

Celebrations over we headed back with the family before returning to our home in California. With no more Majors before the following Easter I had decided to limit the number of tournaments I would play in. We had found a nanny but I still wanted to spend more time with little Dawn.

The End of a Career.

Five years on Richard and I sat at home, with Dawn and Gail, her nanny, watching the annual Sports Personality of the Year. For us it was mid-afternoon as we had decided not to travel to the UK. The family were coming to the States for Christmas and, in any case, I had been in the short-list five times without winning.

Those first few years of marriage and being a mother had been good although I had only one Major to my name until this sixth year when, against all the odds, I had won four on the bounce. Only a bad week at the Woodlands had denied me the grand slam but I had won the Women's Open for the third time.

The programme was well underway when the doorbell rang.

"You're not expecting anyone, are you?" I asked Richard who shook his head, a little nervously, which raised my suspicions.

Gail spoke up. "Come on Dawn, let's see who's there, shall we?"

Dawn was already halfway to the door and, looking back, nodded. "Hurry up, Gail. I want to see."

A few moments later, four people entered with apologies. Three were carrying the paraphernalia of a television crew and the fourth was, I couldn't believe it, Rory McIlroy.

"Why didn't you tell me?" I demanded of Richard, who was now grinning his head off.

"And spoil the surprise?"

I had already got up to greet Rory, who was also smiling. "It has been too long since we first met, Sophie."

"I have never forgotten how you helped that two-bit amateur. I could never have made the leap without your support."

"That I will never believe." He grinned. "Now we do need to get ready and make sure we have a link back home."

I looked back at the television to find that they were talking about why I was on the list. "What a waste." I said.

"Sophie, you've come closer than any golfer since Tiger to completing the grand slam in a year and you could still hold all five titles after the spring. The BBC clearly think you should win even if they cannot control the vote."

"Rory, I've been here so many times before..."

At this point, Gail returned with drinks for everyone accompanied by a starstruck youngster. "Are you really Rory McIlroy? My Mom's hero?"

"You must be Dawn, and yes I am Rory; not sure about the hero bit, though."

Richard took the opportunity to speak. "Dawn makes her Mum tell her bedtime stories about her time playing golf and that time in Augusta, when you helped Sophie, is her favourite story."

"You haven't won as many Majors as Mom, have you?"

"From the mouths of the young." Rory laughed. "I am in good company there. Do you know how many golfers have won as many as your Mum?"

"Jack Nicklaus."

I was stunned, how had my five-year-old daughter learned that? Dawn looked up laughing as only a child can. "Daddy told me!"

Now it was my turn to chuckle. I should say that that little one already had a junior set of clubs and had made it clear that she wanted to learn how to play!

"Miss Jordan?" One of the camera team interrupted. "Sorry, we are now live."

Back in the UK, the result of the vote was being announced. The top two had finished and it was the final name. "The Sports Personality of the Year is Sophie Jordan-Simms! Sophie sadly is not here but we can talk to her at her home in California and ask Rory McIlroy to present her with her trophy. Rory are you there?"

"I am Peter, and it is my pleasure to make this presentation. I can remember first meeting Sophie back when she was a frighteningly good amateur. Just before she won her first Major. I thought she would prove good but I was wrong. She proved to all of us that she should rank amongst the greats both male and female. Sophie, it is a privilege to be able to present you with this award."

I sat there having difficulty breathing. Forget the stress of that first hole tee at St Andrews. This was far harder.

"Thank you, Rory. Thank you everyone back home for voting for me. I could and should thank everyone else who have supported me throughout my career. They know who they are and they know I love them all. There is one person who helped me that you don't know about. Rory said he met me all those years ago. I had just suffered my complete set of clubs being destroyed in a freak accident a few weeks before the Chevron Championship. We were desperately trying to find replacement shafts and couldn't, even at the Masters sales tent. Rory talked to the team there and convinced them to give me a set of the most up to date clubs. At his cost if necessary. Three weeks later, with clubs I could only have dreamed of before then, I won the Chevron. Rory, thank you."

There was a silence in the room but back in the studio the audience were applauding.

The following year I would come close to winning the Chevron but failed by two shots. The winner was Ko Song who was almost apologetic at stopping my attempt to hold all five Majors at the same time.

I was not to know then that that would be the last Major I would ever play. Two weeks later I blacked out and fell on some steps in the garden.

The next thing I remember was waking, in a hospital bed, to hear Richard quizzing someone as to how I was.

"I am sorry, sir. For the moment, I cannot give you an answer. Until your wife regains consciousness, we can only hope that what the initial X-ray suggested is wrong."

"What do you mean?" My voice startled them and, in truth, me as it sounded very croaky.

Then I started to panic. "Why can't I see you?"

Richard was first to react, he was sitting next to the bed and was leaning over me cuddling me as far as he could. For the second time in my life, I sensed that I was festooned in cables and other medical equipment.

"It's all right my darling, you're going to be fine." His kiss was for a moment reassuring before I could react otherwise.

"Richard, you never were a good liar, why can't I see you?"

"Miss Jordan, it is good that you have woken. We need to carry out some further examinations. You have suffered a severe concussion and have been in a coma for three days. You hit your head in the fall and we still have several tests so that we can identify what the damage is, what is temporary and, if anything is permanent. For the minute, don't worry about your eyes. They have medical bandages over them, part of the injuries involved blood loss which flooded them." The doctor, at least I assumed that was what he was, sounded confident but I sensed that he was telling me nothing useful. "Nurse, the patient needs rest and sleep for the next twenty-four hours."

I could feel myself becoming drowsy. "Wait, when can I go home?" I am not sure there was an answer as the sedative took effect and I fell back into a dreamless sleep.

I learned later that I had been rushed to the local A&E and spent those three days in an intensive care unit. The news had spread like wild fire amid the golfing community and messages of support had come from all over the world, from both sides of the game and even from other sports. After that day under sedation, I was subject to a variety of scans and a few, frustratingly long, days later the specialist returned with a mix of news.

"Sophie, firstly, the good news is that there is no permanent damage arising from your fall. Your vision will slowly improve as the blood specks are gradually absorbed, which may take a week or so."

I looked up at him from my bedside chair. "And the bad news?"

He took a slow breath. "The ultrasound scan of your head has identified an abnormality; we think it is a tumour. At this stage we need to carry out another scan. The bad news is that the growth is located very close to the spinal link to the brain. Any operation to remove it will be fraught with dangers. For the moment, that initial operation to obtain a biopsy will be safe and I would suggest that that is carried out in the next two or three days. Once we have the results, we can then plan how we might proceed."

To say I was shaken is to understate matters, Richard was with me and had obviously been told beforehand.

"How long has it been there? Can you tell? Why didn't I feel it?" And then I thought a bit more. "I get occasional headaches or perhaps neck aches. Could that be the cause?"

"I wish I could tell you but it is impossible to yet. We may be able provide some answers once we have the biopsy."

Days later and I heard news that was as good as I could have hoped for but not as good as I would have liked.

"The object is benign, there is no evidence of any malignancy but we don't know exactly what it is. I do believe that it is what caused you to blackout."

"You suggested that the growth is badly located. Why is that?"

"It is attached to the principal link between the skull and the spine and is wrapped around the spinal cord. The risk of removing it, is that the cord will be damaged and you will be left paralysed. There is also a serious risk that you will not survive the operation."

"And if it is left?" I was getting irritated by the struggle to extract critical data from him. This was my life we were talking about.

He looked unhappy at having to be the bearer of bad news. "There is no certainty but it is likely that, in time, it will paralyse you. I suspect within months. After that there is no doubt, in my mind, that it will cause your death."

"Then why are you hesitating? It seems that doing nothing is not an option."

I was now in a mix of shock, misery that I might not see my little girl grow up, that Richard would be left on his own and anger at the procrastination of my medical advisor."

"Sophie, I hesitate because an operation might do no more than speed up the process and I could not find any record of a successful removal. Until I looked overseas, that is."

I gritted my teeth; Richard was sensibly staying silent. "Go on."

"My research found one surgeon who has successfully removed a similar growth but she is based in the UK."

At this Richard interrupted. "Can we travel safely? I mean by air."

The surgeon thought for a moment. "I do not feel it should be a problem."

Two weeks later we arrived back in England. An appointment booked with the surgeon named by our US advisor.

I say named but Richard had refused to tell me who the surgeon was. His excuse was that he didn't want me disappointed if we found ourselves faced by someone else.

To my surprise the surgeon was not based in London but in the Midlands not far from our home town. We arrived at her consulting rooms to find that she had been delayed in theatre and had asked the senior member of her team to stand in for her. I knew that that was not unusual but would have admitted to some irritation and impatience. Until the door opened.

"Chrissie! What are you doing here?" I couldn't but think that my old friend should have been elsewhere. We hadn't been able to meet up for some time and, though I knew she had taken the step to move on from being a Doctor to becoming a consultant surgeon, I wasn't aware that she had made such good progress. Surely, she couldn't have risen to this level already, that took years, didn't it?

"Sorry, Sophie. My boss is still in surgery and she's asked me to start the consultation. She shouldn't be too long, so if you'd rather wait?"

For the first time since the blackout, I suddenly felt positive about the future or at least as much as I could be.

"If she thinks you are good enough, how could I wait, Chrissie? Oh, it is so good to see you again."

"Right, then." Chrissie opened the file in front of her and, at the same time, logged in to the desktop sitting to one side.

Over the next quarter of an hour, she took me through her and her boss's understanding of the diagnosis sent to them by the American medical team. Then she dropped a bombshell!

"Mrs Painter doesn't believe that the object we can see in the scans is a tumour and the biopsy analysis is unclear, it seems to be no more than muscle. There is no hint of anything malignant but I admit that we are confused. There is no doubt that there is something there and it must be pressing on the spinal cord. That would explain the headaches you have been having. It was also probably what caused the blackout."

I looked at my friend, concerned to see her worried at the same time as she struggled with the uncertainty.

"Chrissie, what do we need to do then? If it isn't a tumour, what could it be?"

Before she could answer me, the door opened again and an older woman came in. "Mrs Jordan-Simms. Pleased to meet you. My apologies for not being here when you arrived. I assume that Chrissie has explained where we are at."

I nodded before Chrissie told her boss that she had only just talked about the odd nature of the growth.

The consultant smiled. "So, you haven't told your friend what you have suggested is the problem?"

Chrissie nodded. "I felt you would prefer to handle that."

That caused me to wonder what it was that had her so uncertain that she was holding back. That wasn't the Chrissie I knew and loved.

It became clear that the consultant would have been quite happy for Chrissie to tell all. "Sophie, may I call you by your first name?" Continuing without waiting. "My colleague has suggested that the object is in fact bone covered by muscle. That at some point you damaged your neck and, as sometimes happens with bones, the body's defence mechanism has tried to compensate for the damage by growing replacement tissue. It isn't common but the growth has not stopped. We will need to operate but the good news is that it should be possible to remove a portion of the object which will reduce the risks."

"When should we act?" I was rapidly becoming attuned to the idea that the sooner the better.

"I have already put you on my list for next Wednesday." Mrs Painter smiled. "We will need to run some pre-op checks before then but I do not think we should wait."

I looked across at Richard. He inclined his head as he does when supporting me, as he always does.

"What are the risks?" I felt I needed clarity.

"Assuming my colleague is correct, the best outcome will be that we can remove enough to release the pressure on the cord without damaging it. I should tell you that it is likely that a further repeat of the operation will be needed in perhaps ten years. You see, we can't promise that the growth will stop."

"Worst case?"

"Despite the concerns of the US team, you are unlikely to die on the operating table. I won't lie though, there is a possibility that you will be paralysed. Perhaps a five per cent chance but I can assure you that we will work hard to avoid that."

"Then we go next week." It wasn't that there was really a choice but I felt better for making that decision.

"Mommy, are you okay?"

"Yes, my little one. The doctors will make me better."

"I love you, Mommy."

"I love you too, Dawn. And your Dad does too. He will be with you while I am in the hospital, but you must let him visit me. Your Nan will look after you."

A week later and I was recovering from the operation when Chrissie came to my room. She was clearly a mix of emotions and I decided to take the initiative.

"Come on, Chrissie, tell me the worst."

She took a deep breath. "The boss sends her regards. She gave me the task of telling you how well we did. And," she took another breath. "the downside."

I should say that I was, at that minute, feeling as well as I could have expected. Now I was feeling very nervous.

"Sophie, we've removed most of the growth. It was a mix of bone and muscle. I think that the original injury may have been a result of that evening when you lost your leg."

"So, you've got rid of the problem and I'm not paralysed. What could go wrong now."

"There's no easy way to tell you, Sophie. The spinal cord was already damaged. You are not going to be able to play golf, safely, again. The stresses put on your neck when you swing could be fatal. At best the damage would leave you paraplegic. I'm sorry, Sophie, there is nothing we could have done to improve matters."

I looked at her as she ended my career and realised that no matter how bad I felt, poor Chrissie was feeling worse. She must have hoped that she could rescue me; that her calling to be a brilliant surgeon would be enough. Now she faced the truth; that not all things can work out well and I sensed the tears behind her professional face.

"Oh, Chrissie. Don't cry. It's not your fault and you've given me years to look after little Dawn, and Richard. I've had a great career, done wonderful things. Now I'll just have to change tack. I'll teach if I can. You never know, perhaps I can join Mr Grump on the commentary team. There's lots to look forward to and that's due to you and your boss."

It sounded as if I was talking off-the-cuff, but in truth, I had rehearsed different words during the run up to and immediately after the operation. How I would react to whatever I was faced with. Chrissie and her colleagues had done better than I could have hoped for. I had expected to find myself in a wheelchair for the rest of my life. They had given me a chance at a full life, if not the life I had become used to.

Later my love and I sat talking.

"Richard, I'm sorry but you're going to have to find someone else to caddy for. You are fired!" I grinned at the one person who I knew would be by my side for ever.

PART SIX – NOW.

After that – Sophie.

And so, it came to pass. We sold up in the States and moved back to our home territory.

We were able to take on the mantle first defined by Nick Faldo supporting talented young golfers and, in due course, I was invited to join one of the television commentary teams.

Dawn was growing into an excellent golfer in her own right, determined to follow her parents and, I suspected, wanted to do better. I did try to ensure that playing golf was really what she wanted. I had seen the difficulties faced by other children of top sportsmen and women, but she was adamant that there was no other career for her. She did, I was glad to see, work hard at school. My misfortune had shown her, once she was old enough to fully understand, that she should be careful.

Rob and Teri continued touring until they too had a child, James. Like us they settled in the Midlands and Teri remained at home, most of the time. Rob continued to perform well on the tour and, eventually, he joined that elite set of players by winning the US Open. The Open and The Masters still elude him.

Looking back, I was fortunate to be surrounded by friends as well as family. Their support throughout my life had made my success possible. That support was even clearer after I was forced to retire. To this day, I know that Richard and I will never be alone and that provides the best outcome anyone can hope for.

I continue to work with James, I find it difficult to call him Dad, helping with improvements to artificial limbs and quietly supporting Anita and her team with financial and other help. This was supposed to be done in confidence but I guess it was always going to leak out.

The letter, from the Palace, came as a complete shock. The King wished to make me a Dame! Please would I confirm that I wished to accept! The citation listed my services to golf and to charities including the NHS.

Did I wish to accept? In due course I was honoured to receive the award from the King himself, with Richard and, to her delight, Dawn, being allowed to attend.

His Majesty asked her what she wanted to be and our smiling daughter answered him with confidence. Far more than my own at the same age, I felt.

"I want to play golf like my Mum did, your Majesty."

His response startled me. "I understand that you already have that promise, Dawn. I wish you well."

After then – Rob.

My life had improved by quite some way with the ongoing support of Teri, who did eventually agree to walk up the aisle and marry me. Time passed and, while I continued to rank in the top forty, sometimes as high as top ten, a Major victory eluded me until two years after our son was born. We had named him, James, after that wonderful man who had saved Sophie's career.

Over time Teri and Sophie had become good friends; as had Richard and myself. Of course, having a child limited the amount of time that Teri could spend on the road with me but she was there when I finally broke my Major duck by winning the US Open.

This happened a year after the stunning news that shocked the golfing world. That Sophie would never be able to play the game she loved again nor break Nicklaus's record.

We met up shortly after, when she interviewed me for Sky! I am not sure that I could have coped with such misfortune half as well as she has. I rather feel that I would have refused to accept it, just as I had, at first, been unwilling to accept the cancer diagnosis all those years ago.

Life goes on and Teri and I are still together. I do wonder why she stays with me but her sisters have told me that they have never known her so happy. I guess that that is where my luck has come from. That and the mischievous youngster who keeps us busy all the time when I am at home. He has had such an effect on me and I am pleased that I can, at least, limit the number of tournaments I need to play each year.

Unlike Sophie's daughter, James is looking to follow his aunt into football and shows promise in that sport. If he proves half as good....

PART SEVEN - THE FUTURE?

St Andrews; the Women's Open.

"Sophie, today is the day. Does this take you back to your first appearance here?"

"It does, Laura, in spades. Now I will be down on the course following that one group. I'm sorry if that limits my part in the coverage but I will be back afterwards."

"Give her our best wishes, Sophie. Now folks, we rejoin the action on the course."

"Thanks Laura. We are down at the first tee and I am sure all the viewers know why this group will be followed with interest."

The starter calls up the next player.

"On the tee, the Amateur Champion, Dawn Jordan-Simms!"

*** *** ***

About the Author

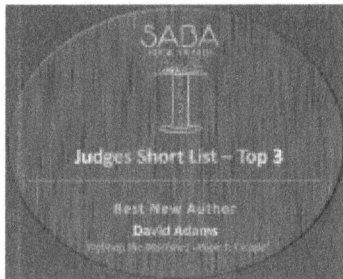

David Adams was born in England in 1952 and spent his working life in finance. First as a banker until, as he puts it, he saw the light and switched from poacher to gamekeeper spending most of his career in Corporate Treasury functions as Group Treasurer for a number of multinational companies. Now retired he spends what little free time he has playing golf, walking the family dog and, on occasion, looking after the grandchildren with his wife Marion.

His first book – ESCAPE – was shortlisted for Best New Author 2020 achieving Runner-Up

Other Books by the Author

Fighting the Machines Saga

1. Escape
2. Contact
3. The Hunt – for Allies

"They had it coming to them!"

No, they didn't but have the murderous actions of the killer destroyed the young golfer's career before it starts and left injuries that will stop her winning true love?

Sophie must overcome the loss of her leg while Rob struggles to cope with the aftermath of cancer.

This is their story of determination, love, and a lot of golf.

Milton Keynes UK
Ingram Content Group UK Ltd.
UKHW010754110923
428455UK00014B/660

9 798223 938279